Soldiers of Gaia

Lacey Jones with Rebecca Jones

Lacey Jones

Rebecca Jones

Lacey Jones

To the memory of our mother, Susan Jane Jones, and to my mentor, Ethel (Bubs) Fraser.

Prologue

"We three," Inanna said, passing her hand over a bowl of still water. The reflection of her young, beautiful face folded softly into itself and sank beneath the surface.

Ripples formed and chased each other around the perimeter of the concrete basin. The wavelets twisted and built an image of the Triple Goddess: Maid, Mother, and Crone. A light wind brushed softly against towering evergreens that encircled the three women standing on a cliff carved deeply by tides. Stars, pinprick holes in the blue-black sky, provided the only light.

Brighid, the Mother, nodded and circled her palm over the bowl. "These five."

The water subsided and rippled counterclockwise. The Goddesses watched the water form images of five people, three women and two men, ranging in age from a four-year-old child to an ancient-looking woman in her seventies.

The Cailleach nodded and spread her fingers over the gently churning water. "This one," she said, and the water stilled. In the center was the image of a young man with dark-blue eyes and days-old stubble on his face. He was handsome in an unkempt way with longish hair tousled over his forehead, trailing beyond his collarbones. His straight nose came to a point at the tip, drawing attention to his full lips. Prominent cheekbones and a strong chin added to the effect, making the man look like a Viking warrior from long ago.

Inanna tilted her head to the side and said mischievously, "*Ooh*, lucky me!"

Brighid hushed her with a *tsk* causing the Cailleach to cackle in enjoyment. All three positioned their index fingers over the bowl, hovering above the image's forehead.

"Anoint them," the Cailleach said.

In unison, they touched their fingers to the water and the ripples began anew. Rapidly, the purls gathered speed until small waves raced against the edge of the bowl. The water began to stack itself, twisting into a fluid tornado contained within the basin. The geyser whipped in a furious motion against the Goddesses' fingers but did not spray or leave the confines of the basin.

As it rose to its full height, eye level to the Goddesses', Brighid spoke.

"I scry with my third eye

"Gaia is dying, we three know why

"Creation to destroy: decree

"Blessed be, so mote it be."

The three withdrew their fingers from the spinning water, and the ferocity dissipated. The Goddesses bowed their heads over the bowl.

The water reflected nothing but the dark sky.

Declan gasped and pushed himself into a sitting position on his bed. His breath came in short pants as sweat rolled from his hairline due to another one of those weird dreams that seemed way too real. He flattened his palm and dragged it down his wet face and around his neck, then stopped and looked at his hand. His face was wet, but his neck was dry. What the hell? He patted the sheets: dry. Pillow: dry. Why was his face wet? He pinched his long fingers over the bridge of his nose to ward off the impending headache of another fitful, sleepless night.

Declan flopped back onto his bed and glared at the ceiling. Goddamn leak in the goddamn roof. That would have to get checked out tomorrow. This crap trailer home wasn't worth the price he'd paid—and that wasn't much. He squinted his eyes shut to retrieve a bit more sleep and had almost drifted off when his eyes flew open.

It wasn't raining. It hadn't rained for days.

Shemar woke abruptly as water ran into his eye.

"What is this shit?" He ran his arm over his brow and cheeks and looked over at his bedmate. "Girl, did you just spit on me? You did not just spit on me!"

The woman opened one eye and smiled lazily. "Baby, I might have drooled on you, but no, I didn't spit on you."

Shemar looked over at the open window. "Damn. Rain is getting in, baby. I have to close the window."

He moved his large frame from the bed to the window and, grabbing the lever, prepared to shut it. Then he leaned out the window and looked over his street: the concrete, the streetlights, the cars along the side. There was no sign of rain. He shook his bald head and closed the window.

"Damn," he whispered.

The old woman rocked quietly on the deck with her face lifted to the sky. Her eyes were closed, and she was smiling. There were shimmering drops of water gliding around the deep creases of her face. She did not hear—or did not acknowledge—the whiny plea of her daughter-in-law from behind the screen door.

"Mama! It is far too late for you to be out here! And it's windy! You will catch a chill. How will I look after you with all these others to care for?"

Mara raised an eyebrow slightly in sardonic amusement. If that girl had to look after anything other than finding a pair of matching socks, she would have a nervous breakdown. Mara continued to rock and, to drown out the whining, she started to sing.

"Mama! Fine! Just remember that I told you to come in, and you wouldn't listen! I am telling Leonid."

Mara chuckled and shook a crooked old finger toward the sky. Those ladies were going to get her in trouble—again. Good. It had been too long since she was in trouble, and she was bored. She let the drops of water slide into her mouth and down her throat. Reclining deeper into the chair, she idly wondered how much longer it would be before it rained.

Father Benedict knelt in front of the cross at the front of the church and lowered his head to his folded hands. The church was empty, except for himself and a bat or two in the rafters. At this time of night, the church was usually closed but the priest had been granting refuge to a few of the local homeless lately. There seemed to be so many more of them these days, and so few places for them to go. He did not judge, nor particularly care, where they came from. It was enough that they sought shelter, food, and companionship. Benedict could provide most of those things. But lately, the Church had been reluctant to continue to give shelter to the homeless.

Tonight, there had been no knocks at the door from people seeking guidance or sanctuary, so he was going to say his prayers and go home to get some sleep. Lately, his dreams had been invaded by three women. They were familiar to him, but strange. He wondered if he had seen a movie or read a book that prompted this feeling of recognition. There was one in particular that he felt a kinship with, and while he would like the dream to cease due to its intensity and insistence upon waking him, he felt he would miss the old one. She seemed ancient and wise. He laughed a little at his peculiar train of thought and shook his head.

Water splashed against his praying hands, surprising him. Puzzled, he lifted his hands to his face and felt water. He looked up at the altar, but there was no holy water in the basin. With narrowed eyes, Father Benedict searched the stained-glass windows for appearances of cracks before he realized it wasn't raining.

Annalee's mother opened the door and peered in at her daughter. Four-year-old Annalee giggled to herself and clapped her hands together in her room. A small nightlight of a dragon lit up the area by the door. Her brown eyes crinkled, and she chirped as she reached out her pudgy toddler hands to clasp something unseen.

"Annalee!" Yenay chided. "Are you talking to the faeries again? You tell them that your mother said you need to go to sleep, or you will be a little crank-asaurus in the morning!"

She swept Annalee up in her arms and touched her nose to her daughter's. Annalee giggled again, more softly, and reached up to inquisitively touch her mother's face. Yenay wondered, not for the first time, what it was about the touch of her little daughter that made her forget why she was angry, or sad, or worried. The child had a way of looking at her, and touching her, that washed away anything that stood in the way of happiness and contentment.

"Annalee, if I could bottle up your kisses and sell them, we would be rich, rich, *rich*!" She tickled her under the chin and placed her back in her bed.

Annalee looked over at the dragon and sleepily said, "Night, night, Tatsuya."

Yenay stroked her daughter's dark, soft hair gently. She tilted her head slightly, her brows drawing together as she lifted her damp hand to her lips. Where on earth did water come from? And why only on Annalee's face?

The young Navajo man slipped noiselessly through the woods. The leg-hold traps snapped in futile aggression as he tripped each one placed by hunters he had watched earlier. He had been at this for hours, but that was okay. He had learned to sleep during the day and live at night. His father had said he was a nightcrawler. His mother was gentler and said he had a different circadian rhythm than most people, but that in itself was a gift. One of many she claimed he had.

Ho'kee slid down the trunk of a tree and sat in the moss. He unpacked a knapsack of water, fruit, and a sandwich then looked up through the canopy of trees. Oddly, he felt drops of water hit his forehead and trickle down his cheeks. He stood up and adjusted his lean to. After ensuring that it was waterproof, he lay underneath it and continued to munch his sandwich. Every so often, a certain red fox with a slight limp would hover around the edges of Ho'kee's little camp. He had made a habit of sharing his food with the little guy who, due to one of those evil things Ho'kee was springing, could not do much hunting on his own.

While they gave each other space, there would not be any *Dances with Wolves* scenarios. Ho'kee turned his head to his side to watch the little creature eat his share of the sandwich and brushed away water from his face again. He must have camped closer to the waterfall than he'd thought. Strange, though, that only his face was getting wet.

Part One

Chapter One

D eclan was still glaring at the trailer's ceiling when a crow started screeching outside at sun break. He threw his muscular forearm over his face and pushed out an exasperated sigh. He switched his glare to the blank canvas perched on an easel, mocking him for his lack of inspiration. And lack of drive. And lack of imagination. Or purpose.

The crow screeched again, and Declan shot out of bed, flung the screen door open, and yelled out at the bird. "Off! Get off with you! Do you know what time it is? Six in the bloody morning! That's what time it is, goddamn bird!"

The crow cocked its head and curiously gazed at Declan from where it sat perched on the power lines which dipped and crossed haphazardly in the trailer park. He dipped his long beak to his talons and groomed himself, completely unperturbed by the outburst.

Declan stared at the crow and moved onto his deck. "Did you hear me? I said get lost!"

The crow, seemingly fully engaged in this game, dipped his beak down and screeched. Declan stood with his hands on his hips in his boxers and bare feet. An elderly couple carefully walked along the outskirts of his site boundary, exchanging worried looks with each other.

Declan nodded his head toward them and raised his finger to point to the crow. "Little bastard screeching at me first thing in the morning! Before coffee! Don't you think that's rude?"

The crow gazed at Declan, his black eyes glittering. He was silent.

Declan yelled at him again. "Oh, so *now* you aren't going to say a word! Now that other people are listening, you have nothing to say?"

The crow dipped his head and scratched his talon along his beak again. The couple shuffled quickly past, maintaining a large distance between themselves, the crow, and Declan. Declan stomped back into the trailer and slammed the screen door behind him. As soon as the couple was out of eyesight, the crow screeched.

Declan ran his long fingers through his dark blond hair to get it out of his eyes. Refusing to cooperate, a tousled forelock fell back into his eyes. Resisting the urge to grab a pair of scissors and be done with it, he started to make coffee. He didn't have much left in the way of coffee grounds, and there was no money coming in until the end of the month unless he sold a painting, but that was as unlikely as the crow beginning to speak English to him. The world did not seem to be very interested in art. Interested in stockpiling supplies? Yes. Assembling bunkers for a war on itself? Sure. Accumulating more money by the one percent who already had too much? Every damn day.

Declan cracked his knuckles to break himself out of these thoughts. Accurate though they were, they didn't do much to enhance his current bleak outlook on life at the moment. He looked out the window, his dark-blue eyes clouding as he snatched at a sweet memory flittering in his mind.

He saw waves of green across low hills dotted with wildflowers and crumbling stone fences. Woolly sheep gnawed at the ground, calmly lifting their heads occasionally to stare into the distance. He heard, then saw, a waterfall creating pools in the smooth rock formations below. Within the waterfall were ledges where he could crawl up the inside of the fall from bottom to top. He looked up to the clear, blue sky. There were no trees around the area.

Declan smiled as he saw himself under the fall, arms outstretched, and body being drenched by the clean, clear water.

A car horn honked, and Declan snapped out of his daydream. He had to brace himself against the kitchen counter as the jolt back to reality felt more physical than mental. Steadying himself, he frowned as he considered he'd never been anywhere like that, as far as he could remember. However, the intense sensations of the earthy smell and the feel of cool wind on his sun-warmed skin seemed too real to be dismissed as a lovely bit of woolgathering. Looking down at his muscular chest, tufted with soft curls, he saw water drops clinging to him.

He spread his arms wide to see similar drops on his biceps and forearms. "What the actual fuck?"

The screen door opened, and Declan looked up to see his brother Niall watching him with amusement as he held a box against his body.

"You doing ballet practice, bro? Arms out, a little pirouette?" Niall laughed and did a mincing turn in his heavy work boots, jeans, and stained baseball cap.

Declan glared at him and dropped his arms to his side. "What do you want, Niall?"

"Nice. I brought you a care package. Coffee, cream because you aren't a real man, whole wheat bread because you are a fucking hippie, some apples...other crap." As Niall put the box on the counter, Declan rested his hand on his brother's shoulder.

"Thanks, brother," Declan said.

Niall shrugged and turned. "No problem. I promised Mom I would look in on my weird artist little brother from time to time. Make sure he didn't starve. Or have to eat paint. Mind you, you did enjoy a dirt clod every now and again when you were an ankle biter. Weirdo."

Declan sat at the lop-sided kitchen table and twisted the stem from an apple. The brothers were quiet for a moment before Declan spoke. "Do you miss her?"

After a pause, and still staring out the window, Niall replied, "Yup. Every day."

"Me too."

Niall sighed heavily and put the coffee on. He slid the container of cream on the table in front of Declan. "For you, milady."

Declan laughed and poured a generous helping into his cup. He looked up at Niall and spoke thoughtfully. "She would not be happy with how the world has turned out in the last twenty years."

"No. She would not."

"Spooky how everything she said was going to happen is happening. I can't decide if she was a visionary or saw the writing on the wall."

Niall poured out the coffee into cups and sat across from Declan. "Both. I think she must have had eyeballs in the back of her head, covered up by all that red hair. She knew what we were up to all the time. Even knew when we were thinking about getting up to something. A mother's instinct, I guess."

Declan stirred his coffee and looked at Niall. "I think it was more than that. She used to get really upset sometimes after we would startle her out of one of her daydreams. Not upset with us, but with the daydream, or vision, she'd had. Remember that? She would break out of those strange states, hypnotic almost, and be crying. Then she would hug us and say things like, 'It's going to be up to you.'"

Niall shook his head. "Not me, buddy. She said that to you. Never me."

A sharp, insistent rap on the screen door startled the men. Declan jolted, spilling coffee onto the already stained table.

"Declan O'Neill! You are a week overdue on your pad rent." The strident, whiny tone of the park manager, Tisdale, caused both men to poke their fingers in their ears to stop the piercing pitch.

Niall looked sharply at Declan. Declan's face flushed in anger, and he pushed himself away from the table. He plunged his hands into the pockets of jeans hanging over a kitchen chair and pulled out a wad of bills. Declan flung open the screen door and crossed his arms over his defined chest, the result of hard work evident in his body. He looked down on the balding, slight man who had to look up—way up—to meet Declan's hard stare.

"Bullshit," Declan said. "You've been too drunk to crawl to the door to get the money, Tizzy."

Tisdale's face, splotchy and crisscrossed with burst blood vessels across his nose, bore evidence to this claim. His shaking hands, reaching out for the money, supported it further. If not for the riffraff in the park, Declan could slide the money under Tisdale's door, but with the amount of B and Es, that wouldn't work. Tisdale stuffed the money in his pockets haphazardly, swaying dangerously close to the deck stairs. He shook his finger at Declan and stumbled down the stairs, muttering to himself. He made his way to the golf cart that he drove around the park.

Niall joined Declan at the screen door. "Why do you stay here, man?"

"Except for Tisdale, it's an okay site. The old ladies keep me fed, and I provide the eye candy." Declan swept his hair out of his eyes slowly and dramatically, then kissed his own shoulder.

Niall rolled his eyes and glanced over at the bare canvas. "Not much work?"

Declan shook his head. "Not much inspiration. Getting odd jobs here and there, but art doesn't seem to be appealing to the masses—or the minority—these days. But that's not why I do it. To be honest, it's been so long since anything inspired me, I can't remember why I do it. Other than to frustrate the hell out of myself."

Niall stood up and put his coffee cup in the sink. "You do it because you have a gift. A few of them, actually."

Declan's mouth curled up in a sardonic twist at the mention of his 'gifts.' If they were gifts, he had yet to see anything but the downside of his frighteningly accurate glimpses into the future, and his unnerving ability to inadvertently read other people's thoughts.

Those 'gifts' made him feel more of an outsider than he already was—and not much fun at a party. But Niall was right. He was a hell of an artist—or used to be.

"No beautiful Muse these days?" Niall asked. "What happened to Bambi? Barbie? Boopsie?"

"Brittany. We didn't share the same interests. She likes money. I don't have any."

Niall adjusted his baseball cap and opened the screen door. "Want to get together for beer and burgers on the grill this weekend? My place?"

"Absolutely. What can I bring?"

"Pie. Ask Mrs. Woods for a blackberry pie. No! Wait. Ask Mrs. Moore for an apple pie. No! I want Mrs. Denver's chocolate cake."

"I have to fix Mrs. Greer's deck so you will be getting strawberry rhubarb crumble."

"Works for me."

Niall got into his old Chevy truck and headed out of the park.

Declan's eyes clouded, and he had to grab onto the railing to keep himself from falling over. He knew what was coming, and knew he was powerless to stop it. These glimpses into his future, other people's future, events that hadn't happened yet were never sunshine and rainbows, and they were rarely wrong. If he fought them, he developed a migraine and they showed up anyway. If he sat quietly and watched the story unfold, he could get away with knowing what he didn't want to, but no migraine. He sat down, and stared out toward the woods, waiting for the vision to envelop his mind.

On a barren cliff overlooking night-blackened ocean waves, three women stood around a fountain. He recognized these women. He had seen them in some dreams he'd been having lately. The ones that kept him up at night. He saw the young one, the middle-aged one, and the ancient one. The water in the fountain was in a high, frenetic twist and he could see faces in the water. He could see the face of a large, bald Black man; a tiny Asian child; an old Russian woman; a handsome young Indigenous man; and the kindly face of an older white man. He watched as the water spun counterclockwise back into the bowl, stilling under the gaze of the three. Then he watched as the youngest of the three, the beautiful blonde with startling blue eyes, turned toward his gaze and seemed to lock on to his mind's eye.

She spoke to him without moving her full, pink lips. Her voice, in his head, was lyrical, sweet, and haunting. "Declan O'Neill. Watch for me soon."

Just as quickly, the vision cleared and his eyes refocused. He came back to the present as Mrs. Greer shook his shoulder with great concern on her lined face.

Shemar walked into the hospital security cubicle and stood at the doorway, coolly regarding the overweight, redheaded man. Nelson sat with his feet propped up on the console and his cell phone high on his chest as his pudgy fingers tapped at the keys.

"You should ask for a raise, Nelson. You work too hard."

The man drew together his bushy eyebrows in concentration as he drawled, "Right? Keeping my eyeballs on the world, buddy. I have a sixth sense. I know when to look up."

Shemar scanned the video screens and rolled the toothpick between his teeth to the other side of his mouth. "So, Sylvia Browne, why aren't you all over the homeless guy panhandling in the waiting room?"

Nelson's wide eyes caught sight of a dirty, unkempt man approaching each patient waiting in the hospital lobby and putting his hand out in a begging gesture. He shuffled far too close for personal, and probably hygienic, comfort.

Nelson sighed and dropped his feet to the floor. "Shoeless Joe is at it again. That guy really burns my marshmallows..." Nelson took a closer look at the screen and slapped his palms on the console. "Oh fuck. Bubba has ahold of him!"

Shemar turned on his walkie-talkie and donned his security guard cap. "Let's go."

The odd pair sprinted from the cubicle, adjacent to the waiting room. They approached an obese, florid-faced security guard with a crew cut who had a meaty hand wrapped around the neck of the disheveled young man, inching him up the wall by his neck. The patients in the waiting room watched in horrified silence. A little girl started to cry.

A matronly nurse, almost a pound-for-pound match to the security guard went to take the guard's arm. "Bubba! You see here! There is no need for—" She gasped as Bubba flung out an arm and pushed her roughly back. Shemar caught her as she flailed backward.

"Back off," Bubba yelled. "I told this piece of shit for the last time to fuck off and lookit what we got. He came back for more Bubba lessons in listening. This time he just might need real medical attention when I get through with him."

Shemar gently moved the nurse out of the way and positioned his considerable bulk in Bubba's peripheral sight. His six-foot, ten-inch frame carried none of the excess fat that Bubba did. His shirt buttons strained at his chest and the sleeves threatened to split at the biceps. His voice was dangerously low, smooth, and controlled. "Put him down, Bubba. Nice and easy. This isn't how we do it."

"Don't get in my way, Shemar. You are too soft on these piles of crap. This guy is going outside with me, and we are having a one-sided conversation about manners."

Joe's eyes were bulging, and the tips of his toes fought to gain ground. He tugged uselessly at the hand around his throat. When he turned pleading eyes to Shemar, Shemar nodded slightly and put his hand on Bubba.

Immediately, Shemar was suffused with an anger so heated, so strong, that it blinded him. His body felt on fire from the inside out, but his actions were focused, his gaze steady and icy. Bubba gasped with shock and looked at his arm, in the leghold trap of Shemar's hand. His other hand let go of Joe's neck in a spasmodic response to the shaking that began to rack his body from head to toe. Joe slid down the wall and crawled to Nelson. Shemar continued to hold Bubba's gaze—which had switched abruptly from hate to fear—as well as his arm and forced the trembling man to his knees.

Bubba's body began to jolt, and his voice, thready and frightened, was barely above a whisper. "Please, Shemar. Let me go. I don't feel good."

Something shifted in Shemar. The gaze between them broke, and he let go of his grip on Bubba. He rocked back as if whatever had been controlling his body had vacated, and he looked in apprehension around him. Nelson looked worried, but the visitors looked relieved and began chattering nervously and with admiration. Joe stood up and promptly made his way down the line of seats. Nelson helped Bubba into the security cubicle, then came back out to deal with Joe. He had Shemar's lunch bag in one hand.

Shemar spoke decisively. "Sit with Bubba. I'll deal with Joe."

Nelson saluted Shemar. "You got it, big guy. Here's your lunch bag. You are always giving it to Joe, so I saved you the trip."

Joe wasn't a bad guy. He was a homeless dude who didn't do well in shelters, had a few mental problems, and had an aversion to showers. Shemar moved his imposingly large frame gracefully down the hall, catching respectful glances and unabashedly appreciative stares from the people lining the sides. He came up behind Shoeless Joe quietly and listened to the disheveled young man with dirty dreadlocks make his pitch.

"Hey man, I know you must have money. Spare some for me, will ya? I haven't eaten for days. Maybe even a month. Maybe a year!" His whiny voice took on an aggressive tone as he leaned into the face of a seated patient. Joe's victim pulled his head back, turtle-like, probably from the smell of Joe's breath. Joe's hands shook badly as he extended them farther into the startled man's face.

Shemar folded his thick, powerful arms across his Herculean chest.

Joe's victim looked up to see Shemar glaring down at Joe, and his worried eyes closed gratefully as he said, "Thank you."

Joe looked confused. "Um...you're welcome?"

Shemar deliberately bumped against Joe, sending the transient off balance.

"Hey! Watch where you're— Ah, fuck. Shemar."

Shemar rocked back on his heels a bit and put a hand on Joe's bony shoulder. At this close range, the most potent weapon Joe had was his smell, but it was formidable.

"Out, Joe." Shemar spoke in a low timbre, a dark velvet voice that rumbled up from his chest.

"I am working here, man! I got a right to be here! I have a right to medical aid!"

"And you are going to need it if you don't get out of this hospital right quick, son. I am not always gonna be around when Bubba is, and you got him riled."

The pair strode to the entrance of the hospital. Once outside, he marched Joe across the parking lot and dropped him onto a picnic bench in a rest area.

Joe looked contemplative for a moment before speaking again. "Shemar, I got nowhere to go."

"Yeah, you do, Joe. I found you a shelter with showers, clean clothes, and meals. It's always been your choice, man. I am not doing that for you again. And you are not coming back here. Why do you keep doing this to yourself?"

Joe shrugged his thin shoulders. "I don't know, man. I don't want to be this way. I never wanted to be this way. Hey, man, I am just glad it's you today and not that other guard. Nelson's okay, but Bubba—"

Shemar's face darkened at the mention of the florid-faced, nasty-tempered redneck with a crew cut who seemed to delight in roughing up the panhandlers who made the mistake of looking for handouts in the hospital. Shemar didn't fault Bubba's work ethic; he was always on time, on the floor, and great with the waiting patients and families. However, he had a brutal method of crowd control, especially when it came to the marginalized population.

"Joe, from here on in, this is a no-go zone. I don't want to see you here. I don't want to see you bugging these people who are upset already, and I don't want to see you hurt. You're a good kid, but you are a mess, son."

Shemar pulled out his wallet and gave Joe a twenty-dollar bill and a card. He had a feeling the money wasn't going to buy sandwiches, but at least the kid would have the card of the street outreach counselor Shemar knew and respected. Shemar thrust his lunch bag into Joe's cavernous chest. "Get going, Joe."

Joe took the money, bag, and card before scrambling away from Shemar.

After watching Joe do his strange quick lurching step down the street, Shemar turned back to the hospital. His face clouded as he thought of Bubba and the conversation he was going to have with that igno-rant blowhard—again. He wondered what it was in Bubba that brought out such a rage within him. He didn't hate the loud-mouthed schnook; he didn't hate anybody. But when someone around him flew into a rage, it seemed to set something within himself off. He became someone he didn't recognize. He scared himself.

It was like something, or someone else, took over his body, mind, and soul. His strength was maxi-mized. His focus was laser pointed. His conscience took a back seat. He had even tried counseling for this strange quirk, but the psychologist was unable to tap into the rage to bring it forward. Shemar never knew what would set it off, but there was always a strong chance that when he witnessed manipulation or physical harm being done to someone or some-thing vulnerable, that rage was going to blind him. When that happened, that darker version of himself, that version that felt ancient and deadly, would take control.

"Ho'kee! Ho'kee, dinner is ready!" Ethel yelled from the back stairs out to the woods beyond, more out of habit than actual anticipation of her only child answering her or acknowledging her call. She sighed and went back into the house where her husband was sticking his finger into the simmering sauce. She struck him in the back of his neck with a towel. "Get out of there, Abe! That is a disgusting habit."

"Eating?" asked Abe with his mouth around a tomato sauce-covered finger.

"Sticking your nasty fingers in my sauce. Troglodyte." Ethel used her hip to shove Abe aside so she could stir the sauce. "Go yell at your son to get his butt in here for dinner."

Abe looked at Ethel fondly. "Why don't we just lock the door, light the candles, pop open some wine, and pretend he's finally moved out?"

Ethel turned and reached out to her husband, lowering her lashes flirtatiously and pouting her generous mouth. "You say the most romantic things. Wine. Ho'kee moving out..."

Abe laughed and stepped out the back door. "Ho'kee! Get your skinny ass in here or your dinner is going to that damn fox you keep feeding!"

Abe listened to the wind for a minute. He heard cicadas, the throaty call of bullfrogs, and wind in the tops of trees, but no twenty-year-old son. He sniffed the air. It was definitely going to rain. When it rained, Ho'kee usually had the sense to sleep inside, but that was about the only time. He had a comfortable room with a nice-sized bed, a TV that rarely got turned on, and stacks of books that remained unread. Abe shrugged. It could be worse. He worked with a lot of guys who couldn't get their adult kids out of bed, never mind out of the house.

Ho'kee showed no interest in moving out, and that was fine with Ethel and Abe. He was no trouble. He wasn't a lot of help around the house but wasn't a complete slob. He worked at a security firm and did contribute to the finances. All in all, he was a great kid. Abe wished he could feel closer to his only child. Ethel was closer, she seemed to 'get' him. But Abe didn't understand the boy at all. He didn't seem to have any friends, male or female. He was a good-looking boy, a bit on the lanky side. He had the high cheekbones of Abe's family, the full lips of his mother, and large dark eyes that were almost black. Abe rubbed the back of his neck. Maybe he was a late bloomer. Abe honestly did not care if Ho'kee's romantic interests were dudes or dames, as long as he was happy. And as long as he eventually moved out with said partner.

He couldn't really talk to the boy. Ho'kee always seemed to be in another world, a place Abe could not access. They had done the father-son things when Ho'kee was younger. The fishing, camping, and hunting trips. Ho'kee would not pull the trigger on the hunt. The last time Abe had lost his patience, urging the boy to make the kill, to pull the trigger, Ho'kee had laid the rifle down and walked away. He had walked all the way home and had refused to get in the truck. Abe knew then he had lost the boy to something, or someone, else. Abe was no longer the man Ho'kee thought moved heaven and earth, and that made Abe a little sad.

They'd started worrying about Ho'kee around his eighteenth birthday. He was still the same gentle, quiet, thoughtful young man at home, but neighbors were beginning to talk and complain. Granted, the nearest neighbors were miles away. However, one of them, an old trapper who kept close to the river and only came into town when he had to, walked onto Abe's property, shaking his fist and holding three sprung leghold traps in the other. Abe had a sinking feeling he knew what the fuss was about. He promised the old trapper he would look into it but assured him it was more likely some of those conservationists and ban-the-fur trade Greenpeacers were behind it. Not Ho'kee. The old trapper admitted he had not actually seen Ho'kee spring the traps, but he had seen him around the trapline, walking slowly and carefully, like he was committing the placement to memory. But he hadn't actually seen the boy spring a trap.

When Abe tried to talk to Ho'kee about it, he was met with a hostile glare and a response of absolute silence. Abe's stomach sank. He knew it had been Ho'kee. This bond he had with animals was eerie, going beyond affection, and more of solidarity. Ho'kee refused to hunt with a rifle. That last time, when he had put the rifle down and walked home, was the last time he used anything but a bow and arrow, and the last time he went hunting with his father. Then he began sneaking out of his room at night. Well, not really sneaking, given the boy was eighteen, but he came home weary, dirty, full of twigs and leaves, with some blood stains he claimed to have come from a scrape, or a fall, or a blackberry bush. Ethel didn't buy that. The boy's skin was messed up, but the clothes seemed as if they had been taken off, set aside, and put back on.

Now the neighbors were reporting seeing a large, silver-gray wolf around. Abe had a feeling Ho'kee might have befriended this creature, feeding it like he fed that damn lame fox. He had tried to talk to Ethel about it when the sightings first occurred. She had stiffened and her mouth dropped open. She had stared out the window, digging her fingernails into her palms. She had gone pale, and almost immediately, worry lines etched her beautiful face. Abe had asked her what the big deal was. It was a wolf, albeit a big one, but it didn't seem to want to harm anyone or anything except a few wild hares and deer. She asked Abe the strangest question, "What color do the neighbors say its eyes are?"

Abe's brow furrowed and he pulled his head back to study her.

"What? Eyes? Damn. Now that you mention it, the old trapper said it was the strangest thing. When he laid eyes on it, he noticed that it didn't show an ounce of fear. It looked straight at him, and its eyes were blue. Not the usual yellow or amber, but dark blue."

Ethel had reached for a chair. She had barely dropped into it before her legs collapsed from under her. They had not mentioned the wolf again, and that had been two weeks ago. Whatever had set her off, she refused to discuss it. Since then, Ethel had been trying to get Ho'kee to open up to her, but the boy had shut down.

As a child, Ho'kee used to live for the times Ethel and he would have story time before bed, picnics on the weekends, and early evening swims in the river. Ethel regaled him with stories of his lineage, and by far his favorite was the shapeshifter story. He was thrilled to hear about a man turning into a bear, or a frog, or a bird, and vanquishing the enemy. He told Ethel one day he was going to become a shapeshifter and destroy all the bad things and bad people who threatened those who could not help themselves. He didn't want to be a hero, he wanted to make the world a good place again. Ethel assured him he was from a long line of shapeshifters and could be anything he wanted. Abe chastised her later for putting these ideas in the boy's head, but she laughed and said Ho'kee would grow out of this stage. She wanted to keep his imagination, his belief that he could change the world, alive for a little while longer. She was not laughing at this idea.

It probably was time for him to leave home and set himself up in a place closer to the city, closer to his work at the security firm. He had been hoping to get a full-time spot in the hospital, and it would probably be better for him to be closer when the casual calls came in. Abe nodded and promised himself he would talk to Ho'kee when he got home. He gave one last glance around and noticed at the edge of the clearing, that pretty fox with the lame leg. He was watching Abe and put his long ears back. He dipped his snout and pawed at the ground delicately. Abe snorted and yelled back at Ethel.

"The boy is long gone, but his pet is here. Let's give it Ho'kee's dinner."

Behind the fox, completely invisible under the dark canopy of approaching nightfall and lush evergreens, a large silver-gray wolf watched Abe, its blue eyes never leaving Abe's face.

Father Benedict walked quickly by the information station on the first floor and stopped in front of the hospital chapel. He dug around in his cloak to find the keys and slapped his hand against his forehead. He had left the keys at home. He had been in such a hurry to get to the hospital to see a church member who had been admitted for pneumonia, that he had forgotten the chapel keys at home. He really wanted his Bible from the chapel. This particular parishioner took great comfort when he sat at her bedside for an hour, talking of local current events, and ending with a hopeful reading from the Good Book. He readjusted his glasses, which had slipped down his nose, and shook his head in frustration with himself and his foggy old brain.

"Benedict, you have the mind of a sieve," he muttered under his breath and glared at the doorknob.

A powerful forearm plunged in front of him with a tiny silver key in a massive dark fist. Benedict rocked back in surprise and almost collided with the security guard's chest, which was seemingly carved from rock.

The guard pulled back from opening the chapel door and spoke gently, his voice rolling deep and resonant. "There you are."

Benedict turned to look up at Shemar's face and smiled in gratitude. "Thank you, son. I feared I was going to have to make something up when I visited Mrs. Ritchie and I was dreading it. I fear that woman knows the scripture better than I do, you see. Oh, I read it on a daily basis, but I also watch a bit of *Coronation Street* and *Jeopardy!* However, Mrs. Ritchie does not. That good woman would not spend a minute of the day not in contemplation of the Lord and His words."

Shemar laughed, a real laugh that started in his belly and spread to his face, showing blindingly white teeth set off by full lips. "I like *Jeopardy!* myself. This job can get tedious. Alex Trebek keeps my mind snapping when it threatens to close up shop. I'll get the elevator for you."

Father Benedict held up his hand. "I thank you, Shemar, but I'll take the stairs. I don't get as much walking in as I used to, and I have to keep in shape. The women's Bible study once weekly group seems to bake as much as study and presents me with their decadent spoils every Sunday. I am a weak man, Shemar." He patted his rounded stomach. "A weak man indeed."

Shemar laughed and put his key ring back against his belt and turned to walk away. Benedict let himself into the chapel and closed the door behind him. He sank unsteadily onto the settee. These little bouts of dizziness, these recent bothersome periods where his heart would inexplicably race and pound against his chest wall like it was seeking freedom, were getting more frequent. He had hidden it for close to six months from his parishioners and coworkers. They always presaged something strange happening to him or around him. He hadn't seen a doctor—yet.

Lately, there had been strange episodes at the hospital and at his church. In the last two months, he had been called upon to pray over two parishioners. One had ongoing, crippling migraines. Months of medical tests and hundreds of dollars in alternative treatments had yielded no reason, and no cure, for the migraines. The young man, Hal, called Father Benedict in tears one night. He had decided to end his life. He couldn't deal with the ongoing pain any longer and felt he had run out of options. The priest had broken all posted speed limits to drive to the young man's apartment, and once he was there, prayed for all he was worth to have Hal let him in. After a few minutes of pleading, begging, and vaguely threatening conversation, the young man let him in. Benedict did a quick scan of the apartment and saw a large bottle of rye and several bottles of medications beside the bed. An unfinished letter was waiting for Hal's hand to pick up the pen again. Benedict took the man's hands and led him to a sofa. He sat beside him and asked if he could pray with him, just this one last time. Hal nodded—he had nothing to lose. The priest bent his head in prayer and placed his hands upon the man's head.

Immediately, his warm hands went ice cold. Father Benedict kept his eyes tightly closed and continued to pray. His hands became fiery hot and tingled as if every nerve had been exposed. It felt as if a surge of electricity was melding his hands to the man's head. The man began to whimper. The priest prayed louder, his voice taking on an edge he didn't know he possessed. Latin words rolled from his tongue and filled the room, reverberating off the walls. His hands continued to surge with heat and vibration, and Hal reached up to grab the priest's hands. He could not break the grip. Father Benedict lost himself in the experience; it seemed like he was on the outside looking in and could do nothing to stop what was happening. His eyes flew open and all he saw was a waterfall of color, an emerald-green light sparkling and flashing.

The room, the man, and the priest were encompassed by this light. A peace came over him like he had never known before in his life.

Hal's eyes widened as he held fast to the Father's wrists. He stared into the priest's eyes and stopped crying. He began to smile, then he started to laugh with abandon. "It's gone! The headache...it's *gone!*"

There had not been a return of the migraines for the young man. He had returned to work, returned to church, and had become Father Benedict's champion, much to the priest's chagrin. He didn't know what had happened but had a strong feeling Archangel Raphael, the patron saint of healing, had something to do with it. Father Benedict did not always see eye to eye with church doctrine, especially when it came to the stories of archangels and superhuman saints. But this...this was beyond any earthly explanation. He would have put it down to a once-in-a-lifetime mutual prayer experience if it hadn't been for Gladys two weeks later.

A devoted parishioner and all-around lovely lady, Gladys had been steadily losing her eyesight. There were no cataracts or retinal problems. Once again, tests had been inconclusive as to what was causing the encroaching blindness. She had started to retreat from the charity work they both loved. She stopped baking for the post-sermon coffee klatches. When she stopped coming to Sunday service, Father Benedict paid a home visit. Gladys lived with an adoring niece who helped as much as Gladys would allow her. Now that she was bumping into walls and furniture, and tripping over her beloved corgi, Gladys was spending more time in bed. She wasn't listening to the radio or tv. She was considering her options. She knew she was going to have to learn to use a cane. She was going to learn Braille. It was all so overwhelming to a seventy-year-old lady. Father Benedict listened to her at her bedside, and failing to find anything of substance to say, he simply took her hand. She smiled and patted his hand.

"There is an eye mask on the bedside table. It helps when the light gets too painful. Could you put it on my eyes, please?"

"Of course, my dear."

Benedict retrieved the cloth and leaned over to place the mask on Gladys' closed eyes. The temperature descended uncomfortably cool Shivering, he leaned over further to secure the mask. In seconds, his hands became unbearably hot and started to tingle.

Father Benedict went pale and whispered, "Oh no..."

Gladys made a sharp intake of breath as those hot, vibrating hands touched her temples. She reflexively reached for the priest's wrists, but his hold could not be broken. A jolt of what felt like electricity moved in strong, fluid currents from those hands to her temples. Father Benedict's eyes flew open wide, and he saw rainfalls of shimmering green sparks. Ancient words of healing fell from his lips, but he didn't recognize the voice as his own. He squeezed his eyes shut, and the vibration stopped.

He dropped his hands from Gladys's temples and looked at her beseechingly. "My dear! Gladys, I am so very sorry! I don't know what happened."

"My God, Father Benedict!"

Her frail fingers reached out, touching his face, and a radiant smile creased her face.

"I can see!"

There had been no return to the blindness, temporary or otherwise. Her doctor could not explain it and seemed disinterested to try, advising her to accept the wonderful stroke of fortune and move on. Gladys happily accepted the gift and joined Hal in praising both God and Father Benedict. Now the word was getting out about the laying on of magical hands by the priest. Father Benedict was less than impressed with his newfound stardom, even if was just contained to his little town. He eschewed the spotlight, uncomfortable even standing in the shadows of the choir, quite anonymous. In addition, he was at a loss to explain what was happening and why. He loved the healing that had happened to the two members of his flock, but he was also a rational man who believed in medicine and science. He did believe in the power of prayer, but the sight of green sparkling rain and physical electric currents was too much to simply accept, even for this man of God. He prayed over it. Mostly, he prayed that perhaps there were others like him that he could meet and thereby pronounce himself sane.

Benedict shook himself out of his woolgathering. He had someone to see. He tested his stance and, feeling normal—or as normal as he could, given his recent circumstances—he opened the chapel door for anyone needing sanctuary and left the room.

Behind him, in a picture of Raphael, an aura of emerald green pulsed above the archangel's beautiful head.

Mara burrowed around in her large garden toward the back of the property. She could hear her children and grandchildren laughing and arguing all the way to the back acreage. Pulling herself slowly to a standing position, she pressed a hand on her back, pushing her tummy forward and, in amusement, cracked her spine from bottom to top. Lifting a huge zucchini to eye level, critiquing its size, color, and shape, she smiled. It would win a prize or two back in the old country, that's for sure. But not here. Here there were not too many garden produce contests. Too many regulations in these contests, for one thing. All kinds of rules, demands, fees, fines, foes, and fums. This whole island seemed to exist within regulations, with the exception of her slice of heaven right here.

She looked up to the top of the hill where the family restaurant sat and patrons waited to be seated. From there, the patrons could see the acres of farmland used to provide fruits and vegetables to the kitchen. They could even see the outline of a large, clear lake in the distance. To Mara's satisfaction—her order, actually—they could not see her own cabin set against the base of the mountain and in front of the lake. Mara spent the majority of her time on the farm and by the lake, raising the crops and harvesting fruit. She demanded a rules-free zone in her own space.

She loved her grandchildren fiercely but being told to stop driving them around the acreage in the back of a beat-up truck filled with hay was still niggling at her. It was bad enough to get the directive that she had to bundle these children in bubble wrap before allowing them to come anywhere near the farm; it was worse that it came from her uptight daughter-in-law. So, the children stared at her from the family restaurant where they worked part-time as servers, cooks, and dishwashers, and gazed longingly at the back of the truck as it bounced back and forth from the gardens to the kitchens. Mara fondly thought of the youngest ones, her great-grandchildren, naked as peeled apples, hollering like Tarzan—or, in Leonid Jr.'s case, George of the Jungle—and plunging butt first, knees pulled up to their chins, into the refreshing freshwater lake at the end of the acreage. Her daughter-in-law had been fit to be tied when she came early this morning to pick them up for church.

Annika had watched in horror as the makeshift swing—a rope tied securely from a tree—carried the children individually, and often two at a time, to the deeper end and left them there to screech, holler, tread water, and splash each other. Mara was, as usual, hip-deep in the water herself, encouraging the children to swing farther, body bomb harder, and splash higher. And when they began to tire and shiver, she was there to wrap them in thick towels and sit them in front of a low fire, sipping sweet hot tea from her thermos and munching on her fresh sourdough bread slathered with churned butter and honey. It struck Mara as odd that Annika did not mind the unrestrained hijinks or the starch and sugar-laden choice of breakfast as much as she minded the children, aged three to six, running around naked.

"Please don't encourage them, Babushka!" Annika would plead, her nervous hands threading her skinny fingers like a ball of yarn.

"Don't encourage them to what? Be comfortable in the skin the Goddess gave them?"

"And *that*, Babushka. Please stop filling their heads with this nonsense of the Goddess," she pleaded. "I've been approached by other mothers at church who say my children are heathens."

"And this is a problem because...?"

Annika, her finely featured face in an uncomplimentary twist of frustration, pointed one of her red-tipped talons toward Mara. "These are *my* children, Babushka. I respect that you raised your boys on your own, and you did a good job. They are all fine men. But I had my work cut out for me to bring Leonid into God's grace, and I will not have you undermining my children's religious education!"

Mara watched her impassively, shining a just-plucked orchard apple in her wide apron. Mara blinked slowly, as the woman before her appeared to be much more mongoose than human with those nails, that hissing, and that tiny face. She smiled slightly and offered Annika the apple.

"No sugar. No fat. No starch. I will not instruct the children in the ways of the Goddess."

Because the Goddess will do that Herself, Mara thought but did not say.

Annika sighed heavily and snatched the apple, biting into it furiously. She turned from Mara and began her trudge back to the restaurant.

Mara called to her, "Would you like a ride? I am afraid Domovoi owns the passenger seat, but the back is nicely lined with soft hay!"

Mara caught the eye of her Russian wolfhound, staring calmly out from the truck's passenger seat. The wolfhound let out a long, bored grumble and settled his chin on the window. Annika lifted her hand without turning around, and Mara chuckled. She swore she heard a sisterly cackle coming from the direction of the lake. With a beaming smile, Mara lifted her skirts and kicked off her shoes. She was going to the lake to catch up with her Ladies. The restaurant was closed now for a week, and the grandchildren would be begging to come help her with canning, jamming, pickling, and going in search of lake monsters. Mara was discouraged from coming up to the house or restaurant. Her old-world dress, her strong accent, and her dirty fingernails embarrassed Annika. Mara was very happy to stay at her cottage on the lake and provide the jars of preserves, baskets of fruit, and an assortment of baked goods that the restaurant sold in its gift shop.

She was often sought out by friends of friends to consult tea leaves or read palms, but, of course, Annika would never speak of it. She would collect a portion of the fee, call Mara on the phone to let her know to open her reading room, and send her husband Leonid with the seeker to consult Mara. Mara had a powerful gift, many repeat clients, and a strong word-of-mouth network. By mutual decision, there was to be no advertisement of this service in any paper. While it might be a novelty to some, it was a revered and serious gift to Mara and a potent threat to others.

With the afternoon to herself, Mara seated herself in front of the lake and patted the wood stool at her side. Immediately, a large, ugly toad leapt beside her, croaked vociferously, and then settled himself. Mara watched the lake and listened to the wind as it picked up in its intensity. She placed her leathered hands in her lap and fixed her dark eyes on a small pool of water at her feet. Slowly, independently of the lake, the pool formed small ripples. The waves chased each other around the perimeter of the pool and ceased. Mara stared intently.

Inside the pool, she saw the images of five other people. She did not recognize their faces, but she felt their power. She also felt their inability to harness, or even acknowledge their own power. As she studied each image thoughtfully, she grimaced slightly at the sight of the handsome young man who needed to be fed, and smiled broadly at the image of the chubby little Asian girl who seemed to look right back at her from the pool. Mara gave a little wave to the child and, to her delight, the child curled and uncurled her plump fist in acknowledgment. Ah. The child would be the strongest of them all.

She reared back a little when she saw the large, beautiful African American man. His power was raw and unacknowledged. That much power in a man without guidance on how to use it worried Mara, but she had faith in the Ladies. They knew what they were doing when they chose him. She also knew she had been called to help him and she accepted the mission graciously.

She grinned when she saw the benevolent priest studying a cockle shell. He played with it in the sunlight, catching the rays and smiling delightedly when he put it to his ear. She watched him on the cliff above a calm sea with his church in the background. He was a gentle soul and, as he got older, his empathy became stronger. Lately, he was becoming concerned as his regular laying on of hands had become a sensation. Anyone from a toothache to chronic pain had sought him out and been cured. He had no idea what to make of this. He had caught the attention of the diocese, who wanted to send an exploratory team to research him. Father Benedict was a spotlight-shy man. He did not understand his power and was loathe to lay claim to it. Mara felt a kinship with the old soul but had a profound sense of loss when she watched him. She could help him understand and work with his abilities, but she couldn't stop what was going to happen to him. What already had its teeth in his body.

She widened her eyes when she saw a young Indigenous man running through the forest. She rubbed her eyes and looked again; the boy was shapeshifting. A Navajo shapeshifter, a Diné. She had heard of them, but she had not seen one. She watched as the boy picked up speed in the forest, his feet seeming to barely touch the ground. He leaned forward, almost doubling over, and his face narrowed sharply. Mara watched, fascinated, as the boy's skin sprouted thick, black fur. His face elongated farther, and his ears shifted upwards. He dropped to all fours, and his haunches lifted. A thick tail uncurled behind him, and the boy was a wolf. A magnificent, looming wolf. The wolf sat back on his haunches, his long tongue lolling from the exertion. His pricked ears twisted, and he stopped panting. He sniffed the air and turned startlingly blue eyes toward Mara. She touched her chest and inclined her head toward the wolf. It stared at her briefly before dipping its wet snout and blinking once. It stood up and resumed its journey. Mara wiped away tears of gratitude that she had lived this long to see this. To be able to be part of this.

Her intention settled on the handsome young man who looked to be of Celtic descent. She put her finger against her nose and nodded at the image. She thought but did not speak.

"Oh, you are a handsome devil. You probably have a trail of broken hearts behind you."

The image jolted. The wide blue eyes of Declan looked around, a smile played at those full lips, and she could read the words he was saying out loud.

"Thank you. But not as many as you evidently think."

Mara sat up straight and her eyes flew open wide. She watched as Declan's eyes did the same. He didn't know. He suspected, but he didn't know. He had the gift of telepathy, and it was strong. But he had been denying it all his life. Mara cocked her head to the side and watched him wave a long-fingered hand across his face. He looked irritated. She wondered if he was hearing voices in his head again and was putting his telepathy down to that lifelong excuse. She sensed a power from this man that she had never felt before. There was more. His telepathy was one gift, but this one—this one had another gift and Mara sensed it was stronger in him than anyone she'd met in her long life. She didn't know what it was yet, but she knew the Ladies were going to have a hand in developing it.

Mara pushed a bare toe into the pool to set it stirring again. Scrying always made her so tired. She pushed the toad out of the way to use the stump as a lever to get up, then she saw something stir in the pool's reflection. She slowly sat back down again; her breath held.

She saw an abandoned city with crumbling concrete and tattered flags, untended fields going to seed. A multitude of animals looked bedraggled and hungry. She smelled decay and saw clouds of insects swarming over prone, rotting mounds. She peered closer. The mounds were black with strips of brilliant white bone contrasting sharply. She pulled back in horror.

"We must hurry."

Yenay lay in bed, listening to her little girl chattering away in her room. Not for the first time, Yenay thought of how lucky she was to have a child who had never had a tantrum or colic and rarely cried. Yenay didn't understand her child's calm and asked her family members if this was a common trait in babies in their family. The amount of laughter that met that question had not been heard before or since in any family gathering. Her mother and her aunts were quick to give her anecdotes about her own behavior up to Annalee's tender age of four. Apparently, Yenay's daughter had not inherited her mother's ear-splitting screech or miserable morning personality. Nor did Annalee refuse to sleep in her own bed. Yenay smiled and turned onto her back, trying to hear what Annalee was saying. It sounded like she was talking to someone and giggling.

Annalee had so many imaginary friends. Yenay knew her daughter would be a writer— probably a best-selling author—with such a creative little mind. She could also be a healer of some kind. She had this uncanny ability to calm the most agitated person or animal. She would often try to touch the afflicted party, but Yenay was always quick to pull her away. Then the child would simply look at the despairing or angry subject, wave her chubby little fingers in an open and closed fist motion, and babble some complete nonsense. The result was eerie. The subject of her attention would immediately become serene, and look confused as if they couldn't remember what on earth had set them off in the first place. People always smiled and mimicked Annalee's open/closed fist toward her, often laughing. The animals would sit quietly, tails curled around their bodies or wagging furiously, bowing to her gracefully or rolling on their backs for tummy rubs. Yenay put it down to the open, innocent beauty of her child's pretty face. For the sake of humanity in general, she hoped little Annalee never grew out of that ability.

"Mama?" Annalee's sweet voice carried through the rooms, inquisitive and bright.

"Annalee?"

"Mama!"

"Annalee!"

Annalee erupted in high high-pitched, delighted giggles. Yenay waited, hearing the tiny footsteps hit the floor and charging her room. Her little daughter stopped at the open door, clapped her hands together, and grinned happily at her mother.

"Mama!" She stretched out her arms.

"Annalee!" Yenay stretched out her own and Annalee trundled as fast as her short legs would carry her to her mother's bedside. She bounced onto the bed and curled into Yenay's warm arms. Yenay closed her eyes and inhaled the scent of her baby. Annalee giggled beneath her.

"What doing, Mama?"

"I am smelling how delicious you are, my dear. I think I may have you...for breakfast!"

Yenay growled and made chomping noises near Annalee's ear. The little girl laughed and squirmed.

49

They both settled in the bed, Annalee playing with the ever-present stuffed iguana she had picked out herself from the toy store. Out of all the teddys, horsies, and kitties, she had insisted on the lizard.

"What we doing today, Mama?"

Yenay played with the child's soft black hair. "Excellent question. What should we do today? What would you like to do today?"

Annalee looked thoughtful and piped, "Beach!"

Yenay smiled. Annalee loved to explore the beach. She was fascinated by tidal pools and could spend hours studying those miniature worlds. She would move things around to see the living creatures, but would never harm anything. She didn't crush mussels to watch a feeding frenzy of the hermit crabs and fry. She watched, and she babbled. Gulls would quiet themselves around her. They didn't seem to feel threatened by her presence and would watch her from a short distance, going about their own business. Playful sea otters would wrestle each other and scrabble up and down the shore to Annalee's delight. They didn't seem to mind her presence either. They actually seemed to enjoy it and would perform acrobatic acts in the water to hear her belly laugh.

Yenay smoothed Annalee's hair back from her forehead. Annalee had gone quiet, absently toying with the lizard. Yenay frowned and put her lips to Annalee's forehead. She was warm. She wasn't damp with water like the other night, nor was she sweating, but she was so warm. Too warm.

"Annalee, sweetie. How are you feeling?"

Annalee turned glassy eyes to her mother. Her cheeks were splotching with an unhealthy glow. "Tired, Mama. I feel hot."

Yenay threw the blankets off the bed and gathered her daughter in her arms. Moving quickly to the bathroom counter, she dug through the cabinet drawers and pulled out a thermometer. Yenay pushed it on and passed it over Annalee's forehead. One hundred one.

"Okay, Miss Annalee, you are getting into a bath."

Ordinarily, this would have been greeted with squeals of excitement and a frenzied collecting of assorted toys for the bath. This morning it was met with quiet.

"Okay, Mama," she replied wearily.

Annalee didn't protest when Yenay helped her get undressed, and this caused Yenay further concern. Her daughter's independence chant, several times a day, was, "I can do it myself!" but there was no battle cry this morning. They got into the bath, and Yenay had a sharp intake of breath at the surprise of the cool temperature, but Annalee did not respond. She sat in between Yenay's legs, her arms limp at her side. Yenay squeezed water over her daughter's head and shoulders, but there was no reaction. No giggles, no sighs—nothing. Yenay pressed her lips to Annalee's temple, and her own eyes widened in apprehension.

She bundled Annalee out of the cool bath and placed her on the counter again. Annalee was having trouble sitting up straight without support, she seemed to be tired and weak. Yenay passed the thermometer over her forehead again. One hundred two.

"No," whispered Yenay. She bent forward and tried to catch Annalee's gaze. The child, who would usually lock eyes with her mother and stare into her own brown depths, could not meet her gaze. Her stare was glassy, off in the distance. Yenay briskly rubbed Annalee and applied a cool cloth to the child's neck, armpits, forehead, and then her ears. She checked Annalee's temperature again.

One hundred three.

Yenay wrapped her child in a thick towel, grabbed her car keys and the stuffed iguana, and proceeded to break all speed limits toward the hospital.

Declan was glaring at the empty canvas in front of him when his phone went off. He reached over to the kitchen counter to silence it but saw the number for the hospital displayed. He gripped the phone tighter as a cold sense of dread traveled from his head to his toes. Niall. He answered the call. "Declan O'Neill."

"Mr. O'Neill, this is Haida Gwaii Hospital. Your name was given by your brother, Niall."

Declan clenched his strong jaw tightly. He held on to the counter, his forearms flexing with the fierce grip. "What happened?"

"Mr. O'Neill, there was an accident at your brother's work site. He suffered an injury that required several stitches. He has been given narcotics to alleviate the pain but is in no condition to drive. He may be released, but only into your custody. Could you come and pick him up?"

Declan let go of the breath he had been unconsciously holding and closed his eyes in relief. "I will be right there."

Ho'kee was shoveling scrambled eggs into his mouth at an alarming rate when his phone shrilled. Ethel looked over, amused—and a little disgusted—when Ho'kee put the phone to his ear and mumbled, "Hello?"

"Ho'kee? It's Jack at the security firm. Listen, we've had to let go of someone at the hospital. Can you come in and orient with...give me a minute..."

Ho'kee heard the sound of shuffling paper.

"His name is Shemar. And hey, you do this well and the admin likes you, it could be the full-time permanent gig you want."

Ho'kee nodded his head but couldn't swallow the overload of eggs. Ethel picked the phone out of his hand and spoke into it.

"Hi, Jack, this is Ethel. Ho'kee will be there right away."

She handed the phone back to Ho'kee, who gave her the thumbs up, crammed a piece of toast into his mouth, and then bolted to his bedroom to get his uniform.

Mara was flinging a bale of hay from her truck bed to the horse pen when she caught sight of the water trough at the side of the barn. The water was still and an image floated upwards. She dropped the pitchfork at the sight of Annalee in Yenay's arms, rushing toward the local hospital emergency doors. She hauled herself into the truck and peeled off the property onto the dirt road leading to the main drive, hay flying behind her.

Shemar was posted at the emergency entrance when he saw the young Asian lady, a child in her arms, running toward the doors. He watched as she tried to move around the ambulance attendants who were beside an elderly man stretched out on a transport bed. The attendants looked annoyed, and one held up his hand to block Yenay from getting ahead of them. Shemar heard her panic-stricken voice as she tried to talk to the attendant, who glared at her and beckoned Shemar to come over and deal with this line jumper. Shemar moved to intercept her from getting in front of the old man. His low voice was firm but gentle.

"Ma'am, the lineup for emergency starts there. You are behind this gentleman."

Yenay's hoarse voice caught in her throat as she tried to catch her breath. "My daughter has a fever! It came on so suddenly. We need help!"

Shemar looked at her calmly. Tears streamed down her face and worry choked her breath. He then looked down at the child in her arms, and his mouth tightened. The child's eyes were closed, her face was flaming with fever.

"Gloria! Gloria, come here!"

The solid nurse that had confronted Bubba shuffled her bulk from the entrance cubicle to join Shemar. She took one look at Annalee and concern immediately creased her face.

"We need to get your daughter to a doctor, right now."

Yenay turned frightened eyes to Shemar. He put his arms out for the child and Yenay handed Annalee over. For the first time in over an hour, the child stirred. She opened her dark eyes slightly and a hint of a smile tugged at her pretty mouth. She tried to reach up to Shemar, but she was too weak.

She whispered, "Shango," and dropped back into unresponsiveness.

Shemar reared back as a wave of recognition battled his denial. Something ancient, something primitive fought its way from his heart to his head. He looked down at the child in his arms, at the hostility building in the waiting patients, at the growing panic on the young mother's face, and he let the primal feeling take over.

Instantly, his huge figure seemed to loom even greater over the hospital waiting room. His voice thundered. "*Still!*"

The crowded waiting room came to a complete halt. People stood staring at the angry godlike figure before them. They quickly sat down and watched in open-mouthed awe as their possessions were flung from the aisle to the sides of the walls without being touched by any hand, providing a clear passage for the dark man to take his tiny sacred bundle into the emergency treatment area. Gloria and Yenay followed close behind.

Shemar strode into the triage room and all eyes turned toward him; all movement stopped. A complete silence descended; nothing but the sound of life-saving machinery could be heard. "Pediatrician!"

A slight, older man stepped quickly from another cubicle and stood in front of Shemar. The doctor opened his arms for Annalee. Shemar's arms closed reflexively around her.

The doctor inclined his head slightly and spoke gently, "Shemar. I will take care of her. You have my word."

He handed the child to the doctor and withdrew his hands. The energy that had flooded him dissipated, and he stood there blinking, wondering what the hell had just happened.

The doctor was administering to Annalee, brusquely demanding tests and assistance. Gloria held onto Yenay's shoulders, keeping her close. No one dared to ask either one to move aside or wait in the hallway. Cautious glances still flicked toward Shemar, but the main focus was on the child.

Abruptly, the doctor lifted his head and looked steadily at Shemar. "If you could return to your post, I have this under control. I think you are making the staff a bit nervous."

Shemar nodded once and turned on his heel. The doctor called his name before he left, "Shemar! Good work getting her back here. She wouldn't have made it much longer. We will do everything we can."

As he left, he swore he heard her delicate voice in his head again, "Shango."

He looked down at his hands. One was clutching a stuffed iguana. This must be Shango. He paused and walked back to the cubicle. He put the toy on a table just outside the drawn curtain and turned away.

He needed to calm down. He stopped at the security cubicle and spoke to Nelson, who fell back in his chair, staring up at his co-worker in a new light.

"How did you...what happened...sweet baby Jesus, Shem..."

Shemar removed his hat and wiped the back of his hand over his brow. He shook his head. "I need a few minutes, Nelson. I am going for a walk outside."

Declan was at the bedside of his brother when they heard the alert over the system.

"Code Blue. Triage. Code Blue."

He went to that place he always did where no one could follow him. Declan stared straight ahead, seeing nothing, and watching everything. He didn't fight the wave of dizziness. He gripped the sides of his chair and his eyes fixed on the wall behind Niall. He saw a little Asian girl fighting for her life that was slipping away in fever. He saw a crowd of anxious medical personnel around her, an older doctor barking orders, and a panic-stricken young mother. The image expanded as the child's arm dropped lifelessly to the side.

Declan sucked in his breath as a green aura filled the image and a benevolent-looking priest lay his hands on the child. The child's chest rose with life.

The voice of the beautiful woman he had seen in his dreams clearly filled his mind. "Find him. Save her."

Declan sat bolt upright and stared at Niall.

Niall waved his fingers at Declan, obviously recognizing that his brother had just had one of his visions. "Go, little brother. *Go!*"

Declan ran out into the hallway, pleading for guidance to find the priest.

Ho'kee pulled up on his motorcycle outside the hospital. Taking off his helmet and grabbing his knapsack, he checked to make sure he had packed his security guard uniform and was not surprised to see a bagged lunch from his mom. Smiling, he decided not to move out, ever. No way. Ho'kee stopped smiling when an unfamiliar and unpleasant odor permeated the air. Ho'kee's back rose instinctively, and his lips curled in a snarl.

He narrowed his eyes and scanned the area for the source of the stench. There were so many people around that he couldn't spot the Carrier of that smell in his human form, but he couldn't shape-shift here either. Often, the Carrier was doing no harm at that moment, but they carried the smell of intention. They smelled rotten, and it was more potent when they were activating.

After picking up his helmet, he strode toward the hospital entrance, running his fingers through his long black hair.

His sharp hearing methodically singled out conversations, in search of the Carrier.

"Please tell me he is a new doctor here."

"Please tell me he is anything but a doctor here."

"We have to find a home for Mom. I can't take her, and she can't live alone anymore."

"Jesus, that was close. Another few inches and his leg would have been amputated."

"The little girl. Find the little girl."

Ho'kee stopped short and looked at the sky. He cocked his head toward the copse in the distance. The mumbled commitment came from the Carrier—low, secret and whispered, but he heard it. He bared his teeth and broke into a run to get to the ER before the Carrier did. He would think of an excuse for his haste to his new supervisor when he got there, but he had to get there. He didn't know who the little girl was or why she was a target of the Carrier, but it didn't matter.

He was in a position to try to thwart intentional harm, and he had learned to trust this feral instinct of his by now.

Mara parked her beaten truck beside the shiny new cars in the parking lot and slid out of her seat. She would normally lock the door, but she was hoping someone might steal it. At least, that's what she usually hoped. Today she wasn't thinking of anything besides the little girl. She had to find the Others, the ones whose faces she had seen in the water, and bring them together.

She wasn't sure how she was going to do this but had faith that the threads she needed to pull the scene together would present themselves. Hitching up her heavy skirts, she moved quickly to the hospital entrance. The shapeshifter darted ahead of her, his black hair flying behind him, a feral intensity in his run. She grimaced and picked up her pace.

Father Benedict laughed and leaned away from Gladys. She had been admitted for heart palpitations and was linked to an interesting machine that blipped along contentedly—for now. He patted her hand and adjusted his glasses. "Now, my dear, I must take my leave. It is Sunday tomorrow, and I haven't a clean thing to wear. I simply must do a wash."

Gladys laughed and shooed him with her free hand, the other held captive by the pulse oximeter. He walked out of the room and rubbed his hands together in an attempt to warm them up. That was strange... He'd felt too warm just minutes ago in the stuffy four-bed hospital room. He turned toward the elevator lobby.

Declan hit the second floor and ran to the nurse's station.

The unit clerk did not look up as she flipped pages but welcomed him with an irritated voice. "Yes?" she snapped.

Declan put his hands on the counter. The movement flexed his forearm muscles. The unit clerk looked at the forearms, and her eyes traveled to the face in front of her. Immediately, her demeanor changed. She turned the papers upside down, grinned widely, and smoothed her voice. "Well, good afternoon! How may I help you?"

Declan arched an eyebrow and leaned slightly forward, his white T-shirt straining at his sculpted chest. "Is there a priest here?"

The unit clerk's smile twitched, and she looked at a notebook beside her. She traced a well-manicured nail down the lines and announced triumphantly. "There he is! Father Benedict. Room 312, visiting a parishioner. He hasn't signed out yet so he must still be up there. Do I get a reward?"

Declan ran his eyes over the unit clerk in a way that left nothing to guess about his intentions.

The sweet voice sounded in his head again. *"Go now, Declan O'Neill."*

Declan stood straight and bolted for the stairwell.

Father Benedict's hands went ice cold as he stood by the elevators on the third floor, waiting to go down. He held them up to look at them, curious. His fingertips turned an almost blue-green before he plunged them into his frock pockets and squinted at the lights above the elevator doors. The usual red lights were glowing a brilliant green. A wave of dizziness came over him and he turned around to sit on the couch in the lobby area. He closed his eyes and pinpoints of green light sparked behind his lids. His eyes flew open as a handsome young man crouched in front of him, grabbing his shoulders. He heard the words from the young man's mouth and swore he felt those words push into his head, crowding into the green light.

"A little girl needs you! It has to be you!"

Father Benedict allowed the man to help him to his feet, and together they ran for the steps as the elevator buttons faded back to red.

In the triage area, the doctor looked helpless as the child's arm dropped to the side of the bed. Father Benedict watched, but no breath filled the tiny chest.

The doctor stood back, giving the priest room. "She's gone. You should administer last rites."

A woman, the child's mother he assumed, screamed from behind him. Gloria, the emergency room nurse, held her as the young woman tried to wrest herself away.

Benedict moved to the cot and laid his hands on the child.

He closed his eyes and the ancient language of Latin poured from his lips, his voice not his own. A brilliant green aura enclosed both Benedict and the child. The aura seemed to start pulsating. The priest's hands grew hot as if they were being thrust into flame, but he did not remove them from the child. He rocked slowly, the dead language rolling off his tongue. He lost himself in the waterfall of emerald lights and allowed the energy to flow in vibrations from himself to the child. The aura swelled around them, pulsing faster.

A single, hard jolt of power seemed to wrest itself from his heart, through his hands, and into the child. The aura stilled, and she opened her brilliant brown eyes. Benedict smiled down at the little girl, and she smiled up at him.

She whispered, "Raffie."

The aura dissipated quickly, fading into the air around it.

The priest gathered her up and held her close. The woman could not stop crying and clutched at her daughter when the priest held her out.

The doctor leaned forward and rolled the temperature over the girl's forehead. "Ninety-eight."

Father Benedict leaned back slightly on the hospital bed behind him, not trusting his ability to stand on his own. Several nurses clasped their hands in prayer and grabbed their crosses. Others clasped each other's hands and whispered, "Blessed be. Thank you, Goddess."

He looked over to meet the bright, healthy eyes of the child. He waggled a finger at her, which she clutched at playfully. "You gave us quite a scare, little one."

The little girl pouted a bit and looked thoughtful. She pointed to the man who had brought Benedict and exclaimed loudly, "Dagda!"

The man smiled and waved his fingers at Annalee.

She grinned shyly and gazed at the priest. "Raffie," she lisped.

The doctor looked puzzled. "Father Raffie?"

Benedict laughed and shrugged his shoulders. "I think that might be this stuffed iguana on her table."

The doctor laughed and leaned in close to the priest's ear. "We are going to need to talk."

"Of course, doctor. But let me rest. I will be in the chapel." Father Benedict looked over at the strange man and crooked his finger in a come-with-me motion. The two of them walked out of the triage area and into the waiting room.

Ho'kee strode up to the security enclosure, hyper-aware of his surroundings. His instincts told him the little girl was safe for now, but the Carrier was still in the area. He scanned the people in the waiting area, but no one there had the fetid stench. From what he could tell, the Carrier hadn't come into the hospital yet. That was good, that gave him the advantage. He deliberately shut down his heightened hunting senses. He pushed the bell outside the enclosure and was greeted by a homely, red-haired man with a big grin.

"Ho'kee Bidziil? Hiya! I'm Nelson." A freckled, pudgy hand closed around Ho'kee's in a firm grip.

"Come on in! Shemar is...uh...right behind you."

Ho'kee knew that. He sensed a coiled presence behind him that felt both caring and fierce. This presence could belong to a savior or a destroyer, or both. Ho'kee could feel the man towering over him, and he wasn't short. He grinned slightly at Nelson and turned around and stared at a chest that might as well have been the grille of a Mack Truck. He tilted his head upwards and caught the calm stare of what was quite possibly the largest man Ho'kee had ever seen.

The man grinned, and his smile was blinding and welcoming. He thrust out a huge hand and enclosed Ho'kee's warmly. His voice, a deep, rich bass, filled the security booth even though he was still outside of it.

"You must be Ho'kee. We are damned glad to have you aboard, son. I hear great things about you from Jack. We had to let go of the previous guard rather abruptly—"

"He was an asshat," piped Nelson.

Shemar glowered at Nelson, who sat down and pulled his hat down his forehead.

"I'm Shemar. I will be orienting you tonight. You can use the locker room behind you to change and lock up your stuff. Did you bring lunch? Cafeteria closes at five, so if you need food for later—"

Ho'kee held up his knapsack and looked a bit shamefaced. "My mom packed a dinner for me. She always does that."

Shemar's smile got even bigger, and he belly laughed. "No shit! My mom does the same thing, and I am a damn sight older than you. I don't live at home anymore, and she still cruises by here, each shift, with a bag of something she cooked up."

Nelson pushed his cap back and lunged for the paper sack on the console, the bag obviously the origin of the rich, sugary smell permeating the air. He pulled out a cinnamon cake donut and sank his teeth in it, groaning and closing his eyes. "Oh, sweet baby Jesus. Will your mother marry me, Shemar? I promise I will make a good daddy to ya."

Shemar leaned over and snatched the bag from Nelson and then extended it toward Ho'kee. "Forgive my coworker's lack of manners. He actually was born in a barn and still lives there."

Ho'kee went to reach for a donut, but a stench filled his nostrils. He flinched and pulled back. His eyes narrowed and scanned the emergency room entrance. His muscles tightened and a low growl began in his throat as he saw the Carrier. His eyes widened slightly as he fastened two people in his view. A middle-aged woman with gray-blonde hair cut short, but fashionably, entered slightly ahead of her escort. Her face was serene, a small smile playing at her carefully-lipsticked mouth. She wore a long, pale gray coat, and her boots were a high-end match to the outfit.

Ho'kee's upper lip curled as he watched her incline her head toward the admitting nurses. She was rancid, but the source of the strongest scent stood beside her.

An elegant man had his well-manicured hand on the woman's elbow. He was the most handsome man Ho'kee had ever seen, and he had never smelled a more rotted soul. The regal gentleman smiled at the nurses. Most of them fawned over him and placed gentle hands on his expensive jacket. In return, he would look deeply into their eyes, place his own hand over theirs and bend his salt-and-pepper head toward their lips to hear them. The gesture was profoundly intimate, and he used it with practiced ease.

The woman beside him slipped her hand through the crook of his elbow and administered a bit more force to spur him forward, but he did not fight this. He laughed and patted her hand, shrugging and looking charmingly sheepish.

Ho'kee's eyes never left the man's face, although his hands really wanted to fold over his nose and mouth to stop the fumes that he had to contend with. No one else seemed to share his impression of stink around this couple. Ho'kee stood by the security cubicle and watched how others interacted with them. He tried to hear what they were saying, but there was no mention of a little girl.

The well-dressed man stood upright and looked intently around the waiting room. His eyes met Shemar's, and he bent his head in unfriendly acknowledgment of the guard. Shemar returned the cold greeting.

The man continued his visual assessment, and his gaze fastened onto an elderly woman in layers of skirts sitting unobtrusively in the waiting area. Ho'kee narrowed his field of vision to watch the man's face and was repelled and fascinated by the fact that the man's pupils were slitted like a snake's.

The older woman seemed to feel a malevolent presence circling her. She sat straighter in her chair and pulled out a talisman. As she held the pendant, she scanned the room. Her eyes met those of the snake-eyed man and his face clouded. He shook his head sharply and as quickly as the authentic reaction took place, it was replaced by a fake public smile.

Nelson scrambled to his feet and quickly made his way to the well-dressed woman's side. Shemar watched her, expressionless.

His voice was flat as he gave Ho'kee a synopsis of the characters. "Reverend Mother Beatrice. Hangs around like a bad smell. Tight with a few of the board members. Especially the CEO there, Nicholai Zlo."

Ho'kee did not take his eyes off the couple. "You are not a fan," he remarked to Shemar.

Shemar sighed deeply and shoved his hands into his front pockets. "No. I am not. I am a big supporter of the Big Guy Upstairs, but I don't get the feeling she and the Good Lord speak the same language. She is very intense. Not very tolerant of those who don't think like she does. We have a chapel here. There are interdenominational services on Sunday, we have visiting rabbis, healers, coven members, and priests of every denomination. That bugs her. There is only one way in her book, and it's her way. She's a lot to process."

"And the guy in the handmade tailored suit. That is Nicholai Zlo," Ho'kee stated.

"Yes. CEO of Haida Gwaii hospital foundation. He has a 'vision' for the foundation."

"That sounds charitable, but I am thinking it isn't?" Ho'kee asked.

"You are very perceptive, son. To his followers and investors, he can do no wrong. Anything he touches turns into pure gold. It is usually at the expense of affordable housing, shelters, low-income subsidized developments, and treatment centers. Anything that can be torn down to be replaced by something more luxurious and accessible by those with a lot of money is expendable to Mr. Zlo. That includes the marginalized people living in and using those places."

Shemar's eyes clouded. "He has been lobbying for years to change the fee structure of this hospital. Fortunately, he can't quite manage it due to some long-term humanitarian members of the board and legal regulations, but he tries. He would like to see private care for those who can afford it. He would like to turn away those who can't. Which would be a big part of our demographic population. He has a bug up his butt about marginalized people. Actually, I think it's people in general. I think Zlo would be quite happy to see only a select few of the human race walking this earth."

Ho'kee's dark eyes searched Shemar's. His voice was calm and low when he replied to Shemar's musings. "You are absolutely right, sir."

Shemar's brilliant smile flashed in his dark face again and his good nature resumed. "Sir! I gotta tell Nelson. I am *sir*. I like it. It suits me."

Mr. Zlo was expertly greeting the employees and certain, but not all, patients in the waiting room. The Reverend Mother had split from his side and was spending time with the better-dressed patients, pressing prayer beads into their hands and arranging her face in a mask of sympathy and concern. Zlo was speaking to one of the ambulance attendants when he straightened, his face becoming devoid of any emotion. His jaw visibly clenched, and he looked over at the Reverend Mother. She looked up to catch the telltale tic of frustration at the side of his mouth, almost imperceptible under the carefully groomed black beard.

Mr. Zlo was very unhappy.

Ho'kee watched the exchange and focused on the words as the woman hurried to Zlo's side. The handsome man lowered his immaculately styled salt-and-pepper head and smiled expertly as he hissed to the Reverend Mother. "Find a little girl. She was resuscitated by Father Benedict. She was supposed to have died."

The Reverend Mother looked confused. A moment later, she nodded brusquely and moved away from him.

Ho'kee held his breath. That was the voice he had heard outside.

The Reverend Mother spotted Nelson and beckoned him to her side. Nelson quickly adhered to her, and she placed a gentle hand on his shoulder.

Shemar spoke quietly to Ho'kee in a low voice. "We better do some crowd control or Zlo will never get out of there. And I want him out."

Nelson was fawning over the Reverend Mother, her hand still on his shoulder. Ho'kee noticed her nails were bitten to the quick. She stopped talking to Nelson abruptly, and her spine stiffened. She removed her hand and turned slowly to face Shemar. The trace of a sneer began to tug at her nose, and when her eyes flicked over to Ho'kee, her jaw clenched.

Ho'kee felt bad intent wash up to him, stop, and recede like a wave back to its owner. Her hard stare bore into his inscrutable black gaze. He could feel her pull back from him as if she were unsure of her footing. If she were a cat, she would be hissing and arching her back.

Instead, she spoke to Nelson in a southern drawl, never taking her eyes off Ho'kee. "Nelson, please go and help Mr. Zlo extricate himself from his people, will you? He is so kind, he doesn't know how to say enough. I would like to take a moment to catch up with our dear Shemar and his new friend."

Nelson tipped his fingers to his cap and left the three standing there, a silence fraught with tension binding them together.

She abruptly broke her gaze with Ho'kee and looked up at Shemar. "Shemar, my dear. How is your mother? I do wish she would come to one of our One True Vision Sunday services. Oh, what a pleasure it would be to enfold her in our flock, especially our choir. Her voice is legendary and worthy of a truly professional coterie. It seems a bit wasteful to tether that gift to such a tiny, neighborhood assembly."

Her words were completely devoid of warmth or sincerity. Ho'kee tilted his head slightly to the right, trying to estimate her age, and consciously trying to tamp down the stench by alternating with mouth breathing.

Shemar did not smile, and his response was as cool as her address. "She is well, Reverend Mother, thank you for asking. I believe she is loved and valued right where she is in the Baptist congregation, ma'am."

Reverend Mother Beatrice drew her brows together as if such an idea was completely beyond comprehension. "Yes...well...perhaps someday. Are you going to introduce me to this dashing young man?" Her pale gaze locked onto Ho'kee's dark look, but neither extended their hands in greeting.

"Reverend Mother Beatrice, this is our newest security guard, Ho'kee."

She tilted her well-coiffed head and narrowed her eyes slightly. "Well, isn't the hospital fortunate? And do you feel fortunate as well, Mr. Ho'kee? Being a man of immigrant or Indigenous status and being hired here must fill you with gratitude."

Ho'kee felt an intense heat flare from the big man beside him and felt his own anger rise to accompany it. He looked down his aquiline nose at the woman in front of him and spoke firmly and proudly. "Descendant of the land, and multiple generations on this island, ma'am. I am Diné."

74

Beatrice felt her blood rush from her face and stepped back from the two men. Just as quickly, she rearranged her controlled mask. Her voice held a nervous treble. "I see. If you two men will excuse me, I must attend to spiritual matters with the board. I have an appointment and I fear I have made myself quite late."

Shemar inclined his head slightly, and Ho'kee smiled, raising his hand in a gesture of goodbye.

She took a step forward to walk between the men to the elevator lobby and decided against it. Pulling her jacket tightly around herself, she took a sharp right and went to the staircase. Once she had closed the door behind her, she sank to a seat on the step.

She gripped her twisting stomach, feeling slightly sick. Where on God's earth did that wicked boy come from? She knew it was impossible, but she swore that boy could look right through her. Nevertheless, she felt stripped bare, scrutinized, and found unworthy. A flare of anger suffused her. She was the one who judged others. She would not have that feral-looking boy judge her! She dropped her head in her hands. She had to get herself together.

She needed a reason to have the board fire Shemar and that boy. Shemar had remained unmalleable, and under his tutelage, the boy would be just as unsympathetic to the Vision and too sympathetic to the undesirables. She had to be careful. A dismissal without proper cause would ignite a ruckus within the hospital and bad publicity that they could not afford. That big man was a well-loved presence in this establishment, but he was becoming a thorn in her side.

His regard for her was obviously dwindling. He had liked her at first, and she had worked very hard to maintain the façade of a nun who loved all, regardless of station in life, but it was exhausting keeping up that image. He seemed to be in the right place at the wrong time and whenever her mask had slipped, he had seen her authentic self; the self she had a strong feeling that the Indigenous boy saw instantly.

If only she could help bring Mr. Zlo's vision to realization faster; the community, the province—in time the world—would see how beautiful it was. Unfortunately, it involved cleaning up and eradicating the dregs and leeches of society. While she understood this completely, most people outside of the Vision did not. However, she had known the Vision was picking up more followers all the time. More people were seeing the light, and Mr. Zlo was the beacon.

She had to get direction. She grabbed a handrail and pulled herself up. As she was beginning to ascend, she swore she heard a woman's voice, authoritative and booming. It echoed around the small space, bouncing off the walls.

"*Cyka!*"

Startled, she looked around. Nothing. There was no one in the area. Shaking her head, she picked up her pace.

Mara glared at the image in the sink of water in the hospital washroom. She had watched the handsome couple enter the hospital but had not had the opportunity to scry until now. She looked at her own image in the mirror and traced a finger over her heavily lined forehead. That prioress was despicable, and the man was terrifying and vaguely familiar. She had physically and mentally felt his hatred for her, yet she knew they had never met each other.

Mara had come in behind them in the ER. She'd watched the large Black man and the young Navajo man be set upon by the Reverend Mother, so she sank into an aisle chair to observe. She watched the young man with the ability to shapeshift. It was obvious he could do it at will, but he had not yet learned to control it completely. He was learning quickly and would become remarkable, but he needed guidance. His ability to smell dark intent was reassuring. His instinct would not be manipulated by outward appearances. He was going to be invaluable.

She watched in apprehension as the Black man fought with the rage that so badly wanted to be freed. He had not yet learned that the more hatred and rage that lived in the person he was focusing on, the more his own fury would be fed. There was so much of that hatred these days; this world was so very angry. Little wonder that Shemar was having more difficulty keeping that power in check. His gift could be precious, but without guidance and control, it would be lethal. For himself as well as others.

She had watched as they had put the run on that repulsive woman. Mara could not read her thoughts, but she certainly heard her hateful words and had to physically distance herself before she spat on the bitch. She also had to get away from the man. He had glanced behind him as she walked through the doors. She watched him as he surveyed her attire and lack of makeup or jewelry with disdain. She then stared directly back as his gaze locked on to her own. She watched a flicker of recognition widen his eyes slightly, then he shuttered his gaze by becoming engrossed in what an older doctor was whispering into his ear. The hatred in that look took her by surprise. She went to the washroom to settle herself and try to see where the prioress was headed, and to get a better read on the man. She passed her hand over the water and peered intently into the sink.

"Show me the child."

An image quickly assembled itself in the water. A young mother was protectively cradling her child against her shoulder. They were coming out of the ER triage area. The little girl was safe. She saw a dissipating green aura around the child and knew the priest had laid healing hands on her. Mara smiled as the little girl popped her head up and seemed to look directly at her from wide brown eyes.

"Nainai!" she chirped happily, extending her hands out, opening and closing her fists.

The young mother stroked the child's hair and whispered soothingly to her. "Soon, sweetie. We will see Grandma soon."

Mara grinned and opened and closed her fist to the child before passing her hand over the water again.

"Show me the telepath."

The water stirred, and the telepath's face came into view. Mara squinted as another face began to appear from inside, then alongside the young man's. The older man had Declan's mouth, but with more lines around the full lips. His chin and upper lip wore a thick, clean beard the color of fresh snow. His hair was full, like Declan's, but streaming past his shoulders and the same bright white as his beard. Those same dark-blue eyes glittered with amusement and magic, but the older eyes also held wisdom. The slight arrogance of the younger man wasn't present in the older. Mara leaned forward to see better as the older man rose from a carved chair, his strong hand on a staff beside him. His robes were rich and elaborate, and he wore a crown of gold and greenery. Majestic and powerful, he stood tall, and Mara saw hundreds, if not thousands, of people kneeling before him with heads bent in deep respect. She watched him lift a crystal orb from its stand and set it to spinning before him, with only energy to suspend it. Mara sighed deeply, with reverence, and watched the face of the old God fade into young Declan's face.

The young man was leaning forward, chatting to a lovely unit clerk who was twirling her hair and sliding over a piece of paper. Mara squinted and sent a thought to Declan, trying out his ability to receive, and listen to, telepathic messages.

"Move on, young man. You are needed elsewhere."

Declan looked annoyed and said to the unseen voice, "Okay! Okay. I am leaving now."

She laughed as he looked surprised with himself.

"Declan, you are some fries short of a Happy Meal. Who are you talking to?" he bickered with himself as he ran down the stairwell.

Mara passed her hand over the still water again. "Show me the priest."

She watched as the image came into focus, and she frowned. The gentle priest was in his chapel, talking to his God. He looked confused and troubled. However, his worry was not what concerned her. An ominous black aura hung around the priest, almost clinging to his skin. It was an aura that did not want to be there but needed to be. Mara closed her eyes. A tear slipped out the side of each one.

A knock at the door set the water to shaking and the image dispelled. Mara plunged her hands in to wash her face. It was time to assemble the Others. She opened the door and strode out to the waiting area.

Ho'kee inclined his head slightly, his eyes still on the door the Wicked Witch of the South went through. The scent of imminent danger was gone, but the unpleasant odor of her ignorance, bigotry, racism, and bullying lingered. He looked back at the waiting room. Nelson had evidently been successful in getting Zlo out of the area. The stench was no longer overwhelming.

Shemar put his hand on Ho'kee's shoulder. "You handled that woman well, son. If I didn't know that ice ran through her veins, I would swear you got to her and, man, it was beautiful. My mother is gonna hear about this, and she is going to insist you come for dinner."

"I don't think either one is what they pretend to be. Well-wrapped packages of explosives."

"Good deduction, Ho'kee. She is getting stranger by the day. She used to be all right. Always wound tighter than a clam's ass at low tide but nice enough. Something changed in her when Zlo became CEO of the hospital, and she became his puppet. She isn't nice anymore."

Shemar looked over at Ho'kee. "Let's go. Already two hours into your shift and you haven't got your uniform on yet. I ought to dock you half a day's pay for that, son."

Shemar grinned widely and turned toward the security cubicle. He paused as a large-boned, older woman walked determinedly toward them.

Ho'kee saw her as well, but her scent was not dangerous, it was comforting. She smelled like his shimá sáni—his grandmother. Her eyes glinted from the distance, a lively spark in the heavily lined face. She could be seventy, she could be one hundred and seventy; it was impossible to tell.

She stood in front of them, her smile confirming a lifetime of taking excellent care of her teeth. She was tall for a woman. While she was large-boned, she was not overweight. That face spent a lot of time outdoors. When she extended her leathery hand and enclosed Shemar's, and then put her other hand over top in an informal, comforting grasp, he knew those hands still did hard work.

She spoke in a heavily accented, deep voice. "Hello, hello! We finally meet."

Ho'kee blinked rapidly. Shemar's smile faltered a bit, but he shook her hand back. She looked expectantly, waiting for them to respond as if they'd understood the foreign language she spoke.

The woman gave Shemar a puzzled stare and swung her gaze to Ho'kee.

He smiled sheepishly and shrugged his shoulders. "Sorry, ma'am. I don't understand either."

"She has a strong Russian accent. Let me translate for you." All eyes turned to a young mother holding a dimpled girl in her arms. The mother turned to the elderly woman and spoke Russian rapidly and fluently. After a brief exchange, the mother turned to face the two men. "This is Mara. She understands English well but doesn't get the opportunity to practice speaking it much. She said she will slow down her speech for you. I'm Yenay. And that is my Annalee."

"You speak Russian?" asked Shemar.

Yenay nodded and met his dark eyes with her own. "Yes. I am an interpreter. I've been good with languages since I was little. Started picking up words and phrases when I was younger than Annalee. My mom said I started talking too much for just one language and took on a few more. My father was an interpreter as well. He worked in refugee services. I follow in his footsteps, and I think Annalee does as well."

Seeing the three people before her, Annalee started to clap delightedly, pointed to Ho'kee, and said loudly, "Woof!"

Ho'kee smiled and tipped his finger to Annalee. "Now *that*, I speak."

Yenay rolled her eyes. "Honestly. I don't know what goes on in this child's mind. I think she saw your necklace, which is absolutely beautiful." Her eyes indicated the silver wolf pendant on Ho'kee's chest. "Wolf." Yenay enunciated to Annalee, who continued to grin disarmingly.

Ho'kee watched Annalee, convinced that what the little girl saw was something far more than the wolf pendant.

Mara looked relieved and began to speak to Yenay in earnest. Yenay moved her bundle to her other hip, but it was obvious she was drained of strength. Yenay slid Annalee so her little feet hit the floor, and the child immediately made her way to Mara, opening and closing her fists. Mara crouched down, opened her arms wide, and waited for Annalee to come into them. Annalee went into those arms eagerly.

"Nainai!" shouted Annalee.

Yenay shook her head and spoke in Russian to Mara. "She is calling you Grandma. I don't know why. Her grandma is my mom. Short and Chinese."

Mara bounced Annalee and spoke to her animatedly. Annalee nodded, smiled, and held up the stuffed iguana for Mara to admire.

Shemar and Ho'kee, still looking baffled, said nothing.

Yenay put a hand on Shemar's arm. "I wanted to find you and thank you for everything you did. I don't want to think about what might have happened if we had to wait."

Shemar placed his own large hand over Yenay's. "No need for thanks, ma'am. We were in the right place at the right time."

"It was so much more than that, but all right, I understand. Oh, and it's Ms., not ma'am."

Shemar looked over at the child and Mara sensed that he was suffused by a protective urge. She suspected his reaction to the child was almost universal. There was something in this little girl that brought out the best in almost everyone around her. The urge to help, the need to be better, to do better; to save.

Annalee must have sensed Shemar's eyes on her. She twisted in Mara's hug and held her chubby arms out to Shemar. He put his huge hands out for the little girl and Mara deposited her gently into them.

Again, a fiercely protective energy radiated from him. She sensed that he was devoted to the care and protection of Annalee. He looked over the child's head at Ho'kee. Mara followed his gaze and saw the reflection of that devotion to the child in the young man's eyes.

Annalee leaned back in Shemar's arms and commanded him. "Down! I want to go down!"

Shemar deposited her on the ground, which she hit running. In a split second, she had left the group and charged down the hallway.

Yenay yelled after her, "Annalee! Annalee, stop right now! Turn around and get back here this minute, you little beast! Annalee!"

Ho'kee looked on in admiration as Yenay went after Annalee. That little imp could run! He didn't pick up any sense of impending danger, so he stayed back. Shemar looked a bit nervous. Mara had a wide smile, her hands on her hips, having seen this scenario countless times in her long years as mother and grandmother. Quite suddenly, the child stopped and dropped to the floor on her small, jean-clad bottom. She watched the double doors, transfixed.

Ho'kee sniffed. There was no threat in the air, but there was a strong, powerful scent. It was thick and it made his head cloud. He involuntarily growled low in his throat, not being able to place this scent and feeling disconcerted by that.

Yenay caught up with Annalee and bent down to pick her up.

Mara closed her eyes, her face inscrutable. She looked as if she'd slipped away somewhere inside her mind.

Declan ran his hand through his hair and winced at the onslaught of words and images in his mind. He brought his long-legged advance to a halt and placed his fingers against his temples to try to stop the incessant throbbing that was matching his heartbeat. There was complete silence around him in the hallway, but the chaos in his head was staggering. He rooted his feet to the floor in a wide stance. Holding his arms out to balance, he closed his eyes and raised his head. Giving himself over to the cacophony in his mind, he began to rearrange the images, slotting them where they needed to be, filling in the jigsaw puzzle to make it whole.

An old Russian woman, skilled in the art of the Craft, watched him carefully from calm, wise eyes. She held a basin of water on her lap. Candles surrounded her in a dark forest. She sat on a stump, sharing space with a large bullfrog.

A handsome young Indigenous man ran through the forest, springing traps, shedding his shirt, jeans, and shoes. The boy's face elongated, and as he dropped to all fours, his back arched sharply, and skin became fur. His mouth stretched far back to accommodate sharp canine teeth, and a silver-gray wolf stood where the boy had been seconds before. The wolf stopped abruptly, sat back on its haunches, curled its tail around itself, and stared directly at Declan, its eyes a startling blue.

A huge Black man with a gentle smile became engulfed by an ancient warrior God of fury. The rage, the power, of this God was terrifying. He saw the God open his mouth to release bolts of lightning, his eyes burning with fire. The man within the God fought to maintain his humanity.

He saw the priest he had met earlier. There was a pulsating green aura around him, ethereal and healing. The aura seemed to be otherworldly, he could see no connection to animal, place, or thing. He forced his mind to separate out the Others as he concentrated on the priest. Declan's eyes flew open as he saw the outline of wings.

The little girl the priest had saved appeared as older, impossibly beautiful. She was dressed in white with a water jug in her right hand and a willow branch in her left. She was everywhere and nowhere specific. She was loved worldwide. He knew she was responsible for a return to humanity, community, compassion, and love. He could also feel that she was loathed by a few whose mission in life was to eradicate those traits and ensure the destruction of humanity.

The voice that had been urging him on this far wove into his mind. "You are all integral to her survival, and she is integral to the survival of humanity. She needs you to save her."

Declan pushed through the double doors and stopped. He saw the faces of the Others. He inclined his head toward the older woman in sudden recognition. She calmly nodded back.

The little girl jumped to her feet, shouting, "Dagda!" She clapped her hands and went running to Declan, possessively clinging to his hand and pulling him to the Others. She pulled him into the odd little circle and pointed to each person. "Baba Yaga! Shango! Woof! Mommy!"

She looked puzzled as she sought out the fifth member and couldn't see him. She looked worriedly at the elderly woman. "Where's Raffie?" she asked.

The older woman looked questioningly at Declan.

He studied the child for a moment and realized what she was asking. "She wants to know where Raffie is. I think she is referring to the priest, Father Benedict."

The woman shook her head and smiled slightly. She caught Declan's eyes, and her voice rang true and clear in his mind. "I am Mara. Speak to me in thought. You don't need to know languages. The Universe hears thoughts and images, not spoken words. I will speak to you in the same way, I have some small gift of this. However, your ability is unlike any I have ever encountered." Then she proceeded to tell him the names of the Others before him.

Declan broke her gaze and looked around him. He picked up the thoughts of each of the people around him. It was chaotic, disconcerting, and downright embarrassing.

"Shango," whose name tag read Shemar, was thinking about how he would tear Declan apart if he hurt the little girl. Declan respected this, still in awe of this man's power.

He looked over at Yenay, who blushed slightly and cast her eyes down. A smile tugged at his mouth, and he heard her think, *I would not kick him out of bed for eating crackers.*

Ho'kee had sniffed the air slightly and his face registered a small amount of disgust as he thought, *This dude smells like he is in heat.*

Declan glared Ho'kee and bit out, "Nice. I was running the staircase so yeah, I smell ripe. Jerk."

Ho'kee reared back slightly and looked at Declan in disbelief thinking that he would have to watch himself around this mind-reading slut. This man in front of him radiated raw, untrained power. Declan crouched down and spoke gently to the child. "Sweetheart, Father Raffie is in the chapel. He is fine. We are all going to see him now."

Annalee clapped her hands and then placed her small palms on either side of Declan's face, peering intently into his dark-blue eyes. "You will take us there?"

Declan reached up and wrapped a large hand around Annalee's forearm. "I will take you there, and I will follow you anywhere." Declan straightened up, still holding Annalee's hand. He walked slowly toward the Others.

Shemar was in front of the rest, his imposing figure filling the aisle. Declan couldn't imagine anyone being stupid enough to pull any shit whenever this guy was doing security guard duty. He stretched his hand forward, and Shemar clasped it firmly and warmly. Declan spoke first. "Declan O'Neill. I think I was summoned here."

Shemar nodded his head, a fine sheen of sweat across his bald head. "Shemar. I seemed to be in the right place at the right time."

Declan put his hand toward Mara. She put her hands on her ample hips and narrowed her eyes at him. She laughed and opened her arms to him. "Give me a hug, mind reader."

Declan gratefully gave himself to the old crone's fierce embrace.

She pulled back and patted his cheek. "If I were a hundred years younger..."

He grinned, winked, and patted her hand. He then turned to Yenay.

She looked at him unsurely. "She called you *mind reader*. The wanting to be younger to...you know...I get that, but..." She hesitated and blushed furiously. "Why did she call you mind reader? You understand her accent so well, do you speak Russian?"

Declan shook his head. "I don't speak any other language but English, but I seem to be able to hear thoughts and see images in all forms. Images and visions don't have a particular language."

Yenay blinked rapidly. Her eyes looked at her daughter in confusion. "What does Annalee have to do with all this? I am going to be honest; this is all very strange. It's been a really long day and Annalee has been through the wringer. I am going to take my daughter home now. Thank you for everything, all of you. I would really like to see the priest who helped save her, but then we are leaving."

Declan lay a hand on Yenay's shoulder. Annalee changed allegiance and gripped her mother's hand. "I don't understand this myself, but I am in agreement with finding the priest, a quiet place, and figuring this out."

Declan removed his hand and turned toward Ho'kee. The two men studied each other quietly. Neither made an effort to shake hands.

Ho'kee did a critical visual assessment of the man in front of him. Again, Declan could hear what the wolf was thinking. He thought Declan was pretty—for a guy. Tall, well-built, arrogant, condescending, know-it-all, smelling like a cougar in heat.

Declan smirked and folded his arms in front of him. He arched an eyebrow. "Gee, thanks for the compliments."

Ho'kee narrowed his eyes at Declan and stepped forward to close the physical gap between them. He spoke low in a rasping, menacing voice. "If we are going to work together, and I think we are going to have to, you stay out of my fucking head without an invitation, Kreskin."

Declan was eye to eye with Ho'kee. He did his own assessment of the man in front of him. Unbelievably good-looking in a chiseled feature way, if you liked that kind of thing. Tall, built for speed, lean and graceful. Black eyes that betrayed nothing of his thoughts. Arrogant, condescending, know-it-all.

Declan blinked rapidly when he put the connection together. Crap. This twerp was exactly what he was accusing Declan of being. However, the boy was committed to Annalee, Declan knew that. Ho'kee was in this, and for that reason alone, Declan knew he could trust him. Declan put out his hand. "Deal."

Ho'kee clasped the outstretched hand firmly, never taking his eyes off Declan's. Declan stared back at those dark, slightly predatory eyes and knew that with this guy around, Annalee had a guard dog that would give his life for her. Declan looked around the Others and then down at Annalee, who was bored and slinging the iguana in a windmill. They would all give their lives for her. She was the one who would save the millions. Declan broke the handshake and spoke to the Others.

"Let's go find Father Raffie."

"Benedict," corrected Shemar. His voice was thoughtful.

"Father Benedict. I just remembered his name."

Declan looked at Annalee again. When he had more time, he was going to figure out what this Dagda/Raffie business was all about. "All right. Let's go the chapel and find Father Benedict Raffie."

Mara, who had remained motionless, observing everything and saying nothing, expelled a long-held breath. "Finally. Too much talking."

She motioned Shemar to lead the way, and the group advanced.

Father Benedict remained seated on the chapel sofa. The encounter with the child had taken so much energy out of him, he was still feeling lightheaded. He brought his hands up to his eyes to study them from nails to the end of his lifeline. He briefly thought how much he would like to be able to 'read' his palm, then laughed at himself. A fortune-telling Roman Catholic gypsy priest. Wouldn't that impress the Vatican?

He wished he could understand what was happening around him and in him. He had heard of people being conduits for divine healing. He'd heard of the miracles that laying on of hands could perform. He wondered how many of those healers got a late start in their lives on that gift. He wondered what he was supposed to do with this gift, how permanent it was. He knew he was going to have to talk to the ER doctor and let him in on the strange sensations of his hands, and probably allow a battery of tests to be done. He was intrigued as well as confused, but he wasn't frightened. Not for himself and not for his gift.

He did feel great peace around the little girl. There was something in her, around her, and about her that lifted him. He sighed and looked heavenward. "I ask only for understanding of this gift you bestow on me. Why me, Lord?"

Father Benedict laughed again at the forlorn plea. How many times had he heard that nugget in confessions? *Why me, Lord?* He continued to giggle, and stood up, wiping his glasses on his shirt.

He heard a step, then many steps, enter the chapel, and he put his glasses back on. He blinked rapidly at the sight of the group and then drew a slow gaze over each of them. Shemar. Declan. A handsome Indigenous youth. A wise-looking older woman in a Russian-style dress. A pretty Asian woman. Holding the pretty woman's hand, was the child. Annalee broke her grip from her mother and ran to Father Benedict, arms outstretched.

His heart swelled as he crouched down to catch her in his arms. His eyes filled with grateful tears. "Bless you, child. Thank you, God."

Annalee turned to the group and pointed at Benedict. "Raffie! This is Raffie."

Declan scanned the room and his eyes rested on a stained-glass mural. "Raphael. Raffie is St. Raphael."

Father Benedict rose from crouching and followed Declan's gaze. "So, it is," he said softly. "The patron saint of healing."

Declan looked steadily at the Others. "I think we are Descendants. Annalee can see who we are and where we came from. We need to go back to our families and learn more about our heritage. Our 'gifts' are from them. The name Annalee spoke to each one of us; we need to take it home with us and talk about it."

Yenay began shaking her head. "What does Annalee have to do with any of this? She is a child!"

Declan crouched down again and gently spoke to Annalee. He pointed his finger at Shemar. "Shemar," he said.

Annalee also pointed and chirped, "Shango!"

Shemar looked completely confused. He shrugged and spoke, "I'll ask Ma."

Annalee continued to move her finger in a circle and chirped at the next person. "Woof!"

Ho'kee's mouth set in a grim line. He looked around as if he didn't want to share his guarded secret, but he understood this group would find out. "I am a shapeshifter. I am Wolf."

Yenay passed her hands backward, looking for a safe place to sit as if a wave of lightheadedness came over her. Shemar took her elbow and guided her to the couch.

"Raffie!"

Father Benedict looked up at the stained-glass mural. "St. Raphael."

"Baba Yaga!"

Mara smiled and clapped her hands together once, nodding solemnly at Annalee.

Annalee turned and pointed to Declan. "Dagda!"

Declan's forehead creased. Benedict sensed the title was familiar to the man, like he'd heard it before but could not remember the context.

Declan placed a hand on Annalee's soft head. "And you, Annalee?"

Annalee pointed at herself and said clearly, "Bodhisattva Quan Yin."

Yenay visibly paled and a tremor started in her. "No," she whispered, but the glow radiating from her daughter contradicted her.

Father Benedict removed his glasses and wiped at his eyes. He gazed at Annalee fondly and spoke softly, reverently. "And a little child shall lead them."

In his office at the top of the hospital building, Zlo stood rigid, staring out the window. He did not see the panoramic view nor the groups of people coming and going. He didn't see the push of journalists attempting to get in to get an exclusive with the "Healing Hands Priest" and anyone who was willing to claim witness to the miracle. He didn't see the security force expertly keeping the journalists out. He didn't acknowledge the quiet knock at the door nor the entrance of the Reverend Mother.

His voice chilled the already cold room. "The little girl lived."

Reverend Mother Beatrice folded her hands in front of her and answered firmly with as few words as possible. Zlo despised unnecessary talk. "She did, sir. A true miracle. Donations to the hospital are already pouring in. The press would like an exclusive with the priest and yourself."

Zlo remained standing, his face impassive. "I will have Lorraine set it up. You may leave."

At the top of Zlo's chest, hidden from public view by the expensive suit, a thick labradorite stone on a leather strip began to glow. Zlo closed his eyes, feeling the stone begin to pulse and send waves of heat through his body. He whispered, "Mentor. I am listening."

Declan walked up the trail to his mobile home, still lost in thought. He had dropped off Niall at his home, promising to be back the next day. He needed to think, he needed to process. He needed to wake up if this was all a really strange dream. If it wasn't, he really needed someone to tell him what the hell was going on, why this motley crew was all brought together, and where they were going. He stopped walking; his feet rooted to the ground as he stared at the figure seated on his trailer steps.

Her white-blonde hair curled to her small waist. Her full lips smiled with happiness. Her wide, sky-blue eyes gazed warmly at him. She stood to greet him in denim cutoffs and a white T-shirt. She was the most beautiful woman he had ever laid eyes on. She was the girl in his dream of the Three Women. Her voice, melodic and sweet, wrapped around his mind like a song.

She reached out a hand in invitation. "Declan O'Neill. I am Inanna. We are going to be together while you seek answers."

Chapter Two

Declan walked into his trailer behind Inanna and closed and locked the door. He leaned against the door with a goofy smile on his face as he watched Inanna fill the kettle and intuitively know where to find mugs, spoons, tea, and sugar.

He was still happily bewildered. "Inanna. That is a beautiful name. What does it mean?"

She put the mugs of tea on the kitchen table and met his gaze. He wondered if he would ever not feel weak in the knees when she looked his way.

"It means 'Lady of Heaven.' I picked it myself before I came here."

An alarm began to ring distantly in Declan's head. Was she beautiful and crazy? That would be just his luck. "You chose your name? Before you came here to my place?"

"Of course. I could have any name at all when I came to this realm. I decided on Inanna."

Yes. Beautiful and nuts. A perfect artist's muse. "Are you a professional muse? Model?"

"No. I am not a model. I am a Maid."

"Domestic Goddess!" He winked and tilted a finger toward her.

"Now you are getting closer," she teased.

"My brother is going to love you. He thinks I only date women who are pretty but bright as Alaska in December. You will change his mind, Inanna."

She looked at him a little sadly. "Declan, I won't be meeting your brother. That is not my purpose here. I am going to be with you until the full moon, then my time is over. Only you will see me during this time."

Declan put his palms flat on the kitchen table and sighed dramatically for effect. He was already formulating plans to change her mind, but she didn't need to know that. "Damn it. I knew you were too good to last." He looked at her and smiled again. "But you know what? I will take every second I have with you. Until you have to turn into a pumpkin, or a frog, or whatever is going to happen on the full moon."

Inanna sat at the table and motioned for him to join her. "Declan. You have suspected for some time that you have gifts not shared by your brother, and not shared by any other you have met."

Declan's brows drew together, and his mouth tightened. "How did you know that? Did Niall tell you? Did Niall put you up to this? Is this a really rotten joke?"

Inanna regarded him calmly. She reached out and smoothed a wayward lock of hair from his forehead. "You look so much like your mother. I am so grateful to be chosen to guide you."

Declan looked confused. "My mother? You knew my mother?"

Inanna smiled gently and touched her finger to his full lips. "Very well. The Others have family present that will be able to help them understand their abilities and where they came from. I was chosen to help you with that, on behalf of your mother. We don't have a lot of time, Declan. I am going to ask you to trust me and touch me."

She pulled her chair around to face Declan, close enough that their knees were touching. She reached out and wrapped her hands around his forearms. He placed his large hands around her delicate wrists. "Close your eyes, Declan, and touch your forehead to my forehead."

Declan thought to himself this was the weirdest foreplay he'd ever been part of. He wondered if it was some New Age tantric yoga stuff.

Inanna giggled and her body sent movement into his. "Don't open your eyes, and this is not foreplay. I can certainly feel the blood of the Dagda running in your veins."

"I keep hearing that name associated with me and quit reading my mind. It's a buzzkill."

Inanna laughed again, then took his hands and placed them palm down on the tops of her thighs. Declan decided this bit of foreplay actually showed promise. She placed her hands on his thighs the same way, and Declan's member swelled in response. He opened one eye to see if Inanna noticed. She kept her eyes closed, but the sultry smile playing around her lips told him that she did indeed notice. He closed his eyes again.

Inanna spoke softly,
"Thoughts in darkness, be in light
Come to me in second sight.
Thoughts of others, let me see
This is my will, so mote it be."

A wash of colors twisted in Declan's brain, much like a DNA helix. The helix unwound and formed several sigils, one after another. Alchemic symbols unfolded, turned, and flowed into Freemason symbols. He watched, mesmerized, as each symbol flowed into the next without interruption in haunting transformations. Inanna's lilting voice entered his head, lulling him into a deep trance.

"The Universe does not recognize dialect or language as we know it. It recognizes thoughts, images, intention. You are so very gifted, Declan. You've been able to read minds since before you were born in this time. Reclaim your ancestry. You are of Dagda."

Declan felt hypnotized. He spoke quietly, "My mother..."

"Was also gifted, but not as strongly as you. I haven't seen your kind in a very, very long time."

"Long time? You aren't even out of your twenties yet."

"Shh. Age is irrelevant, and you are incorrect. Focus on my thoughts."

"You mean quit talking, but you are saying it in a nice way." Declan grinned but kept his eyes closed.

Inanna squeezed his thighs gently. "You never opened your mouth in that conversation."

Declan's eyes popped open, and he broke the forehead bond. The beautiful images retreated quickly from his mind. He frowned at Inanna. He tested out his voice and realized she was right. His mouth was dry. He hadn't been using his voice to communicate. "This is really strange, but so many things are beginning to make sense in a weird way."

She smiled and cupped his face in her hands.

He grasped her wrists in his strong hands, loving the feel of her fingers on his face. His dark gaze burned into her sky-blue eyes. He spoke to her via his thoughts. "Tell me more. Show me more."

Shemar pulled open the screen door of his childhood home and shouted into the empty space. "Mom!

There's something I need to talk to you about." He dropped his hat and gym bag on the kitchen table and flung open the fridge door. He heard his mother answer his call.

"Shemar, you yell like dogs howling at a dinner bell! I better not see your greasy hat on my table or that nasty gym bag stinking up my kitchen. And if you still have your shoes on, I'm going to wear them to kick your backside out the door."

Shemar shut the fridge door, tossed his cap onto the coat rack in the hallway, slid his gym bag to follow it, and kicked off his shoes, one at a time. They smacked into the bag like curling rocks. He slumped tiredly into a kitchen chair and rubbed his bald head. A skinny old black cat leapt onto the table and butted Shemar's chin with its head. His mother, Olivia, circled behind him and dropped a kiss on his head. She bustled about, pulling down dishes and placemats, before shooing the cat from the table. The cat rounded immediately and vaulted into Shemar's lap, kneading and purring. Shemar idly scratched its war-torn ears.

"You could have given me a call to let me know I had someone besides me, myself, and I for dinner. Now I have to set a fourth place."

Shemar was quiet as he watched his mother. Olivia was a beautiful woman in her fifties. Her black hair was gracefully wreathed with gray, and her gently lined face glowed with health and love of life. She was widowed when Shemar was six, and she never remarried. She was devoted to God, Shemar, the Baptist congregation, and her cats, in that order. Shemar got to know his father through photographs and videos. He looked like him—handsome features, a blinding smile, and early baldness. His mother was short and curvy while his father had been of average height and well-proportioned. The physical resemblance to his father ended there as Shemar was far more heavily muscled and significantly taller.

Olivia stopped bustling and put a hand on her hip. She arched an eyebrow at her son and put her other hand on his shoulder. "You are not going to tell me you are going to marry that woman. Don't get me wrong, she is a nice girl and got a nice way about her, but she isn't for you. Your mother knows that. Don't give me that look like you don't know what I am talking about, Shemar."

"No, Mom, I am not going to marry Jackie. She isn't the marrying kind."

"Then what are you wasting your time for? You aren't getting any younger, and I want some grandbabies on this big lap."

"Okay, Momma."

"Don't you 'okay, Momma' me. Set the table and tell me about your day."

Shemar continued to stroke the cat. "Mom, who is Shango?"

Olivia's mouth dropped open. She blindly grasped for the table, her shocked gaze on Shemar's face. Shemar leapt up, dislodging a squawking cat, and guided his mom gently into the chair. Olivia sat in silence, the look in her eyes both fearful and worlds away. Shemar had rarely seen her like this. He had a distant memory of this look when she received an afternoon phone call telling her that Shemar's father had suffered a major heart attack and had died at his desk in a real estate office. The result of an autopsy had shown a pre-existing heart defect that no one had known about.

Shemar grabbed a glass and some water and wrapped Olivia's hands around the base. "Momma, drink this, please. You don't look so good."

Olivia curled her hands around the glass but did not raise it. Her usually robust voice came out in a hoarse whisper. "Where did you hear that name, Shemar?"

Shemar laid his large hands over his mother's. "A little girl about four years old was in the hospital with a critical fever. Momma, I think she died on the table, but this priest laid his hands on her, and I swear she started to breathe again. She is all right now but when she came to, she looked at me and said 'Shango.' She actually called me by that name twice, so I don't think it's an accident. And this guy I met today has this weird kind of mind-reading trick. This is a long story but fast forward to the end of the day, the mind reader mentioned we were all 'Descendants' of whichever name the little girl was calling us."

Olivia slowly shook her head as tears gathered in her eyes. "You were to be spared, that is the deal I struck with the dear Lord. You weren't to be touched by the past." Olivia grabbed her son's hands and straightened in her seat. Her stare was fierce when she looked into his eyes. "You better tell me the long story, son. Start at the very beginning, and don't leave anything out, especially about the child, the priest, and the telepath."

While Shemar laid out the story, Olivia remained motionless, her eyes giving nothing away. When Shemar reached the part of losing control over his temper and moving in almost a blackout state, Olivia squeezed his hands to the point of pain. When he finished the story, he sat back, waiting for her response.

She released the breath she had been holding. "Stay here," she said getting up. "I need to show you something."

When she came back, she was armed with a photo album and an ornately carved wooden box. She dropped the book on the table and opened it to a carefully written, painstakingly detailed family tree. Shemar scanned the dates but did not see a "Shango" first or last name anywhere in the past or present. He traced the familiar branches with his fingers and stopped at the name of his great-grandfather who had immigrated from Nigeria. There were no names before his on the paternal side.

"Our family was not always a God-fearing Baptist one, son. At one time, your father's family worshipped the Yoruba gods, the Orishas." She was clutching the box fiercely. "There are still those who believe in the Orishas. One of the Orisha is a God named Shango. He is considered the most powerful and most feared of the Orishas. God of thunder and lightning, he is said to spew fire. He is worshipped for his courage, his sense of justice. He is a protector from evil, a warrior. He is moral and magical. He is also destructive and wrathful. It has been centuries since there has been any indication that he lives in human form again. I was hoping for centuries more. On your father's side, you are a Descendant of Shango."

Olivia carefully placed the carved box in front of Shemar. He got the sense that the box was pulsating. He felt both revulsion and an overwhelming attraction to whatever was in that box. He knew whatever was inside needed him as well. Olivia backed up a few steps. "I made a promise to your father that I wouldn't hide your past. I didn't want this thing in my house, but your father...that was the one, the only thing he would not budge on. It moved with us everywhere. I could hide it in the attic or the basement, but we both knew it was always there. It came with your father, and with all fathers before him. I promised him regarding your past, that if either you went looking for it, or it came looking for you, I would give you this box and tell you what I know about your ancestry. I was hoping—I was praying—I would never have to do this. It's in your hands now, Shemar."

His face was grim as he assessed the box. To anyone else's eye, it was an ornately carved box, adorned with sigils whose meanings were long forgotten. To Shemar, it held the answer to what was happening to him, and in him. It held the answer to who and what he was becoming.

Olivia placed her hand protectively on his shoulder. "Your father said he couldn't open this box, nor could your grandfather, or generations of men before him. The box can only be opened by the incarnate of Shango. I understand if you need to do it. I understand if you won't. There is a big part of my heart that doesn't want this to be true, but there is a bigger part of my soul that knows...well, it just knows."

Shemar nodded and picked up the box in both his hands. The pulsing energy immediately swarmed around his hands, as if it were looking for something. The wave inched its way up his forearms, causing his hair to stand on end, encircling his biceps, and creeping its way to his shoulders. The wreath snaked its way down Shemar's body to his toes and branched out to the floor. The wreath reared back when it touched Olivia, who shuddered and swatted at something she couldn't see. Traveling up Shemar's back, it waited briefly at his neck. He felt unable to move like the energy was binding him. He had never felt so powerful, so clear and focused. He sensed the energy speaking to him in an ancient tongue, and he answered in the same tongue.

"Continue."

Olivia sat across from Shemar, tears filling her eyes.

The energy wave surged over Shemar's head and began to flow into his eyes, his ears, and his mouth. Shemar felt a raw, unearthly strength flood his body as if he were going to explode. He stood up and clenched his fists at his side. He opened his eyes, and Olivia stood as well, backing up and grabbing at her chest. His eyes were blood red. He seemed to be looking at her and through her. His body trembled and he seemed to swell in size in front of her, threatening to go through the ceiling and expand through the walls. His hands reached for the box on the table and the lid flung open on its own. He reached down and picked up a weathered, sharply edged small statue. The statue, in his hands, began to glow the same color as Shemar's eyes. He lifted the statue in one hand and raised it up, above his head. His thunderous voice shook the house like an earthquake. "Shango!"

Olivia watched in horror as the essence of her son seemed to leave that body. In his place stood a warrior in full battle dress; the statue had become an *oshe*—a double-headed ax—gripped tightly in his hand. The warrior opened his mouth and a roar erupted that caused the mirror in the hallway to drop and shatter. Olivia sank to her knees and clasped her hands in prayer as the warrior deity loomed over her. He watched her for a moment, reading her energy, and lowered his oshe. There was no anger, fury, or hatred to fuel him.

Then he stood quite still. Shemar's voice came back to him, frightened and confused. "Mom?"

Olivia looked up and saw her son again in those dark brown eyes. She reached out her hand to Shemar. "Right here, baby. I am right here."

Shemar stared at the statue in his hand and gingerly placed it in the box, closing the lid. "I understand," he whispered.

Mara sat in her sagging lawn chair looking out over the lake. She folded her arms across her chest and closed her eyes, feeling every day of her seventy years today. Reaching up and untying the scarf around her head, she pulled out pins and a cascade of silver waves spilled over her shoulders and down her back. Running her fingers through the thick tresses, her eyes remained closed. She listened to the wind in the trees, the various calls of wild birds in the air, and smelled the sharp tang of incoming autumn.

Crossing her arms over her chest again she spoke in her native Russian. "Good afternoon, Annika. Please get a lawn chair, over by the stump, and sit beside me. You make me uncomfortable buzzing about like a bee."

Annika walked a few steps to the chair, returned to Mara's side, and awkwardly perched on the edge of the seat, unable to make herself comfortable. She shuddered at the sight of a large bullfrog on the stump beside her and did her best to ignore it. Mara raised an eyebrow and smiled slightly. The princess would feel a pea in a dozen feather mattresses.

"What is on your mind, daughter?"

Annika stared out at the lake, hesitant to speak, which usually meant she needed something from Mara, and it was a big favor. Mara let her stew; she wasn't going to offer to do a damn thing.

"Babushka. I need to apologize for earlier. I was wrong."

Mara went still. She was expecting to be asked a favor, not to hear an apology. Mara did not respond, it wasn't time. She continued to feel the sun on her face and kept her arms crossed, sensing there was more.

"I spoke to Leonid. I told him I had asked...no...that I had told you...to keep my children out of your teachings." Annika glanced over at Mara and then down at the ground. "He was very angry with me, but I am not apologizing because he is mad at me. I am apologizing because I should not have said what I did. I have no right to say those things. They are your grandchildren, and they are beautiful souls. I talk to others in my church, and in my language club. I watch other children in the restaurant, and I realized that our children are the gentlest, kindest, most compassionate children I have seen. I know that is largely because of you."

Mara reached out and took Annika's hand and patted it.

Annika took a large breath and continued. "I know I wasn't around much for them when we got the restaurant up and running, and then with the side catering business and the storefront. You are always there to pick them up, play with them, teach them, take them places, and create things with them. Leonid reminded me that they learned these things from you. Your son thinks the world of you, and I do too."

Mara smiled slightly and looked over at Annika. "My son is a good man, and the children are a credit to our family village that raised them. My ways are a part of that education. There is no such thing as too much knowledge. I thank you for what you say. You make me proud to be your mother-in-law."

Annika smiled weakly and got up from her chair. She looked at the lake and down at Mara. "Could I ask you something?"

Mara inclined her head slightly.

"What is it that you do, when you see things happening to other people, in other places? Are you reading the future?"

Mara looked thoughtful. "I was given the gift of scrying. Some people use crystal balls, or firelight, or candle wax. I was given water as my element. I am able to see things that are going to happen or could happen. I usually see things that are happening right now, but in other places, to other people."

"How do you do it? How did you learn?"

"I am quiet, I am listening. I knew I had this gift as a child, among other abilities."

"Like the herbs you grow and use. I know people come to you for cures."

"I don't cure anyone of anything. I act as a guide and support only. I can help, sometimes I can heal, but I don't claim to cure."

Annika pulled her shawl closer. "I am not comfortable with these ways. They are magic."

Mara laughed gently. "That is fair. I am uncomfortable with your ways as well. As long as you aren't doing the magick, you don't have to be comfortable. You leave it to me, and the guides before us and the guides long after us."

Annika fiddled with the cross around her neck. "Would you like to come to dinner tonight?"

Mara smiled and shook her head. "Thank you, Annika, but no. I am going to be rather busy over the next while. I really don't know how long. I may not be around much at all. There are a lot of jams and jellies for the store in the garden shed. The eldest are going to take care of the cows and chickens while I am busy. They know what to do."

Annika looked concerned. Mara rarely left her property for any reason. "Is everything okay? Is there anything we can do?"

Mara closed her eyes again and leaned back in her chair. "No, child. Everything is not okay, but it will be. What you can do is have faith and compassion and if I ask you to do something in the next few weeks, please just do it. Don't ask why. Just have enough trust in me to do it."

Annika was pulling at her fingers. A sure sign she was nervous and wanted clarity, but to her credit, she sighed and tightened her shawl around her shoulders and did not ask for elaboration. "Babushka. You have my word."

Ho'kee tossed and turned in his bed, staring at the ceiling and staring at the wall in equal measures of time. He didn't want to talk to his mother or father about his dual nature, but he knew he was going to have to. He'd had time to realize what he was, but he had not yet completely accepted it. He had heard stories about shapeshifters and Skinwalkers in his Navajo culture. One was revered and the other was abhorred. According to legend, he may have the blood of both running through him, and he shuddered. He thought of that day years ago when he had been awakened to the ability to shift.

He and his father had been out fishing. On the way back, they had heard a plaintive wail. His father had tried to get him to move along, saying that the trappers had a right to make a living too. Ho'kee could not ignore the wail, it seemed to be calling to him. He had stopped and looked at his father directly, eye to eye. He was not a child, and he couldn't be dragged home anymore. Abe knew his only child had a kinship to wildlife that no one he had ever met shared. Ho'kee was a good fisherman, but if you put a gun in the boy's hands, it was getting dropped on the forest floor. The boy believed others had a right to their livelihoods, but he would not support the leg hold trap. He recognized that cry of pain as a victim of the violent device.

Abe put his hand on Ho'kee's shoulder and said softly, "Do what you need to do. I won't be far behind you."

Ho'kee set off toward the crying, his fury building with every step. He pushed his way through the forest, training his eye for the telltale signs of hunters and trappers. He stopped and listened. The crying was becoming fainter. He had to hurry.

He angrily fought his way through the underbrush and deliberately sprang a leghold trap he saw covered in moss. The viciousness of the snap infuriated him. The cry had turned into a whimper, and he couldn't locate it. The sound wound through the top of the trees and fell into the bush. Ho'kee tripped over a fallen log and yelled, gripping his ankle. He wrapped his hands around it, already feeling the swelling of a badly turned foot. Ho'kee looked up at the sky, seething with anger.

He realized he was seeing the sky, trees, and forest with alarming clarity. He could identify where each rustling leaf was coming from and heard a lake bird calling from miles away. Releasing his ankle, Ho'kee was mesmerized as the swelling dissipated, and his ankle, his foot, his whole leg was slimming. The cry sounded again, but this time he recognized where the anguished howl was coming from. Ho'kee knew exactly where the victim was.

He hunched over beneath low-lying branches and sprang back into action, aware that he was moving faster than he was before. His feet were so light on the forest floor he was almost dancing. Feeling his muscles bunch and his back arch, he dropped his hands to the ground. Looking down in a surreal moment of awareness, he recognized the large silver-gray paws of a wolf. Ho'kee kept running and felt the wind against his face; dodging logs and rocks and gliding over fallen trees. He ran down a steep river embankment with sure feet and sprinted across the stream. His ears twitched, the cry clear and the area precise in his mind. He broke through a clearing and saw a young red fox, its paw clenched in the teeth of the trap.

The fox looked at him in resignation at first, then directly into his eyes. They stared at each other for a second, and the fox's ears folded back as it bent its head to chew again at its own foot in the claw. Ho'kee's large paws straddled the trap, and his full weight came down on the levers. The trap opened, and the fox drew out his leg. Ho'kee jumped back and the trap snapped uselessly back to the ground. The fox limped away from the trap but kept its eyes on Ho'kee. Ho'kee sat back on his haunches, overcome with sudden fatigue.

He felt his back straighten. His legs splayed out in front of him, and his hands on the ground by his hips. Ho'kee looked around him curiously, but not frightened. His ankle was swelling up again. The little fox watched him warily from a distance. Ho'kee sat for a few moments longer, getting his strength back. He heard a crashing in the forest, probably a very pissed-off trapper. His ankle buckled as he attempted to get to his feet. The little fox retreated out of sight as Abe came into the clearing with Ho'kee's clothes in his hand.

Abe looked amused as he spoke, "Found these by the stream. Decided to have a dip and a nap, did you?"

Ho'kee looked for a sign of anything else in Abe's face that was going to ask for an explanation.

Abe picked up the snapped trap with bits of fur and blood on the savage teeth. "Found the critter, did you? Not too damaged to just let go? If it is poorly, I can put it out of its misery, Ho'kee."

"No! No...it's okay, Dad. It's going to have a limp, but I think it's ok. Young red fox."

Abe nodded and dropped the trap. He threw Ho'kee's clothes at him. "Get some clothes on before we go home. You sure got ahead of me fast, son. You've been training or something?"

Ho'kee struggled to get his jeans on, leaning against a tree. He yelped when he tried to put his running shoe back on the injured foot.

Abe's eyes widened in alarm, and he slid his arm around Ho'kee's waist. "Lean on me, Ho'kee. That looks like a nasty sprain you took. Damn! Ho'kee, look! Those are massive wolf tracks in the area where the trap was! That thing is huge! I'd love to lay eyes on that monster someday, from a very safe distance."

Ho'kee got the other shoe on. He leaned on Abe as they arranged themselves for the trek home. As they were leaving, Ho'kee noticed the little red fox watching him from the outskirts of the clearing.

That was two years ago. He had become more adept at shifting, and more careful. He had been sighted as a massive silver-gray wolf only a couple of times. The little red fox had become a companion, one that would never be housebroken or kept in a cage. In all the world, only that fox knew his secret. Ho'kee had a feeling that was all about to change, and he knew he needed to tell his parents.

How did he even begin that conversation? *Hey, Mom, remember great-grandmother going on about Skinwalkers and shapeshifters being part of our lineage...well, funny that should come up because...*

Ho'kee clutched his pillow to his chest and blew his breath out. He got up and looked out the window. At the outskirts of the property, the fox was happily chewing on a large bone Abraham had flung to him. The fox twitched his ears and looked directly at Ho'kee.

"I know," sighed Ho'kee. "I will tell them."

"You don't have to, Ho'kee. They already know. I told them while you were at the hospital, meeting the Others."

Ho'kee whirled around to the open door of his bedroom. Uncle Dan stood there. He wasn't sure which side of the family Uncle Dan hailed from, if either, but he had been around for years. To hear others talk, he was outliving Rip Van Wrinkle. Ho'kee looked at Uncle Dan in surprise, he hadn't seen the old man for ages. Sometimes when a family member would have a naming ceremony or a gathering in the long house, he would see Old Dan there, looking well over one hundred years old, laughing and eating with equal gusto.

"Uncle Dan! How did you—? When did you—?"

Uncle Dan smiled, showing all his own strong, white teeth. "Refreshing to talk to a young man who doesn't know everything. Come, Ho'kee. Let's talk outside."

Ho'kee pulled a blanket around himself and followed the old man out. He walked quietly beside him, alternating between feelings of confusion, fear, foreboding, and irritation. He was tired after this afternoon's introduction to the Others. He was fearful of his parents' reaction to the news that their only child was a shapeshifter. He knew that this 'gift' was about to turn into something less playful than springing traps, running through forests, and making buddies with little red foxes. He was irritated because at this moment he just wanted to be a normal young man doing normal young man things.

"You are right, Ho'kee. This gift of your forefathers is much more complicated than it seems right now."

Old Dan sat at the edge of the clearing and idly reached out to scratch the ears of the little fox who had crept silently up to the two men. Old Dan rooted around in his medicine bag and pulled out dried meat, holding it out to the wild creature who gingerly took it in his teeth and gnawed.

Ho'kee sat beside Old Dan.

"You have been given two years to learn how to shift. Now I am going to tell you where this gift comes from and how to use it. I am also going to tell you when to cloak it and when to set it free."

Ho'kee watched Old Dan carefully.

"Only your parents, myself, and the Creator know about your gift," Old Dan said. "Your mother has suspected for a long time. Your gift comes from her side of the family. It hasn't been seen for generations. Your father had no idea. He will have trouble accepting this, but he loves you, and he respects the old ways. He will come to an understanding and be able to help you."

Ho'kee looked over at the fox, laying its sleek head on its front paws. "I am a freak."

Old Dan shook his head and grimaced. "No, Ho'kee. You are a gift. Could you light a fire? I want to show you things in the flames."

Cardinal Josef peered at Father Benedict over the steeple of his fingers. His shaggy eyebrows were dancing wildly as he listened quietly to the story the priest was telling. He did not say a word, but his face betrayed amusement, concern, sadness, and hope all in the fifteen minutes it took for the priest to unburden his heart and mind. The Cardinal watched his childhood friend and seminary brother fight with inner demons during the tale.

Father Benedict, at the end of his story, took his glasses off and wiped them on his tunic. His voice was weary. "There you have it, Cardinal. The whole story. I am sorry you got dragged into this. That was not my intention."

The Cardinal nodded solemnly, his fingers still steepled. His bright, dark eyes watched the declining sun's rays play through the stained-glass windows. He put his hands on the armchair and gazed at Father Benedict. "Benedict, call me Josef, please. This 'Cardinal this' and 'Father that' takes much precious time when it is between God, you, me, and St Raphael. I know the news report was not of your doing. Quite a scene took place when you laid hands on that lit-

tle girl. There are newspaper articles already and social media has gotten wind of it. I think Hollywood
is petitioning the Vatican for permission to find an
actor to play you in an upcoming movie based on
this whole experience!" Josef smiled lopsidedly and
added, "They would have to find someone really, really old."

Benedict laughed and put his glasses back on. He
looked thoughtfully at Josef. "What do I do? This is no
longer a secret. I don't understand why it is happening
or how long it will go on for. I couldn't get into my
own church last Sunday due to the crowds. I did an
outdoor sermon but really, Josef, all anyone wanted
was to be touched and healed."

Josef smiled warmly and reached out to take Benedict's hand. "That is all anyone ever wants from their
priest. To be touched in some way, to be healed in
some way. They want to be heard. You accept this gift
gratefully, Benedict, and use it as long as you have it.
But we do need to reign this in somehow. Unfortunately, I don't believe you will be safe now. You have
what many others would take great pains, and inflict
great pain, to obtain. Some will want to study you,
dissect you while you still live. Others will see you as
an ATM and beg to manage you, make you rich and
famous, and knowing you as long as I have, my friend,
I can't think of anything you would dislike more than
being famous."

Benedict sat back and sighed. "You believe me."

Josef nodded slowly. "I would believe you even if I hadn't seen and heard the reports from your congregation and the ER doctor. St. Raphael uses many people as his instrument, but in you, Benedict, he has infused the whole orchestra."

Josef leaned forward, looking directly into Benedict's eyes. "Benedict. Is there something else? Are you unwell? I realize you are exhausted but there seems to be something else. Have you seen a doctor recently?"

Benedict smiled ruefully. "No. I keep meaning to and then this happened and keeps happening. I think I am actually a bit fearful of what doctors might find. I have not been feeling well the last few months, Josef. Unable to do my usual long walks without being utterly drained. Flights of stairs wind me after one floor. Dizziness, even before the 'healing hands' started. I don't want to hear 'I am sorry to diagnose you with doddering old age.'"

Josef grinned mischievously. "That ship has sailed, my friend." He then looked concerned and patted his friend's hand again. "Please see the doctor, Benedict. Actually, I will have one sent to you. I think it is best if you take yourself off somewhere, away from here, for a while. You can be of little service to others if you are not well yourself. Come back to Italy with me! Stay with me a while, old friend. We will plump you with pasta and relax you with red wine and sunshine. Ah, it will be wonderful!"

Benedict smiled gratefully at Josef and shook his head. "You could not be kinder, and I could not be more fortunate to have you as my friend. But, Josef, something is telling me that I am needed here for now. There is something of great importance about to happen, and I believe, in my heart and mind, that I am to be part of it. It has to do with the child and the odd little group of us that met at the hospital."

Josef looked resigned. "I understand, Benedict. Promise me when this is completed, you will vacation with me in Italy? In the meantime, there is a location in the northern part of this island utilized for sabbaticals, seminars, and empowerment retreats. It is owned by a friend of mine and currently unused. I would like you to go there. Think of it as being sent on a mission. Until it is completed, you may not return. I already have someone to take over your parish. It is a large compound with cottages. Perhaps the Others would come with you? It would be a safe haven for all of you right now, out of the spotlight. These events at the hospital seem to be gaining people's interest."

Benedict looked wearily at the stained-glass mural. He could hear the security guards outside the chapel attempting to move people along. Not only was his church being engulfed by the curious and desperate, so was the hospital. The increase in people, traffic, and phone calls was not to anyone's benefit. Josef was right. He should leave for a while.

"Josef, I accept your offer with gratitude. I will contact young Declan right now and propose this, and I believe he will be as thrilled as I am."

Yenay swung open the screen door of her home and yelled into the house. "Ma! Mom, get in here and tell me right this minute what the hell is happening with my baby!"

Silence was far too rare in that house. It meant someone was hiding something somewhere.

"*Ma*! I need some answers from you, and you are not going to put me off any longer. This has been coming for a long time, like four years, we need to talk."

Yenay bent down and put Annalee's feet on the floor. The little girl broke into a run toward the living room. "Annalee! Don't run in the house. *Ma*!"

Annalee stopped and put her hands over her ears. She grinned and put a finger to her lips. "Shhh! Mommy. Gramma is hiding. I can find her, but you need to be quiet."

Yenay sighed and sat down on the couch. If Annalee still had the energy to search this huge house for her diminutive Gramma, then she could do just that. Yenay waved a hand in Annalee's direction. Instead of taking off, Annalee folded her legs under herself and closed her eyes. Yenay watched her with confusion. What on earth was she doing? Ah. The little munchkin was probably tired from this extremely emotional day and needed to nap instead of playing hide and seek.

"Gramma is in the sewing room. In the closet. Pretending to look for thread. She has blue in her hand. But funny Gramma is sewing a red hat for me!"

Yenay slowly got up from the couch and locked the front door behind her. She reached down for Annalee's hand and then they quietly went up the stairs and down two rooms. Yenay pushed open the door to the sewing room and saw a recently abandoned project on the sewing machine. A red hat. She drew in a breath and crossed the room, pausing briefly in front of a closet door. She flung the door open and looked down at her mother holding a spool of blue thread in her hand.

"Gramma!" Annalee put her hands up to take her grandmother's. She knew not to jump into her grandmother's arms. Her gramma wasn't old, but she wasn't strong. She also looked like she had been crying.

Yenay's initial anger gave way to concern. "Ma? Annalee is okay. It was scary, but she is okay. I am sorry I couldn't tell you more over the phone, but let's go into the kitchen. I will make tea and we can talk, okay?"

Tina nodded and let herself be guided by Annalee. She looked up at her daughter and whispered, "You know, then. That she is a Descendant."

Yenay's face tightened, and she whispered back, "I know she is a little four-year-old child who is precocious and beautiful and who I can't get enough of, but this 'Descendant' business is bothering me. This is the second time I have heard it today and I need an explanation. You can tell me exactly why we left China so quickly, why it was imperative that Annalee be born here, and why you have kept me in the dark about my ancestry."

Tina took her daughter's hand with her free one. "I will tell you everything, Yenay."

Zlo stared into the flames of his fireplace intently. He pulled off his labradorite pendant and held it in front of the fire. The fire danced in reflection against the polished piece. The iridescent effect illuminated the natural striations of the stone, mimicking leafless branches against an early evening sky. He thought again of his life, his career, his belief in the Vision, and, as always, his Mentor. He credited everything he had, and was, today to his Mentor.

Nicholai had always been ambitious, and many would say arrogant. He would agree to the ambitious label. He had goals, a timeline, and an image in his mind of what his life was going to be. He would not allow barriers, or even boundaries, to halt the progress of his pursuit. He worked constantly, tirelessly, and rigidly. As the only son of a successful—and ruthless— investments broker, Nicholai learned that acquisitions were expected and necessary; people were easily traded commodities. When individuals were no longer useful to a project or purpose, they were to be set aside. People drained his energy and they were unreliable, but they were a necessary nuisance. Nicholai had never known his mother and was strongly discouraged at an early age to ask questions about her. His father told him she had simply been a 'vessel' and when her usefulness was over, she was no longer part of the equation. The family unit had always been his father, himself, and a presence called the Mentor. Nicholai was cared for by a succession of emotionally distant nannies. They were never unkind, but they were not loving. He was a job they had to do, and if they developed maternal feelings toward the lonely boy with the haunted, dark eyes, they found themselves out of that job quickly.

He had overheard a conversation between his father and the Mentor when he was six. The Mentor, an elegant, regal-looking older man who occupied the mirror in front of his father, was saying quietly to his father that 'the child was the promised one, the strongest one to appear in centuries of this lineage.' He remembered peeking around the door, wondering, with a bit of jealousy, who this child was. The Mentor had slowly turned his gaze from Nicholai's father to Nicholai, and a small smile had turned up his lip. Nicholai was tempted to shrink back from the door, but he heard the Mentor's voice in his mind, not his ears.

"Come forward, child. Come forward and stand next to your father."

Nicholai opened the door fully and walked in, standing beside his father. His father's face flushed an angry red. The boy knew better than to simply walk in when the Mentor and Stanislaus were in a private conversation. He seized the boy's shoulders in a painful grip and shook him hard. As suddenly as he started, he gasped and tore his hands from the boy. Stanislaus looked at his reddening palms, already beginning to form blisters. Glaring at the boy, he raised a hand to strike him, but his hand was painfully pulled back behind him by an unseen force. In a moment of clarity, he looked at the Mentor, sitting serenely in the mirror, watching Nicholai's father with sardonic amusement.

"It is time the child got to know me better, Stanislaus. He is in this room at my bequest, sent telepathically. At his tender age, he is already stronger than you. You will never lay a hand on him again, do you understand, Stanislaus? I have given you wealth, power, status, and security. I can just easily drive you into poverty, shame, and ruin. I am the reason you exist. I could be the reason you cease to be as well."

Nicholai looked warily between his father and the Mentor. He had seen the Mentor several times, always in the mirror, and he had been sternly warned to never bring the Mentor up in conversation with anyone. The Mentor turned his full black gaze on the child, and his pupils became slits. He raised his finger and beckoned the boy closer. Nicholai felt his father's fear. Stanislaus was not worried for the boy's safety; he was worried that he could become obsolete very soon.

Nicholai raised his arms to his father. Stanislaus lifted the child and put him on the table that the mirror sat upon. Nicholai curled his legs under his bottom and sat quietly in front of the Mentor. The Mentor's serpentine smile had spread over his features.

He spoke to the child gently. "Nicholai, I am going to ask you to do something, and I want you to know that I have complete faith in you. Do not ask why. Do not tell me it is impossible. I know you can do this, son. I want you to take your hands and put them against mine in the mirror. Then I want you to hold my hands just like you do when you go for a walk with your nanny."

Stanislaus stiffened as his son placed his small palms against those of the man in the mirror, and then curled his tiny fingers around the withered, pale knuckles of the older man. The Mentor closed his eyes.

This was the child who could free him. This was the Descendant who could bring him across the realm into Gaia, and the Mentor's work on the eradication of humanity could begin in earnest. The centuries of Descendants before Nicholai were malleable and earnest, but not one had shown the promise and connection that this child already did. He would be raised to believe he was working for, and leading, a Vision of a perfect society, with perfect people living in perfect homes. Once that had been accomplished, the Mentor would be in a position to take possession of the body, mind, and soul of the powerful man this remarkable boy would become.

The Mentor reached behind his neck and pulled an iridescent stone, strung on a thick leather cord, over his head. He passed it into the child's hands. Nicholai gazed at the crystal in wonder. It was the most beautiful stone he had ever seen. In his hands, the stone began to glow, as it did against the Mentor's chest.

"Yes. Yes! Nicholai, you are the chosen one. Whenever you want to talk to me, you say the words 'Mentor, I am listening,' and I will be there. Promise me, son, that you will never take that piece off. Never, ever."

Nicholai nodded solemnly, his small hands cupping the glorious treasure. The Mentor pinned Stanislaus with a warning glare. "You will remain to raise the child, but under my direction. Do you understand?"

Stanislaus nodded slowly. He was not to be terminated. Yet.

The Mentor leaned forward, placing his chin on the back of his hand and staring at Nicholai. "Oh, my child. I have waited so long to meet you."

Chapter Three

D eclan pretended he didn't hear the phone at his bedside. He was completely consumed with staring at Inanna in his bed. His gaze slowly traveled from the top of her silver-blonde head, over her forehead, and to gently arched brows. Her eyes were closed in sleep. Long dark lashes fanned her sculpted cheeks. He lingered on her full, pink lips. Even in sleep, they curved into a sweet, sexy smile. Her long neck gracefully sloped to strong, sculpted shoulders. His fingers reached out almost involuntarily to sneak a lift of the blanket covering those full, firm breasts...

"You should probably answer the phone, Declan."

Declan's fingers froze in midair. "Ah...feck."

Inanna laughed and grabbed his hand. She kissed his fingers and rolled onto her side to face him. "It is Father Benedict. If it were anyone else, I would encourage you to continue your inspection of my body."

"Don't go, okay? Don't leave. I promise I won't be long."

Inanna smiled gently and cupped her hands around his face. "I am here, with you, until the full moon. No matter what."

Declan grabbed the phone flipping onto his back. He didn't check to see who the caller was, he knew she would be right. He put the phone to his ear as her warm hand slid down his body and grasped his rigid shaft. He yelped into the phone. "Hel-lo?"

"Declan, Father Benedict here. We met at the hospital the other day."

Declan couldn't help but smile at the warmth and joy in the priest's voice. He wondered if this man ever had a bad day. "Of course. That was quite a day."

Declan reached over with his free hand and curled it around Inanna's, who continued to playfully stroke him. He grunted when she squeezed and let go before blowing him a kiss and getting out of bed.

"I am sorry, Declan. Did I catch you in the middle of work?"

"No, it's okay. I am just getting...up." Declan looked down at the tent in his lap and smiled. He looked over at Inanna making coffee and caught her gaze. He curled his finger in a come-hither sign. Inanna batted her eyelashes and turned away, bending far over the sink to fill the carafe, and sending blood surging into the steeple.

"Oh dear. Is it that early? I apologize, Declan, but I feel that time is of the essence, son. Something happened the other day, and I know you are aware that it wasn't a...how do you say it...a one-off?"

Declan became aware of a shift in the energy of the room and through the phone lines. He was shaken by the image of a headstone, lovingly cared for, and a name etched in it above a timeline that was not long from now. He looked over at Inanna, standing rigidly at the kitchen sink. She turned slowly to meet his gaze and put the coffee pot down.

"No, it wasn't. I felt that as well. Are you all right? Have you seen a doctor recently or plan to? I...I'm not talking about the healing hands or the presence of St Raphael. Is there something else going on?"

The voice on the other end of the phone was silent.

"Father?" Declan put his feet on the floor and gripped the phone harder.

"I thank you for your concern, Declan. I had been feeling a bit off before all this started. I keep meaning to see a doctor about my fatigue and these headaches. But then I think I am just getting old. Well...older. That nice doctor in the ER asked to examine me out of purely scientific curiosity. I think I should let him."

Declan sighed with relief. "Good. That's great news."

"Declan, we need to assemble the Others. I know there may be resistance, but I feel there is something we have all been gathered to do. I believe that the Others realize this as well, as much as they may want to deny it. I have been offered a place for us to gather. I would like to go there now and get it ready for us to stay a while."

Declan felt a panic threatening to take over him. "What? Now? But...but there are things I have to tend to here. I just started something new, and I can't just go off and...ow!"

Declan planted a hand over his ear where a well-thrown sock bundle had struck him. He cast an annoyed glance over at Inanna who stood in front of him, her arms crossed over her chest and a stern look on her face, although her lips were smiling.

She crept into his mind. "Settle down, Declan O'Neill. I will be there with you."

Declan nodded and gave her his most charming lop-sided smile. He spoke almost gleefully to Benedict. "I will contact the Others."

"Thank you, son. I will be in touch when the accommodations are ready."

"Goodbye." Declan put the phone down. "I am really glad he is going to see that ER doctor. I am getting the feeling that he might be a bit sick. The doctors will get him sorted out and on the road to rec—" Declan stopped talking. He looked over at Inanna. Her blue eyes shimmered with tears, and she shook her head sadly.

Shemar sat in the darkness of the living room, staring without focus at the carved box. Olivia sat beside him on the sofa, her cup of tea growing cold for the third time in as many hours. Shemar's phone rang beside him, but he made no move to answer it.

Olivia glanced at the phone before she got up and answered. "You have reached Shemar's phone. This is Olivia."

Shemar looked up when, a few seconds later, she said, "I know who you are, Mr. O'Neill. I heard about everything."

Declan was silent on the other end of the phone.

Shemar watched his mother concentrate on the table, on the window as if trying to prevent the caller from reading her thoughts. Then she said, "I understand, Mr. O'Neill. I don't like any of it, but I understand. I would pray with all my heart that I didn't, but that would not prevent what is happening. I only want to support Shemar and that little girl. This all has to do with her, doesn't it?"

"Yes," Shemar heard Declan say through the phone. "Yes, Olivia. It does."

Olivia pressed her lips together to keep them from trembling and stifled a sob. She handed the phone to Shemar.

He reached out and took it but linked his fingers with his mother's before releasing her. "Declan. Where are we going from here?"

Mara tossed a bale of hay into her truck and stopped abruptly. She cocked her head and listened to the silence. Thrusting the pitchfork into the ground, she went to the well and hauled up a barrel of water. She tied it in place and leaned over. Passing her hands across the water, she peered intently into the depths. She saw Declan.

His eyes were focused on something in the distance. She smiled slightly as she thought how extraordinarily beautiful this man was. If he were any prettier, he would be winning the local beauty pageant. She saw him laugh. A large smile revealed his white teeth and the gentle lines around his mouth deepened. She heard his thoughts as they entered her mind.

"Mara, this is the property we are meeting at. We will be there for a while, at least until we understand why we were brought together. Can you meet us there this afternoon?"

Mara recognized the old place and nodded. She formed her words and pushed them to Declan's mind. "I know where it is. I will be there."

She passed her hand over the barrel and lowered it back into the well. She smiled again as she saw her granddaughter Nikita dancing toward her.

The young girl had her earbuds in and was singing along to her music. She stopped and bent down to talk to a stalk of wheat. Mara knew that she was actually talking to the fae. Nikki already presented with some of the gifts of her lineage. She and Mara were inseparable, much to Annika's annoyance. Nikki tossed back her long, brown hair and giggled. She looked over at Mara and waved. Mara watched her with pride as Nikki made her slightly gangly, fifteen-year-old way to her grandmother's side. She stood tall already, up to Mara's shoulder, and Mara was a big woman. Mara put her arm fondly around Nikki. The girl looked up at her with light green eyes and winked. Mara winked back and pulled up the barrel again. She tied it and sat on the edge of the well as Nikki passed her hand over the surface.

Father Benedict dropped his suitcase on the hardwood floor of the foyer. After adjusting his glasses, he put his hands on his hips and gave a low whistle. This refuge was definitely what the good doctor would have ordered, had the priest actually gone to see him before coming up here. He promised himself that as soon as the group had come to some understanding about who and what they were, he would have the tests and erase that niggling fear that something was not quite right in himself...present circumstances of green auras and healing hands aside.

Father Benedict laughed at himself again and went to pick up his suitcase when a sharp stab of pain sliced through his head. He dropped the case and pressed both hands to his temples, trying to squeeze the pain into submission. His eyes clouded and for a moment, he could not see. He dropped to his knees with the onset of vertigo and then eased himself into a sitting position. The pain subsided and his vision slowly returned to normal. He pulled off his glasses and shook his head, squeezing the bridge of his nose. After placing his palms on the floor, he pushed himself back to his knees, then stood.

A wave of nausea hit him, and he leaned against the doorframe. He really had to get more rest.

The long hours, lack of sleep, and these new turns of events were playing havoc with his well-being. He would be of no use to anyone if he got the flu now. Chiding himself, he resolved to pick a room, unpack, and make a cup of tea. Heck, a whole pot of tea. And a pot of coffee. The Cardinal assured him the pantry was fully stocked. He could put together his delicious, if he did say so himself, cheese tea buns. Puttering would give him something to do until the Others came. Declan would be calling them all about now, so he best get himself familiar with this sprawling place so he could be a proper host.

He found a smaller bedroom, quiet and a bit darker, on the second level. Light seemed to be bothering his eyes lately. Well. He certainly was becoming a complaining old fart, wasn't he? After putting his few clothes away, he wandered down a corridor and managed to find the kitchen again. He filled the kettle and went to turn the faucet off when he heard a sickening thump against the window in front of him. Startled, he put the kettle down. Seeing a mark on the window where something had struck the glass, Benedict hurried outside and knelt on the ground in front of the window.

On the grass, eyes closed and body still, lay a small, beautiful goldfinch.

"Oh dear. Little one, I am so sorry this happened to you. Come, I will find a place to bury you, so you aren't carted off by some opportunistic cat."

Benedict picked up the small bird and stroked it absently as he walked toward the gardens in the back. He cupped his hands around the bundle and looked around for a shed where a shovel might be. As he stood there, he was suddenly aware of his hands growing cold.

He closed his eyes and held his breath. It was happening again; he could feel it. The tips of his hands now tingled with warmth, and a surge of heat flooded his fingers. Tipping his head skyward, the wave of light-headedness was replaced by a feeling of euphoria. He looked down at his hands and opened them slowly.

The little finch sat quietly in his palms. She blinked, ruffled her feathers, chirped, and took off in flight. He held his hands in front of himself and watched the strange green aura dissipate.

Ethel walked onto the porch and looked out at the outskirts of the clearing. Ho'kee sat sprawled in a wooden Adirondack chair, a blanket encasing him. The remnants of a fire were in front of him. She saw the woods behind him rustle a little, and she smiled when the little lame fox stretched and yawned. She walked toward her son with two steaming mugs of coffee. As she sat next to him, her eyes teared up with gratitude and foreboding. Her sweet, intelligent, compassionate...shapeshifting son. A sob broke from her throat and startled Ho'kee awake.

He looked over at her and smiled. "Mom. You brought coffee. I love you so much."

Ethel laughed and handed him a mug. "You had a visitor last night. Someone besides Little Red behind us."

Ho'kee nodded and sipped at his coffee. "Yeah, it was so strange. I haven't seen Old Dan for years and he just shows up to talk to me about all kinds of things."

Ho'kee looked anxious and put his mug on the chair arm. "Mom, I need to talk to you about something."

"Yes. I know, son. You are a shapeshifter. Old Dan paid your father and me a visit. To be honest, Ho'kee, he only confirmed my suspicions."

Ho'kee's face flamed. "I'm sorry if you are disappointed in me, Mom. Now that I know what I am, I am not afraid of it. I am going to learn more about who and what I am. Old Dan will teach me."

Ethel's face was sad as she reached out to touch her son's hand. "Ho'kee. Old Dan died yesterday afternoon after he came to see your father and me. Yet I have no doubt at all that he will be back to teach you for as long as you need him."

Ho'kee looked stunned. The old man had spent the night with him, he knew it! He had reached out and actually touched...no. No, he didn't. He never did touch the old man. "Oh man. So, I just spent the evening talking to a ghost."

"Spirit, Ho'kee. Yes, you did. He promised us he would be with you on this journey. You are going to be part of something that will change this world for the better, Ho'kee. I am so very proud of you. I have never, ever been disappointed in you, sweetheart."

Ho'kee lowered his eyes so his mom couldn't see the tears gathering. He swiped at his wet cheeks with his blanket and saw Abe come out to the porch with a phone in his hand.

"Son! It's for you. It's Declan O'Neill."

Yenay peeked in at her daughter watching television. Annalee chortled at the sight of Oscar the Grouch. She loved the old sourpuss. She rolled from her tummy to her back and tried to watch the television upside down. "Mama!"

"Annalee!"

Annalee twisted herself into a pretzel and watched Oscar from in between her legs, palms planted on the floor. "Mama, the phone is calling. It's the pretty man we met yesterday."

Yenay looked quizzically at her daughter from the kitchen bar and her mouth tightened as the phone did indeed ring. She looked at the caller ID. Declan O'Neill. She tossed her kitchen towel over her shoulder and answered. "Hi, Declan."

"Yenay! Good to hear your voice. How is Annalee?"

She gazed fondly at her daughter who was now standing on one leg in imitation of a flamingo on the screen. "No worse for the wear whatsoever. No fever, no aftereffects. Like the whole thing never happened."

He spoke, quietly but firmly, to break her attempt to brush it aside. "But it did, Yenay. I spoke with the others. We are going to meet at a site that Father Benedict has arranged. How soon can you and Annalee come?"

Yenay's eyes narrowed as she glared at the phone in her hand. Her tone was angry and clipped. "Now look, Mr. O'Neill."

"Declan, please."

She drew a sharp breath in and held it. "Mr. O'Neill. I will not under any circumstances allow Annalee to be drawn into whatever this is. I know there is some strange knowledge she has about 'Descendants' but she is far too young to understand what any of it might mean."

"I understand your concern, Yenay. However, I have a feeling that the older Annalee gets, the more pronounced her gifts are going to become. You have probably already noticed things like how strangers respond to her smile, how no one she meets wants to break contact with her, how her presence alone in a room can change the energy immediately, always for the better."

Yenay closed her eyes, tightening her grip on the phone.

"You've probably noticed the little things too. She knows when a phone is going to ring and who will be on it. She knows where someone is when they are hiding."

She held her breath. Those were just flukes.

"They are not flukes, Yenay. This is who Annalee is, who she is becoming. You spoke with your mother?"

"Yes. She told me that neither our maternal nor paternal line had claims of descendancy from Quan Yin."

She could tell by the silence on the other end that Declan did not believe her. He had every right not to. She was lying.

"Annalee's father?"

Yenay expelled her breath. She was ending this call right now. "I have no idea, and we are finished talking. Don't call us again, we don't need or want..."

Yenay opened her eyes and caught her daughter's gaze. Annalee stood in the doorway, her little palms pressed together. She bowed her head slightly to her mother and said softly, "Quan Yin."

As she raised her little head, shots of gold light flew from her center, surrounding her in a shimmering, intense glow. The little girl was completely peaceful within the golden orb with her hands outstretched.

Yenay dropped the phone. Her hands came up to her mouth as she watched her daughter morph into an image that she herself had only seen in history books and carved statues. Her little girl was a golden image of a beautiful woman, with a willow branch in her left hand and a jug of water in her right. She shimmered in a white and gold robe and smiled serenely at Yenay.

She raised a hand to block out the overwhelming brightness of the light. Tears ran down her face as she felt the purity, kindness, and compassion of the image before her suffusing her body and mind. She cried out, sinking to her knees, bending her head to the presence before her. "Quan Yin!"

Suddenly, a tiny hand patted her gently on her shoulder.

"Mama!"

She looked up at her daughter with wonder and grabbed her close, causing the child to squeal in delight and surprise.

Annalee picked up the phone on the ground and handed it to her mother. "Pretty man is still on the phone, Mama. He saw everything."

Yenay gulped back a sob and grabbed a pen with her shaking hand. "Where are we meeting, Declan?"

Declan looked over at Inanna, ethereal and beautiful in her white skorts and tight blue T-shirt. She caught his gaze and laughed. He was never going to tire of that sound.

"Eyes on the road, Declan O'Neill. I am all too mortal at this time."

"You are a goddess, my beauty. But you do say the weirdest shit."

Inanna laughed again and caught his hand. She lifted it to her mouth and kissed his fingers.

"Do you want to meet the Others? I know they would love to meet you."

Inanna smiled a bit sadly and turned her gaze to the road in front of them. "I will in time, Declan, but not this time. I will be with you, always at your side, but they will not see me. None but the child will see me."

"I am not going to lie to you and say I understand, but I honor how you feel. However, before we get married, you have to meet my brother."

Inanna squeezed his hand. "I am your muse, your lover, and your guide, but I won't be your wife."

"That's okay. I can live with that. You modern-age women. As long as we stay together."

Inanna was silent, her head turned toward the window, watching the scenery. "This is a beautiful area."

"Yes. Father Benedict said the retreat was tucked away. Perfect for hermits, nature lovers, celebrities avoiding paparazzi, and visiting clergy."

"Father Benedict is a good man."

"You know him?"

Inanna traced her finger lightly over the window frame of the car. Her voice was reflective. "I do. In a matter of speaking. We have met in his dreams."

Declan drew his brows together in confusion. "Wait. You visited him in his dreams as well? You and the two other women?"

"Yes. We visited all of you."

"Then why can't they see you? Why can't they meet you? If they've already seen you, doesn't it make sense that they meet you face to face?"

"I am not part of their journey in this form, only part of yours."

Declan tightened his grip on the steering wheel. His jaw muscles worked as he thought about what he was going to say, and how he was going to say it. Bugger it. He was just going to blurt it out. "Inanna. You are leaving me when this is over, aren't you? Whatever this is."

She looked at him with sadness in her eyes. "Yes."

He squeezed her hand and gave her a tight smile. She was going to change her mind; he was sure of it. He would be the kind of man a woman would never leave. He knew he could change her mind. He was sure of it. Kind of sure. Her sweet voice brought him back from his dark mulling.

"I think that is it, up ahead! Oh, Declan, it is absolutely beautiful."

Declan looked up to see a three-story structure resembling more of a vacation home than a humble rectory retreat. It looked like it was made of stone, brick, and glass. Two wood decks wrapped around two levels, and the third had a widow's walk. He let out a low whistle. "I think we are going to need a map for the interior of that place. Or strategically placed bits of popcorn scattered behind us."

Declan pulled his car in tightly behind a clean, compact VW Bug. He opened his car door and stood up to see Father Benedict emerging from the house, wiping flour-caked hands onto a tea towel.

"Declan! Welcome! You are the first, thank goodness. I will need some help getting rooms organized. I got caught up in baking cheese scones."

Declan shut his door and waved to the priest. He walked around to Inanna's side. "Father, I want you to meet someone. This is..."

He opened the passenger side door, but Inanna wasn't there. There was no indication that she ever had been. Even the coffee cup she was drinking her latte from was gone. Declan blinked rapidly and closed the door.

The priest looked at him quizzically. "Declan? Do you have someone you want me to meet? I am sorry I don't see anyone there, but I am old, and my glasses don't always work well."

Declan dropped his head slightly. "No. Well, kind of. My brother gave me some family albums and my mom's journals. There is some reference to Dagda in there. I thought we could do some research. So, Father Benedict, meet the Dagda journals."

Benedict looked instantly relieved that he wasn't going blind, and Declan wasn't completely mad. "Ah! Of course. Excellent idea."

Declan sniffed the air. "You are a great baker. Those smell downright heavenly."

The priest laughed and tossed his towel over his shoulder. He put an arm around Declan's shoulders to guide him inside and stopped suddenly, looking at the branch of an evergreen tree in front of the kitchen window. Declan followed his gaze, and saw a beautiful little finch on the branch, tilting its head toward the two men. Beside the tiny bird was a large black crow, cleaning his beak with his talons. Side by side, the odd couple seemed completely at ease with each other. The little finch chirped, startling the crow. The crow fluffed his feathers and called out.

Declan narrowed his gaze at the big black bird. "Did you actually follow me all the way here, you obnoxious rook?"

The priest looked from the birds to Declan, a bit uneasily. "Friend of yours, Declan?"

Declan looked skeptical. "We have a mutual friend." Declan glared at the crow and stage whispered, "Do *not* shit on my car."

Father Benedict's smile was genuine amusement as he watched the exchange.

Declan walked ahead of the priest toward the house. "More like an albatross. Shrieks like a banshee. I don't think it's the same one that hangs around my house though. That would be a long flight for him. I don't think we're that close."

Declan pushed the door open as Benedict tilted his head and studied the crow. The crow tilted his head in response and leaned over to touch its beak gently and affectionately to the finch's head.

"If there is one thing I have learned beyond the shadow of a doubt, young Declan, it is that the impossible does not exist."

Mara put the old heap of a truck in park and, be-cause she didn't trust the beast, looked around for large rocks to put behind the back wheels. She spotted two in the beautiful, but slightly unkempt, garden of wildflowers in the center of the roundabout. She kicked away the hem of her dress and marched over to the first boulder. She crouched down and lifted the rock into her arms. She started to straighten up when the lovely young man with dark-blue eyes stepped in front of her.

"Mara! May I help you with that?"

Mara gave him a wide smile and inclined her head. Declan reached out to take the rock.

"Please let me lift that for you."

Mara grinned more widely and deposited the rock in Declan's arms. His eyes flew open wide, and he grunted at the unexpected weight. Mara pointed to the back wheels of the truck. As Declan struggled with placing the stone, Mara lifted a second, heavier one, and almost tossed it behind the second back tire. She stood with her hands on her hips as Declan rose up and looked at her with respect.

"You are really strong, Mara."

Mara's hand flashed up and then down in a dismis-sive gesture. She gave the tires a kick with her boots to check the stability and turned back to Declan. She cleared her mind so he could read her thoughts and tapped the side of her head.

"Strength and incredible beauty in one package. It is surprising how humble I have remained."

Declan smiled. "Father Benedict has your room ready. May I show you to it?"

Mara looked a bit sad at the mention of the priest. She latched her gaze onto Declan's. "How is he?"

Declan looked at her quizzically. "He is fine. He seems a bit tired, but he's done a lot in a short amount of time with coming here, getting things ready, baking cheese biscuits."

Mara watched Declan closely for a few more seconds and decided now was not the time to share her concerns about the priest's health. She clapped her hands together and ushered Declan in front of her to get her suitcase while she pulled out a dark bag from the cab of the truck.

He hesitated as Mara stopped and opened the bag to retrieve a large vial of black salt. He raised an eyebrow. Mara dropped the bag and opened the vial. She studied the surroundings briefly, then shooed Declan inside.

Mara closed her eyes and whispered an incantation. She opened them and methodically began to chant as she spread a wide circle of black salt around the premises. At the end of the circle, she closed the vial, put her hands on her hips, and lifted her face to the sky. "So mote it be."

She walked into the house and heard that delightful priest's voice.

"Mara! I thought you would never get here! I need help getting the tea and scones ready and this young lad is hopeless in the kitchen."

Mara hugged the priest fiercely. Benedict returned the hug just as fiercely. No words were needed to communicate the feeling of hope and kinship between them. They broke apart, and Mara busied herself finding butter for the scones. She reached into that bottomless bag and lifted out her homemade jams, jellies, and lemon curd. She looked around the kitchen at the artistic display of well-used, high-end cooking tools. She gave a low whistle.

"*Damn*, something smells good in here!"

Shemar's voice reverberated through the house as he strode in, filling the large space with his frame. He winked at Mara, who winked back. He gave a low whistle and looked around the kitchen. "Damn! Oh! Sorry, Father, I didn't see you there." Shemar looked a bit shamefaced as he put his hand out to shake the priest's.

Benedict laughed. "No need to apologize, Shemar. I often use that turn of phrase myself. Especially when smelling exceptionally delicious cheese scones."

Declan appeared behind Shemar and took that moment to appreciate the sheer size of the man before him. The man was built like a tank and just as unstoppable. "Hey, Shemar! Glad to see you."

Shemar turned to extend his hand to Declan. His wide mouth curved into a smile. "Declan! Good to see you again, man. Have you heard from Yenay?"

Mara's eyebrows rose at the warmth that was infused into that name. She smiled a little and looked over to Father Benedict. He was cleaning his glasses but smiled as well and winked at Mara.

Declan ran his hand through his hair and looked up at Shemar. "Ah...yeah. She isn't feeling too enthused about this, but she and Annalee are on their way."

Benedict replaced his glasses and pulled on oven mitts to take the biscuits out. "I understand her reluctance to continue this exploration in regard to the little girl. However, I don't believe procrastination or turning a blind eye will help her with who, and what, Annalee is becoming."

Shemar sighed heavily. "I have to tell you guys something, but I will wait until the others get here."

Mara cocked her head to Declan, sensing a shift in Shemar as his figure tightened with anxiety.

Declan put his hand on Shemar's shoulder. "Something happened when you spoke with your family, didn't it? Something shifted in you."

Declan's eyes widened as he saw a figure flash quickly through his mind and retreat just as fast. "Oh man. Shango."

Mara sat down heavily at the mention of that name. Father Benedict froze at the stove.

Shemar crossed his arms over his chest. "Yes. But I don't want to get into details without Ho'kee and Yenay."

Seemingly on cue, the sound of a motorcycle outside rumbled through the kitchen. Mara looked out the window to see Ho'kee park his bike and remove his helmet.

He tossed back his long black hair and sat on the bike for a few moments. She could see that his senses were fully engaged in his surroundings. There was a wariness in his survey. He was at ease on the bike, tuned into the area around him. She watched him as his gaze slowly traveled in a half circle. Then he gracefully got off the bike, and, while he was detaching his knapsack, he scanned the second half circle behind him. Seemingly satisfied, he pulled the sack to his shoulder, grasped the helmet, and began striding to the front door.

Ho'kee looked the building up and down and gave a low whistle.

Shemar came through the door and pulled the young man into his strong handshake. "Good to see you! Saw you checking out the scenery there. Anything to report?"

Ho'kee smiled broadly and patted Shemar's huge shoulder. "All quiet on the rectory front, sir!"

Shemar laughed and put his arm around Ho'kee's shoulders. "Come on in! Man, you have got to see this place. I think only the celebrity monks stay here."

"Like celebrity rehab monks? Into the communion grape juice?" Ho'kee joked and then almost knocked over Father Benedict who was coming out from the kitchen. "Oh Jeez. I mean—rats. Sorry. I was just kidding."

The priest laughed and put his hands on the young man's shoulders. "No offense taken, son. I have known a few of my brothers of the clerical collar to be a bit too fond of the 'grape juice.' I myself enjoy a glass or two every so often. I think there may be a selection of monk-made wine in the cellar, actually. Would you like to go downstairs and see if you can pull up a bottle or two to go with our dinner tonight?"

"On it! Just gonna drop my stuff in my room. Where in this labyrinth is my room?"

Shemar pointed up the stairs. "I took the corner left. Declan took one level up, the center. Father is on this level. The other 657 bedrooms are up for grabs."

Ho'kee laughed and took the steps two at a time to secure the room beside Shemar.

Shemar watched Ho'kee climb the stairs and smiled, feeling a bit 'uncle-ish'.

Declan came to stand beside him and looked up. "Ho'kee?"

"Yeah. Good kid. Smart and resourceful. Reminds me of myself at that age. Almost as handsome as I was too."

A snort followed by a peal of laughter caused the guys to turn around. Yenay had a hand over her mouth and the other was holding onto Annalee. She spoke in between gulps of laughter. "I apologize, Your Most Royal Good Lookingness. We didn't mean to startle you."

Shemar's eyes shone as he looked at Yenay, and she returned the interest. Annalee's cheeks dimpled when she looked up at Declan, and she opened and closed her little fist.

Mara's voice preceded her as she bustled into the foyer, chortling, and speaking Russian. "Angel! Come see Babushka and give her the hugest hug ever in the history of huge hugs!"

Annalee squealed and pulled herself away from Yenay, pumping her four-year-old legs as fast as they would carry her. Mara crouched down to gather the force of the child as she launched herself at the old woman. Yenay gasped in fear—the child was like a rocket launcher—but Mara closed her arms around Annalee delightedly and lifted her, spinning her around as the child laughed.

Declan winked at Yenay and stage whispered, "If a wrestling match between the Russian Babushka and

Shemar the Gorgeous breaks out, my money is on Grandma, just saying."

Yenay's laugh burst forth, and Declan smiled conspiratorially.

Ho'kee leaned over the upstairs railing and called down. "Munchkin!"

Annalee looked up and waved her arms at Ho'kee. "Woof!"

Father Benedict walked in from the kitchen wearing a frilled apron adorned with embroidered apples. Yenay bit her fist to prevent a second round of laughter, but none of the others were as kind. He put his fists on his hips and pretended, unsuccessfully, to look stern.

When the laughter subsided, he spoke in his gentle, happy lilt, "Cheese scones and tea are served for the famished travelers! There may be a spot of something stronger for those who need it."

He winked and crooked his finger in a beckoning motion to the kitchen.

Chapter Four

The Descendants sat quietly in a large wood-beamed living room, gusts of wind battering with futility against thick paned, floor-to-ceiling windows. They all gazed at the snapping fire inside a stone chimney, lost in their own thoughts.

Ho'kee sat cross-legged in front of it, occasionally pushing at the logs and dropping another piece on. Annalee lay sleeping, her head on a pillow in Yenay's lap. Yenay absently toyed with her daughter's hair as she looked over at Declan sitting at a long table, pen to paper, furiously scribbling.

"What are you writing over there, Declan?"

Ho'kee snorted and flicked a piece of sap into the fire to hear it snap. "Doodles Declan."

Declan arched an eyebrow in Ho'kee's direction and spread his hands over his work. "Oh, young shapeshifter. I have so much to teach you. This is a timeline, working backward. I am going to try to find the common link that drew us all together to the hospital at that particular time. There might be something in our shared backgrounds that will give us a clue as to why we were each chosen as the reincarnation of our ancestors. I am open to any helpful suggestions, and the floor is open to whoever wants to tell their story first."

The Others all turned their gazes to Declan. He sat with his pen poised over the chart and gave a loud, dramatic sigh. "All right, all right! Since you are all so nosy and persistent with your pleas to hear my tale, I will go first."

Ho'kee threw another piece of pitch into the fire, prompting several rude sounds to emanate from the flames, much to the amusement of the gathering.

"Here is me. Declan O'Neill. Born to Susan and Ronan O'Neill, may they both rest in peace."

Mara inclined her head in acknowledgment of Declan's loss.

"One brother, Niall."

Ho'kee laughed outright. "Niall O'Neill?"

Declan cocked his head to the side as he added to his line. "My da was a bit fond of the gargle. He couldn't think of a thing when my mother had my brother, hence when he was asked for the boy's name, he thought of one he couldn't possibly forget."

A round of interested and amused looks met this declaration. Shemar uncrossed his arms and laughed richly.

"Ronan was killed in a work accident when I was four. We had no extended family in Ireland, and my mother did not want to stay there. She said we needed to be somewhere else, and she knew it was in Canada. My mother had one sister, and she had stayed in touch with her since Aunt Brionne emigrated to British Columbia twenty years before. She and my aunt talked briefly on the phone and within a month we were on our way to join her in Shirley, on this island. Mom worked for Aunt Brionne at her nursery, eventually becoming a partner.

"I was about seven when I realized Mom had this uncanny sense of knowing what was going to happen before it did. She would just freeze, right in the middle of talking or walking. She would just stop. She'd stare straight ahead, not blinking. Most times it was something small like she would say, 'Your brother just fell off his skateboard. Again. He's hurt his knee. Again.' Other times, she would start to shake and sit down and cry. She would talk out loud, to someone or something I couldn't see, and ask, 'How do I stop this? Why show me if I can't stop this?' She would never tell me what the big things were, but when we saw the news covering mass murders, plane crashes, political protests turning violent, she would show no surprise, just sorrow."

Declan stopped talking for a few minutes, his hand tracing over the timeline, marking where family members were born and died.

"She spent a lot of time with us at the seashore, every chance we got. It was almost ritualistic with her. If there was an abundance of bioluminescence in the waves, we would often be there all night, and miss school the next day. I remember so many small fires and burying ash in the morning."

Father Benedict, his fingers steepled together, peered over his glasses at Declan. "I am sorry for your losses, son."

"Thank you. She died when I was in my teens. She knew she wasn't going to live to a ripe old age. She made veiled references to leaving a lovely corpse, not one withered into ropey sinews. I found her when I got home from school one day. She was lying on her bed, very peaceful, like she knew what was coming and prepared herself. Her affairs were all in order. She wanted to be cremated and sent into the sea. She had a funny peculiarity in those instructions. It had to be done at night, and it had to take place when the bioluminescence was strong."

Declan scanned the timeline with his eyebrows drawn together in concentration.

Shemar shook a thick finger in Declan's direction. "I know that look already, Declan. You are making a connection."

Ho'kee got up and went to stand behind Declan, pulling his long hair back from his face. "Bioluminescence," he said and drew in his breath. He repeated the word for the others to hear. "Bioluminescence."

Declan's eyes seemed focused on the paper in front of him, but Inanna's sweet voice was lilting hauntingly in his head. She was repeating those words like a prayer, or an incantation. Her voice threaded through Ho'kee's raspy one.

"Oceans. Transcendence. Bioluminescence."

Declan looked at Mara. Her eyes grow wide as she heard Declan and Ho'kee speak the incantation together. Unseen by anyone but Mara, a faint blue aura undulated beside Declan.

Benedict removed his glasses, gripped the chair arms, and leaned forward. "Declan, think back. When did you realize that you shared a gift with your mother? What happened?"

Declan gazed unseeingly at the timeline. Images of the past formed a jagged jigsaw in his mind, and he tried to move the pieces around to see where they fit. "I was four. No one had told me, but I remember standing up in the sandbox of the neighborhood playground, knowing at that moment that my father had died. I had been swinging, and all of a sudden, looking up at the sky, I got a bad headache. I stopped swinging and squeezed my eyes shut, putting my hands over my ears. That sometimes helped to stop the headaches. When I opened my eyes, I saw my father in a crumpled heap at the bottom of the monkey bars. I remember running home, flinging open the door, and looking at my mother's face.

"She was trying so hard not to cry; she could barely speak. I remember my brother turning off the tv and watching from the couch. I remember she got down on her knees and stretched out her arms to me. I hugged her and talked to her. I told her it was ok, that she didn't have to talk, I knew Da had died. I remember Niall starting to cry and getting drawn into the hug. She pulled away from me, holding me at arm's length, and asked me how I knew that. She had just moments ago gotten off the phone with the hospital. My father was a window washer. He had fallen off the scaffolding several floors to his death.

"I told her I just knew. I didn't have it in me to tell her about the vision I had seen, but the way she looked at me at that moment, really looked at me. 'Chosen. My son from my line, you are the one.' She tried to teach me how to work with the ability, and how to accept it. I remember her trying so hard to keep me 'normal' and trying to teach me when to use it and when I wasn't supposed to. She worked hard with having me try to control it. I remember Aunt Brionne looking at me sadly and saying, 'I am not so sure this gift isn't a curse.' Then Mom got sick with cancer. I don't remember her ever going to a hospital or talking about treatments. The lessons stopped. I was about twelve when she got sick. After she died, something in me changed. I couldn't read thoughts anymore, and I no longer had visions."

"Did you perhaps decide you would no longer read?" Father Benedict's voice was calm and soothing. "And would no longer have prophetic visions? It is often a teenager's reaction to something they have no control over. All or nothing. They fight tooth and nail to have it, or they abandon it altogether. It sounds like the latter, son."

Declan nodded. "Aunt Brionne raised us until we were big enough and ugly enough to find our own ways. We moved here, to Nanaimo. There was more work for Niall in construction and a larger art market for me."

Yenay smiled and clapped her hands together. "I knew I had seen your work! The art gallery downtown, the foyers in a few of the banks? You are a gifted artist. I love your work!"

Declan smiled back and bowed his head. "Doodles Declan thanks you, lovely lady."

Ho'kee laughed and then drew himself up sharply. "Wait. So, you really do read minds. That was no fluke at the hospital. You are a telepath, and you are a prophet."

"I am a telepath. I have a gift of prophecy. I am very, very rusty in both areas. It's been almost two decades since I worked with these gifts. But I've met someone who is guiding me and pulling things out of me that I never knew existed! It's incredible and terrifying and..."

Declan stopped abruptly and cast an apprehensive glance at Benedict.

The priest clapped his hands together. "Oh son! I am not doing anything that you can't do for yourself, I am merely part of this funny little ensemble, trying to fit the pieces together."

Declan sighed quietly with relief and went rigid when Ho'kee leaned in close to his ear. "You were with Her," Ho'kee said. "I can smell Her on you."

Declan narrowed his eyes and turned his face to Ho'kee's. Their foreheads almost touching. "Not. Your. Business. I stay out of your head, you stay out of my bed, *comprendez?*"

Ho'kee smirked, and put his palms up in mock surrender, backing away. He went back to the fireplace and prodded the flames with a poker. Declan continued to glare at him until Shemar broke the quiet.

"Ho'kee, you are Navajo, right? How did your family come to the island?"

Ho'kee looked over at Shemar sharply, not prepared to tell his tale. He then looked at the curious eyes of Father Benedict, the kind and wise old eyes of Mara, the guarded and protective ones of Yenay. He stared briefly at the sleeping innocence of Annalee, her arm wrapped around the stuffed iguana, lying on her mother's lap.

He wouldn't look at Declan. He knew Declan wouldn't go into his head, Ho'kee could feel this guy kept his word, but he still didn't want to look at him. Declan unsettled him. The idea of the Goddess with Declan unsettled him. He shook himself out of these thoughts and looked back at the fire.

"Our people were the Athapaskans. We have been here for over a thousand years. Many Navajo went south, through the plains, through the mountains. There are big populations in America. But my family stayed here in western Canada, many of us made Tofino our home. Mom and Dad run a bed and breakfast up there. There is just me, no brothers or sisters. We have a lot of family up there, all very close. My grandparents died before I was born, but I got really close to an honorary great-grandfather, Old Dan. He was everybody's great-grandfather. I talked to him just before he died."

Ho'kee involuntarily lifted his gaze to meet Declan's. There was no judgment in Declan's eyes, but there was an unspoken question of why Ho'kee was choosing to lie. Ho'kee shook his head, his long hair spilling over his face, and he drew in a long breath.

"Fuck that. Sorry, Father! Sorry, Mara! That just came out. I was going to sit here and lie to you, but I can't. I did see Old Dan again, but I saw him after he had died. We spent the night outside, in front of the fire, and he told me about my bloodline. He told me a few things I already knew, and a few things I didn't want to know. He talked to me as sure as I am sitting here talking to you, but he'd died the day before. So, I was talking to a ghost and you probably all think I am loco."

Ho'kee stared into the fire, positive that if he turned around, he would see pitying gazes on his new friends' faces. He only turned when he heard Shemar's bass voice.

"That is incredible. I had a whole conversation one night with my dad. He had passed away when I was six, but last year he came to me. I was trying to tell myself it was just a dream, but man, the clarity, the feelings, it was too real to chalk up to anything other than real as it comes."

Ho'kee smiled in relief. "Right? Exactly. I woke up outside, my mom handing me a cup of coffee, but the blanket I put around the old man to keep him warm in front of the fire was still there. I know things about myself now that no one else does. She knows I am a shapeshifter. She knew when my father told her about the blue-eyed gray wolf the farmers and fishermen saw. The shapeshifters in our bloodlines were various animals, but always with blue eyes."

Ho'kee went quiet again and pushed his hair back with his hand. "Old Dan told me I am the Descendant of a shapeshifter and a skinwalker. That's not what I wanted to hear. Skinwalkers are not revered in our culture. They are usually malevolent and in general, feared and despised."

Yenay's hand had paused above Annalee's head. She asked quietly, "What is the difference between a shapeshifter and a skinwalker?"

"Skinwalker is a harmful witch. The term is never used for healers. Shapeshifting to a wolf, like I do, is the ability to do that at will. Old Dan said centuries ago, a union between a skinwalker and a shapeshifter led to a Shifter child on my mother's line. I am that Descendant."

Mara smiled slightly and leaned forward to place a firm, wrinkled hand on Ho'kee's forearm. "I understand the questionable gift of having both a destructive force and a healing nature living inside you at the same time. I will help you come to respect, and be able to control, that darkness."

Ho'kee gazed at the old woman thoughtfully. "Thank you, Mara."

Declan poised his pencil in midair. "Ho'kee, do you remember anything to do with bioluminescence when you first shapeshifted in Tofino?"

Ho'kee's black eyes widened in surprise as he saw the scene replayed in the flames of the fire. That day he shifted, running after the fox. He remembered his feet, his paws, glowing beneath him, kicking up water sparking with light. "Yes. I was close to the ocean, in the woods. I could hear it. I was shifting, or transcending, and I was running through water that was bioluminescent."

Declan marked his grid. He put his pen down and spoke quietly. "Have you tried to shift into any other form since you talked to Old Dan?"

Ho'kee stared at Declan, a sneer pulling at his upper lip. "You mean put on the skin of something dead and see what happens? No, Declan. I haven't."

Yenay looked shocked at the abrupt reply. Father Benedict and Shemar looked at Ho'kee with something uncomfortably close to pity. Mara folded her arms and glared at Ho'kee.

Declan only looked thoughtful, unaffected by Ho'kee's snarkiness. "Does the animal have to be deceased in order for you to shift?"

"I don't know, okay? Not when I become Wolf, but I don't know about anything else. Old Dan didn't know either. He said that usually a skinwalker had to wear the skin of the animal to shift, but as a mixed-blood Descendant I might be different."

Ho'kee pushed his hand through his hair, off his forehead in frustration. He looked over at Declan, his anger subsiding, and he spread his hand, palm up, in a gesture of incomprehension. "I am afraid to find out."

Father Benedict drained his sherry glass and raised an eyebrow toward Ho'kee. Ho'kee unfolded himself and went to the side table to retrieve the sherry. He poured a generous amount into the glass for the priest.

He then stood back and said quietly, "Tell us your story. Why did you come to this island? When did you know you were a Descendant?"

The priest tilted the glass slightly to his lips. Then he shot the contents of the glass down in one gulp. He put the glass down and took his glasses off. "I came here because this is where I was guided to. I was in a seminary in Rome, obtaining my degree. That is where I met Cardinal Josef, we attended most classes together. The Cardinal had high expectations of himself and his education. I was in the running with him and saw myself in robes befitting a member of the Vatican! But God had another idea."

He polished his glasses on his frock and put them back on. "I had a premonition, of sorts. I was in bed, but not asleep. My eyes were closed, and I heard the ocean. We were nowhere near an ocean in our seminary. I thought Josef was pulling a prank, thinking that if I heard waves or water, I would have to get up and...um.... relieve myself all night long. I looked all over my tiny room for a recording device, but there was nothing. I decided it was probably a recording being played too loudly in a room above me, so I lay back down and closed my eyes. An uninvited thought, more like a voice, crept into my head. It was telling me I was not meant to stay in Rome. There was a place I was to go to, make a home in, and it had parishioners to serve. I was a bit annoyed. I wanted to stay in Rome, but I don't refuse an invitation from God, however much I don't want to go to the party."

Shemar laughed.

"I remember demanding this intrusive voice in my head show me where it thought I should be going. I was treated to a picture in my mind's eyes. I saw a pretty little bay, tiny lights of a small city in the twilight. I saw a greenish-blue tinge to the waves that were edging the shoreline. The light on the water was bioluminescence. I asked the bishop the next day if he would give me guidance. He knew that Josef and I were intent on staying in Rome and working within the church there. We were walking and he stopped abruptly and put his hands on my shoulders. He told me he'd had a dream the night before, and he swore he had heard ocean waves. He said he felt pulled to send me to a parish on an island, but he couldn't decipher where it was in his dream. All he could ascertain was the same as me; the island had bioluminescent waves. We went into his study and culled the 'please send a priest to such and such location' files. There were many islands, and a number of them boasted bioluminescent oceans. As we assessed each request and looked at pictures of the churches and the area, we both grabbed onto one at the same time. We both spoke at the same time, 'This is it!'"

He looked around at the rapt audience. "Uncanny and uncomfortable, I must say. It was a photograph of a little church in Cowichan Bay, on Vancouver Island. There was a small, detached cabin on the same grounds as the church, and both were beside the ocean. I left for the island within the week. As for St. Raphael, I am afraid I can't give much information on this peculiar trait of mine. I know very little of my background, having been raised in an orphanage. I was never adopted, so I aged out of care and joined the seminary. I cannot say for certain if the term 'Descendant' applies to me, but I can't dismiss it either. I did not have this ability until recently and although it is a gift from God to be a healer, it is difficult for an old man such as myself to adjust to."

Mara snorted and made her dismissive wave toward him. "Rubbish."

Yenay laughed and lightly tapped Mara's arm.

Declan made a few marks and looked up at the priest. "When did you first realize you had this gift? What happened?"

The priest looked thoughtful and traced his finger around the rim of his sherry glass. Ho'kee made a move toward the decanter, but Father Benedict smiled and shook his head.

He took his glasses off and traced his eyebrow with the tip of his forefinger. "The very first time it happened, I put it down to an aberration. I believed it was a 'fluke,' as you concisely said, Ho'kee. Later, as this gift appeared more frequently and with greater intensity, I realized that 'aberration' was the beginning of this chapter of my life. I was in Cowichan Bay, doing my nightly stroll. I came across a young buck that had been hit by a car and left to die on the side of the road. I called the wildlife rescue center and they promised to send out a volunteer as quickly as they could find one to see what could be done, if anything. I watched the poor thing struggle to breathe. Blood was coming from its nose and mouth. Its eyes were staring at me, I felt like he was asking me to do something, do anything. I remember asking the creature, 'What can I do?' At that moment, I felt my hands go ice cold, which was not seasonal. It was October; chilly but not freezing, but I felt as if I had plunged my hands into an ice bucket. Just as quickly, they started to tingle, and my skin felt like it was being pricked by fire. It became so intense, I looked around for water to put my hands into, to settle the heat. A mudpuddle, a curbside drain, anything. Behind me was a small beach, so I pushed my hands in there. I took off the top part of my cassock and drenched it in the water. I came back to the buck, and he was no longer breathing.

"His eyes were open and staring. I felt grief, that I had left the scared creature to die alone. My hands were now throbbing. I looked at them, and this strange, soft green aura was surrounding them. I thought this was probably a malfunctioning streetlight casting its shadow, so I shrugged the concern off. I was going to call the rescue center and tell them there was no hurry, but I wanted to make sure the deer was gone. I put my tingling hands on the creature's neck to feel for a pulse, and a sensation wrapped around me, threaded into me, became me. It was warm, it had a pulse of its own, it was soothing and calm. It matched my heartbeat, and I couldn't break it. I watched that green aura travel to encompass the deer and my hands, and once it was complete, the buck startled.

"I stepped back, and the deer got to its legs, unsteadily, but it did. It watched me for a moment, then darted off across the road. I looked down at my hands, and they were normal. I decided, for my own mental health, that the deer had only been stunned and I was mistaken about its lack of heartbeat. I looked up to verify the streetlight was working again, but there was no streetlight. I decided the green glow was due to the water in that area of Cowichan Bay."

Father Benedict paused. "It is a popular evening kayaking destination. Its bioluminescence is stunning."

Shemar gently replaced the sock Annalee had taken off in her sleep, and his rich bass voice filled the room. "My family came here from Nigeria, years ago. I was raised Southern Baptist, but it never really caught on with me. My mom, Olivia, is an anchor in the local chapter. She was heavily invested in covering all traces of the family's previous faith. To her way of seeing things, and it's not without merit, following that faith came at a very high price."

Yenay watched him curiously, her hand stilled above Annalee's head.

"We were believers in the Orisha. I am a Descendant of one of those lines. I am Shango."

Mara shivered and Ho'kee got up to place a blanket around her shoulders. She accepted gratefully and motioned to Shemar to continue.

"I knew something was off about me for a while. Mom said I didn't have much of a temper, but I would get seriously worked up when I saw injustice or brutality, in any form. Even as a child, this fury would come over me. I didn't have the words, and that frustration would just enfold me. Things would move around the house; I mean dishes flying, windows breaking. Mom figured the house was built on a fault line and had surveyors come around. It wasn't a fault line. There were scenes right out of Stephen King's movies; door cupboards opening, appliances starting themselves up. It never happened when I was calm, only when I was in a fit. Mom called in a priest a few times, thinking the house was possessed. It wasn't the house. Mom dove hard into the church when I was about twelve and really concerning stuff happened with me. If I saw someone getting bullied, I would go into a rage and fly at the bully. I've always been a big guy, and the recipient of my fists never came out the winner. I'd get especially protective with little kids, animals, older people, people that didn't fit the so-called mainstream. I ran into a big problem. Once I started, I couldn't stop; I would lose myself."

Shemar clasped his hands together and looked out the window. He struggled with his words. "There was a neighbor who took to beating his dog one night. I heard him yelling, and I heard the dog crying. It was the most heartbreaking, awful sound. Something deep within me snapped. All I remember is looking out the window and feeling this hatred come over me, watching that piece of shit looming over his dog. The next thing I remember, my mom was waking me up the next morning. I had the dog sleeping beside me on the floor. My hands were bloody and bruised. The neighbor came over to our house and handed over the leash and dog food to my mom. When he saw me, he backed away, crossing himself, stumbling back down the steps. I tried to talk to him, but he took off faster than a roadrunner. The neighbor wasn't about to press charges because he'd have to admit to what he had done, and he was obviously terrified of me. His face was a mess, and I did that. The only thing I slightly remember about laying that beating on the guy is the dog crying. I kind of remember the dog whimpering, seeing the guy below me, and I stopped.

"After that night, my mom doubled down on her work for the church. She kept talking about a pact she made with the Lord, and I didn't ask. I didn't want to know. She'd been through so much with me already. She said it was time to eradicate the past, and she tried. I tried too. We managed to get through my teens with her praying and me keeping to myself. Then I got older, and I was finding it harder to lock that part of me down. Now I get a feeling that Shango needs to be out, and he's gonna fight me until he gets the power."

Shemar put his hand over Yenay's, who had reached out to place her palm reassuringly on his shoulder. "I experienced becoming him, transcending to Shango, recently. I was holding a carving, and I couldn't stop the transformation. The scariest part of that was I actually almost became him. I thought like him, looked like him. It was the first time I consciously tried to meld with Shango, but on some level, I was holding back. There was something of myself still there because I came back to my mother's voice. But man, this being just took over my body and mind."

Father Benedict's eyes were wide. "How unsettling for you, son!"

Shemar played with the second sock Annalee had kicked off her tiny feet, his thumb filling it heel to toe. "I have the feeling Shango could do serious damage, and I know for sure right now I am not able to control him."

Declan studied the timeline. "Where were you born, Shemar?"

"Nanoose Bay, here on the island. Mom told me I was not waiting around to get to the hospital. I was early and I was insistent. By the time the ambulance got there, Mom was holding me in her arms. She had me in her own bed, in our home. Dad had run next door to get the neighbor who was a midwife, and part of the congregation. In a matter of two calls, half the church was there to help. I was a healthy boy. Mom said she was glad I decided on the night because she could look out the window at the stars, sky, and ocean, and feel and smell the breeze."

He was silent for a moment. "She said the bioluminescence that night in the bay was staggering."

Mara pulled her blanket closer around her and smiled at Yenay. She spoke quickly, her voice firm and controlled. "I brought my family here to Nanaimo. We bought a large piece of land and built a restaurant with a house beside it. The cabin that sits at the back of the lot, beside a pond, was built for me, by me. Russia was unsettled, and it looked like my family was going to have to split and go various places to get work. No one wanted that, it isn't our way in my family. We stay together, we move together. We are born, we age, we die, and we start all over again; together.

I had a vision when I was scrying one day. I had to scry secretly. Where we lived was not tolerant of any faith being practiced. The town despised followers of Christ, Buddha, Allah, the Goddess, and all other Higher Powers equally. The government was to be worshipped. The government was to be our supreme being.

"As you have no doubt surmised, I did not fit in well there. Alas, neither did my Christian daughter-in-law, atheist son, and undecided assorted other children and siblings. My husband had left several years ago, looking for himself. I hope he found himself. I certainly did not care enough to search for him."

Yenay bit off a laugh, and Mara gave her a lop-sided smile.

"I saw an island in my water bowl," Mara continued. "It was beautiful. Surrounded by ocean, filled with trees, run rampant with wildlife, and a climate that made farming yearlong possible. I saw the restaurant, the house, and the cabin. I saw my children and my grandchildren living together, playing together, and staying together. I spoke to my oldest son Leonid and his wife, Annika. We made a family decision to emigrate."

Mara's lips thinned as she thought back to those days. "My faith, my craft, and my way of life were not accepted where we lived. Studiously ignored for the most part, but not accepted. I am a Descendant from a lineage of witches, and our history traces back to the Baba Yaga. I have always known who and what I am, my mother made sure of that, and her mother before her. I had only sons, and none of them showed an interest or an aptitude for the craft. My daughter-in-law, Annika, is Christian. She is less tolerant of my craft than my sons are, but because I am an excellent grandmother, great-grandmother, cook, and wise woman, she keeps her opinions mostly to herself. She follows her path, and I follow mine."

Mara grinned as she looked up at Ho'kee, who was watching her in fascination. "My granddaughter Nikki, she is truly a Descendant. She is hungry for knowledge, almost greedy for it. She will be a powerful witch when she comes into her own. I was about Nikki's age when I realized the extent of my gift. All of humanity is blessed with abilities, some are more pronounced than others. I learned to scry at a very young age, gazing into those musical balls that tip upside down and rain snow on skaters. I began to be able to see things in other mediums, but the strongest visions and my deepest connections came from water sources. Lakes, tidal pools, any bowl of water, especially salt water from the ocean."

She folded her arms over her ample chest and tilted her head back. "The first time I realized how strong my gift was, I was in my early teens. I had been scrying for a while and was able to see shadows and identify some images but not much more than that. Then, one autumn day, I was at the pond, talking to my familiar..."

A circle of confused eyes met this declaration.

"I will explain later. Anyway, I was speaking with him and was idly watching the water, and I passed my hand over the surface to move a lily pad. At that moment, a picture as clear as a portrait formed under the surface."

Mara took a deep breath, held it, and let it out slowly. "There was a fire. I saw my mother inside the house, flames around her, trying to beat it down. I watched as she looked out the window at me, and the glass exploded. I ran home as fast as I could, and dove into my mother's arms, crying and telling her what I had seen. She didn't dismiss me. She looked worried but told me that she would be careful due to my sighting. Several days later, at school, we heard a fire engine screaming its way out of the town. We were a very small community, and the school was not far from my house. I started to shake.

"I moved my legs as fast as they could carry me out of the school. My teacher yelled at me to stop and sit, but I was too frightened to stop running. I ran to my house, and watched, horrified, as the roof collapsed into the house. The house was completely engulfed by fire. I heard the windows explode. I started to scream when I felt a powerful pair of arms draw me away from the fire. It was my mother. She had believed me when I told her about the vision and had taken precautions. She remembered what I had told her, and when she had run into the kitchen after smelling smoke in the dining room, she resisted her first instinct to try to beat it out. She closed the door, pulled my siblings to safety outside, and watched as the fire doubled and tripled upon itself in seconds. If she had waited one minute more, she, and probably my younger brothers, would not have survived."

Mara opened her eyes and caught Declan's intense gaze. "It has become stronger since then with my seventy years on this earth. My mother had me in a birthing pool, I slid into the water from her womb. I remember my mother telling me that the midwife cleaned me up after the birth, using charged seawater. The water was gathered from the Russian River Estuary. It is known worldwide for its bioluminescent beauty."

Yenay reached out and clasped the old woman's hand. Mara squeezed her hand gently. Yenay looked down at her still-sleeping child. She looked up and caught Declan's steady dark-blue gaze. She had a sharp intake of breath. She didn't think she would ever get over how unfairly beautiful that man was. She watched him give her a slow, devastating smile and inclined his head slightly. Shemar watched the exchange warily. He visibly relaxed when Yenay stretched her feet to touch his strong thigh. Ho'kee rolled his eyes and stabbed the logs with a fire poker. Father Benedict and Mara exchanged indulgent glances and sipped their tea simultaneously.

"Declan, I lied to you. My mother told me everything. I could not, I would not, accept that my baby girl was anything but a sweet four-year-old angel. Now I know she is so much more, but I need to protect her. I need to keep her safe from everyone and everything that will come looking for her as she gets older, and as this innate power she has gets stronger. I thought if I denied what was right in front of me, what I have witnessed since the day of her birth, I could convince myself she had been spared this 'gift.' But that is not protecting her. That is shielding her from who and what she is: a Descendant of Quan Yin."

Yenay's gaze settled on Annalee. "I knew when she was born, she was special. I was told it was going to be next to impossible for me to have children. All I wanted through my years of travel, education, and high-profile jobs was a child. I didn't yearn for the nuclear family model. I was never interested in being a stay-at-home wife of a successful husband, as much as my mother wanted that for me. She wanted me to feel stable and secure, to want for nothing. Those wants and needs were never in my makeup.

"I traveled with my father when I was old enough to do so, on diplomatic assignments all over the world. I loved that life. I had relationships, but they inevitably ended when the topic of settling down came up and relaying the medical opinion of my unfriendly womb. But the yearning for a child got stronger. So, I decided to go ahead and have one session of IVF done. Just one.

"The odds of my getting pregnant were negligible but there was something in me that kept knocking at my heart and my mind's door to do this, to take that chance. I talked to my mother who, to her credit, did not try to talk me out of it. I passed all the required tests, paid the required money, and asked for an anonymous donor. There was little hope for success, but I had promised myself to take this chance; then I became pregnant. Delightfully, healthily pregnant.

"I had no morning sickness; I had no crying jags. My body stretched to accommodate little Annalee, but I did not suffer any of the common complications. Annalee was truly a miracle. I took it all happily in stride, but my mother, Tina, was more wary. She had started to place her grandmotherly hand on my belly in my first trimester, and the joy that was in her face was astonishing. It was as if this peace and serenity, this absolute thrill of life, leapt into her being when she touched my stomach. At first, she was ecstatic, but then she got nervous. She said it wasn't like the thrill of being a grandma. It was almost otherworldly, this sense of calm, of happiness. I think, then, she realized Annalee was not going to be a typical child.

"Mom began to get very nervous. She started to suggest we leave China and move. I was not averse to the idea. The thought of raising her in a wide open space, on a pastoral hobby farm, had a sweet appeal. We had no close family in China. I was shunned by a large part of our family for being unmarried and proceeding to get pregnant. I had a job that could take me anywhere. I thought about it, but mom got more fearful and insistent all the time.

"I started looking at other cities, but mom was focusing on other continents. Then she was honest with me one day and told me that she feared for this child being born where we were. She would not be accepted. She would be treated badly by other children and their parents. My mother isn't given to flights of fantasy. The reasons she gave for leaving were sound. So, we went in search of the perfect place to raise this little girl. I used every search engine I could find, and my mother went to the local tea leaf reader."

Mara nodded sagely at this mention.

"I went with Mom to see the reader. I waddled in, all six months of me, and sat down. I remember the reader watching us strangely. She seemed frightened that we were there at all. She poured the tea, and as she was looking from the leaves to us, she became more agitated. She mentioned that my child was in danger being born here. There were those who did not want her born at all. She made veiled references to those people already knowing that my child would become the hope for humanity that many did not want to see. I got angry, insisting that the anonymous donor would never find out who his sperm had been given to, and no one would come looking for my child.

"The reader just became more upset, insisting that we had to leave as quickly as possible, go as far away as we could, and not tell anyone here where we were going. She moved the cups. Although she was shaking so hard, I am surprised she didn't dislodge the leaves. She told us to find an island, surrounded by glowing waters. We would be safe there, for a time.

"Now I was scared too. I know so many people would have put this 'fortune telling' down to nonsense, and how could such a well-educated, well-traveled, sophisticated woman as myself put any faith in this? Well, I did, and I do. We asked about the threat, who they were, how to find them. However, the reader was beside herself by this time, saying that we had to leave because even being in the presence of the unborn child, the Descendant of Quan Yin, was dangerous to her own life.

"She herself was in danger from those whose existence depended on the Goddess of Mercy and Compassion not being reborn. We sold our home and belongings and moved to this particularly beautiful island we found that was surrounded by 'glowing waters.' Also known as bioluminescence."

Yenay struggled to shift her position without disturbing her child. The little girl was pliable as a wet noodle as she was manipulated into a different pose. She continued to grip the iguana in a dreamless sleep. "I knew my mother's suspicions were valid the day Annalee was born. It was a birth without pain, without need for medication. My body accommodated her transition into this world easily. She came out smiling; a happy, joyful baby. The doctor who delivered her, a gruff old man, was transformed in front of the stunned medical staff.

"He was laughing, his furry eyebrows dancing, as he swaddled my baby himself, shooing away the nurses who tried to scoop her from him. I watched as this man's heavily lined face lost years, his eyes devouring the baby, his cooing to her as completely alien in that room as a stork with a bundle would be. He had tears wetting his cheeks as he held her, proclaiming her to be the most beautiful child he had ever laid eyes and hands upon. It took considerable strong-arming by my mother and the head nurse for him to relinquish her to me. As soon as I held her, I understood exactly what had happened to him, because it happened to me.

"I held this precious girl, and a happiness, a pure love, came over me. I know a lot of it was motherhood, I understand that, but there was something else in her face. She is hope. She is mercy. She is honesty and kindness. They had to pry her out of my arms to weigh her, do some blood tests. I watched her transform each and every person who touched her. Their worry lines disappeared, and they bathed in her glow. They were kind to each other and laughing together. Staff were coming up from the ER to see her, and she responded to everyone. She never cried. Oddly enough, there were a couple of nurses who refused to lay a hand on her, almost as if they were afraid of her. My mother was omnipresent. That lady was always protective of me but with her granddaughter, she became a warrior.

"People can't help but respond to her energy, and if she touches them, and being an affectionate little girl, she often does, that look of hope, kindness and love comes over each and every one. No one remains unmoved by her. You all have been touched by her, you have seen it and felt it yourselves. Now I am in fear for what the future holds for my little girl. I don't know how to raise Quan Yin. I don't know how to keep her safe from the part of the world that wants to drain her, or that part of the world that would do her harm."

Ho'kee got up and walked over to Yenay, who was wiping tears from her eyes. He crouched beside her and took her hand. "I pledge my life to the protection of your daughter. I knew it when I first saw her, I am a guardian."

Shemar placed a large hand on Yenay's knee. "As am I," he assured.

Father Benedict put his hands together in prayer and leaned forward. "As am I."

Mara put her hand out to cup Yenay's face. "As am I," she pledged.

Declan put his pen down and crossed the room. He crouched on the other side of Ho'kee and put one hand on the sleeping child and one hand on Yenay's arm. "As am I," he promised.

Annalee stirred and stretched her little limbs. Her eyes widened in happiness as she surveyed the group huddled around her, gazing at her fondly. She smiled up at Yenay and then suddenly was transfixed by the fire. Yenay's pulse skipped.

"What is it? What do you see, baby?"

Annalee's dark eyes were filled with tears as she stared at her mother in grave concern. "There is a man looking for me, Mama. I don't think he likes me."

Yenay closed her eyes, her face going pale.

Unseen by anyone but the child, Zlo stared solemnly into the flames in his fireplace. His pupils contracted to slits. "Oh, child. You are indeed incredible. We have been expecting you."

Chapter Five

Declan, up in his room, watched Inanna as she watched him. Her voice was expressionless, her eyes flat and emotionless. She scared him right now.

"Who is this man that Annalee is talking about?" he asked. "Is he a threat?"

Inanna nodded. "The creature Annalee is talking about is a dark deity known as Chernobog. He would be the reason for her extinction if he could manage it. He 'mentors' particular people who may already share some of His vision, but they never know the extent of His vision until he is done with them. The appearance of a Deity who is the embodiment of hope, mercy, and unconditional love among human beings would anger and terrify him. He has already tried to kill her, but she has been anointed by the Goddess and given protection. It was the actions of yourself and the

Others, acting on behalf of the Goddess, that saved her."

Inanna gazed out the window and raised her eyes to the sky. She closed them and mouthed a silent prayer. "Chernobog exists for one reason, Declan. To eradicate humanity from the face of the earth. He despises the human race. He doesn't care about race, gender, or status, but he uses these attributes to pick his subjects—the ones who will follow him and worship him. They will do anything on his behalf. He has his followers believing that a particular strain of humans will save the earth, and this strain can be created through genetic selection. He then uses that belief system he has created to turn his followers on each other. Unfortunately, he has been successful for many purges. For Chernobog to survive, to flourish in this world and be able to eliminate the species, he has to work faster and harder before Quan Yin grows up and amasses a worldwide following. Or he must find a way to kill her before she matures."

"Who is he mentoring? Who is his most powerful follower right now? And how long before he ascends to become Chernobog?"

Inanna lifted a crystal orb from the table and held it in front of her face. As she spoke, her gaze never left the sphere. She gently slid her fingers around and underneath until it was spinning slowly on its own. Declan watched, fascinated, as the orb clouded and cleared, unsuspended by hand or string, in the middle of the room.

"Chernobog only uses Descendants of his own line, and he grooms them from a very young age. He would never allow anyone to ascend to his status. He descends into them, gradually and cleverly, until he overtakes them completely and is in their body and mind. In effect, he eats his own. However, even in human form, he cannot last long in this realm before he begins to lose his magic and his influence. But he doesn't need much time to wreak havoc and unleash widespread hatred."

The sphere continued to spin slowly, refracting light beams of rainbow onto Inanna and Declan.

"His magic is powerful and deadly. He has had centuries to perfect his craft of cloaking. He has been able to keep the identity of this particular Descendant from the Goddess so far, but you, Declan, you can unmask this Descendant."

"How?"

"You will know the time, the place, and the Other you will need. The Goddess will guide you, but She cannot fight this battle for you. She will be with you, She will fight beside you, but She can't take your rightful place in this battle."

Declan sat heavily on the bed, staring before him. Inanna reached up and grasped the orb gently, drawing it back to her and placing it on the bedside table. She sat beside him and placed her soft hand on his shoulder. "Declan. My time here is almost at an end. I have done what I was tasked to do."

Declan turned a heartbroken gaze toward her. He reached up and cupped her beautiful face in his hands. He whispered, his voice rough and cracking. "No. Please, Inanna. We need you. I need you more than ever. You can't leave! I was hoping you would stay with me through this, and long after this is over. I have never had a connection like this with anyone. I love your mind, I love your spirit, I adore your face. You are my muse. You are so compassionate, kind, patient, and full of love for life. I want to marry you, Inanna."

Inanna smiled sweetly and sadly. "Oh, my sweet man. If I could do, and be that, I would be the most fortunate woman in this realm. It is time for Brighid to guide you. You have seen her in your dreams. Where I am goals, intentions, and building, She is expansion, solidifying, and protection. This is her time. You need her now."

Declan pulled Inanna to him and held her tightly, his chin buried in her soft cloud of hair. "If I don't let you go, you can't leave."

Inanna pulled from him easily, despite his strong hold. She leaned her forehead against his and moved her thoughts into his mind. *"We have tonight. Once more, I am your lover, your muse, and your guide. I will have shown you and taught you everything deemed necessary and done a few things I decided to do just because I wanted to."*

She broke contact and moved over to the edge of the bed, where she slowly began to undress. Declan gazed at her hungrily, not daring to blink for fear of missing a second of her ethereal beauty. She was absolutely perfect. His throat felt thick, choking on a familiar sense of loss. He knew, on some level, she was not of his world, but he spent an awful lot of emotion wishing she was.

He pushed his hand through his hair and caught her gaze. "Annalee. She is safe here? Right now?"

Inanna smiled and tossed her silver hair over her shoulder, running her long fingers through it. "Yes. For now. She has protection around her and above her. But you and the Others need to stay aware. Chernobog is an entity whose existence depends on her demise. He will not be easily defeated, and he has thousands of followers who will go to their death doing his bidding."

Her hands stopped, and she gazed out the window. Shadows fell over her face and his youthful Goddess looked weary. "Mara was right, we don't have a lot of time. Heed the Baba Yaga. This is not her first encounter with this particular evil, and she is becoming aware of their shared history. The Goddess is strong, and the spell has held. If Chernobog could have killed her by now, he would have. Do not underestimate him. He has existed for centuries, in countless forms, under countless names. He has come close to realizing his reason for existing a few times, and he is close again."

Declan got up and went to Inanna. He stood behind her and wrapped his arms around her waist. They both looked out the window watching a blue-eyed wolf roughhouse with a feisty red fox. A talkative crow egged both sides on from the safety of a tree branch. An uninterested bullfrog sat still, blinking slowly and ignoring the shenanigans.

"So, his sole reason for existing is to destroy the earth?"

Inanna was silent for a moment, watching the animal group until the little fox darted into the forest, the silver wolf on his heels. "He wants to keep the earth. He would like nothing more than the earth without humanity in it. Chernobog seeks only the death of Man's body and soul."

Mara filled her crystal bowl with water she had collected from the ocean bay behind the retreat. She set it on her bedside table and sat down. She took off her head scarf and pulled out her hairpins. Her white hair tumbled out over her shoulders and down to her waist. She pulled her gnarled fingers through it and closed her eyes. She opened one eye to survey her position, relieved to see the ring of black salt around her. She thought she may have forgotten that step, and she instinctively knew that was a step she absolutely could not do without. She chanted softly in Russian.

"At night I scry with my third eye
It opens when the silence speaks
it doesn't tell me when or why
it gives me only phantom peeks.
Into the crystal orb I gaze
and Spirit gazes back at me
I follow wraiths within the haze
and whisper soft 'so mote it be.'
By candlelight the spell will start
by moonlight call the ghosts to talk
by daybreak I bid Spirit part
until next time we meet and walk."

She opened her eyes and passed her hand over the still water. It began to circle from the inside, spreading to the edges of the bowl, and then stopped. The water became smooth as glass. Mara peered in, and her lips tightened.

She saw Annalee bound by a heavy cord. She was blindfolded and a scarf was tight around her mouth. Mara knew this was a vision of something already in the making. Someone wanted to take the child and keep her mute. Mara noticed the heavy cord was glowing, its colors fading from green to blue, and red to yellow. A closer look revealed that the cord was not keeping her from moving her limbs, it was to keep someone else from touching her. The cord was fraying at the ends; it was in danger of unraveling.

Mara passed her hand over again and an image drifted up from the bottom. A crudely carved Nigerian artifact rippled under the water. It seemed to fold in on itself, then splay out, and the piece began to glow a dark rusted red. The sculpture changed hues, darkening the water with discarded color. It leeched out the rust and became the brilliant color of freshly spilled blood. The piece throbbed and exploded in the water, dissolving before her eyes.

Concern creased her features as she watched a large silver wolf with blue eyes draw back its lips to display sharp, white fangs and furiously launch its heavily muscled body at a target, but Mara couldn't see who, or what.

She drew in a ragged breath as she saw Father Benedict's body become completely engulfed by the green aura. He raised his hands to the sky in prayer, and then lowered them down in front of him to lay healing hands on someone, or something.

She passed her hand again over the bowl and watched intently. The water began to roll around the bowl, and a mist formed in front of her. She watched in fascination as the mist began to draw the shape of a Celtic knot. Beneath it, in the water, a second image began to form. She saw a large wooden staff. She knew that staff—it had two ends; one to take life, and one to restore life. It was the *lorg mór*. She stared as the staff tilted from side to side, then slowly lifted from the water. It stood before her, the image large, the power unfathomable. It could only be wielded by the Dagda, the ancient Celtic God of Druidry and Magic.

She passed her hand once again, and the water began to churn rapidly. She grasped the arms of the chair and drew back involuntarily. She saw Him. She knew Him. An older man with long, black hair and sculpted, strong features. A thin-lipped mouth devoid of warmth but alive with cruelty. Intense, black eyes stared back at her, the thin, arched brows above them rising slightly in recognition. Those dark pupils widened, then narrowed to serpent-like slits.

Chilling laughter filled her mind and words were hissed at her. "Not this time, old hag. You won't defeat me this time."

Father Benedict sat up in his bed, his face slick with sweat. He felt unable to breathe. He groped for his bedside light and snapped it on. The room was flooded with light, and he took a quick inspection of all four corners, putting his glasses on for a closer look. He calmed himself and took several large breaths, counting to five and letting them go slowly. He put a finger over his wrist pulse and willed it to slow down to a pace that wouldn't give him a heart attack. The house was fairly quiet. He could hear the heavy footsteps of Shemar, directly above him, apparently also unable to sleep. He pushed the covers off and gingerly touched his feet to the floor.

Just minutes before, this room had been closing in on him; the ceiling was lowering, the floor rising, the walls shifting and moving inwards. It was becoming his coffin. Then he'd heard a laugh that chilled him to the bone. He wanted badly to shake off this feeling of being watched, but he knew that even if he could rid himself of that thought, he shouldn't. He should trust his instinct. His faithful gut had very rarely been wrong. He sat on the edge of the bed, feet firmly planted on the floor, and nearly left his skin when he heard a soft rap at the bedroom door.

"Father? It's Shemar. Are you all right?"

Benedict looked heavenward in relief and moved toward the door. "Shemar! Yes, yes, son. I am all right."

He opened the door to see Shemar's dark face lined with concern.

"You yelled out. Is there something in the room? Is it a spider? 'Cause, man, if it's a spider, you're gonna have to get Ho'kee or Mara's pet bullfrog. I don't do spiders."

Father Benedict looked way up at the imposing, rock-solid structure in front of him and started to laugh. "Oh, Shemar. Thank God for you. No, no, it wasn't a spider. Come in, come in."

Shemar stepped in and closed the door quietly behind him. Benedict went to a small side dining suite and carefully lowered himself into a chair, still feeling unsteady. He took off his glasses and rubbed his eyes. Shemar sat opposite the priest and waited.

"I am afraid I had a truly disturbing nightmare."

Shemar remained silent.

"The room was trying to suffocate me, bury me alive."

Shemar folded his arms over his chest and clenched his jaw. He spoke softly. "There was laughter."

Father Benedict's eyes widened in surprise at Shemar's statement. "Yes! It was rife with cruelty, malevolence..."

"Evil."

The priest nodded slowly. He reached out to place his hand on Shemar's forearm. "You heard it."

"I did. I had a different dream but heard the same laughter."

The priest gently squeezed Shemar's arm.

Shemar got up and walked to the window. He opened it a little to let air in and heard a bullfrog. He scanned the edge of the woods, and his gaze softened a bit when he saw a little red fox leaping into the air, trying to catch a talkative, swooping crow. A large silver wolf sat to the side; its thick tail curled around its paws. Its ears twitched, and it turned its eerie blue eyes toward Shemar.

Shemar inclined his head slightly to the wolf and drew away from the window. "In my dream, I was holding that artifact my mother gave me. It started to heat and burn into my hand, but I couldn't get rid of it. I tried to pull it off, but it scorched deeper into my palm. It was charring both my hands and starting to burn down my arms. I couldn't move. I couldn't stop watching it. I knew that it was going to burn me alive, engulf me, and I was powerless to stop it. I opened my mouth to scream, and I heard that laugh. I woke myself up, and I heard you yell as well."

The priest tightened his dressing gown over his pajamas and slid his feet into a pair of fuzzy slippers. "I believe a cup of tea is in order, Shemar. I am willing to wager that the Others are awake as well, with dreams of their own."

Shemar swung the door open to find Yenay, her fist poised to knock, fear in her eyes. Annalee was leaning away, using her mother's hand as an anchor while she skated around her in stocking feet. She squealed in delight at seeing Shemar.

She lifted her arms to be picked up by him. "Shango!"

Shemar bent to receive the missile attack and let her climb over his back to ride shoulder style. Her head almost grazed the high ceilings, and she delightedly touched the rafters. Shemar reached over and took Yenay's hand. He squeezed it gently and smiled at her.

She looked up and gave him a tentative smile back. Annalee rocked forward and back on her high 'horsie.'

Three of them made their way down the winding staircase. Father Benedict paused to cast another glance around his room. He caught sight of the pendant that he had taken off and put beside his bed. He picked it up and put it back on. He kissed it before laying it on his chest. "St. Raphael. I don't think I want you out of my sight for a while."

The foursome entered the kitchen to see Declan already pouring two pots of tea. He pointed to each pot and spoke, "Mara's recommendation. One to get to sleep and stay asleep, one to invite good dreams, as opposed to the ones that brought us all here together in the middle of the night."

Ho'kee let himself in through the kitchen door. He was disheveled, but his eyes were bright and alert. He pushed his hand through his tangled hair and picked out bits of twig and leaves, frowning at them and depositing them in the sink. Mara stood in the doorway, tightly tying her bathrobe around her. She bustled forward and began plucking out the debris from the sink and shoving it pointedly in the compost bin.

Ho'kee grinned at her. "Sorry, Mara."

Mara took his chin between her fingers and smiled at him, tapping his cheek lightly and muttering in Russian.

Ho'kee looked over at Yenay, who was unsuccessfully trying to hide a smile.

"She said good thing you are so cute."

Ho'kee laughed and raised his hand to give a high five to Annalee, towering over him on Shemar's shoulders.

Declan put the pots and mugs on the long kitchen table. Mara set out two plates of cookies. Ho'kee lunged for a handful, and she smacked his wrist, placing a stacked sandwich in front of him.

"You've been doing sentry duty all night. You need real food. Cookies after sandwich."

He looked surprised, then smiled and thanked her in between mouthfuls.

Declan held his gaze on Ho'kee until the young man looked up. His black eyes were wary, and he willed his mind to blank. "Ho'kee. When do you sleep? Have you had a disturbing dream recently?"

Ho'kee looked uncomfortable and slowed his chewing, delaying his response.

Yenay reached up and took Annalee from Shemar's shoulders, dropping her into the booster seat beside her. She made a cup of warm milk and put it in front of the little girl, who held a sugar cookie in each hand. Yenay directed a disapproving look toward Mara who lifted her shoulders in surrender.

"Ho'kee?" Declan asked again, his voice firmer.

Ho'kee pushed the plate away from him and folded his arms across his chest. He glanced at Father Benedict, who nodded his head in encouragement. "I sleep during the day. That's why I look for evening and night work. I can't sleep at night, never could. Yes, Kreskin, I had a disturbing dream the afternoon we got here. I got wood for the fireplace, then I went to my room to sleep for a bit."

Declan caught Ho'kee's reluctant gaze.

"Ok, fine. I will tell you. Just stay out of my head."

"I gave you my word, Ho'kee. I stand by it."

Ho'kee shrugged out of his leather jacket. Mara placed a mug of warm milk in front of him. He put a hand up to refuse it and she frowned, pushing it back in front of him. He sighed and wrapped his hands around it. "I saw Old Dan. He was inside a fire circle, chanting. He was dressed in ceremonial clothes, and he was holding his staff in both hands like he was getting ready to spike it into the earth. I was feeling good about the dream, but then I heard laughter, and it wasn't good. Old Dan's eyes opened, and he was melting into the fire. He didn't look scared, he just chanted louder. The laughter got louder as well. I saw myself as Wolf, on the outside of the fire, I couldn't get to Old Dan. The laughter got stronger as Old Dan melted."

Ho'kee drew a shaking hand over his face. He glared angrily at Declan. "I couldn't get to him. I couldn't save him. I had a sickening feeling that Old Dan's spirit was being attacked because of me, and I couldn't save him." Ho'kee toyed with the mug handle and pushed it away from him. "This is fu—I mean...messed up."

Annalee climbed down from her booster seat. She took a sugar cookie and toddled over to Ho'kee. She stood at his side and stretched out her arm to offer him the cookie.

Ho'kee smiled at her. "Hey, Munchkin. Is that for me?"

Annalee nodded happily. "There is a good-dreams wish on this cookie for you. If you eat it, you can sleep tonight and not have any more bad dreams."

Ho'kee lifted Annalee to his lap and took the cookie. "Where did you learn to put these kinds of spells on cookies, Munchkin?"

Annalee tilted her head back and grinned up at Ho'kee. "I didn't. An old man did. He said his name was Hatalii, but you would know him by another name."

Ho'kee's arms stiffened, and he raised his eyes to Declan, they were blurring with tears.

"Old Dan. The Navajo name for medicine man is *Hatalii.*" Ho'kee ceremoniously dipped his cookie in the milk and savored each bite.

Yenay put her head in her hands. Her shoulders were shaking. Shemar reached over and let her lean into his solid frame. Her words came out in tight breaths. "This is too much. This is all just too much. She is four years old."

Shemar rubbed her back and asked quietly. "Did she have a nightmare?"

Yenay stopped and looked at him. "No! I had a nightmare, but she didn't! When I woke up, she was still right beside me in bed, laughing and babbling!"

She slapped her hands on the table, causing it to shake. Her voice started to rise with frustration, fear, and anger. "I saw my mother. She was in a chair, and she couldn't move. She was staring at me, and I heard her voice in my head telling me to stay where I was. There were thin strings, knife-like, all around her, crisscrossing her body. I knew if I took a step toward her, one would slice into her. She kept her head high, just staring straight ahead. I heard that laugh that you are all talking about. I was losing my mind, trying to get to my mother, but it was as if she herself was preventing me from getting too close. Even as she was facing that torture, she was pushing me away, saving me."

Yenay stopped to catch her breath, winding her hands together. She looked up at Shemar with tears in her eyes. "I knew she was sacrificing herself for me and Annalee, and there was nothing I could do. When I woke up, Annalee was playing with her iguana and babbling to her 'Ladies,' whoever they are."

Declan leaned forward and stretched his hands out. He took Yenay's hands in a warm clasp. "There is an entity we are up against. His name is Chernobog."

Mara's ruddy complexion went white. She stared into space as Declan told the Others what he knew of the creature responsible for their nightmares.

"He can't hurt her here, in this space. He knows she is with us and that she has protection. We are not the only ones protecting Annalee either; the 'Ladies' she speaks to are very real. We know them as The Goddess. That laugh we all heard belongs to a creature that tried to get to her earlier. He found out who Quan Yin is on this earth, and he went after her. That is why the hospital could find no physical reason for the fever. The creature tried, but he failed because we were all brought together in time by the Goddess. Now Annalee is stronger because she is surrounded by us and by The Goddess. However, he is getting stronger as well. He has more followers, and is gaining more followers every day, every minute, by inciting hatred, discord, rage, separation of spiritual and physical."

All eyes turned to Declan. Father Benedict clasped his hands in prayer and lowered his head. Mara grasped the symbol of the Goddess around her neck and prayed. Shemar looked angry. Yenay looked frightened. Ho'kee closed his eyes, processing what he had just heard.

Annalee slid from Ho'kee's lap and circled around to Declan. She scrabbled up to the seat beside him and took his face in her tiny hands. "Dagda. The Ladies want us to say hello to our ancestors."

Declan's face flickered momentarily as he thought of the possible ramifications of proceeding with this experiment. Then he thought of the certainty of their futures, and Annalee's, if they did not.

He heard a strong, female voice with a gentle Irish brogue enter his mind. *There will not be full ascension at this time. It is not the right time. This is not the right realm.*

Declan took Annalee's small wrists in his hands and looked into her bright, shining eyes. He saw the incredible beauty she would grow up to be and the power she would yield, if the Others could keep her out of the hands of Chernobog's followers. He closed his arms protectively around her small body and he lifted her up. She wound her tiny hands in his hair and whispered, "*Tá creideamh agam ionat.*"

His eyes widened to hear his mother's voice say those familiar words: "I have faith in you." Declan clasped his hand around the back of her little head and looked intently at the group gathered before him.

"All right, my people. Let's see what our ancestors have given us."

Shemar and Ho'kee remained stoic, leading the way out of the house. Mara grabbed her bag of magic and followed. Yenay took Annalee from Declan and walked by his side to the clearing a short distance from the house. Father Benedict brought up the rear, winding his rosary through his fingers. They gathered in a circle around a fire pit that had not been lit for some time.

Declan raised his head and spoke. "May the God and Goddess of our understanding be with us. Mara, would you do the honor?"

Mara inclined her head slightly and crouched down. She lifted the bullfrog gently from his comfortable spot on the velvet pouch and pulled out a vial and some black stones. She handed a stone to each of the Others as she sprinkled black salt around the perimeter of their circle. She returned to her spot and filled her cupped hands with a sparkling mound of ground powders. She waited for Declan.

He looked over to Father Benedict. "Would you invoke your Higher Power?"

The priest touched the cross against his chest and closed his eyes. "My Lord, I pray that you make me a channel of your presence. Your will, not mine, be done."

Declan inclined his head toward Mara. She stepped forward and flung the dust in the fire pit circle, an enchantment rolling off her tongue in her native language. Immediately, sparks lit and thin, sharp flames began to flicker in the center, quickly filling out and expanding to the edge of the rock circle. Yenay gasped, and Annalee stretched out her palms to the warmth of the fire from the safety of her mother's tight arms. Ho'kee grinned and gave a respectful bow to Mara. Shemar's eyes were black, his gaze locked on the fire, his hands held tightly together. Father Benedict reached over to take Yenay's hand.

Declan stepped forward. "By the power and the intent of the Goddess, I ask that I be united with my ancestor, the Dagda."

He reached into the pouch he had brought with him and pulled out the crystal globe. He held it aloft in his hands, gazing at the fire through the crackle quartz orb. He pulled one arm back to his side and held the globe in his right, lifting it higher. He balanced the orb on the tips of his fingers, and then slowly pulled his fingers away from the bottom. The crystal ball hung in the air, glittering with the firelight. Declan gently pushed on the side and the orb began to spin slowly. The Others watched, transfixed, as the hovering ball's rotation accelerated, shooting glints of multicolored light from inside and outside the orb. Declan closed his eyes, and when he slowly opened them, his dark blue eyes were a glittering topaz. He looked up at the sky and dropped to one knee.

The orb began to spin faster, images flickering and disappearing in its depths. The wind picked up in the trees, and Ho'kee's ears pricked, hearing a call he couldn't identify. Father Benedict watched in fascination, Mara watched in admiration, and Shemar watched in solidarity as Declan's physical presence began to change. Yenay held Benedict's hand tighter, fear engulfing her, and Annalee squealed with delight and clapped her hands together.

"Dagda!"

The Dagda rose from one knee and stood magnificently before them. His long, silver hair hung past his shoulders, the wind picking it up to stream behind him. His snowy beard was cropped short, enhancing the strong jaw and wide, generous mouth. His thick, white eyebrows arched regally, and he had both large hands, laden with heavy rings, on hips that were covered in steel gray armor. The chink of chain mail joined the sound of the wind in the trees, and the Dagda stretched his finger to slow down the mad cycling of the orb.

His voice was thickly accented and rolled like warm waves over everyone gathered in the circle. "Merry meet! I am the Dagda. I am Druid and King. I am magic and wisdom. I have dominion over life and death, time and seasons. I am a fair God and a leader of warriors. See me and know my Descendant Declan O'Neill."

Yenay stared in open-mouthed awe at the figure before her. He was a God, and the most beautiful man she had ever seen in her life. Father Benedict discreetly rubbed his glasses and replaced them, a smile turning up his lips.

Ho'kee gave a low whistle, followed by a whispered, "Well, I'll be damned..."

The Dagda threw back his head and laughed, winking at Ho'kee. His gaze lighted on Mara who began to sink to her knee in a bow. "Baba Yaga, please do not bow to me. We are equals. You are a Queen and a warrior. This is who we are to each other. We are bound as warriors in allegiance to the ascendancy of this child, Descendant of Quan Yin."

With this, the God went down on one knee before the child, but the top of his head was still far above the standing figure of Yenay.

Annalee grinned widely, her eyes dancing with excitement, and she cried out, "Dagda!"

The Dagda rose and turned his shimmering gaze to Shemar, who stood strong and fierce in front of Yenay and Annalee. "Shango. Let us meet as equals, ancient God of Fury."

Shemar swallowed and stared hard at the Dagda. Ho'kee crouched beside him, watching as a dark, thin red mist began to twine from Shemar's closed fist. The large hand held fast onto an ancient-looking relic that started to glow, the light emanating from the spaces between Shemar's fingers. Shemar seemed to be fighting an internal battle, sweat breaking from his forehead and his rigid posture beginning to shake with tension.

The Dagda silently touched the orb with his finger, and the crystal flashed an image of Annalee, her arm dropping to the side of the bed in the ER. It flashed an image of Bubba with his hand around Joe's neck, sliding him up the wall. It flashed an image of a greasy-haired man raising his fist above a chained, crying dog. With this final image, Shemar's eyes closed. When he opened them, they were glowing red.

The artifact in his hand was pulsing; its heartbeat could be heard throbbing from Shemar's fist, from within the ground, within the fire, through the trees. Yenay involuntarily shrank back, shielding Annalee. Father Benedict stood firmly beside her, his face betraying a mix of dread and alarm as he watched what was happening to his friend. He crossed himself and kissed the crucifix that hung around his neck. He stared at the transformation taking place and prayed. Mara moved quietly behind each person, and put her hands around theirs, securing the black stones within their palms. She approached Ho'kee and crouched with him. He reached out and held her hand in his own.

Quickly, the red mist thickened and twisted, spilling over Shemar's hands and flowing up his wrists and down his torso, wreathing him in an energy that seemed to be breathing. It coiled around his legs and onto his feet, twining upwards and outwards over the big man's back and shoulders. It seemed to hesitate only slightly at his neck, but then created a shroud of crimson and cloaked Shemar's head. The Others watched the red mist branch out on the forest floor, searching. The mist approached each watcher as they stood rigid, and it crept back as each one clutched the black stones. It reared back violently as it approached Father Benedict as if it had tried to touch something that would certainly destroy it. Yenay tried to leave the circle, her arms tightening so hard around Annalee that the little girl was struggling to get free.

"Mama, you are squishing me too tight! Red cloud won't hurt us, Mommy."

Yenay turned from the circle to see the Dagda standing in front of her. She would have pushed Declan out of the way, but this was not Declan. The God was immense, glowing, and the protection she felt from him eased her immediately.

"Descendant of Quan Yin is right, Yenay. You do not have what the red mist seeks, and your lover needs you both. He needs a reason to come back from Shango."

Yenay swallowed, searching those ethereal blue eyes. When she saw a glimpse of an image of the three of them together—Yenay, Shemar, and a teenaged Annalee—she turned back to the fire.

She dragged her gaze upwards to see the crimson cloud had become a blanket of flame outlining a large, dark man. An explosive roar from within the effigy shocked the forest into action. The familiars—the crow, fox, bullfrog, and finch—that had gathered outside the circle bolted as a group into the depths of the copse; their eyes glowed from safe hiding spaces. The tall trees bent sideways with the force of the roar of the wind and the combustion. The fire Mara had started leapt skywards and threatened to spill over, but the circle she had drawn kept it confined. In unison, the Others gathered around Mara and Father Benedict, with the exception of the Dagda, who stood face to face with the Nigerian giant of a God who was emerging from the flames.

Shango's eyes glowed a brilliant red. Bolts of energy cracked from His body like small lightning bolts. The warrior was clothed in full battle dress, and his massive hand gripped an *oshe* where the tiny artifact had been. He wore a brass crown glittering with garnet jewels and a heavy dark red gladiator war kilt. Heavy gold bands circled biceps striated with thick muscles. As massive as Shemar was, Shango was four times his size. The God of Fury stood silently in front of the Dagda, taking a silent measure of the Celtic God before him. The Dagda stood at a respectful distance, his eyes never leaving the red orbs of Shango.

Shango opened his mouth to speak. Ho'kee remembered what Shemar had said about fire coming from the God's mouth. He reflexively raised one hand to his face and pulled Mara behind him with the other.

"At ease, Navajo shapeshifter. I am not in full ascension. No fire or lightning bolts will be sent from my mouth. Dagda, it is an honor to go into battle with you."

The Dagda bent his silver head in acknowledgment. "Shango, God of Fury and Destruction, it is my honor to serve with you."

Shango's eyes never left those of the Dagda. "I am Shango, God of Thunder, Fire, and Lightning. I am the most powerful and feared of my pantheon. I am a seeker of justice and slayer of enemies. See me and know my Descendant Shemar Akinyemi!"

Annalee's eyes were wide with wonder, but the child showed no fear at the sight of the God. She whispered, "Shango."

The Dagda turned his opaque eyes to Ho'kee and smiled at the young man. Ho'kee stood mesmerized before the two Gods. He could hear his own heartbeat and felt his pulse begin to quicken.

"Wolf," the Dagda said, "we ask to be honored with your transcendent presence."

Ho'kee looked around him uncertainly. He had never shifted when he wasn't running. He wasn't sure he knew how. He felt a second of resentment with being commanded to shift, but just as quickly realized it was a request, not a demand, and it was necessary. He looked up at the Dagda and spoke quietly. "Dagda, how do I shift without running?"

The Dagda inclined his head once and touched the orb hovering above the fire. Ho'kee watched it as it expanded, rising and stretching wide. Within the larger orb, Ho'kee saw his familiar forest and the little red fox catching and releasing its own tail. The orb started to spin slowly, drawing him into its images. The speed of the cycle increased, and Ho'kee felt his heartbeat rising to match the images flying past him as if he were there running. He could feel the soft ground giving in to his paws. He felt the wind through his whiskers. He could hear the ocean in the distance and the stream close by. He heard the mystical call of a great horned owl and felt the terror of a small mouse darting between his legs.

As Ho'kee was drawn into the orb's images, the Others watched the young man's ears elongate and his nose sharpen. Fur sprouted from his arms, and he dropped to all fours, his back arching, his clothes splitting and falling from his transcending body. The Wolf growled deeply as it shook off the remnants of humanity. It snarled, black lips pulling over deadly canine teeth. Its massive nails were sharp and long, digging into the earth as it grounded itself. It stood in attack stance, its gaze level and assessing. It took measure of the beings around the circle then looked up at the sky, closed its eyes, and stretched its throat out. A howl erupted from the core of the Wolf and ricocheted off trees and stones. The wind answered with its own moan and entwined, the eerie call lifted over the treetops and flooded the darkness.

Father Benedict felt tears prick his eyes. The Wolf was beyond magnificent. It was otherworldly perfect. He felt Mara reach for his hand, and she looked up him, her own eyes filled with grateful tears.

The Wolf looked around itself and lowered its great head to gently retrieve something from the ground and then moved toward the Dagda. The Dagda lowered his hand, and the wolf dropped a silver necklace in his palm. The pendant was an intricately carved portrait of a wolf. It pawed at the dirt slightly, and sat beside the Dagda, its massive tail curled around its lower body. It caught the eyes of each of the Others with its own light blue ones, resting for a few seconds longer on little Annalee.

She stretched out her hands, a loving smile dimpling her cheeks, and she affectionately said, "Woof!"

Wolf blinked slowly and sank to the fire circle floor, stretching its paws in front. From the copse, the fox padded over to the side of Wolf and curled up beside him. Wolf looked over and nuzzled the small creature with his long snout.

The Dagda looked over at the Others and spoke, "This is Mai-Coh. His name means Howling Winds. Of all land creatures, Wolf has the strongest metaphysical powers and is the greatest hunter. He will give the ill peace; he will give the strife-laden harmony. He will defend his tribe against invaders. He will lead us in the hunt and battle at our side. We are beholden to the Navajo shapeshifter. Look upon Wolf and know his Descendant Ho'kee Bidziil."

The Dagda stopped the orb from spinning, and it contracted to its original size. It began to turn slowly again. He stepped forward through the flames of the inner circle to stand in front of Mara. Yenay shrieked and shielded Annalee's eyes, but the child protested and pulled her mother's hands off. The Dagda was completely unhurt. He gazed down at Mara, his eyes glinting in the starlight. Mara looked deeply into them and saw that they had the color of the moon.

The Dagda reached for her hands and clasped them warmly. His voice, low and melodic, with a strong Irish lilt, was hypnotic. "My sister, Baba Yaga, would you do us the honor? I long to see you again after all these hundreds of years."

Mara bowed her head in deep respect and stepped back from the Dagda. She lifted her arms to the sky, tilted her head back, closed her eyes, and chanted.

"As above me
So below
I ground with Earth
With water, flow
Fire lights path
Air blows song
I honor Earth

And Spirit strong
Ancestral Mother's
Will be done
Goddess grant
We be as One."

The Dagda took a step back as the woman in front of him joined her hands together above her head. Mara's physical shape began to shift and fade. The lines of her face and the sharpness of her bone structure softened and blended together. She was disappearing beneath a symbol that was darkening and growing.

Yenay whispered, "No!" She made a move toward the symbol taking over Mara, but Father Benedict hooked his hand around her elbow and pulled her back forcefully.

He whispered in a firm but kind voice, "Mara is the eldest of us and by far the most knowledgeable. This is her path. She is safe."

Yenay allowed herself to be pulled back to the priest's side. She watched as the symbol began to turn slowly, in the opposite direction of the crystal orb still hovering over the fire.

The symbol became faceless and legless, its elegant form in perfect curves and lines. On each side in its womb area, an infinity circle glistened as if built by millions of perfect crystals. Above its head within a perfect circle was a five-pointed star, and on either side of the star, a crescent moon facing outwards. It turned slowly, floating in perfect alignment with the earth and sky. The Others watched as one side glittered with magnificent light and reflection, and the other side shone with a dark red circle in a body of obsidian black. The warmth of the light side seemed to calm the fire, but when it turned, the fire leapt to life, snarling and sparking. A wild wind whipped up, and trees groaned before its force. The flames of the fire bent in the wind, and the forest debris rose in twists, scattering twigs, leaves, and branches.

The Dagda, Shango, and Wolf remained motionless, while Father Benedict huddled with Yenay and Annalee. In the chaos, a disembodied female voice echoed through the area. It seemed to come from everywhere and nowhere. It descended from the sky and ascended from the earth. It was commanding but calm, and the language was universal.

"Be warned, those who seek or encounter the Baba Yaga. She may be your greatest ally or your greatest foe, depending on your purpose and the condition of your soul. She is the keeper of wisdom and the old ways for her family and her community. She rules over the elements of air, earth, fire, and water. She understands and holds the knowledge of life and death. She is a healer and a destroyer. She will tell the truth to those with the courage enough to seek the honest answer. She is an enchantress and ancestral Mother. How she appears to one, as beautiful or as baleful, is wholly subject to one's own mind and intention. Look upon the Baba Yaga and know her Descendant Mara Yahontov."

The symbol continued to rotate slowly as the wind calmed and the fire returned to its safe height within the stone circle enclosure.

Annalee watched the symbol in wonder, her little fists opening and closing in her greeting to Mara. "Baba Yaga," she whispered.

The Dagda stepped in front of Father Benedict, a peaceful smile on his broad, handsome face. The priest looked up from behind his small-framed glasses and returned the smile, albeit with a bit more apprehension. The Dagda rested his large hands on the priest's shoulders and Benedict felt a warmth born of respect and inclined his head to the God.

"Dagda, I am not a God, nor do I profess to be a Descendant of one. I am a child of the Lord, and I have been blessed with an ability to help others, that is all. I am not sure how I can be of service, but I stand ready to serve our hope for humanity: Annalee, Descendant of Quan Yin."

The Dagda tilted his head to the side and studied Father Benedict. The Dagda stepped back and held his hands in front of him. "It is you who does us the great honor of embracing Spirit in every aspect of being. I would like to pay my deep respect and gratitude to St. Raphael."

Father Benedict nodded and took his glasses off, handing them over to Annalee, who immediately tried them on, giggling. The priest laughed and gazed steadily at the fire. He moved his cassock aside and knelt on the ground, bringing his hands together in prayer. He closed his eyes, and the pendant about his neck began to glow with a soft green light. "St. Raphael, pure spirit, medicine of God. I pray to you, our guide in journeys, our consoler in our illnesses, patron saint of healers. I ask you to honor me with your presence and grant the great grace of purity to prepare me to be the temple of your Spirit."

The green aura spread gently from the pendant, gliding over the priest's chest, enfolding him in a colorful blanket. Sparkles of emerald green lit upon Father Benedict, draping him in a softly shining cloak. The Others watched as Father Benedict rose from his knees, eyes still closed, and pressed his cold hands together. Behind him, an image rose, outlined in gold. Enormous wings spread out, spanning the size of the circle and lifting toward the sky. Beneath the wings, an archangel bearing a staff and wearing a loosely draped tunic towered over Father Benedict. The angel's long, dark hair tumbled to his shoulders, and his dark eyes rested on the Others peacefully. A slight smile turned up a corner of his generous mouth, and Yenay caught her breath. He had the same smile as Father Benedict.

Wolf raised himself to his haunches and pushed his snout against the little lame fox. The fox looked up at Wolf and pulled his long, red ears back against his head. Wolf nudged the fox again, and the fox limped over to the priest. The fox sat in front of the priest and curled his tail around his haunches. The little animal looked down and then up, gazing at the priest, and then lifting its stare to the glowing archangel behind the Father. The fox lifted its misshapen, lame paw, and Father Benedict reached out to take it.

Immediately, the archangel's wings opened, and a flash of green lit the night sky. Swirls of shades of green twined above the trees, and Father Benedict felt the familiar heat displace the icy cold in his hands. St Raphael's beautiful eyes closed, and as He stretched out his hand to place on Benedict's head, the priest held the fox's paw, and the green aura encompassed them all. The fox whimpered slightly as an energy current surged through the priest to the fox, but neither let go. St Raphael's haunting, soft voice drifted around the Others. "I am St. Raphael; I am He who heals. I am the Angel of health and refuge of sinners. I am the patron saint of those who travel by land or sea or air. I heal the wounded and ill and bring comfort to the dying. I am peace, I am serenity, and bright with the resplendent glory of God. See me, and know my presence in this Descendant, Father Benedict Aurora."

As suddenly as it happened, the aura began to dissipate, and the image of St Raphael faded from sight. The priest opened his eyes and opened his hands. The little fox drew out its paw and gingerly set it on the ground. It pressed harder, and harder again. The fox sat down, uncertainty on his face. Then the little creature squealed and pounced at the ground with both its front paws and its mouth open. It began to bark, a slightly shrill and high-pitched sound, and pranced delightedly. It went into a playful attack position and launched itself at Wolf, who rolled the little animal with a gentle paw swipe. The Dagda watched the priest with concern and stepped forward to steady the man who swayed slightly toward the fire. Benedict put his hand out for his glasses, and Annalee pressed them into his palms.

Her eyes were shining with unshed tears. "Raffie."

The priest gave a self-conscious laugh and thanked the Dagda. "This gets harder to come back from each time it happens. I am not as young as I once was."

The Dagda smiled gently and put his hand on the priest's shoulder. "None of us are, my brother. None of us are." The Dagda stepped back into the circle and faced Yenay and Annalee. Gently he said, "It is time."

Yenay closed her aching arms even tighter around Annalee. She stared at the Dagda. "I am not giving her to you."

The Dagda's expression did not change, and his voice did not alter from its powerful, gentle lilt. "She is not yours to give or to keep, Yenay. She belongs to no one; however, Quan Yin would dwell in the hearts of everyone."

With that statement, the Dagda and Shango both lowered themselves to one knee and bowed their heads. Wolf remained seated and placed a paw on

228

the rambunctious fox to keep it still. Father Benedict made his way to Shango's side. He gingerly placed a hand on the warrior God's massive shoulder to lower himself to kneel. The warrior did not look up but reached out a hard, steady hand for the priest to use. The symbol stopped spinning. The sparkling, crystal side gleamed with the fire's reflection.

Yenay looked around her in rising anxiety. "What are you doing? What's going on? We...we've had enough of this. I am taking my little girl—"

"Mother, stop. Put me down."

Yenay pulled her head back to look at Annalee. The child was looking at her from the eyes of an ancient soul. She didn't fight her mother, but she released her grip on Yenay, forcing her to let the girl slide to the forest floor. The child faced the Others and dropped into a lotus position. She placed her fingers together over her knees in a sacred mudra and closed her eyes.

The forest surrounding her was bathed in a warm, golden glow. Everything in the vicinity was gilded—tree branches, stones, and the faces of those that surrounded the fire. The auric field became so bright that Yenay had to shield her eyes from it, and the Others bent their heads further. There was a flash of brilliance from the halcyon center, and a feeling of complete peace came over each and every living being surrounding the child who was no longer a child.

The crow and bullfrog carefully came forward from the forest and watched. Birds lit on tree branches and wild animals crept to the outside circumference and lay down in the warm, golden circle, hunter beside prey. Yenay lowered her hand and looked into the warm, compassionate eyes of Quan Yin. The Others raised their heads and felt a thick, gentle blanket of serenity and love wrap around them. Father Benedict wiped at his eyes discreetly.

Quan Yin's smile exuded a peace that enveloped all around and before her. Her thick, black hair shone like onyx, reflecting the firelight, the sheen of her gold aura, and the crystal brilliance of the Symbol. It hung past her shoulders to her small waist like the broad wing of a blackbird, and she was crowned with a headdress of gold embroidered with red beads and tassels. Yenay clasped a hand over her mouth as Quan Yin began to lift from the ground, still in the lotus position, to a position slightly above the fire flames. She was cradled in the soft petals of a lotus flower and clothed in a delicate, shimmering white robe. A Phoenix symbol in pure white jade was clasped around her neck, and her wrist bore a blue jade dragon bracelet. Beside her sat a peacock, preening itself, unconcerned with anything but its close presence to the Goddess. In one hand, Quan Yin held a gracefully carved vase, and in the other, a silvery willow branch. From her height, she spoke, and her melodic, hypnotic voice caressed all who heard it.

"Soldiers of Gaia, guardians of Quan Yin, please rise."

The Others rose from their bended knees.

Shango stared at the Goddess, his red eyes glowing, and put a massive hand under Father Benedict's elbow to guide the priest to a standing position. The priest's eyes opened in wonder as he realized he hadn't put one iota of effort into that maneuver. Shango's hand had worked like an elevator. He would have liked to mouth a 'thank you' to Shango, but he could not take his eyes off the otherworldly vision before him. He felt tears threaten to gather again, as he bore witness to Her perfect beauty. He admonished himself for being such a soft old fool. They heard the Goddess laugh, a sound that prompted every creature before Her to smile in response.

"My good Father, you are anything but a fool. You have been chosen by your Lord. He has complete faith in you. Please have it in yourself."

Yenay collapsed to the ground, sobbing. She was overwhelmed by the pure radiance of the Goddess. She wrapped her arms around her stomach, gulping for air. Suddenly, she felt warmth, and a flow of serenity suffused her body and stilled her wracked nerves. Gentle fingers at her chin tilted her face up, and she looked into the shining dark eyes of Quan Yin.

"Yenay. Mother of Annalee. You grieve for the child's lost innocence."

Yenay nodded, and her hands wrapped around the soft, strong forearms of the Goddess. "She is only four years old."

"I understand. She will always be your child, Yenay. She will be your child at every age, and every stage. She will need you to guide her, raise her, love her, and teach her."

"How? How do I raise Quan Yin?"

"You do not. You raise Annalee."

Yenay cast her eyes down and used her sleeves to wipe away tears. When she looked up, Quan Yin was still in her lotus position, above the fire. Yenay blinked. How did she stand before her and remain above the fire? How could she be in two places simultaneously? Then she remembered the legend. Quan Yin was given many arms and many heads to attend to all that she needed to. She could be everywhere at the same time. The Others stood in silence as the gentle Goddess spoke again.

"I am the Bodhisattva Quan Yin, the One Who Hears. I meet you in mercy and compassion. I wish to be present to heal Gaia, and Her people, when the people who have strayed from the path of kindness and love return to it. I wish to be present to continue to walk hand in hand with those of humanity who already walk this path. I wish to be present to help rebuild the great damage done to Gaia and Her children that has been done by those who do not honor humanity or the earth. I will not be present if I do not have my soldiers. My existence will end, and so will humanity. There are those who yearn for this to happen, but there are many more who, by turning their faces away from the threat, assist the outcome that will be my demise. My anointed ones, you have been chosen for your dedication to Gaia, Her children, her land and seas, her creatures. You have been chosen for your wisdom, your courage, your gifts, and your hope for humanity. Gaia and humanity are indebted to you and the most certain risks you have pledged to take. I bless each of you and honor your hope with my own. Look upon me and know my Descendant, Annalee Sun."

Quan Yin then placed her vase beside her and used both hands to touch the willow branch. Each branch began to glow golden, and a vision of Quan Yin appeared before each of the Others. At the same time, they were anointed with the nectar in the vase she had beside her, a gentle finger pressed a drop of shimmering bioluminescent water against each forehead. Each lowered their gazes, and when they raised their heads, the Goddess of Mercy and Compassion was gone.

Declan looked over at Shemar and raised his hands to his face. The beard was gone. He couldn't see over the tops of the trees anymore. Shemar reached over to put his hand on Father Benedict's shoulder, the presence of Shango gone. The priest gazed fondly at the little red fox who stretched his paws up along Ho'kee's blanket-wrapped thigh, as if to show him the miracle that had happened. Ho'kee gratefully tightened the blanket that Mara had quickly shrouded him in when Wolf began to dissipate. Mara looked over at Yenay, who was scooping Annalee up in her arms, weeping quietly and trying to stay strong.

Annalee looked over her mother's shoulder at the Others and smiled a tired smile. "The Ladies said we need to go to sleep now. They have work to do, and we need to rest."

The Others quietly returned to their rooms, no one speaking. They closed their doors behind them. One by one, they got ready for the night ahead. Mara took her vial of black salt and stepped outside, circling the house, sprinkling and chanting, the bullfrog following a short distance away, giving voice to his presence.

Ho'kee watched her from his window, and flung food down to the little fox, the crow occasionally intercepting the goodies. Father Benedict knelt beside his bed, a rosary in his hand, and began to pray. Shemar knocked gently on Yenay's door. She opened it and pulled him in, Annalee giggling behind her. Declan closed his door and walked to the beautiful woman in front of the fireplace, bathed in the glow. He wrapped her tightly in his arms and breathed in her scent—apples, evergreens, honey, and the ocean. He looked into her crystal blue eyes and opened his mouth. She lay a soft, long finger on his mouth and leaned in to claim his lips with her own.

Chapter Six

N icholai Zlo stepped in front of the podium on the outdoor stage and, arching his eyebrow, gave the microphone an amused look. His brilliant smile disarmed the crowd in front of him and his deep, strong voice carried over the congregation. "I will not be needing this little guy. I have a big voice, and I carry a big Vision!"

The enthralled audience clapped and cheered. Security stood at either side of the stage, watching the predominantly Anglo-Saxon, male, expensively dressed contributors gaze at Zlo.

"My people," Zlo continued. "My trusted, empowered Visionaries. We are growing in number and growing in strength. We are those who have seen the truth. We refuse to meekly assimilate into society's deplorable 'victim'-oriented morass. We want, no, we demand personal accountability on the part of each member of our contributing society. We can no longer afford to break our backs for those who willingly pile their miserable excuses for draining our precious resources on us. We are exhausted, and we deserve so much more, my people. You work hard and you should be rich, but are you? Are you reaping the rewards of dedicated service to your work, or are you watching your hard-earned funds create a comfortable environment for those who continue to make poor life decisions? And I know, my friends, that you have not been asked this question by those who thrust their greedy hands into your pockets, so I am going to ask you this question because I care about you. My friends...how do you feel?"

A disturbing, tension-filled quiet settled over the crowd as they thought about this question. Gradually, and then quickly, fists were thrust in the air and shouts began to rise from the throng.

"Cheated!"

"Robbed!"

"Used!"

"Lied to!"

Zlo grimaced with understanding and nodded sagely. He extended his hands in supplication and drifted them down. The horde responded by quelling the anger he had stirred in them.

"Now, my people. Now is the time to embrace and act on our Vision."

Zlo took a breath and casually swept back a perfect-ly coiffed lank of hair that had fallen on his broad forehead. The crowd was quiet save for the occasional clap and call for "Vision." He scanned the crowd and carefully selected a few individuals to make direct eye contact with.

"We do not hate the marginalized. However, they are there by choice. We will not condone the actions of drug addicts, but we do not hate them. We will not welcome the homeless, the mentally ill, or the addict into our home, but we are willing to provide housing in an area where their actions, for which they are responsible, do not jeopardize our children, our loved ones, our elderly, or the very lifestyle that you and I have fought so hard and so long to create.

"The Vision believes that a perfect society is possi-ble, even inevitable, with the proper rules and guid-ance in place. The Vision believes that even the dere-licts are allowed space, and we will build these insti-tutions where they are fed, clothed, treated, and kept warm. These institutions will become their forever homes, they will be safe there, and, by keeping them safe, we keep ourselves and our children safe.

"We have tried mercy and compassion. These at-tributes, while noble indeed, have done nothing to solve the problem. We need action. My people, you and I have the solution. We have the solution. It is the Vision. You have tried, my friends. You have tried so very hard to be patient and understanding. That has made the problem worse, through no fault of yours. We now live in a society where these attributes are a weakness, not a strength. We vow to support those less fortunate than ourselves, but in a dedicated, structured environment that they may not leave, for their own safety. The alternative to this? Well, it is unfortunately all around us. However, we can fix this. This is what people with the Vision do. We fix that which is broken and then instead of waiting for the next break, we rebuild the infrastructure so breaking does not happen. Failure is no longer an option.

"Dig deep, my people. Dig deep and help me create the society you deserve, the society you truly want, although it is not politically correct for you to say so. My friends, I do not care about politically correct words. I care about you and a better world for generations yet to come."

Zlo stood back; his hands rested on the podium, and he bowed his head reflectively and with humility. "I will only ever do your will, I pledge that. Tell me what is truly in your heart, tell me about your Vision, and if we are in alignment, we have the power to change everything. Take the power back, my people, and let me be your instrument of devastating eradication, so we may rebuild, replant, and rebirth our society."

In the sea of adoring faces, one watched Zlo with curiosity. Joe stood still and straight, threading his sobriety chip through his fingers, listening to the man at the podium. Kibbles the terrier sat quietly on Joe's feet. Freshly bathed and clipped, with a new leash and collar, he caught the attention of a few nurses who were skirting the outside of the group on their way to work. A number of the pretty women smiled at the handsome young red-haired man who probably looked vaguely familiar to them. Joe smiled back as they bent to pet the friendly little terrier. Gloria bustled her way through the crowd to stand beside him and the man at Joe's side.

She hugged Joe fiercely and her eyes teared up as she raised her hand to brush away the thick fall of red hair over his forehead. She looked deep into his clear, green eyes. "Joe. I don't have the words. You look wonderful."

"Thanks, Gloria. Could not have done it without my kick-ass sponsor. Thank you for lending him to me."

The man beside them both reached out an arm to wrap around his wife's shoulders. The man continued to glare at Zlo from behind his dark sunglasses.

"What does he have against people like us, Jack?" Joe asked.

Jack sighed. He put a large, comforting hand on Joe's shoulder. "Fear, Joe. He is terrified. He is scared that he will lose what he has and scared that he won't get what he thinks he needs. That sort of fear looks like hatred. He would rather hate than move outside his comfort zone to try some empathy. Men like Zlo have zero interest in people like us. It would be easier on his mind if we all got shipped to some deserted island to fend for ourselves. To keep his conscience clear he would supply the basic necessities of survival by helicopter drop."

Gloria stared at Zlo with contempt. For all his handsomeness, his beautiful speeches, his artful and practiced way of pretending to connect with people, she had told Joe she was quite happy to stay outside the six-foot-pole range of him.

Zlo stepped away to thundering applause. He stepped off the platform to greet and gladhand, while Mother Beatrice collected four-figured checks. With security ahead and behind them, they smiled and chatted and shook hands with almost everyone in the large group. Still smiling, they waved from the hospital entrance and stepped inside.

Once inside, Zlo looked at Mother Beatrice, his smile immediately dropping from his face. They took the elevator to the office at the top of the building. Zlo strode in first, and flashed his smile at his secretary Lorraine, who blushed prettily.

"Hold your calls, Mr. Zlo?"

"Lorraine, your beauty is only enhanced by your extraordinary, and a little eerie, powers of perception. You are always taking care of me."

Lorraine's smile radiated.

Zlo and Mother Beatrice strode into the office and closed the door behind them, taking their respective seats. Mother Beatrice had requested an audience, and it had been granted.

Zlo drummed his fingers impatiently and watched the Reverend Mother Beatrice with irritation. He had a place to get to and a thing to do. This incident that occurred in the ER was a media circus. While chaos in other people's lives could be quite beneficial to his plans, he couldn't stand it in his own very ordered world. While he didn't mind the positive media publicity of an in-house priest with healing hands, he resented not being able to control the parties involved.

After reviewing the security camera footage with that oafish security guard Nelson and the Reverend Mother, who seemed to know everything about everyone, he was able to obtain the names of Shemar, Yenay, Declan, and Father Benedict. The other two that seemed to be irritating Mother Beatrice—the old lady and the Indigenous boy—Zlo had deemed irrelevant.

He'd sent personal invitations to each of the primary players in that ER spectacle to attend the fundraising speech and join him for an afternoon lunch, and not one had responded. The hand-delivered invitations had been returned to him unopened yesterday. That was rude, to say the least.

He had no doubt they would each connect with him at some point in the next twenty-four hours. After all, he was Nicholai Zlo, CEO of Haida Gwaii and creator of the Vision. Zlo continued to stare at the Reverend Mother, who was continuing to blather on about something or other. If she didn't know so much, and adore him so blindly, and was so useful to the Vision...

"I do believe, Mr. Zlo, that is what needs to happen to ensure the Vision stays on point."

She sat back and stared at him with those unblinking fisheyes of hers. Zlo had absolutely no idea what she was talking about because he was deliberately not listening, but oh, how he really loathed people telling him what they thought needed to happen concerning the Vision.

Whatever she'd been saying had clearly been out of line because fear filled her eyes at his lack of response.

"Oh, Mr. Zlo! Sir, I am so very sorry," she rushed to say. "I misspoke. I, in no way, meant to suggest that I know what needs to happen, I do not. The Vision is my life, my purpose, Mr. Zlo. I get too passionate, I know, and I—"

Zlo held up a hand to stop her and dropped his palm flat on his desk. He didn't smack the desk. Displays of anger were emotional and gauche. "Please, Reverend Mother. I accept your sincere apology. No one is more loyal to the Vision than you are. In that direction, you must realize what a boon it is to this hospital, to the bigger Vision, that our own in-house priest can perform medical miracles. Of course, we do need to rein him in a bit. He is a bit too old to be without supportive protection from some press and the unworthy of society. Not every person deserves his touch, we must be cognitive of that."

The Reverend Mother stared at him with confusion on her face. "But, Mr. Zlo, that is what I have been trying to tell you; he's gone. Father Benedict and Shemar left after the ER incident. I wanted to have words with the man about the silliness of his parlor tricks before I brought my concerns to you, but he has left. His parishioners are being attended to by a novice."

Zlo's expression went from calm to a simmering, cold fury in flat seconds. He refused to release Beatrice's frightened eyes from his stare.

His voice was flat and cold. "Where is he?"

Beatrice's voice trembled. "No one knows, sir. He and Shemar left the same day. The young Navajo security guard as well—all three are gone. Jack at the security firm said Shemar took personal time off and asked that the Indigenous boy not be trained with anyone but him. Jack agreed. I knew nothing about Father Benedict taking leave until I went to the chapel. Apparently, Cardinal Josef had arranged that."

Zlo sat frozen, which frightened her more than any outburst would. He wouldn't break his gaze from her, and she couldn't see what was going on in those fathomless depths. He pushed an intercom button at his desk and spoke in icy, clipped tones. "Lorraine. See the Reverend Mother Beatrice out."

He lifted his finger and stood at his desk. He was a powerful figure, a dark, dangerously handsome man with absolute ruthlessness etched in his face. He extended his hand toward the Reverend Mother as his secretary came in. "Reverend Mother. Once again, I am indebted to your service and your keen observations. I don't know how this organization would operate without you."

"Mr. Zlo. Upon my words as a devout follower, you will never have to find out. I pledge allegiance to you and the Vision."

Zlo nodded and released his grip, and she stumbled backward slightly before nodding and leaving his office.

Zlo walked around his desk and put his palms flat on the surface. A slight tic at the corner of his mouth caused Lorraine to gasp. This was not a good sign.

"Lorraine. Call Tomas and Henrik. I want every name in that strange little group that gathered in the

ER, everyone that gathered around the child. Give Tomas and Henrik their addresses, and if you don't have the information, get the information. Mother Beatrice will be able to help you. Allow them access to the security footage. I want to talk to these individuals, and I am not taking no for an answer."

Lorraine took her leave quickly. Zlo stood at the window, looking out. He was starting to feel uncomfortable about this situation. He couldn't put his finger on what was making him uneasy. This group that Reverend Mother happened upon... Who were they? What were they doing in his hospital? He needed to consult his mentor.

He needed more information. He needed to know how this odd group could be used to further the Vision, or if this group had shown up to throw a wrench in this pursuit. The Mentor would know. The Mentor was the one who had told Zlo that a child was going to be admitted to the ER and was unlikely to survive. The Mentor had told Zlo to attend the hospital and ensure that the child did not leave, alive or dead.

At the time, Zlo wondered why the Mentor cared. He had never shown any interest in the hospital patients, only in the advancement of Zlo's career and the accumulation of funds to promote the Vision. Now, Zlo realized there was something about this child and the bizarre series of events that followed her entrance that was connected. He was getting a feeling that somehow these people were linked with the Mentor.

Zlo strode out of his office, ignoring Lorraine. She did not let her crushing disappointment show on her beautiful face.

Henrik and Tomas stood on either side of the elevator. Zlo stepped inside and they joined him, wordlessly.

Declan floated between a dream and wake state. He felt a strong, gentle touch stroking his hair back from his forehead like his mother used to do. He heard a soft Irish lilt singing "The Gypsy Rover," also like his mother used to do. He hadn't felt this safe in a long time. He reached over to the other side of the bed, but his hand rested on a cool sheet, not on Inanna's warm body. He reluctantly opened his eyes and met the dark jade gaze of a beautiful woman. She was smiling at him with a peaceful and gentle smile. Her incredible eyes were rimmed by thick black lashes, and fine lines creased the corners. Her thick, dark red hair tumbled over her shoulders, and a heavy streak of pure white from her scalp to the ends of her curls framed her serene face.

He fought back a traitorous pooling of tears in his eyes and spoke to the woman, his words sounding strangled. "She's gone, then?"

The fire-haired woman tilted her head to the side and continued to stroke his hair fondly. Her voice was low and soothing. "Yes, Declan, her time with you was done, for now. I am Brighid. I will be your guide for the Full Moon. The Others have been assembled. Now, you and I must lead them into battle."

Declan moved onto his hands, the sheet slipping from his chest. Brighid's gaze never left his face. He was very aware of his bare ass under the covers, and he was uncomfortable. "I am kind of naked."

Brighid smiled widely, her generous mouth accommodating the genuine grin. She laughed a contagious belly laugh that had him smiling back without meaning to. She cupped her hand under the curve of her belly, and he noticed her pregnancy. She rose gracefully from the chair. Declan instinctively reached out to grab her elbow to help her, and the sheet dropped farther.

Declan flushed and grabbed at the cloth. "Shit! I mean, I am sorry! I was trying to..."

Brighid held up a graceful hand, still laughing. "You are a gallant knight, Declan O'Neill. I assure you; I have seen nakedness." Now she arched an eyebrow, before turning away to give Declan an opportunity to get into the jeans that she had placed at the end of his bed. "I will keep my eyes averted until you are clothed."

Declan flushed deeper and muttered, "Thank you, ma'am," as he struggled into his jeans.

"Brighid will do just fine, Declan."

Declan zipped and turned toward Brighid. She held out a shirt to him. She was a little shorter than he was and rounded out perfectly with glorious pregnancy. He felt a surge of protectiveness toward this mother-to-be with a dancing light in her eyes. She reminded him of someone. She reminded him of...

"Mom. You look like my mom."

Brighid reached out and took his hands in both of hers. She rubbed them together. "That is the highest compliment I could receive. I thank you, Declan."

"Will the Others see you?"

"Not right away. Like Inanna, I am here for you. I will be your Muse and your guide. The Others may feel my presence but only you will see me until such time as it is deemed necessary that I show myself."

Declan was a bit sorry when she withdrew her hand. He flipped the kettle on in the ensuite kitchen and pulled mugs down. She stepped over to the swivel chair in front of the window and maneuvered herself down. She glanced over at Declan and with a smile, patted the seat of the swivel chair beside her. "There is so much of your mother in you, Declan. She knew almost from your birth that you had the blood of the Dagda, truer than any others of your line before you." Brighid looked out the window, a little wistful. "I have missed that great God. I have been waiting for him a long time to make his appearance on this earth again."

Declan looked utterly confused, and Brighid laughed.

"Never mind me, Declan. I get a bit strange when I am this far along. Have a seat, we need to discuss what Inanna brought up last night before she left."

Declan went to sit, then jumped back up. "Oh! I made tea. My da said my mother needed almost hourly infusions of tea when she was expecting."

Brighid gave him a grateful smile and folded her hands over her belly. "You are a credit to your species, young Declan. Now, let's talk about how we keep your species safe from this particularly evil force that is hellbent on driving them to kill each other."

Ho'kee took the steps downstairs two at a time and swung into the kitchen, almost knocking over Mara, who was lifting a casserole dish of something heavenly smelling out of the oven. She smiled at him and put the dish on the stovetop and pointed to a full pot of coffee. Ho'kee gave her a bow and clasped his hands in blessing before grabbing a mug.

He turned quickly and almost careened into Father Benedict, who was carrying a laden tray of hot pancakes to a warmer. "I'm sorry. I smell coffee. I will be much better after coffee. All the synapses need to wake up to fire properly."

The priest laughed and stacked plates beside the buffet server on the kitchen counter.

"I will never stand in the way of a young man and his coffee, Ho'kee! Pour me a cup, will you?"

Ho'kee raised a hand and pulled down another mug and stopped short when he saw three guests enter the kitchen at the same time. Yenay, Shemar, and little Annalee arrived in a group with Shemar's arm around Yenay's shoulders and Annalee dragging her mother by the hand. Ho'kee grinned. Good for them.

"Woof!" shouted Annalee, launching herself at Ho'kee. He bent to sweep her up in his arms and throw her up to almost touch the ceiling. Her excited shrieking brought smiles to the gathering around the table.

Shemar gestured toward an unoccupied chair. "Declan?"

Mara nodded and pointed to the plate she was filling with pancakes, bacon, and hash brown casserole.

Father Benedict added a helping of scrambled eggs to the plate and placed it under the warmer. "Mara told me he will be down later. He has had a long night."

Ho'kee smirked and muttered, "Uh huh."

Shemar gave him a stern look, and Ho'kee turned away from him, twirling Annalee in various ballerina poses in midair. They sat at the table, and Benedict quietly said grace while Mara closed her eyes and muttered her thanks to The Goddess.

The priest closed the prayer and lifted up the syrup decanter and started to speak what was on everyone's mind. "So. What do we know about how each one of us came to this island?"

"It was someone else's idea," retorted Ho'kee.

"Besides that, son."

"Something higher, something outside of our own small worlds brought us here." Shemar studied the large stack of pancakes in front of him and added another flapjack.

"Your 'gifts' were granted, or you were made aware of them, when you were touched or surrounded by bioluminescent water," Yenay spoke softly, then looked down at the table and started to twist her napkin. "They are strongest at that time, in those locations." She cast a worried glance at Annalee, who laughed as Ho'kee lifted his empty plate and licked it clean, growling when she tried to take it away from him.

The priest nodded and folded his hands in front of him, elbows on the table. Mara prodded him with a serving spoon, and he withdrew his elbows. She shook the ladle at Ho'kee who placed his plate gingerly on the table.

The priest looked around the table and spoke thoughtfully. "Why were we gathered together at the hospital? We know that Annalee got sick and we were called to attend, but why? We each served a role, but two things bother me. How did the child get so sick, so fast? There was no underlying cause, and her recovery was instant. And why us? Surely there are others in the world who are also Descendants, so why us?"

Declan answered the priest as he came down the stairs. "We were the anointed ones. We were destined to be at that place, at that time, to come together. There was also a push from another force that wanted to flush out any supporters that Quan Yin may have already."

Mara's eyes narrowed as she looked up at Declan. "Chernobog," she spat.

Annalee placed her hands over her ears and squeezed her eyes shut. She buried herself in her mother's lap and started to rock, singing a song to herself.

Yenay closed her arms around the child and shot an accusing look at Declan. "Do you have to? Can't you see the mention of this man or creature or whatever you are calling it, scares her?"

Declan sat at the table and held Yenay's glare. "He is going to try to do more than scare her, Yenay. She is the embodiment of hope, compassion, charity, and love of humankind. She is everything that is a threat to his existence. She is only four and already has this power. As she gradually ascends into who she is, she will only become more powerful, her gifts more far-reaching, and her message stronger than his. He is going to try to stop that, or his Vision, centuries in the making, will be destroyed. He will become unwelcome, and in his worst nightmare, irrelevant."

Father Benedict stood up shakily. He made his way to the living room and placed a hand on the mantle of the fireplace to steady himself. He looked every year of his age, and then some. He whispered, "Is this Lucifer?"

Declan put his hand on the priest's shoulder. "He has many names, but Chernobog was never an angel. He is a ruthless Deity, who was honored by believers so he would not harm them. He was appeased by human sacrifice. There is no way of gratifying him other than with human blood and blind devotion. Unfortunately, his followers become so enraptured by the ideal society he offers, that they fail to remember the reason for his existence. They don't realize that they themselves will be part of the eradication. Chernobog seeks nothing other than the death of man's body and soul."

The stunned silence around the table was only broken by Annalee continuing to sing so she could not hear Chernobog's name. Declan looked over at her and smiled. He crouched in front of her and placed his own hands against hers. He leaned his forehead to hers and moved a message into her mind. "I won't mention that name again, I promise. Not until you are ready to hear it. We will call him something else, so your ears don't hurt, okay?"

Annalee looked up at him with tear-filled eyes. She nodded and reached her arms up. He swept her up and held her tightly. He moved the message to Mara's mind.

She closed her eyes, nodded, and spoke to the Others. "We have to call him something else for now. That name hurts her ears."

"Asshat? Creep Show? Fugly?" Ho'kee's flippant remarks were met with both disdain and laughter.

Shemar tilted his head. "I kind of like Creep Show."

Mara's mouth lifted a bit at the side, but she waved a warning finger. "Do not underestimate this force. He has many followers. Millions. They have followed him for centuries and continue to do so. He can't be eliminated. He can be made weak, but never powerless. He has accumulated great power in these last few years by dividing people."

Declan put Annalee down and caught Mara's eyes. "You recognize him."

Mara sat heavily in a chair beside the priest. She sighed and projected to Declan who relayed her message to the group. "I do. I have seen him strive for his vision of the elimination of mankind for some time. In past lives, and in this one. He has taken this vision a step further now. He has man destroying his own home—Earth—in pursuit of some idea of perfection."

"That must make him very pleased with himself," said the priest.

Mara looked up at Father Benedict; concern creasing her features, she nodded. "He has never come so close to realizing his purpose as he is now," she said into Declan's mind.

Declan spoke quietly. "Mara, you've been down this road before, you know something about him. What is his weakness?"

Mara folded her arms over his chest and her voice filled Declan's head. "His followers are his strength and his undoing. He has to work through them, and there are more good than bad people in this world, despite what the news tells us. But in the face of false information, promises of status, wealth, prestige, and fear-mongering, his followers are growing in number and in viciousness. However, they are human, and mankind is complex. Mankind can be swayed." She reached out and put her calloused hand on Annalee's soft head and stroked her hair.

Annalee looked directly at her. "Did you see him, Mara? When you were once Baba Yaga?"

Mara nodded slowly. This time, Yenay translated for her, "I know I did. I recognize the name. I see his image in the scrying bowl, and the feelings I get are familiar ones. But those memories are from lifetimes ago."

Shemar sat beside Yenay and put his arm around her waist. He rested his hand against her hip, and she moved slightly toward him. His voice was incredulous. "So, this creature was able to make Annalee sick, and he did it just to flush us out?"

Declan nodded slowly. "That is the message I am getting. He was flushing her out as well. He knew Quan Yin had a Descendant in this time, and he went looking for her. I don't think he actually counted on us being there, but now he knows she has guardians. The Goddess came to prepare us for this, then he came to size us up."

"So, we did exactly what he wanted." Shemar's face contorted with anger.

"I don't think so, Shemar. He didn't expect us to band together after that. He expected that we would all go our merry ways and never see each other again. The Goddess anointed us as a group of Descendants in order to protect Annalee from him."

"For the rest of our lives," Ho'kee stated.

"As long as we each shall live. He would not expect that of us, or that we will continue to recruit for this purpose in our lifetimes and for other lifetimes to follow."

"Are we going to have to go head-to-head with this guy?"

"Eventually. He has followers to do his work, and he will be sending them in as part of his demand for human sacrifice. They will go willingly, they will die for his cause, although they have no idea that his ultimate goal is the eradication of humanity. He himself will only go head-to-head with another Deity, not a Descendant. Only another Deity can destroy him."

Yenay dropped her head into her hands. "That doesn't make me feel any better, Declan."

Shemar placed his hand on Yenay's shoulder. His stare was hard and level, holding Declan's gaze. "How do we find him?"

"He needs to take human form to enter this realm. It will take something otherworldly to discover the man or woman he is hiding in. We have abilities and gifts we are just coming into, and I know with absolute certainty, and I have it on excellent authority, that we will find his host."

Zlo lit the candles in his study and pulled the curtains closed. He sat down and faced the large mirror. He pulled off the black cloth and gazed into his own reflection. He deliberately slowed his heart rate and let his mind enter an altered state. He opened his eyes and saw his reflection staring back at him. The labradorite pendant glistened in the night light.

"Mentor, I am listening."

The familiar chill seized him, and the mirror warped slowly. His stomach clenched and he felt sick. He reached out to the desk to steady himself as the mirror undulated. The temperature in the room dropped rapidly, and an acrid stench filled his nostrils.

He repeated the mantra "this too shall pass, this too shall pass" as his fingers began to turn blue, and he fought the nausea with all he had. Suddenly, the chill broke and he was suffused with heat. He looked down to see the labradorite pendant pulsing and glowing. He tore off his tie and ripped open his shirt. Sweat drenched his back and chest and dripped from his forehead.

He leaned over the desk in front of the mirror and raised pain-filled eyes. The pendant's sheen morphed from blue-green to deep blue, the shadowed walls surrounding him. The portal was now open. He squeezed his eyes shut. His stomach settled. The mirror stopped warping. He opened his eyes and saw a different face in the mirror, so much like his own. Chiseled features, a long Roman nose, sharp cheekbones, thin lips.

The face smiled cruelly and whispered to Zlo, "Favored Descendant of my own lineage, I am here."

Chapter Seven

F ather Benedict wrangled his suitcase into his house. "Hello, honey, I'm home!" His jovial call to the house sitter died on his lips when he simply pushed the door open. "Joe? Joe, I'm back! Shemar said to remind you of the meeting tonight. Jack is going to pick you up."

The priest stood in the foyer and pulled off his driving gloves. He peered around the corner, but there was no sign of Joe. Benedict looked skyward and said a quick prayer that Joe had not gone on a bender while the priest was gone. Joe had been doing so well since he got out of detox and the shelter.

The priest shrugged out of his coat and called out, "Joe? I could use some help with the suitcase, and you are far younger and slightly better looking than I."

Then the priest heard a heartbreaking whine from a little dog. Kibbles charged into the foyer and emitted a high-pitched, frantic bark. The terrier grabbed at Father Benedict's cassock with his teeth and pulled the priest into the living room.

"Kibbles! What on earth has gotten into you? Whatever you have done I have already forgiven you. Just calm down, little one, and we will..."

He turned the corner to the living room and stopped. Joe was lying in a pool of blood, and from the look of his face and hands, it was all his own. The young man was completely still.

Father Benedict lunged for Joe and felt for a pulse. "Joe! Joe, this is Father Benedict! Joe, can you open your eyes for me? Please, Joe, please open your eyes."

Joe's face looked like it had been flattened. By hand or boot, his nose was broken, ad his cheeks had bits of white bone protruding from them. There was blood coming from his mouth and his ears. His neck had dark red cord lines at the bottom of his throat.

"Oh...Joe." The priest's eyes filled with tears.

Kibbles whimpered by Joe's side, his terrier eyebrows twitching in concern. The priest's fingers were still wrapped around Joe's wrist when the weak pulse stopped altogether. Joe's head lolled to one side.

The priest lifted Joe's upper body against his own chest and closed his eyes. "St. Raphael. I need your divine help. Please, heal this man through me."

The room grew colder, and his hands turned icy. The familiar sting of heat began in the tips of his fingers and traveled down his knuckles, over his palms, and engulfed his hands. He opened his eyes to see an emerald orb floating between his two hands when, in a flash of light, the orb shot out beams from either side to connect his hands. The green aura then traveled over the priest's body, and he felt calm and strong. The aura wrapped around Joe, forming a cocoon of the two of them. The aura throbbed, and a jolt of energy surged through Father Benedict, blocking out all feeling, all thinking, until all he saw was green. All he felt was peace. Then he felt a stirring from Joe in his arms. He looked down, and Joe was staring up at him from blood-lined eyes that were filling with tears. Joe tried to speak, but blood spurted out.

Benedict used his cassock to clean the blood. "Shh, son, don't try to speak. I thought we lost you for a minute there, but your pulse is becoming quite strong. You've opened your eyes, praise God!"

Joe continued to cry silently, and his eyes darted wildly around him. His brow creased and his breathing became too rapid. Kibbles crawled forward on his belly and licked at Joe's outstretched hand. Immediately, Joe's breath evened out and he closed his eyes. The priest gave thanks as the healing aura drifted slightly above Joe, then sank into his body.

Father Benedict scanned the room, taking note that there were no broken windows, no sign of theft. He really had nothing of much value, but what he did have was still there. Even the envelope with cash in it should Joe need anything during his house-sitting stint was left untouched on the kitchen table.

Father Benedict had a dark thought and asked the troubling question. "Joe, is this drug related? Blink once for no, twice for yes."

Joe opened his eyes and stared at the priest, then lowered his eyelids slowly once. The priest heaved a sigh of relief.

"Joe, do you know who did this to you?"

Joe's lids closed once only.

"Why would anyone do this to you? Were they look-ing for something?"

Joe blinked twice.

The priest did not expect an answer, his query was spoken with horror.

Joe's bruises were fading quickly, the broken bones in his face shifting under Father Benedict's gaze. Joe leaned forward and got to his knees. He reached out and grabbed Father Benedict's bloodied cassock. Joe stared at the priest in wonder and disbelief, feeling the effects of the potentially lethal beating receding. Joe's eyes filled with tears, and he twisted the cassock in his hands as he forced out the reply.

"You."

Shemar pulled up outside Olivia's home and stared in shock. There were two police vehicles in the street and various people were coming and going out of her house. He fumbled with the seat belt and heaved himself out of the car. His looming presence cast a shadow across the driveway and a police officer looked at the shadow and all the way up to Shemar's incredulous face.

"Brett? My mom?"

Brett dropped his pen and paper into his pocket and put his hand on Shemar's bicep. Not for the first time, Brett wondered if this guy was actually brick and mortar, not skin and sinew.

"She's okay, Shem. Your mom is okay. She isn't hurt. She's in the cruiser right behind us."

Before Shemar could turn around, he heard Olivia's voice.

"Baby! Shemar, I am so happy to see you, so grateful, thank God you are all right. You are all right, baby?" Olivia touched her son's face as he bent down to hug her. She was shaking badly.

"Of course, I am, Mom. What happened? What's going on?"

Olivia held his hands and guided him to a bench in the front garden, beneath the living room window. Brett followed closely. "I went to work this morning, but when I got to the church, I realized I had forgotten the music for the choir practice at home, so I had to come back. When I got home, there were two men in the house."

Her voice broke slightly, and Shemar could feel anger rising toward the hooligans that had scared his mother this way.

"Did you give them what they wanted, Mom? No heroics, right? We talked about this."

Olivia looked at her son from frightened eyes. "They weren't robbing the house, baby. They didn't want cash. When they realized I didn't have what they wanted and didn't know where it was, they left. Shemar, they were as cold as ice. They didn't yell or threaten, just calmly walked out the front door like nothing happened. I have no idea how they got in." Olivia twisted her hands in her lap. "Shemar, I have never been witness to anything as cold, as dark, and as wicked as those two men. I could feel them, Shemar. They were the closest to evil I ever want to get."

"What did they want, Mom?"

Olivia's breath caught in her throat, and she started to cry.

Brett spoke quietly, "You, Shem. They wanted you."

Ho'kee stopped his motorcycle outside the house. After taking off his helmet, he shook out his hair. He was hoping Ethel would have something baking. Suddenly, a rifle shot broke the quiet, sending birds in droves from the copse beside the house. Ho'kee threw his helmet to the side and sprinted in the direction of the shot.

Ethel banged open the screen door, her eyes huge. She yelled as Ho'kee disappeared into the woods. "Ho'kee! Ho'kee, no!"

He didn't acknowledge her plaintive cry from behind him. His ears pricked, and his eyes scanned the area. He heard Abe's voice, low and booming through the trees.

Ho'kee stopped abruptly and willed his body to resist shapeshifting.

"Stay the fuck off my property," Abe yelled. "If I see you again, I will shoot first and worry about introductions afterward!"

Ho'kee cupped his hands around his mouth and made a call, the sound of a loon, to his father. Three calls in quick succession. Abe lowered his rifle and lifted his hand to stop Ho'kee's advance. He slowly eased down his hand, indicating that Ho'kee stay still and be silent. They both remained motionless for a full two minutes. Then Abe crooked his finger for Ho'kee to advance.

When he got close enough, Abe put a hand on his son's shoulder and gazed directly into his dark eyes, so much like his own. "Son, did you get in some sort of trouble when you were gone? Mix with the wrong crowd?"

Ho'kee was genuinely confused. "Trouble? No, Dad. I was with Declan, and a priest, an ancient Russian grandma, Shemar, a four-year-old girl, and her mom. We didn't exactly tear up the town. Why? What's going on?"

Abe stared out in the distance before answering. His sharp eyes caught all movement in the forest. "Two very well-dressed men came to the house looking for you. I didn't get the idea it was a friendly social call. They tried to just walk into the house. Remington and I escorted them out and off the property."

"Is Mom okay?"

"She's scared for you, but okay. Any ideas, son?"

Ho'kee stared into the distance with his father. His voice was tight with apprehension. "Unfortunately, yes I do."

Mara flung her burlap bag from the window of her truck. It made a soft thud as it hit the ground. She swung the door open and carefully took out her bag of magic. Placing it gently on the burlap sack, she stood with her hands on her hips, narrowing her eyes at her small cabin. Something was off here. Mara inhaled deeply and arched an eyebrow at the bullfrog, who could not seem to get comfortable on the stump. He was agitated, which was very unlike him. She eyed the door and windows to her cabin and straightened as she looked for the spider web that had been resting in the corner of the front door. Mara had always been careful to open the door just enough to get through, so she didn't disturb the large, peaceful spider and her thick, intricate web.

The web was gone. Several silver threads floated pointlessly from the overhang. She swore and lifted her heavy skirt to walk to the pond to scry. She was halted by Nikki's worried greeting.

"Babka? Oh, thank Goddess you are back! We were worried about you! Dad and Uncle Artur have gone looking for you. I am worried about them too."

Mara turned and opened her arms to her granddaughter as the girl raced into them. "I am well, child." Mara pulled back and lifted Nikki's chin in two fingers. She looked into frightened eyes. "There has been someone in my cabin, yes?"

"Yes. I think they couldn't find what they were looking for, so they came up to the restaurant."

Mara stiffened, her jaw tight with anger. "They?"

Nikki nodded. "Two large men. Not as big as Dad and Uncle Artur though. The men left when Dad and Uncle Artur told them they were all going to discuss something outside. I didn't see them after that. Dad told us to get into our rooms and not to come out until he came back. As soon as he came back, I came here."

Mara hugged Nikki close. "Where are Leonid and Artur now?"

"I think they went to the pond. Is that where you were going, Babka?"

"Yes. Come with me, child."

The bullfrog called out and Mara looked at it, intrigued. She stopped Nikki and put her hand out. "You have something you wanted to give me?"

Nikki looked surprised and pulled a blood-stained cloth from her pocket. "Yes! I almost forgot! Dad dropped this in the garbage after his talk with the two men. He said something about none of it belonging to him, all to the other guy. I thought maybe it could be useful. I don't know why it would be, I'm probably being stupid."

Mara took her granddaughter's chin in her fingers again and raised her face to meet Mara's eyes. "Child, never doubt your intuition. It is a gift from the Goddess and not to be taken lightly. You did absolutely the right thing, and I thank you for it. This little treasure will come in very handy for a binding spell you and I are going to do."

Nikki's eyes sparkled with anticipation, and she hugged Mara again.

Mara spoke quietly in Nikki's ear, "Do you know what they were looking for, Nikki?"

"Grandma, they were looking for you."

Yenay and Annalee came loudly to the front door of their house, singing ridiculous songs and laughing. The second they got to the door, it was flung open, and Tina reached out to forcibly pull them both in.

She slammed and locked the door behind them and made sure the curtains were closed. Annalee stared at her grandmother. She clung to Yenay's leg.

Yenay glared at Tina. "Ma! What the— What in blazes are you doing?"

Tina put a finger to her lips. Her voice was barely above a whisper. "We are being watched. There are two men out there. I have seen them in a car across the street. They haven't come to the house, but I know they are watching us."

Yenay's lips curled upward. "Ma. What did I tell you about that endless loop you watch of *Matlock*, *Perry Mason*, and *Cannon*?"

Tina's face remained strained.

Yenay stopped smiling. "You are serious. There is someone watching the house."

Tina nodded. "I called the police with the make and license of the car, but it was hard to describe the men. The inside of the car was dark. I don't know what they look like. Every time the police came by, they were gone, like they knew the police were coming. They haven't actually done anything, but the policeman said he would find them and have a chat with them. He left his card here. Brett, I think his name is."

Annalee was silent. She continued to cling to Yenay's leg and stare at her grandmother.

Tina spoke out loud, and all three knew she was lying. "I think they were casing the house to try to steal something! They were probably watching our comings and goings to determine the best time to break in, and now that the police are involved, they will go away. Let's put our silver in the safe and hire security guards until the police can catch these men!"

Annalee was slowly shaking her head. Her four-year-old voice was too weary for her age. "It's me. They are looking for me."

Declan braked his car and shut the engine off. He quickly moved to the passenger door to help Brighid out. He looked around the trailer park and saw no one. How did it happen that each time he had a Goddess on his arm, there was no one around to see it?

Brighid smiled her thanks and moved up the steps. The ever-present crow trilled loudly when Brighid stepped onto the deck. She cooed at the bird and stretched out her hand. To Declan's amazement, the bird waddled over to her and dipped its head. She scratched behind its head, and it closed its eyelids. She stroked it fondly over its onyx-colored head. Declan brought up the rear with his bags and the crow flew to the closest tree and began squawking at him.

He narrowed his eyes at the bird. "What is it with you?"

Brighid laughed and stood aside for Declan to open the door. He gasped and dropped his bag. The trailer was the cleanest he had ever seen it. Fresh flowers were on the kitchen table in a pretty glass milk pitcher. The wood panels gleamed, and the laminate flooring shone. The appliances sparkled and the windows were crystal clear.

He didn't think of himself as a slob—well, not really a slob. Okay, okay, he admitted to himself, he was a slob. However, even on a dedicated cleaning day, his place never looked like this. He saw a note propped on the table and picked it up, reading it aloud to Brighid.

"Little brother, you will notice that for once in your slob life this trailer is clean. This was not an accident. Call me ASAP when you get back."

Declan laughed until he saw Brighid's face.

She looked concerned. "You should call Niall immediately."

Declan dialed, and Niall picked up on the first ring.

"Should I be worried about you, little brother?"

"I'm fine, Niall. What's going on?"

"Tisdale called me, having a fit. Two men were in the park, at your trailer. They were giving the creeps to the little old dears who look after you and sit at their windows watching the neighbors all day long. They called Tisdale as soon as the two goons set foot on your deck and looked like they were going to bust in. Tizzy confronted them about trespassing and, apparently, they scared the living shit out of him. Brother, they were not there to buy art."

Declan's jaw tightened. "What did they do?"

"Nothing. They did nothing. Tisdale said it was the way they did nothing that scared him. I thought he was drinking his dinner, as usual, but he wasn't slurring. The old dears all crowded around their decks, so I am thinking the goon squad decided against having witnesses. I came out as soon as Tizzy called, but they were gone. I went in, but nothing was disturbed. All your lady friends came by for a looky-loo armed with goodies, and I couldn't stop them from *tsking* and cleaning up your mess. Truth is, I didn't try. Enjoyed some treats and a couple of your beers while I sat on the deck waiting for the Blues Brothers to show up again and locked up when the ladies were done."

Declan was not tempted to laugh at all. He felt violated. Not by his neighbors, the sweet old dears, but by whoever these men were. He also felt very, very angry. "Well. I owe that tipsy weasel for creating a scene. Did Tisdale say what they were looking for?"

Brighid and Niall both answered at the same time, "You."

Henrik dabbed at the bloodstains on his knuckles while Tomas looked in the car mirror at the gash above his eye. This assignment had been a disaster. That skinny house sitter for the priest should have folded. He should have told them where to find the old man. The violence was so unnecessary and time-consuming. Henrik wanted to make sure the wretch was dead, but Tomas held him back, saying he was going to succumb to his injuries eventually and these leeches on society deserved to suffer. Henrik had shrugged and released the cord wrapped around Joe's neck. Tomas was right.

"Why aren't we bringing them all in the usual way?"

Tomas cursed at the gash and slapped the mirror upwards. "Direct order from Mr. Zlo. He wants them one at a time. They are absolutely not to be brought in as a group or even as pairs. We have permission to escort or drag them in, our choice. However, the child is not to be touched in any way, shape, or form. We aren't supposed to lay a hand on her."

Henrik looked thoughtful. "I didn't think Mr. Zlo liked children."

Tomas pressed his fingers against the bridge of his bruised nose. This odd group was being evasive, and the families were ornery. Tomas had taken a thumping from the Russian guys before Henrik could drag him away. He was pretty sure that the First Nations man would have happily blown a hole in both of them and would be waiting for his next opportunity.

"I don't think it's about that. He was adamant about not touching her. Her mom and grandma can be coerced, but not the little girl. There may be collateral damage in the future, but she isn't to be harmed."

Henrik nodded. A random thought crossed his mind. He wondered if this child had anything to do with the Vision. It wasn't like Mr. Zlo to get wound up about anything that didn't have something to do with the Vision. He shook the idea out of his mind. He wasn't paid to think.

Declan hung up the phone. Brighid was sitting in the recliner with a cup of tea, her feet up. She had found one of Mrs. Greer's pot pies in the fridge and put it in the oven. The trailer smelled amazing. He wished he had more of an appetite.

Brighid sighed and closed her eyes, inhaling the aroma. "I do enjoy these sensations when I am here. I don't get here nearly as much as I would like to."

Declan reached for his glass of whiskey and shot it down, neat. "The house sitter for Father Benedict was beaten almost to death. Our families haven't been harmed physically, yet, but they are scared. Two men were looking for each one of us, Brighid. I don't understand. Why did they try to kill Joe and not touch anyone else?"

Brighid opened her jade green eyes. They glittered as she looked into Declan's troubled blue ones. "Joe was collateral damage. The men who did that don't think in terms of individuals. They think in terms of a doctrine, this 'Vision.' It is a plan for a society that has no room, no patience, no compassion for people like Joe. This is not the first time such an idea has been floated in front of a tired and overwhelmed society. This is the first time it has gained so many followers in such a short amount of time. The biggest difference this time is..."

"The leader."

"Yes, Declan. The leader is someone we haven't had to worry about in a very long time. The leader is a Descendant of Chernobog."

"There are many leaders of the Vision around the world?" asked Declan.

"Unfortunately, yes. But only one of them is Chernobog's Descendant."

Declan curled his hand around the crystal orb left on the table by Inanna. He lifted it to eye level and stared deeply at it. Brighid's lips curved into a smile as she watched him.

He set the orb to spin slowly on his fingers, then carefully removed his fingers. The sphere continued to spin, unsupported. Declan's body was suddenly surrounded by a mist. He felt his features take on a stronger, older edge. His hair lightened to white and streamed around him. His smooth complexion was graced by a snow-white, close-cut beard. The Dagda passed his strong, long-fingered hands over the orb and it lit from within. Brighid rose to her feet when the Dagda looked at the sphere and then at her.

His voice was low and rolled like thunder.

"All right, Chernobog, you realm-hopping ophidian. Whose body have you slithered your way into?"

The Dagda's glittering blue eyes narrowed as he peered at the images within the spinning globe. "I cannot see who the Descendant is. He has had many years to perfect this incarnation and he is cloaking himself well. However, I know of someone who will help us. With her assistance, we will uncloak Chernobog's Descendant ."

Brighid sank to one knee and bowed her head in respect to the Dagda.

He reached out and fondly placed a hand on her shining red tresses. "The Goddess will fight alongside us. It will not be long until this battle takes place. There will be death, there will be angels, and there will be victory. Now, rest, and continue to mentor my Descendant. He and I will become one again soon, in full ascension."

Brighid reached out to wrap her hands around the leathery old wrist. Golden hairs returned to the forearm that seconds ago bore only white hair. Declan reached down with his other hand to her elbow and helped her up.

She laughed as she rose. "I am too pregnant to keep doing that, Declan. Next time your centuries-old grandfather pays a visit, give me some warning."

Declan's grin was disarming. "Duly noted. I will call the Others for a meeting at the chapel."

Chapter Eight

Watery sunlight filtered through the stained-glass windows of the hospital chapel, casting a weak glow around the white room and laying thin ribbons of gold over the wooden pews. Small particles of dust drifted in the rays, unsettled and without direction.

When Declan finished speaking, the room was quiet enough to hear each heartbeat.

Yenay absently put her hand on Annalee's head as the child was trying to climb Shemar. "So, this Chernobog has a Descendant, and he is one of the primary leaders of the Vision I keep hearing about in the media? This leader is actually one of you?"

Declan's jaw clenched. "Yes, and no. He is the Descendant of Chernobog, and he has known this all his life. As a result, he is incredibly powerful. We have only recently been anointed and awakened to our ancestry."

Yenay let Annalee advance from Shemar's hips to his shoulders, keeping her hands at a safe distance under the monkey child to catch her in case of a sudden drop. Her frustration was palpable. "No. No, I do not understand. If he is a Descendant, why is he doing this? Why wouldn't he want to protect her? Why does he want to harm my child when you Others want to protect her?"

Father Benedict steepled his fingers together and looked sadly at her. "Yenay, I am afraid that for all the good that is in this world, there is a lot of evil. A Descendant of Chernobog would be created to be in that dark deity's own image. Well, not quite his image because according to Declan, he won't allow complete ascension, but you understand."

"No! No, I do not understand! I don't understand at all! If this guy is walking around among us, for all to see, why don't you go looking for him? How hard could it be to recognize him? Wouldn't he be wrapped in some kind of aura, like you are when you heal people?"

Declan sat in front of Yenay. His gaze met hers steadily. "He has been at this a lot longer than we have, Yenay. We are only just beginning to figure out who we are, where we came from, and what we are capable of, with the exception of Mara."

Yenay swung a hopeful face toward Mara. "Then you know! You know who he is! You can point him out!"

Regretfully, Mara shook her head. "I am sorry, child. I don't know which human form he is descending into. He is careful to block himself from scrying. I might see something around him when I meet him, but I can't be sure. I have a feeling this Descendant is being stringently guarded for this incarnation."

Yenay looked frightened and turned toward Ho'kee. "You can smell him, right, Ho'kee? Like you did with Mother Beatrice? You smelled that something was off with her, you can do it again!"

Ho'kee looked thoughtful. "I don't know. I can smell bad intent, but it goes off whenever someone is plotting anything that is going to be harmful to someone else. Robbery, assault, stalking, the list is endless. My sense has been so overloaded lately, I find it hard to narrow down who has the strongest, and therefore most destructive, intent in a room full of people."

Yenay became more flustered, her voice rising an octave and ending in a plaintive note. "Father Benedict? You have so many years fighting with evil and the Devil, you must be able to defeat him?"

The priest took off his glasses and gave her a tight smile. "My dear, I am afraid this is something of far greater magnitude than I have ever encountered. I have been face-to-face with people who have done heart-rending, wicked things, but nothing like this. I have never encountered anything like what Declan is describing."

Father Benedict reached out and put a hand on her shoulder as fear deepened the new lines in her young face. "That is not saying I will not go into battle for Annalee. I will go into battle for each one of you, without hesitation."

Yenay's eyes filled again with tears, and she wrapped her arms around the priest. He enfolded her gently.

Annalee watched from Shemar's shoulders. She lay her chin on his bald head and said sadly, "Raffie."

Declan sat down and folded his hands together. "I believe we have all met Chernobog before, as our ancestors."

Yenay turned weary eyes to Declan, her hands still held by the priest. "Declan. You have telepathy, you have prophecy, tell me! Help me! Help me protect Annalee! You, out of any of the Others, should be able to get inside this man's—or this thing's—mind and tell me how to stop this! We need to keep her safe!"

Declan felt as weary in that moment as Yenay looked. "Believe me, Yenay. I am trying. I won't stop trying. But we have to find him first, and that is going to take guidance, patience, and the use of our gifts."

Ho'kee looked up. "So, let's flush this creep show out. Let's hunt him down."

Shemar stood up and stretched to his full height, narrowly missing the beams on the ceiling above his head. "I am with Ho'kee. We shouldn't be waiting for him to strike again before we figure out who he is."

Declan looked thoughtfully out the window. "We need to combine our abilities. We need to send a message to Chernobog and his Descendant that we have figured out the link. We will do something that will get this leader to show himself."

"And Annalee? Our families?" Yenay whispered.

"She will be safest with us. Our families are safer if we are not around them right now."

Shemar looked doubtful until Ho'kee spoke up. "My Dad had them running off the property with a Remington pointed toward their asses."

Mara started laughing as she spoke. "My sons had discussions with them as well, in a language they understood. My granddaughter was able to provide the police with detailed descriptions for sketches."

Father Benedict's voice quavered a bit as he spoke. "Joe is severely traumatized as a result of them. He is being well cared for by Jack and Gloria."

Declan's voice was reassuring. "I doubt those men will revisit our families, there was too much attention drawn. Our families now have protection and security." Declan paused briefly and continued. "We need to find a place to gather again, where the bioluminescence is strong. We need an area of ancient magic."

Mara looked at him curiously and nodded. She patted Yenay's purse and, without a word exchanged, Yenay pulled out a notebook and pen.

Declan's eyes remained closed. He lifted his face to the sky. Again, he listened to something no one else could hear. "Latitude 49.1530 degrees North. Longitude 125.9066 degrees West."

Yenay scribbled it down and held it away from her, squinting. "Might as well be Egyptian hieroglyphics," she mumbled.

Ho'kee laughed and took the paper. He put the coordinates in his cell phone. He studied it, and the cocky smile left his face. His hand dropped to the side, the paper in it. He turned and looked at the Others. Declan raised an eyebrow in question.

"This is my home. This is Tofino."

Shemar placed a firm hand on Ho'kee's shoulder.

Ho'kee stared at Declan, and a wordless communication took place. After a minute, Ho'kee crumpled the paper in his fist and sat heavily on a concrete landing of steps. "Okay. We can do this. My parents will want to be part of this." Ho'kee slid his hand back and forth along the wood railings beside the steps he was sitting on.

"What are we going to do to flush him out?"

Declan pushed his hand through his thick hair, off his forehead. "I am not one hundred percent sure, Ho'kee. Let's sleep on this, and meet at your home in the—"

"Well! Father Benedict and the assortment of heroes I met in the ER some time ago." All eyes swung toward the ramrod-straight figure of Reverend Mother Beatrice in the doorway of the chapel. She was striking in her cream-colored jacket and skirt, well-tailored and discreetly embroidered with silver. She looked otherworldly, haloed by the yellow light of the hospital corridor behind her. "What a grand media circus you brought to town! I would like to be able to say it is wonderful to see you all again, but I would be speaking untruths, and we all know how our Lord frowns upon untruths."

She raised an eyebrow and looked directly at Mara. Her silky voice dripped with sarcasm. "Well, maybe not *all* of us."

Declan slowly turned, taking in the response of the Others.

Ho'kee's upper lip contracted in a snarl.

Shemar crossed his arms over his chest. Yenay pulled Annalee close and stepped behind him. Father Benedict rose slowly, keeping his eyes on the woman in front of him.

Mara's eyes narrowed to slits. She spit out the word, *"Cyka."* Then she slid into a pew, never taking her eyes off the woman. She reached back and pulled her long, braided hair over her shoulder. She stared at Beatrice, and began to unbind her own hair, soft words in her native language rolling off her tongue.

Ho'kee crouched beside Mara protectively. His hearing had likely picked up her incantation. While Declan couldn't understand the language, he felt the spell weave around and past him.

Mara unbound her hair and shook out the long, white tresses. She kept watch on the Reverend Mother.

The ties that bind this woman's heart
Let them fray, be split apart
The knots that choke this woman's mind
Let be unraveled, fast unwind.

She moved a thought into Declan's mind. *"We will not have long with this spell. Make good use of it, young Dagda."*

Declan did not betray any sign of hearing the message but sent one back.

She received his thought as stoically as he had received hers. *"You are a very wise woman, Mara."*

Father Benedict folded his hands in front of him, not the least bit inclined to extend a hand in greeting. His voice was as gentle as ever. "Reverend Mother Beatrice. How delightful to see you again. I trust you are keeping well. It is not often we have the grace of your company in the hospital chapel. To what do we owe such a pleasure?"

Annalee poked her head out from between Shemar's knees and looked up at the Reverend Mother. The little girl made eye contact with her and chirped, "You are beautiful! You look like an angel." Annalee then tilted her head to the side and pursed her bow mouth. "But you are so sad. You think you are mad, but you are sad. Why are you so sad?"

The Reverend Mother started abruptly and gazed at the wide, dark eyes of the pretty little girl in front of her. She seemed taken aback for only a second, but in that second, Mara sensed the woman was marveling at the purity of this innocent child. However, before Annalee's magic could seem to take hold, the woman arranged a tight smile on her face.

"Why thank you, little girl! What a sweet thing to say. I promise you I am not mad or sad today. I hope you are feeling better, dear?"

Annalee started toward the Reverend Mother but was halted by Yenay's grip on the back of her collar. Clearly puzzled, the little girl looked back at her mother. Mother Beatrice seemed to recognize the lioness-like protection in Yenay's face and took a step backward.

Declan stood up and looked at the Reverend Mother, a blinding smile crossing his face. He strode toward her, his hand outstretched. Again, she seemed to be caught off guard as this unbelievably beautiful man moved gracefully toward her. She hesitantly stretched out her hand to accept his strong handshake.

"My name is Declan O'Neill. We did not get the chance to be formally introduced last time we were all together."

Mara watched intently, a slight smile tugging at her mouth as she sensed the woman's confusion.

Ho'kee crouched beside Mara on his haunches, also watching intently. He whispered, "What the hell is he doing?"

Mara tapped her temple lightly. Ho'kee nodded and stood up. Shemar continued to stand guard over Annalee with Yenay close behind him. Father Benedict began to walk toward the doorway to join Declan and the Reverend Mother when Mara reached over and grabbed his flowing cassock discreetly. He stopped, not looking back.

Declan was probing the thoughts of Reverend Mother Beatrice. He was linking with her mind.

Declan directed a thought to Mara. *"Find out what you can about this man Zlo."*

Mara, slowly rebraiding her hair, obviously heard Declan's thought. She rummaged in her bag and located her cell phone. In his mind, she told him that she would text her granddaughter. Nikita would not question anything; she would simply work her technological genius and supply Mara with the findings.

The Reverend Mother had been feeling quite pleased with herself. She had found the people responsible for the media circus and she just knew Father Benedict would be reprimanded by Mr. Zlo for his shenanigans. That Indigenous young man would be fired for his flippancy and Shemar would most likely be put on probation. She had never seen that old witch before and would be quite happy to never set eyes on the evil-eyed harridan again. And what on earth did 'cyka' mean?

But that self-satisfaction was quickly fading, turning into something else.

She looked again at the child and had to fight the urge to reach out to the little girl with outstretched arms. She staggered slightly, fighting the feeling of being so woozy.

She tilted her head slightly as the lovely young man, Declan, put a hand under her elbow. She found herself genuinely smiling in response. What on earth was wrong with her? Her brain was positively fuzzy. She felt so lightheaded. She inadvertently reached out to Declan to steady herself and he gallantly wrapped a strong arm around her waist, his other hand still under her elbow.

His eyes darkened with concern, and he spoke with a strong, smooth voice. "Reverend Mother, are you all right? Let's get you out of here and into some open air. May I escort you outside to a bench for a bit, to get your breath? It is quite claustrophobic in here."

Beatrice blinked up at the young man rapidly. That was exactly what she was thinking! It was so close and confining in here. She was not at all comfortable in this chapel. What a kind young man. He would be well served if she were to get him away from the influence of this mob. She nodded vigorously and placed her hand on his forearm. Declan guided her toward the door.

Declan opened the door and escorted the Reverend Mother outside. He shrugged out of his jacket and lay it on the concrete bench for Beatrice to sit on.

"You are a very sweet young man, Mr. O'Neill."

The Reverend Mother lay her hand on Declan's forearm and straightened her spine. Her mind was beginning to clear, finally. What had happened over the space of about fifteen minutes felt like hours. She could almost see the webbing inside her mind dissolve, the wisps of fog dissipate. She locked gazes with the young man, who was looking back at her with interest. He really was disarmingly handsome. She gave her head a shake.

She wondered briefly at this feeling of dizziness. She probably didn't eat enough at lunch. That's why she reacted to the little girl. That's why she was feeling so fuzzy around this gentle young man as well. What was wrong with her? Why was she out here with one of the people Mr. Zlo had asked her about? What had happened in her head? She really needed to eat something and lie down.

Declan rose and extended his hand toward her. "Reverend Mother, forgive me for being so personal, but you seem awfully tired. I am wondering if you have the time to lie down for a while. Take care of yourself, instead of always taking care of others."

"You read my mind, Mr. O'Neill."

A smile twitched on his lips. "Declan. Please call me Declan. May I escort you to your car?"

Beatrice took his hand and rose. As soon as she did, the fog cleared, and her vision sharpened. She looked at the young man in front of her with fresh eyes. He was too charming. He was too handsome. She didn't trust this man at all. She pulled her hand away abruptly and her usual scornful expression settled into her face. "I am quite capable of seeing myself to my car, Mr. O'Neill. Where is Father Benedict? I still want to speak with him about these vulgar displays of so-called 'healing hands.'"

Declan glanced behind him as Shemar closed and locked the chapel door. "It looks like he's left the building, Reverend Mother."

She looked annoyed and bit off her words. "Since the two of you seem to be so close, please relay this message to him for me. On behalf of the interests of the Board of Directors of this hospital, his magic tricks must cease immediately. I have referred the matter to the CEO, Mr. Nicholai Zlo, and I am currently waiting to hear back, but I am confident he shares my views."

Declan looked at her thoughtfully, his smile didn't dim. "All right. I understand, then, that you are speaking for the Board of Directors and the CEO? So, I should take this concern directly Mr. Nicholai Zlo? I will make an appointment immediately. Better yet, I will gather the Others and we will attend in a group."

"No!" Her artfully arranged facial composure dissolved. She looked panic-stricken. She raised her hands up, palms toward Declan. "No! Please don't do that! I meant only that I had referred the matter. The Board of Directors has issued nothing in reply at this time. I am not speaking for them, and certainly not for the CEO. He feels that the presence of a priest with healing hands could be a boon of media coverage for the hospital, but I am sure he will change his mind once he thinks about it and realizes what a circus act it truly is."

As she was saying the words, doubt crossed her face, then anxiety. She stiffened her shoulders resolutely and clasped her hands in front of her. "Mr. O'Neill, I would appreciate it if you would not mention our conversation to anyone else. I wanted to give you ample time to find another venue for Father Benedict's shenanigans. They are not seemly."

Declan bowed his head slightly. "Duly noted, Reverend Mother."

Beatrice held his gaze for a moment later, then broke it and abruptly turned into the corridor and pushed open the door leading to the parking lot. Declan watched her walk stiffly to her car. She was obviously still wound up about him repeating anything that would prove she had spoken out of turn.

He was still musing when Brighid's voice drifted into his mind. *"What have you unearthed, Declan?"*

He smiled again to himself and moved a thought to her. *"I have just read a very intriguing and disturbed mind."*

Tomas and Henrik stood in front of a very angry Mr. Zlo. His black gaze pinned both of them at once. Tomas tried to break the eye contact, but his gaze was dragged back to Zlo.

His voice was calm, but the ice underneath it chilled Tomas. "So. You did not find one. Not one of these people that were in the ER when this healing of the child happened?"

Henrik's shoulders straightened and he gripped his hands in front of him. "Sir, we found all the witnesses to the event. We interviewed an ER doctor, the one that was going to pronounce the girl dead. We also spoke with the patients that were in the waiting room; those that saw the security guard move things without touching them. We interviewed the junkie drifter who seems to have a friendship with the guard and the priest. We made contact with the families of each of the people that Reverend Mother Beatrice noted were present when the girl was revived and were in the hospital chapel afterward."

"Henrik. I am hearing that you two skirted the perimeter without getting inside. I am hearing that you frightened the families of these people to the point that they may go into hiding. I am hearing that you used ugly, barbaric methods to try to extract information, alerting the police to your presence, and received nothing in return. Incidentally, that 'junkie drifter' is alive, compliments of God's right-hand man, Father Benedict. I see by the marks on your faces that you both had the barbaric methods you used turned against you, and still, you have brought me nothing."

Tomas shivered as the temperature in the room plunged a few degrees. Mr. Zlo's hands were in his pants pockets, but his stance was anything but casual. He seemed spring-loaded. He raised his head and looked down at the two men in front of him. His black beard, meticulously groomed, caught the glow of the lights above him. The same glow cast an aura over his thick salt and pepper hair and illuminated his strong shoulders, which were clad in a Vicuna jacket.

Zlo was both the most handsome and the most terrifying man Tomas had ever met. Zlo turned his back on them and walked to the window.

Henrik and Tomas stared forward, in a rigid military stance. In his peripheral vision, Tomas saw Zlo pinching his long fingers over his eyebrows. That meant Mr.

Zlo was getting a headache. On the good side, that meant he would dismiss them imminently. On the bad side, it meant that dismissal could be for now—or permanently. Mr. Zlo's headaches preempted a personality change in the man that was legendary in the hospital.

Zlo's deep voice was quiet but audible, like thunder after a nearby lightning strike. "Who made the decision to leave the drifter alive? Which one of you showed that compassion?"

Tomas took a step forward, sweat beading his brow. "The decision was mine, sir. I felt his injuries were sufficient to ensure death within a short time. I did not feel compassion, sir."

Zlo turned to look at Tomas, his black eyes glittering. "And yet, you showed it."

Tomas was confused but willed himself not to show it. Did he? Was there something in him that stopped Henrik's final step out of compassion? No. It couldn't be. Not after all this time in service to Zlo and the Vision.

Zlo continued to stare at Tomas. His voice was weary but harsh. "Get out. I will deal with you later. Go home. You have been traitorous to the Vision and useless to me. Do not leave town, we are not done. Go."

Tomas blanched and stepped back beside Henrik. He sharply saluted Zlo and Henrik, then strode to the door.

Without being touched, the door swung open quickly and closed behind him sharply. Lorraine looked up from her desk, her hands in midair, and watched Tomas march purposefully from the office. She looked back at the door, closing on its own, softly clicking shut. He heard her say softly, "I am going to miss him."

He didn't stop to ask her for clarification.

Chapter Nine

"**M**om! Dad! I'm home! And I brought my friends!"

Ethel looked up from her map on the dining table to her son in the doorway. She pushed her glasses farther down her nose to look at him over the rims. "Friends?"

"Yeah, Mom. I texted you. You never read my texts."

"You never text me. You rarely call. And you don't bring me flowers anymore."

Ho'kee grinned mischievously.

"Oh? How many, exactly? Coming for dinner?"

"Coming to stay. We need a safe place to be together until the threat is gone."

Ethel rose from her chair and took her glasses off. "Threat? Staying?"

"Mom, you are repeating everything I say. You're not old enough to start doing that."

"My boy, you started giving me gray hairs when you were three. Start at the beginning and let me catch up on this tale."

Ho'kee stood aside and leaned his upper body outside the open door. "Shemar! Father Benedict! Come on in!"

Ethel moved forward as a slightly overweight, slightly balding priest stepped in. He held his hat in his hands and had the most engaging smile she'd ever seen. There was a peace and warmth that emanated from this gentle man that almost brought her to tears. He clasped both her hands in his warm ones and spoke.

There was a trace of an Italian accent that leant a musical quality to his voice. "Mrs. Bidziil, I am so grateful for your hospitality. You have a beautiful home and exquisite grounds. I have never traveled this far up the island. I am in awe of this rugged coastline."

Ethel held his grasp and smiled at Father Benedict. "Thank you so much, Father. You are welcome here. Since my son is not forthcoming with the reason behind this stay, perhaps you would be so kind as to let me in on it?"

The priest patted her hands. "Absolutely, my dear."

"All right then, I will put on the kettle and Ho'kee can start fixing up rooms for—how many?" At that point, she looked up, way up, to see a heavily muscled, beautiful Black man filling the doorway to the point she thought it might split at its beams. Her eyes widened. "Oh, my. I am sorry. I don't think this little retreat was built with the intention of accommodating men of your stature, Mr. ...?"

He reached out a huge hand that completely engulfed hers, but his grip was so tender, she felt only the softness and warmth of his skin. "Shemar, Mrs. Bidziil. Thank you for your hospitality."

To Ethel, it seemed the room shook with the timbre of his rich voice. An idle thought went through her head; she could listen to this man read the phone book and be entranced. She blinked rapidly and looked into warm, rich brown eyes. "My pleasure, Shemar. I do have one room that can accommodate you nicely. You will have the executive suite. It has a king-size bed."

"Hey!" Ho'kee retorted. "That's my room!"

"You are a freeloading, fridge-raiding hobgoblin. It is Shemar's room for as long as he needs it. Now help me get sheets and towels for our guests."

There was a commotion at the side door and Ethel glanced over to see Abe walk in, then step aside for a strong, mischievous old woman. As soon as the woman was in the house, she clasped her hands in front of her, smiled broadly and winked at Ethel. Ethel loved this grandmotherly-looking lady instantly.

Ho'kee leapt over to her and put his arm around Mara's broad shoulders. "Mom, this is Mara! She's an old witch."

Ethel's jaw unhinged and she gaped at her son, who she knew she had raised better than that. "Ho'kee! You apologize to this lady this instant, or I swear on Old Dan's grave I will..."

Mara belly laughed, and it was so infectious that everyone in the room laughed with her. Ethel tried not to join in the contagion, but Abe was laughing helplessly as well.

A lovely young Asian woman appeared from behind Mara and walked up to Ethel, extending a delicate hand. "Please forgive their rather sloppy manners, Mrs. Bidziil. I am Yenay. This is my friend Mara. She is laughing because she actually is a witch. A multi-generational hereditary witch."

Ethel smiled warmly at the sweet young lady. "Good thing you spoke up, Yenay. I was about to kick my son's arse."

"Ho'kee is a wonderful young man. He is funny, forthright, and headstrong. Not unlike his parents, I think?"

Ethel laughed again and inclined her head affirmatively. She looked down to see a beautiful little girl tugging at Yenay's jeans. Her gaze, luminous in large chocolate brown eyes, fastened on to Ethel, and she graced Ethel with a dimpled, heart-swelling, sweet smile.

"Hi! My name is Annalee. This is my mom. Is Ho'kee really your son? He is too old to be your son. You are very young and very beautiful."

Ethel had no idea what came over her in the presence of this child. She dropped to her knees to take the little hands that were stretching out to her. She gently took those small fingers into her own and a thick surge of emotion coursed through her body and mind. She felt like pure white light, completely happy, completely at peace. She felt a blissful smile touch her lips, and her eyes widened at the sense of light all around and inside of herself. She felt tears spring to her eyes, and she gazed at the little girl in wonder. "Annalee. I am so very, very happy to meet you. You are a very special little girl."

Annalee smiled again and nodded. "Yes. You are Ethel. You have a bed and breakfast now, but you used to track, like Ho'kee. You still do, but now you make people take cameras instead of guns."

Ethel was surprised. She looked over at Ho'kee who shrugged.

"I didn't tell her anything. Munchkin knows things."

Ethel watched her son, who was watching Annalee. She felt the ferocity of his protectiveness of the child. The little girl slowly, gently, disengaged herself from Ethel's grasp. Ethel doubted she herself would have had the strength to pull away. She stood up but could not tear her gaze from the girl.

Yenay smiled and also looked over at Annalee. "She is my daughter. You are correct. She is a very special little girl." Yenay's face clouded over. She whispered to Ethel as Annalee raced into Ho'kee's outstretched arms. "But not everyone wants to protect her. Some would do her harm."

Ethel did not look surprised. Her lips thinned. "There will always be someone or something that needs to destroy anything beautiful."

They both fell silent, watching Annalee being thrown toward the ceiling by Ho'kee and being caught in his large, strong hands. The little girl was shrieking happily. Ho'kee caught her midair and stood to position her two tiny feet on top of his own. She held onto his arms and allowed herself to be waltzed around the living room.

"Mamma! Mommy, look! I am dancing!"

Abe watched the tender scene unfold and picked up a remote from the table. Within seconds, vibrant music filled the big room. Ethel chuckled as Father Benedict took Mara in a somewhat clumsy embrace. Mara laughed and repositioned them both, now leading the dance.

Yenay smiled shyly as Shemar performed a courtly bow and extended his hand toward her.

"May I have the pleasure of this dance, my lady?"

The striking couple glided easily between the two other couples. Annalee continued to chirp happily, and Ethel watched her. The child was incredible. Her touch alone eliminated Ethel's frustration and confusion over the impromptu slumber party of odd people her son had foisted on her. She felt nothing but love, acceptance, and warmth as she kept her eyes on the little girl.

Her connection with the tableau in front of her was broken when a slightly accented, lilting masculine voice filled the room.

"Hi, honeys! I'm home!"

Ethel turned and saw in her foyer, the most beautiful man she had ever seen in her life, or even in her dreams. She inadvertently gasped, and unconsciously continued to stare. Declan smiled at her, and she felt a hot flush begin in her solar plexus and branch out to the rest of her body. The Others waved and shouted hellos to Declan but did not stop dancing. Abe watched his wife watching Declan.

He strode to the handsome young man and stretched out his hand. "Abe Bidziil. The lovely lady is my wife, Ethel."

Ethel berated herself inwardly and stepped forward to shake Declan's hand.

"Declan O'Neill. We are in your debt for this, Mr. and Mrs. Bidziil."

Ethel took the young man's hand and looked into those dark blue eyes. She knew for certain this man had the ability to read her thoughts. She gave herself a mental shake and spoke to him. "Abe and Ethel will do nicely, thank you, Declan. I have a few questions, and my son is being his usual taciturn self. The lovely priest was going to fill me in, but he appears to be otherwise engaged. Do you think we could talk over tea?"

Declan looked into the room and a devastating smile lit up his face, accenting the slight lines around his mouth. "Well, the old devil is cutting a rug with the Russian Babushka," he chuckled. "Absolutely, Ethel. I welcome that. Brighid said to give you, I mean, I think Ho'kee might have mentioned that you are a Nanaimo bar aficionado. I brought some, just made."

"You bake, Declan?"

"I do not. Woefully inept in the kitchen as Father Benedict would delightedly tell you. My friend made these."

"*Oh*! Nanaimo bars!" Ho'kee exclaimed and danced Annalee into the foyer before lifting her to Declan's height to scoop two bars.

"Dagda!" chirped Annalee.

Abe looked closely at Declan. "Dagda? As in the Celtic god of magic?"

"Yes. Part of the long story I am going to tell you once our dance party finishes their fox trot. You know of the Dagda?"

Abe nodded. "Doctorate in mythology, University of Alberta. Go Pandas."

Declan's disarming smile grew larger. "Dr. Bidziil! Am I ever glad to meet you!"

Abe beckoned Declan to join him at the long table. The Others gathered around, and Declan introduced them, as did Annalee.

"Shemar," Declan said.

Annalee corrected with, "Shango!"

Holding his hand out to the old woman, he said, "Mara."

"Baba Yaga," Annalee countered.

"Father Benedict."

Annalee giggled. "Raffie!"

Declan laughed and winked at Ethel and Abe. "That would be Saint Raphael."

Annalee looked up at Ho'kee's chin from his lap. "Woof!"

Yenay laughed. "She has problems with Mai-Coh, so Ho'kee is 'Woof' for now."

Abe looked at them all with what appeared to be bemused wonder. "Quite an eclectic group. Yenay, you mentioned that there were those who are not protectively disposed toward your child. An entity in particular?"

"Chernobog."

Abe gave a low whistle and shook his head. "Heavy hitter. May I ask? Annalee?"

"Quan Yin."

Abe and Ethel drew in simultaneous long breaths and gazed at the child. "My Creator. She is...she could be..."

Father Benedict looked both joyful and sad as he spoke the proclamation everyone was thinking but no one was saying. "The Second Coming. The savior of humanity."

Abe studied the older priest and said quietly, "And a little child shall lead them."

Mara passed her hand over the scrying bowl and peered closely. "Show me this man."

The water remained still. She scowled into the basin and spoke more forcefully as she swept both her hands over the water. "Show me the chosen Descendant of Chernobog."

The water did not move, its depths clear and clean. No images, no shadows, nothing. She sighed and leaned back in her chair. She was not surprised when Declan knocked at her door. He entered and then took a seat beside her.

Looking into the bowl, he said, "He has a block up. The Goddess pointed out that whoever Chernobog has chosen has been groomed since birth and is very good at avoiding detection."

Mara looked steadily at Declan. "You are the most powerful among us. Your gift is ancient but new to you. I know the Goddess is grooming you as well, but this man has several years more experience than us."

Declan took Mara's hand. "This is why we work together; we collaborate. We both have the gift, and if we combine our abilities..."

Mara's troubled eyes became brilliant as she turned this over. "Yes."

Declan moved his chair to sit in front of her. He reached toward her and leaned in. She leaned forward and took his hands. Immediately, the basin between them began to churn. Mara opened her eyes to look down.

Declan whispered. "No, not yet."

Shemar gently pushed the door open to see what Declan and Mara were up to. He started to speak, but stood immobile, watching the scene in front of him. A thin mist was beginning to spiral around the two seated people, eyes closed and clasping hands. The mist threaded between Declan and Mara as they seemed to be combining their prophetic gifts.

They each clung to the other as Shemar heard a low command that seemed to come from everywhere all at once. "Show me."

The mist thickened and twisted into a fog, churning threads of dark and light into a web around the couple. Shemar couldn't move; he couldn't tear his gaze away from the two. Their bodies shimmered with their ancestral roots, their lineage of God and Goddess apparent in their blurred features. A beautiful young woman with cascading dark hair and a wreath of ivy and white flowers crowning her leaned into the young man. The young man was bearded, strong, with the antler rack of a buck, and he leaned into her. The mist wreathed around them, pulling them tighter together.

The wreath twisted and expanded, stretching toward the ceiling, and plunging its way through the roof.

Outside, the little red fox whimpered, pawing at the ground. Alerted, Ho'kee gathered Annalee up in his arms and looked toward the sky.

"Oh my God..."

Annalee thrust out her finger toward the rising, twisting mist moving from the house to the sky. Father Benedict and Yenay stopped gathering firewood and looked up. Ethel and Abe came out to the porch, then down to the group, when the priest beckoned them. All eyes turned to the mist, winding and undulating, expanding over the house.

"Look! The window!"

An ethereal silver glow lit up the window from the inside. A rainbow of colors caught the light. It was hauntingly beautiful.

"What's going on in there?" Abe asked. "I better go in and see."

Abe's arm was caught by his wife. She shook her head. "This is not for us. We may witness it, but we can't be part of it." Ethel turned toward Ho'kee, a look of intrigue on her face.

He moved Annalee to his other shoulder. "What's going on in there, Munchkin?"

"Baba Yaga and Dagda. They are talking. We can't hear them, but the Ladies can."

"Ladies?"

Annalee pointed again to the spiraling mist. All eyes were locked on it as it gathered speed and volume. It continued to expand and whirl quickly.

Father Benedict dropped his logs.

In the black sky, the thick fog was forming the Triple Goddess. Ho'kee clearly saw the young Maiden girl, the pregnant Mother, and his acquaintance in his dreams, the old Crone. He watched as their hands rose together and clasped.

Inside the house, Shemar stood back as the young Goddess and God continued to speak without words, chanting and calling on their brethren.

The young God opened his eyes and spoke forcefully. "Now," he said.

Mara's eyes flew open, and she passed her hand over the water in the basin. The water churned and spat, the depths blackening. The web surrounding them glowed more fiercely as a secondary, dark fog began to try to weave itself into the web, reaching for the young couple. They did not have much time with this portal.

They locked gazes with one another, entwining their fingers together to keep the connection, and demanded simultaneously, "Show me!"

An unholy scream split the sky.

The Goddesses held firm, their spectral figures circling in the air. The dark mist seemed to bump up against the silvery fog and desperately tried to find an entryway.

Inside, the Goddess and God looked into the basin, and a face known to both drifted to the surface. Shemar saw the reflection from his rigid position at the doorway.

He whispered, "Zlo!"

The basin flew from Mara's lap and shattered on the ground. The dark mist retreated as quickly as it had come. The web surrounding the couple began to fade, and Shemar watched his friends' faces and bodies meld back to their earthly images. The ghostly Triple Goddess form shot up into the starlit sky, and the window of Mara's bedroom once again glowed gently with candlelight.

Lorraine shot up behind her desk, her mouth open in shock. She listened as the scream strangled into groans, and heavy footsteps down the hallway picked up a running pace. The office door was flung open, and she stared at Henrik's pale and sweating face. She met his startled gaze as he strode past her and gripped the doorknob to the inner office. Lorraine shook her head slowly, as Henrik turned to stare at her, a look of panic on his face. She moved quickly from behind her desk to join Henrik at Zlo's office door, thereby committing the most heinous infraction in the office by leaving it unattended; she didn't care. Henrik flung the door open, and they both stood still in shock to see the great man Zlo writhing on the floor. She ran in front Henrik and kneeled beside her boss. Zlo was gripping his head in his hands, his face a contorted mask of pain. Sweat dripped from his forehead and upper lip, dampening his mustache and staining his collar. He squinted his eyes shut and emitted another howl that reverberated around the room, shaking the walls.

She put her hand on Zlo's shoulder. He looked up at her from pain-filled dark eyes, and she saw a glint of pleading in them that made her want to pull him into her arms.

Immediately, a furious voice filled the room on the heels of the scream. "Leave! Get out!"

Lorraine and Henrik looked at each other, nonplussed. That was not the voice of Zlo. Granted, the man was under a lot of pressure but lately, almost every week, he seemed to become more commanding and less accommodating, a different man.

At one time he talked, and seemed to listen, to his followers and employees. Now he barely acknowledged their existence. He was even looking different. His cheekbones seemed sharper, he seemed taller, his shoulders broader. A thought had been bugging Lorraine for over a week since their last tryst. She had fallen in love with those deep, dark brown eyes. On their last date, which had been fast, furious, and unsettled, she had noticed that those eyes were black. As black as squid ink.

Lorraine moved closer to try to help her boss to his feet. Zlo was still grimacing in pain, his hands clenched against his ears. If that voice came from him, he was a hell of a ventriloquist. A shadow at the office window caused all three to look toward it. They saw a thick, silvery fog twist sharply and shoot into the heavens. Another guttural cry took hold of Zlo as that voice rattled the window.

"Leave! Get out!"

Lorraine jolted when Henrik took her by the elbow. She wasn't fighting too hard to be guided away. Once outside, Henrick shut the door and heard the lock snap into place behind him. He wiped the back of his hand over his forehead. Lorraine swore she could hear her own heartbeat.

The two retreated to Lorraine's desk, shaking to various degrees.

Lorraine stared at Henrik and spoke tremulously. "We better do as he has ordered. I've never heard him sound like that. I've never seen his migraines this bad."

Henrik looked uncomfortable. "Shouldn't we call up an ER doc? Mr. Zlo didn't look so good."

"No!" shouted Lorraine. "He won't thank us for that. Let's just do as he ordered and leave him alone. I don't think he wants us to see or hear him this way. I think we might be in trouble just for seeing this."

Henrik gave a hesitant nod.

"I...I need a drink. You?"

Henrik shook his head. "You go ahead, ma'am. I will stay out here in case Mr. Zlo calls us in."

Lorraine nodded and went to the executive conference room in search of Glenfiddich.

Inside the office, on his hands and knees, Zlo leaned forward, resting his forehead on the ground. He carefully opened his eyes. The headache that threatened to split his skull in two was abating. A dull, echoing thud had taken its place. He drew his knees forward and sat back on his haunches. He closed his eyes and whispered, "Mentor. They know."

The room temperature plunged. The labradorite pendant against his skin began to burn the center of his chest. Zlo remained on the floor, the room spinning too rapidly to attempt to try to get up.

He heard his mentor's voice, "Yes, my son. It is not your fault."

Zlo felt chilled and then felt a fatherly hand stroke back a sweat-drenched lock of hair from his wet forehead. Zlo opened his eyes in wonder. The Mentor had never touched him before. The relentless throbbing of his migraine ceased immediately. The Mentor was crouched in front of him with a cruel, malevolent smile on his thin lips.

Zlo spoke, his voice raw. "Mentor, I failed you. I should have seen this coming. I should never have let them band together. I should not have let that child leave the hospital. I am responsible for them finding out about me."

Zlo took a ragged breath and continued. "I should have known that since I went looking for them, they would be looking for me. Mentor, they know I am your Descendant, I heard the old witch calling for me, and I saw her again, but younger, and with a young man. I was looking up through water, Mentor, and I saw them looking down at me."

The Mentor cupped his hands on either side of Zlo's head and looked deeply into the depths of Zlo's eyes.

The Mentor's eyes were a fathomless black. His words sounded kind, but the tone was cold and abrupt. "You were not prepared, son. Do you remember my telling you that I was going to protect you from your lineage being discovered until we were ready? Well, this odd-ball assortment of fans the child has collected also has protection from a very powerful source. This source obviously coached them into being able to throw off the cloaking spell we used. This random group would not have the power to do it on their own, they are merely human. They have some interesting abilities, but they are as mortal as you. You had no way of knowing they are being coddled by a higher power; you are not to blame. If anyone should shoulder some responsibility, it is the two men you used to discover who these self-appointed guardians of the child were. They failed you, son. There must be consequences for that."

Zlo kept his gaze on the Mentor, eager to accept this explanation. The Mentor stood above him and reached out his hand. Zlo gripped on, and the Mentor easily pulled the big man to a standing position. They stood together, the mirror on the wall reflecting the eerie physical similarities between the two. The Mentor put a firm hand on Zlo's shoulder. "This is the reason they will not come to you one-on-one. They are now bonded as a group, and that makes them more dangerous to our Vision, Nicholai."

Zlo felt shamed and whispered, "Anything, Mentor. I will do anything to stop that from happening, anything to stop them."

The Mentor smiled and tapped Zlo's cheek, stinging him slightly. "Of course you will, son."

Zlo watched the Mentor intently, a myriad of emotions rolling through him. There were fleeting seconds when he felt that as much as the Mentor had done to bring him so far and so high up in his career, they were not entirely on the same page. When they spoke of the Vision, and Zlo's idea for the forever home for the marginalized who could not live in standard society, he would see a glint of hatred in the Mentor's eyes. He would get a sinking feeling in his gut that seemed to be trying to tell him the Mentor had no love, and no use, for these particular human beings. But then the Mentor would smile, and his soft words of encouragement and understanding would ease that feeling.

The Mentor's eyes narrowed slightly as he looked at Zlo. This Descendant was more intelligent than any of the others before him, with a minuscule touch of empathy that the Mentor couldn't quite eliminate; and those both made him less malleable.

The Mentor was going to have to accelerate his plan, and he would have to be very careful. When plans were hastened, the threads holding them together tended to unravel, but the Mentor did not have any choice.

This group forming to oppose the Vision was already powerful, even if they were hobbled together by a precocious child. He had to find out quickly what was bonding them, besides the child. This was not an everyday assortment of old ladies and priests. There was something far more in each one of these guardians. They were trying to draw him out and they succeeded by identifying his Descendant. No one completely human could have done that. There was something else about each of them that he did not yet have a handle on. Now that they were working as a collective, they were a serious problem.

"Nicholai, I can assure you, these people are not as simple as you think they are. I need pictures of the people your men failed to gather. External interference has compromised my ability to see them in my mind's eye. We also need to find new men for you. The two you have, have been useless. I have one truly great man I will lend to you. He is fiercely loyal to the Vision and will be as faithful to you as he is to me. His name is Gorgo, and I will send him shortly."

Zlo, feeling stronger, leaned back against his desk to respond. "Henrik is loyal, true, and unquestioning. The other has shown a modicum of empathy."

The Mentor grimaced and shook his head. "Unacceptable. Completely unacceptable. He may remain within the Vision, but he must undergo retraining immediately. We will find him another form...I mean, position." The Mentor stood before Zlo and folded his hands in front of himself. "We cannot come this far, to have a group of self-proclaimed 'guardians' threaten to destroy what we have built, what we are still building. They have no right, they have no knowledge, and they have no respect for the Vision."

"I understand, Mentor." Zlo walked to his desk and leaned over. His fingers began to fly rapidly over the keyboard. "I have pulled up frames from security cameras. I have put this group on the screen for you to see."

The Mentor gestured for Zlo to sit at the desk, and he went behind the chair, resting his hands on Zlo's shoulders. "Nicholai, tell me the names of each of these people. You will feel a warmth behind your eyes. I am with you, in that time, feeling what you felt, seeing what you saw. We are together in this, my son."

The Mentor stiffened, and his hands tightened painfully on Zlo's shoulders. Zlo winced slightly as he focused on the image disturbing the Mentor.

They were both looking at the same picture but seeing different things. Zlo saw an elderly woman in old world dress, waiting on a chair in the long line of connected seats. The Mentor narrowed his eyes and saw, on the woman's forehead, the shadow of a crescent moon. He held his breath, watching that symbol of the Goddess glow a soft, but eerie, sapphire color under her skin.

Zlo began the introductions. "The old woman's name is Mara. She is some kind of medicine woman or fortune teller from Russia. Her family owns a successful restaurant in town. When I saw her at the ER, I had a strange reaction to her. She looked at me, and I felt this rage rise in me. I have no idea why. I am sure I am overreacting. She is some frail, helpless drain on an overtaxed health system, and I was already irritated. I am sure that's all, Mentor."

The Mentor grimaced. "She is anything but that, my son. In the realm I dwell, she is known as the Baba Yaga. I am sure you have heard stories of her in your youth. She is not to be underestimated. There is nothing frail or helpless about her. You were right to be wary. I did not expect her to be in this group. She is a formidable foe and usually works alone. She is not who I would imagine to be guarding a child."

Nicholai then enlarged the picture of a huge Black man carrying a tiny Asian child in his arms. "This is Shemar. He is the head of our security department. He has been around for a long time. People love him. I would like to terminate him. He is far too friendly and accommodating for someone in his position, especially with the panhandlers and addicts. We need soldiers, not nursemaids. Witnesses said they thought Shemar had been possessed when he demanded help for the child. It was in the way he moved, the way he spoke and appeared. Unfortunately, none of that was captured on camera. There seemed to be a malfunction when this took place, and the footage was stopped."

"Shango," the Mentor whispered.

"Shemar," Zlo corrected.

Immediately, Zlo's chair spun around, not propelled by anyone's hands. Zlo was a large man, and in excellent physical condition, but the Mentor lifted him by the lapels of his suit as if he were a ragdoll. The Mentor raised Zlo slightly above him and his icy breath, smelling slightly of decay, chilled Zlo's face.

"Don't ever correct me, Nicholai. You need to start taking this extremely seriously. That man *is* a soldier. In my world, he is known as Shango, God of Fury and Destruction. He is a loyal ally and a deadly opponent."

The Mentor dropped Zlo back in his seat and gestured for Zlo to turn back to the screen.

Zlo straightened his tie with shaking hands and then widened the screen on the next subject. "In-house chaplain, Father Benedict."

The Mentor sharply drew in a breath, sounding like a hiss. Father Benedict had one hand far up on Shemar's shoulder, and the other hand was clasped warmly in the big man's hand. His ever-present benevolent smile wreathed his peaceful face, and his little glasses sat slightly askew. Zlo saw an older, balding priest in an old-fashioned cassock.

The Mentor leaned in, his mouth a tight line. "St. Raphael." The Mentor pressed his palms together and inhaled slowly. His words were clipped. "Who else?"

Zlo gave his Mentor a look of concern. He had never seen the Mentor exhibit any emotion at all, but he could feel the older man's seething rage threatening to explode. Deciding, wisely, against saying anything at all, he pointed to the next frame.

A handsome Indigenous youth, about twenty years old, crouched on his haunches beside the old woman. His eyes were trained on Zlo, and his face wore a mask of revulsion. Zlo had not even noticed him beside the woman he'd had such a volatile reaction to. The Mentor seemed to have read Zlo's thoughts and verbalized his response.

"That is his power, Nicholai. He moves without notice and adapts to the most hostile conditions. He moves in the animal kingdom as the leader of packs and while he sees you, if he doesn't want you to see him, you won't. This is a Navajo shapeshifter. There is something more in this boy, but I need time to investigate. He is not a full-blood shifter, but he is something far, far more."

The Mentor did not seem as angry with the sight of Ho'kee. He seemed intrigued. "This is an interesting collective. All differing cultures, all differing spiritualities, connected by one common goal. That child. I know who she is. I've been watching for her appearance for a long time. I did not expect her to gather this kind of army..."

The Mentor's words stopped. He lay his hands flat on the desk. Zlo swore that if the Mentor could have gone through the screen to wrap his hands around the next image's throat he would have.

Declan was lifting a giggling Annalee into the air, her sweet face lit by dimples. Zlo was confused. The Mentor had seen the child before. Why this strange reaction now?

Suddenly, the temperature plunged a few more degrees and the Mentor straightened. His face was unreadable, but his black eyes became larger, filling the sockets.

Zlo said quietly, "Declan O'Neill. A local artist of some talent. He is becoming quite popular."

The Mentor's eyes glittered. "It can't be him. He would never be summoned by anyone, much less a child."

Zlo, remembering his most recent consequence to pointing out an error of the Mentor's, said nothing.

The Mentor leaned close to the monitor, his nose almost touching the screen. "Show me more of this man."

Zlo pressed the frame advance tab and Declan came to life. His brilliant smile matched the child's and his beautiful face tilted upwards.

The Mentor reared back, his head shaking slowly. "The Dagda. I was hoping never to see his image again. I did not expect him to be leading this band of interfering reformers."

Zlo stayed seated and watched the Mentor walking slowly over to the window.

The Mentor turned his head to speak to Zlo. "Nicholai. This is not a group cobbled together by accident. This is far more than I had imagined."

Zlo watched as that dangerous smile etched into the Mentor's profile.

"Fortunately, I thoroughly enjoy a good battle. This one will be epic." The Mentor turned to face Zlo squarely. "Nicholai. These people are like you. They are Descendants."

Zlo looked crestfallen. He knew how powerful he was with the Mentor. Now there were six others on the opposite side of the Vision, just as powerful. Nicholai could almost see the years of work and time he and the Mentor had invested being flushed. His chest felt heavy. He looked wearily at the Mentor, who was regarding him impassively.

"Nicholai. I am going to help you achieve the Vision. However, this next step will require great courage and personal sacrifice. Since you have been under my guidance, you have achieved successes most people only dream of. You have had possessions—cars, houses, boats. You have had any lover you set your eyes upon. You have had more money than you could spend in a lifetime. You have wanted for nothing, as long as you have pursued and preached the Vision. And many times, when you made those morally questionable deals, seduced those lovers knowing you would never want them again after their submission, preached words that sounded foreign on your own tongue, did you not wonder how this was all happening? What would eventually be the cost? No. Because you were never your true self. You have been part of me since we joined hands when you were a child. I have been infiltrating your body, mind, and soul since you were born. You were created for me, Nicholai, in my image."

Zlo gazed dumbfounded into those depthless eyes of his ancient lineage. His mouth dropped open, a shallow breath filling his constricting chest.

"Son, I will need you to tell me that you are mine—body, mind, and soul. If you say those words with utter conviction, my very essence will enter your being and you will never feel the same. You will never have felt so powerful, so in control, so attuned to everything going on around you. You will never have felt so feared and worshipped. Nicholai, you will never be the same man again. We will be truly together, in this realm. Will you say those words, my son?"

Zlo remembered his father telling him that if the Mentor asked his Descendant of this, there was no greater honor. The Descendant was truly the chosen one. In the recesses of his mind, a faint voice called to what was left of his own psyche, a voice he remembered from childhood when the Mentor first entwined his fingers in Zlo's. He remembered seeing an image behind the Mentor, a veiled older woman with a calm and gentle voice.

All these years later, he heard her again. *"Nicholai, it is not too late. This is not your battle. This does not have to be the end of your life. Nicholai, there is a child waiting to be born to you. There is still time to break from Chernobog and help for you to do it. You may still make the decision to live to ensure the survival of humanity, not the eradication of it."*

Zlo stared at the Mentor, all the pieces of his life puzzle falling into place. He lifted his gaze over the Mentor's shoulder and saw the older woman again. Her lined face was troubled. He wondered briefly why she was here. He remembered being told that she would appear at the time of someone's impending death. His mind was horribly clear. "Chernobog? I am the Descendant of the Black God?"

Chernobog's eyes slitted like snake pupils.

Zlo looked at the Veiled One, ghostly and graceful. He looked back at Chernobog, and his voice shook, "There was never going to be a facility, an institute, for the marginalized. There was never going to be genetic perfection through science and selection. This is all leading up to mass eradication, of all human beings."

Chernobog's snake eyes did not blink. His voice became wrapped in a distinct hiss. "You always were brilliant, you had so much potential. You were useful to a point, but you have become a liability. I no longer have time to build you into the leader you could have been. We do not share the same Vision. Yours is a perfect society of perfect people. Mine is an earth completely free of humanity. You still have hope for mankind, even if it is a society that you yourself create. Unfortunately, this hope is going to be the death of you. I can't eradicate this trait from you, so I must eradicate your being. I will be taking possession of your vessel now."

Chernobog stretched his hand; its tendons lengthening and tightening as his nails became talons.

Zlo shook his head slowly and reached out his hand to the Mentor in acceptance.

The Veiled One lifted the covering from her face. A silver tear slid from her clear, crystal eyes.

The Crone reached her own hand out toward Zlo, her voice haunting and clear, *"Do not speak the words, Nicholai. You still have the chance to help with man's salvation, instead of his demise."*

Chernobog's firm voice overrode that of the Crone. "Nicholai. You were only born to serve me. You were created for me. Everything you have done, everything you have become, was because of me."

Zlo closed his eyes. The labradorite flashed blue and began to glow.

He spoke the words.

Part Two

Chapter Ten

Y enay and Abe got on either side of Ho'kee and lifted him to a standing position. His hands were still clamped tightly over his ears, shielding them from the scream. His eyes were wild with pain. He looked beseechingly at his mother as she placed her hands on either side of his face.

"It's over, honey. The screaming has stopped."

Ho'kee gingerly removed his hands and winced slightly as the little red fox emitted a high-pitched whine. Ethel looked sternly at the small animal. It caught her gaze, folded down its ears and curled up into a ball with his bushy tail covering his nose. The crow above him blinked but stayed silent. The bull-frog on the stump beside the fox groaned out a low, rolling croak.

Inside, Declan looked up to see Shemar's expression turn grim.

"I never did like that sleazeball," Shemar said. "Now I know why."

Declan raised an eyebrow and replayed the reading of Mother Beatrice's mind in his own. "What did you find out, Mara?"

"Nikita was very thorough with her research. Nicholai Zlo was raised as an only child to a single father and a succession of nannies. There is no record of who his mother was. His father died unexpectedly when Nicholai was twenty-one. There was no service for Stanislaus Zlo. Nicholai built a reputation for having a golden touch. Anything he willed to succeed would do so and surpass all expectations. Anything, and anyone, he opposed went down in flames. He has the same reputation with his lovers. He has no children, no wife, no other family. He does have a reputation for being utterly ruthless. Some would say unconscionable."

Mara took a breath, letting the Others process the information before she continued. "He is the CEO of the Vision Foundation, which has the Haida Gwaii hospital under its umbrella. He preaches a 'Vision' that his followers are wedded to. Nikita attended one of these meetings with her father to gather information. The attendants were all white, mostly male. Judging by the appearance of the people who attend his high-priced fundraisers and dinners, there is no one under a very high tax bracket in those rooms. What more do you know about him, Shemar?"

Shemar bit out the words, "Take the most racist, misogynistic, elitist path a man can take, and this cretin will lead it. He has no qualms about throwing his employees under the bus. I would imagine his 'followers' get much the same treatment. Cloaks it well, though. He is a master of deception, all the niceness of King Henry VI, all the nastiness of Ivan IV."

Shemar was grinding his knuckles painfully into his palms, cracking them under his fingers. Mara winced, rose from her seat, and placed her knurled, warm hands over top of Shemar's.

Declan tilted his head slightly, listening to a voice no one else could hear. *"The collaboration was successful. You have found Chernobog's Descendant. It is Nicholai Zlo. Well done, Horned God and Goddess."*

Ethel held Ho'kee's wrists in her hands. Ho'kee pulled his hands away, calling out anxiously, "Annalee? Annalee! Where are you, Munchkin?"

Yenay and Father Benedict looked at each other, fear taking hold.

Yenay began to shout. "Annalee! Annalee, come to Mommy, right now! No hide and seek!"

Abe and Ethel's faces went taut, and they joined the small group as Yenay barked orders.

"Father, check the house. Abe and Ethel, outskirts of the forest. Ho'kee, you know hiding spots around here, check those out. I am going to look at the cabins and sheds. And when I get my hands on her and I am going to roll her in bubble wrap. Mara and Declan, could you do those things you do and for the love of all that is holy, find my baby?"

Annalee leaned over, delighted that the funny-looking little creature seemed to be studying her, bobbing its black and white head up and down. It didn't run so much as waddle quickly. She had never seen anything like it before. It looked like a skunk but not as furry. It kind of looked like that weasel that Gramma chased out of her chicken coop. It had bright, beady black eyes that were fixated on her. Annalee loved all animals, but this one made her a bit nervous. It was very cute but smelled awful. She squeezed her fingers over her nose and laughed at the honey badger.

"You need a bath, Mr. Weasel."

The badger stood up on its hind legs and pulled its paws up against its chest. Its nose pointed sharply in many directions in the air. It waddled a bit closer to her. Annalee softly clapped her hands together and went to touch it, but it scampered away from her. A few feet from her, it once again rose on its haunches and sniffed the air. It seemed to wait for Annalee to follow it.

The screech of a crow caught her attention. She swung her gaze up to a tree behind her. That crow that followed the pretty man around was kicking up a fuss on the branch. It was flapping its wings, making a shrill call repeatedly, and shredding the bark with its beak. The badger stretched its mouth in a wide, vicious snarl. It locked its eyes on the crow. The crow shrieked and dove like a missile toward the badger, its long, black talons extended. The badger reared up, its own massive front paws sporting savage claws.

Annalee's eyes filled with tears. She jumped up, crying, "No! Stop! Both of you, stop!"

Both animals were surprised by another human voice.

"Annalee! Annalee sweetheart, where are you?"

The crow abruptly ascended and the badger dropped to all fours. It looked above at the flying crow and emitted a frustrated scream. Annalee clamped her hands over her ears. The badger snarled and retreated quickly into the brush.

Annalee was broken out of her reverie and called out, "Mommy? Mommy, I am right here with Dagda's bird."

Yenay swooped into the underbrush and scooped up her child, squeezing her hard into her body.

Annalee squirmed and whispered, "Mamma. You're squishing me!"

"Annalee, you scared the life out of me! What were you doing?"

Annalee pointed in the direction of the now long-gone badger.

Ho'kee's soft, quick steps brought him to the spot where the creature was. He stood still, an expression of disgust marring his attractive features. "It stinks here, and not ordinary wild animal stink. It isn't anything I've smelled before. Decay, rot, and something else. Like a bog, but way worse."

A low, offended croak erupted from the bullfrog that had climbed onto a moss-covered log beside him. Mara tried unsuccessfully to hide a smile.

"The stench is almost otherworldly."

As soon as the words left his mouth, he dragged his gaze to Declan, who had come up behind him with Abe and Ethel. Declan's eyes closed as he tilted his face upwards and tightened his mouth.

Ethel stood beside Yenay, and gently started to plait Annalee's hair. "Sweetheart, what did you see here?"

"It was a skunk! But not a skunk. Like a kitty! But not a kitty. I called him Mr. Weasel. I think he liked me. I think he wanted me to follow him. Maybe he is lost." Annalee's eyes filled with tears again and Yenay stroked her back.

Ethel spoke calmly. "Oh sweetie, he is just fine. Tell me, was he a skinny little weasel? Black or brown?"

Annalee shook her head firmly.

Ethel smiled and tried again. "Okay, not your typical weasel around here. Was he kind of fat and waddly? Black and white and kind of stripy?"

"Yes! But then he and Dagda's birdie were going to fight! And he stood up! And he had really, really long claws and lots of sharp teeth and I was scared."

Declan looked over at the crow two-stepping on the branch and dipping his head in acknowledgment. Ethel exchanged a worried glance with Abe.

Declan and Mara exchanged a look.

Ho'kee's nostrils flared, and he set off in the direction of the creature, the little red fox darting out from the clearing and into the underbrush, following.

Away from the others, Ho'kee listened to his heartbeat. He picked up his running pace, feeling the forest floor rise up to meet his feet. His eyesight sharpened and his hearing become more acute. His mouth widened, his nose elongated, and he welcomed the familiar sensation of his arms extending to the ground and his chest opening and broadening. His ears pulled back as he picked up the stench of the creature and then raced headlong into the forest. He bared his teeth and gave himself over to Wolf.

Abe took out his phone and then scrolled until he brought up a picture. He enlarged it and showed it to the child. "Annalee, is this the animal you saw?"

Annalee took the phone in her tiny hands and chirped excitedly. "Yes! This is skunk kitty!" She wrinkled her nose again. "He needed a bath."

Abe held his breath and turned the picture toward Ethel.

She shook her head. "Here? Highly unlikely it's homegrown."

Declan leaned over to look. "What is it?"

"Honey badger. Savage creatures. They are cute...to a point. I can see why a child would follow one. Curiosity," Abe answered.

Yenay also leaned over Abe's shoulder and looked at the screen. "But what on earth is it doing out here? Is it a pet that was dumped?"

Abe raised an eyebrow, snapping off the photo. "This would make a lousy pet for anyone except someone as nasty as it is."

Ho'kee returned, picking leaves and twigs out of his hair. "This doesn't smell right. I lost its scent as soon as I got out of the immediate perimeter. There were no signs of it. No burrows, no claw marks, no signs of feeding or feces. I don't think this is a true honey badger."

Abe ran his open palm over his face. "I guess it's too much to hope it is a domesticated mixed breed badger weasel gone rogue."

Declan cast a veiled look to Ho'kee. The young man plucked a final burr from his hair and, in unconscious mimicry of Abe, ran his hand over his face.

Shemar emerged from the bushes and enfolded Yenay and Annalee in his arms. "Is she okay? Are you okay? What's going on?"

Yenay shifted Annalee to her hip and linked her arm through his. "I am taking her back to the cabins. I don't want her to hear any more of this right now, but you need to stay and hear this, Shemar."

Shemar's face was grim as Yenay left with Annalee in her arms.

Declan's low voice took on a warning tone when the child was out of hearing distance. "We know Zlo is aware of us. He knows we are aware of him. He is going to be more on guard and more likely to use his followers to get what he wants. He wants Annalee; we are in the way. He can't kill her as long as she is protected by the Goddess. But if he can get to her, and keep her isolated, he can keep her gifts and abilities from developing."

"Isolated. She would eventually die without human contact. More likely sooner than later. She is only a child," murmured Shemar.

"That would be his most desired outcome," replied Declan.

"He knows he has to get through us?" asked Ho'kee.

"He will not hesitate to kill us unless he thinks we each have something he wants. He may try to persuade each of us, or only a couple of us, to switch allegiance."

Abe sighed heavily. "How do we fight a Descendant—a disciple—of Chernobog?"

"We keep Annalee safe. That is our focus, our job. If and when we are called on to fight, we will each know. We stay together and we help Yenay and Tina raise that little girl. We are her village."

Abe's face was inscrutable as he stared at Ho'kee and Declan, standing together.

Ethel cleared the lump in her throat. "Ho'kee. What is it about that badger that you are not telling us?"

Ho'kee glanced up at the crow who was studying him intently. "It used to be human. It's been shapeshifted, but I have a feeling that wasn't voluntary. I think it was sent to lure Annalee."

At the cabins, Father Benedict hung up his cell phone. Joe was going to be all right. His road to recovery was going to be difficult, but he was showing strength and resilience. He asked Father Benedict to bring him his Big Book, a Bible, and a token for thirty days sober. The priest promised he would have these things in Joe's hands when he got back from this mission.

The priest looked at his own hands. Such ordinary-looking hands. What in heaven and earth had he done to warrant being given the gift of healing? He chided himself promptly. Many people were healers. There were millions of people blessed with the ability to heal others physically, spiritually, and emotionally. He was given this particular ability later in his life, but that did not discount the spiritual healing he had been able to provide in his many years of service.

He went into the kitchen to put the kettle on. He knew the Others had found the child. He wasn't sure how he knew, but a peace settled over him when a whisper blew in his ear saying, *"she is safe."* He had given thanks and promptly called the hospital to see how Joe was doing. He still could not fathom why the man had been beaten so badly. What had he done or said to incur such wrath? Or did he not have to say or do anything? Was it simply that he existed as a man who was not up to their standards, or would not fit in with this disturbing 'Vision?' The priest ran his fingers over his furrowed brow. He still believed in basic human decency. He had to, or he could not do the Lord's work.

He looked up to see Yenay stride in with Annalee in her arms. The child was stoic, but Yenay's face showed traces of tears, old and new. The priest walked quickly into the foyer to meet them. Yenay stopped in front of the Father, searched his kind eyes, and promptly lost the control she'd had up until now. She moved into the priest's arms and collapsed against his chest, clutching at his robe.

Annalee gazed up at her thoughtfully and tugged at Mara's hand. "Come, Babushka. Mommy needs some time with Raffie."

Mara clasped Annalee's hand and conspiratorially whispered in Russian, "I will show you how to make *medovik*! A sweet treat for a sweet tooth, made by a sweet child!"

Annalee clapped her hands happily. "I will find aprons! We are going to get messy!" she chirped delightedly.

Mara placed her large hands under the child's bottom and shooed her into the kitchen.

Father Benedict continued to hold Yenay quietly, stroking her hair and tightening his hug. "Father, you have to fix this. I know you can heal people, so please, heal Annalee and myself. Lay your hands on her and take away this 'gift' she has. Nothing, absolutely nothing, is worth the life of my baby girl. I don't understand why anyone would want to harm her, and I don't want to understand that kind of evil. I need this all to be fixed, right now!"

Yenay pulled away, gripping the priest's sleeves. He gently stroked her hair back from her forehead and his eyes reflected her tears as words became strangled in her throat. "She needs to draw and color. She needs to build dinosaurs with clay. She needs to play Pet Vet and worry about being out of tune on her keyboard playmat, not how she is going to ascend to become Quan Yin and who is going to try to stop her from doing that. Father, you need to fix this!"

"There is nothing broken to fix, child. I have a healing gift, but you don't need healing and neither does your daughter. You need answers and hope. I am afraid I can't give you the first, but I can attest to the other. Your daughter *is* hope. She is the embodiment of hope, promise, and love."

"No. She is a little girl. She will probably grow out of whatever this is, and I need to keep her safe, and I need you to stop it. Take it back. Give it to someone else but not her."

"Yenay. I can't. No one can. She is the chosen one. I pledge to help you keep her safe. You have a circle of warriors who will lay their lives down for her, and these are only the ones we know of right now, that are closest to us. When word of Annalee gets out, that circle will become an army of soldiers, worldwide. I have no doubt about that. Declan has seen it and I do not doubt that young man's prophetic ability."

He pulled her back into his embrace, emotion constricting his throat. "I could think of no better gift than to give you what you ask. A normal life, with a child who is not destined to be the Goddess of Compassion, the savior of humanity. But that gift was never mine to give, and so it is not mine to take away. We may pray for help, understanding, acceptance, and fortitude. I know these will be granted. But to pray that the gift of hope be recalled? I do not feel that prayer will be granted."

Yenay pulled back again and searched the priest's kind eyes. She saw compassion and concern reflected back, but not an ounce of pity. She straightened her spine and nodded abruptly. "This is not over, Father. I am trying to understand where you are coming from but forgive me if the only person in this world that I give a damn about at this moment is my daughter. Now, if you will excuse me, I believe The Goddess of Compassion could use her mother's help in the kitchen, where she can't even reach the counter yet."

Yenay wiped her eyes and entered the kitchen. She promptly yelped. "Annalee! You look like you are about to haunt something. Did you actually crawl into a flour sack?"

Lorraine raised an eyebrow and glanced at the clock, then at Henrik. Henrik checked his watch again. Tomas was going to be in major shit. He had been put on personal leave for retraining and was expected back today, but the only one who seemed to be actually expecting him to be at his usual post was Henrik. Henrik shrugged. Tomas was skating on thin ice. Any second now, Zlo was going to call them in, and Tomas was nowhere to be found. Henrik had told her that he couldn't think of an excuse he could use to save his partner.

It wouldn't matter. He would never lie to Mr. Zlo anyway.

On cue, the office door opened and Zlo's imposing figure filled the frame. He scrutinized Henrik, who stood silent, eyes facing forward. His rich, warm voice, which used to feel like a caress to Lorraine, now held an icy tone that made her shudder.

"Lorraine. No interruptions until further notice. Henrik, come with me please."

Lorraine put Zlo's office phone on 'do not disturb' and walked to the front office door to put the 'by appointment only' sign up. She could feel Mr. Zlo's dark, assessing eyes on her. There were times that look used to make her flush head to toe. Lately, that look held such little passion and such coldness, that all she felt was chilled. It felt like she was being sized up as a possible broodmare and dismissed as anything else. It had been a long time since they'd known each other intimately. He had started to become disinterested in any part of their weekly dates except the rushed, rough sex. He would then put his clothes on, glare at her, and leave. The man had changed, become more distant. His slightly self-deprecating sense of humor was gone. He no longer talked about the Vision with her. He barely spoke with her at all, except to cancel their date two weeks ago. This week, he hadn't even called to cancel. He simply didn't show up. He seemed locked in his own mind and body.

Lorraine realized that if they never shared a bed, or even a date, again, she would breathe a sigh of relief.

Inside Zlo's office, Henrik stood erect.

"I have a project for you, Henrik."

"Yes, sir. I am listening, sir."

"Due to emerging circumstances, it is necessary to accelerate the Vision in certain areas. One particular one, immediately." Zlo paused, making sure Henrik was hearing him, and not paying lip service.

"Tell me what you need done, sir."

Zlo narrowed his eyes, gave a tight smile, and continued. "I need you to assemble a large component of men like yourself. They must be loyal and unafraid to get their hands dirty. I want no questions asked; orders followed to the letter. This army will be an integral part of the next vital step in bringing our Vision closer to fruition. I need them to show no fear and show no mercy to those that oppose our Vision. I need more men just like you, Henrik."

Henrik was careful not to show how thrilled he was with the personal attention and accolades. He had waited his entire service to Zlo to hear those words. "Absolutely, sir! I am honored and will not fail you. I will begin recruitment immediately."

"Unnecessary, Henrik. I brought along an extraordinary man to head recruitment. You will assist him."

Henrik kept his eyes trained forward despite his concern.

Zlo crooked his finger toward the back corner of the office, and, seemingly out of nowhere, an Aryan man with a perfect crew cut appeared directly in front of Henrik. His smile was slightly lopsided. He gave Henrik an almost imperceptible wink from glacial blue eyes. Henrik's mouth went dry and his crotch began to warm.

"Henrik, this is Gorgo. He is my right-hand man and from here on in, your partner."

Gorgo pulled out his hand from the military pose behind his back and thrust it forward. Henrik gripped the strong hand firmly, and his eyes opened wider when he felt Gorgo's finger do a slight, intimate trace against his palm. They each pulled back their hands, reassuming the military pose.

Henrik cleared his throat and spoke in a slightly hoarse voice. "Sir. I am not sure where Tomas is. Will he be part of the recruitment?"

Zlo raised his handsome head and looked down at Henrik, a cruel smile tugging at his mouth. "My faithful soldier. Don't concern yourself with Tomas. He is on a very different mission for me at this moment. He is 'scouting' for me. I doubt you will see him again, Henrik. Certainly not as the man you once knew, but you may be secure in the knowledge he is still in service to the Vision."

Henrik felt the blood rush from his face but did not waver in his countenance. Zlo reached out to put a large hand on Henrik's shoulder.

"Go. Let me know when you two have assembled the Vision army. I will let you know by text where they are to report to. Until then it will be a closely guarded location. This is not an overnight assignment; this will be the army's life. They will live, breathe, eat, and sleep the Vision."

Henrik could not help the beginning of a smile altering his rigid features. He looked at Gorgo, who was staring intently and openly at him. "Sir, it will be the honor of our lifetimes."

Zlo slowly blinked.

Declan held Brighid's hand as she lowered herself into the chair beside the fireplace. She waved her hand in front of the cold hearth and it leapt to life. The logs crackled merrily, and warmth drifted out across the room. She kicked off her shoes and pointed to a blanket on the bed. "Declan, could you give me that blanket? I am a bit chilled. I take this form so rarely I forget how sensitive everything is."

"The form of pregnancy?"

Brighid laughed an explosive belly laugh that caught Declan off guard and made him laugh as well. "No, but fair enough. Declan, come sit with me by the fire. I want you to see something in the flames. I want you to look hard and long, lose yourself in the flames. Tell me what you see. Don't think, just relay what the flames tell you."

Declan sat at her feet, his back against her knees. She reached down and placed her hands on his shoulders. Her lilting voice was hypnotic.

"By my hand, my will and spell
We read the future, see it well
The paths if taken, where they lead
Who thinks what thoughts, who does what deed
This is my will
So mote it be."

Declan passed his hand across in front of the fire. Immediately, he saw the image of Quan Yin beginning to ascend from the ashes. Just as quickly, another flame twisted around her and pulled her to the base of the logs, wrapping her tightly. He watched as a fiery God in full battle gear, a powerful ax swinging at his side, strode purposefully toward Quan Yin and stood behind her. A macabre mask-like face stretched its mouth wide, wide enough to encompass both the flaming God and the bound Goddess. It looked like Zlo, but as the mouth opened in a scream, the face melted, and the mouth laughed. Three sparks above

the tips of the flames exploded, and their smoke twisted together, slowly circulating above the tableau.

Declan didn't blink as the flames rolled back, ban-
ishing the picture, and rolled forward again. He saw a
wolf running at breakneck speed. It was surrounded
by a green aura. He saw the crow stretch out long legs,
and its body became a house. He felt his eyes burn
because he could not look away from the image of
a Giant, a God, with long, flowing iron-colored hair
and a gray beard, the Dagda. The God stared back
at Declan, a brilliant light of recognition behind the
gaze. The God was on one knee, and in his hand was a
lethal club mace. The Dagda smiled slightly and flung
the club mace toward Declan.

Declan suddenly pulled back, and the fire swelled
within the grate, licking at the outsides of its confines.
Brighid firmly pushed down on his shoulders. Sweat
was accumulating on his upper lip. Declan drew the
back of his hand over his wet forehead and tore his
gaze from the fire. He looked up Brighid and drew
himself up. He stood over her and extended his hand
to help her up.

"The Vision followers are coming for her."

Chapter Eleven

Zlo narrowed his eyes, critically taking in the structure of the sterile and reinforced 'safe room.' The doors were self-locking from the outside, with both an automatic and manual feature. The lack of windows made the room dark as midnight and the marble flooring and walls kept the room cooler than most might find comfortable. The effect might be considered hopelessly depressing by some. For Zlo, it was perfect. He scanned the floor-to-ceiling door and a frown creased his forehead.

He looked around him in irritation. "Henrik!"

Henrik strode quickly to Zlo's side. "Sir!"

"Where is the food slot? There needs to be a slot that the guest can be fed through."

Henrik flipped through his worksheets on the tablet and pointed to one. "The designer said no slot. The door needs to be opened in order to provide food. The architect said anything else is inhumane and contradictory to the Vision's ideals."

Zlo's voice brought the internal temperature of the room down a few more degrees. Workers watched their fingers turn blue in a matter of seconds. "Did he? Please bring this man to me and leave us for a while. I must get to know this man who apparently knows my Vision better than I do."

Henrik nodded and left.

Henrik felt a fleeting pang of pity for the guy who was about to have to answer to Zlo. A few people in his employ had gone missing since the start of this project. The muffled, careful whispers said, 'creative differences,' but Henrik had never seen them leave...or come back. He had never seen Tomas again either.

Bubba was outside, bored senseless. He sat on a concrete step outside the peripheral view of other, more focused security guards and sighed heavily. He appreciated Henrik getting him this gig. He hadn't had much of anything since Shemar stuck his nose in his business and got him fired from the hospital. It was surprising to get the call from Henrik saying Zlo was allowing him to hand-pick an army. He didn't think Zlo liked him very much. He was still sure Zlo didn't like him much, but when he met the man again a couple of weeks ago, there was no recognition in those black eyes. There was absolutely nothing except a slight, cruel-looking smile. Bubba shuddered.

Zlo had been a lot of things when Bubba worked for him, but this 'new and improved Zlo,' as Henrik liked to call him, was nothing like the old Zlo. The complete apathy that Zlo looked at him with was disturbing. Bubba shrugged to get himself out of this alien reflective state and caught sight of a weasel in the distance. Wait. No. Not a weasel, too big. And striped like a skunk. Skunk! Oh man. Bubba drew out his pistol and took careful aim. He squeezed one eye closed and pulled the trigger. The shot rang out, ricocheting off a tree and veering wildly off course as the toe of a boot swiftly and painfully made contact with his ribs. Bubba rolled onto his side, crossing his arms over his ribcage and curling into the fetal position.

"What the fuck? What the actual f—" Bubba stopped mid-sentence as a face appeared nose-to-nose with him.

A pair of glacial eyes stared impassively at him. The voice was clipped and emotionless. "Inappropriate and unauthorized discharge of firearms is strictly prohibited and is a punishable offense."

The face hovered above him for a few seconds then rose into the sky. A very tall, crew-cut man of indiscriminate age casually emptied Bubba's barrel. He placed the gun in his own belt and stood with his hands behind his back. Bubba vaguely remembered this guy from the recruitment hall.

He had stood there, rigid and unblinking. The only person he exchanged words with was Henrik, and then it was to say either 'yes' or 'no' to the selection of an army candidate. He hadn't said a word to Bubba then and appeared to be done with him now. He jerked his head to the side, indicating Bubba rise painfully to his feet.

"Don't shoot the animals," the man warned. "Mr. Zlo doesn't like that. You are relieved of sentry duty for the night. You are ordered to review recruitment videos four and seven. Your weapon will be returned tomorrow morning."

Bubba was angry, his usual go-to response. He got up, snarled, and swung his fist toward the man who was treating him like shit. His fist made contact with the man's open palm. The palm closed over Bubba's hand and bent it backward, forcing Bubba to his knees. The man did not appear to be exerting himself at all. Bubba started to shriek, and the man stepped behind him and closed Bubba's windpipe with his forearm.

"You are not deserving of Mr. Zlo. You are a disgrace. You will be removed."

Bubba clutched the iron forearm with both hands, his face flushed crimson. He spit his words at the man.

"Fine with me, you white-eyed freak! Gimme my pay and I am—"

His words were cut off as a hard twist was made by the forearm, and Bubba's silent head lolled heavily to the right. Gorgo dropped the body to the floor and looked at it with indifference. He looked over at the badger, up on its hind legs, paws stroking its nose and whiskers.

Gorgo saluted him sharply. "Scout Tomas! Good day to you."

Gorgo spun on his heel and left the area.

Mr. Zlo looked at the sweating man before him with interest, but not the good kind of interest that Claude was used to. Claude was a good-looking guy, and not unaware of the many nuanced deliveries of intrigue that floated his way. Zlo was looking at him like he was in a petri dish, and he couldn't decide which instrument to use to start the dissection.

Zlo leaned against the front of his desk, his suit jacket flaring out slightly, and folded his arms across his strong chest. "Tell me, Claude, what is the mission statement of the Vision? Preferably in my words, but if your memory is spotty, use your own."

Claude swallowed hard and stared straight ahead.

"Sir! The mission of the Vision is to create and maintain order out of disorder. Clarity and direction out of chaos and deviation. It is to bring mankind back in alignment with its highest purpose and utmost purity. It is the elimination of everything and everyone that threatens to thwart the creation of perfect human beings. It is to discourage individual wants which have run rampant over the collective need for control."

Zlo nodded sagely, but that cruel upturn in his lip belied his serious consideration of Claude's answer. "Claude, as you know, many people find our Vision distasteful; abhorrent even. Some would go so far as to call it evil. They would seek to dismantle the Vision before it has completed its work. How do you suggest we deal with these proponents of this free thinking and free living that has effectively almost destroyed our God-given earth and threatens to eradicate its own kind?"

To his credit, Claude did not hesitate in his answer. "Sir! They should be evaluated as to their possible usefulness to the Vision, reeducated and, if they are not in agreement with the process, they would require elimination."

Zlo nodded somberly. "And if they were children?"

"Excellent opportunity to reeducate and retrain."

"And if they could not be swayed? Would you be able to eliminate them?"

Claude's eyes widened and he impulsively stared at Zlo. "Sir. They may be children of a lesser God, but they are still children. Surely, mercy would be in order."

Zlo shook his head sadly. "Mercy is an odious attribute and none of the Vision soldiers may have this. It is akin to compassion, which is, at its center, the antithesis to what we are striving for. It has no place in the recreation of this world. Unfortunately, you seem to have this dubious quality to some degree. In my experience, compassion is the death of communal order. There is no room for forgiveness of trespasses. Rules are enforced to maintain order. Mankind has been without a world leader for too long. A very wise man once said, *'things fall apart; the center cannot hold; Mere anarchy is loosed upon the world.'*

"When there is order, there will be peace. One leader, one Vision, one race, one creed. The earth will be restored. I am certain you still have *feelings* for the vulnerable."

Claude tried in vain to keep his disappointment from his face. He was to be discharged.

Zlo's raised his eyebrow. "You won't be of any use to the Vision as a guard. However, you may be of some service in scout duty. A fellow soldier, Tomas, showed mercy and did not complete an assignment given to him. He allowed an unfit miscreant to live another day to suck on the teat of this society's 'mercy.' He was given scout duty and has proven most valuable. He may never return to his former...position...but he is well regarded and protected within the Vision. You have probably met him, but for Tomas' sake, his physical structure has been altered. Is this something you would be willing to entertain, Claude?"

Claude nodded eagerly. He could stay within the Vision! He would be well-regarded! He wouldn't be killed. There was no downside to this agreement.

Zlo looked amused. "Rise, Claude."

It was the last time Claude stood at his full six-foot, four-inch height.

Outside the room, Henrik and Gorgo watched the members of the Vision toil hard at creating this living, working, teaching, and evolutionary space. Henrik stole a look at Gorgo. The man was inscrutable. He was physically perfect and had a ready smile that conveyed no warmth whatsoever. He took orders directly from Zlo—all others took direction from Gorgo and Henrik—and used words sparingly. Henrik thought he was halfway in love with the guy already.

In an odd twist to the guy's character, he was committed to a fat badger that prowled the place. It seemed to have free run of the outside grounds, and Gorgo was forever throwing food its way and smiling indulgently at it. He would coo at it, calling it his 'most secret and valuable weapon.' If its smell was what Gorgo was referring to, Henrik didn't doubt that for a second. The badger had come waddling up to him the previous week, but Henrik pushed it away with his foot. Gorgo glared at him but said nothing.

Henrik had put his hands up in surrender. "I would never hurt the little guy. I just don't want him hanging around me. He stinks to high heaven."

Gorgo's beautiful smile beamed and he laughed. "Stinking to high heaven! Oh, that is rich! I rather like that."

Henrik had smiled back in reaction to Gorgo's obvious entertainment but didn't understand. It was undoubtedly better that way.

Henrik watched closely as Gorgo supervised the installation of a monstrous, thick, lead door at the opening of a sterile, white room. Henrik wondered a little about this room. He thought it may be a detention room for Visionaries who were not adhering to the program but then realized Zlo wouldn't waste his valuable time on them. He shrugged off the annoying and useless speculation and concentrated on the task at hand. He knew this must be the room for the 'special guest' Zlo had made reference to.

Henrick caught himself feeling a little bit sorry for whoever this was, and promptly squashed that as well.

He looked up to see Gorgo watching him, with that familiar cruel smirk. Gorgo lowered thick albino lashes in a wink. If Henrik wasn't sure this striking man was flirting with him, he would have sworn he was being toyed with.

Declan continued to sketch rapidly as Shemar described what he remembered of Zlo's personal guards. Mara and Declan had been unable to touch Zlo's mind after the initial contact. It was as if Zlo's mind had completely shut down after that and each attempt to invade his mind was met with nothing. Declan had remembered the families talking about two well-dressed men who had made contact with them. Abe remembered them distinctly, having had a clear view of them at the end of his gun. When he started describing them, Shemar plowed his hand into his palm.

"Zlo's personal security detail! I knew they sounded familiar. These two went everywhere with him and were always outside his door. Between them and Lorraine, it is easier to get to the moon than get an audience with Zlo." Shemar leaned over Declan and pointed a thick finger to one of the pictures. "Even shorter hair. Crew cut. A bump on his nose, like it's been broken."

"Gee. Sounds like a real heartbreaker," Ho'kee quipped.

Yenay stifled a laugh, but Mara snorted in amusement.

Abe, on the other side of Declan, gave his own observations. "Eyes closer together. And a unibrow."

"Heartbreaker just keeps getting better," muttered Ho'kee.

Annalee, perched above Ho'kee on the back of the couch, walloped him with the iguana. "You be nice, Woof."

Shemar watched the sketch come to life under Declan's furiously flying pencil. "Whoa. Man, you are really good! You should sell your work."

Declan laughed good-naturedly. "Believe me, brother. I try."

Abe jumped up. "That's him! You got him! That's the guy. The darker-haired one did most of the talking. He seemed to be in charge."

Shemar scrutinized the sketch, and the names came to him immediately. "Tomas. And the other is Henrik."

Mara abruptly got up to gather her scrying bowl.

Father Benedict reached into his cooler and retrieved a sealed container of holy water. All eyes were on him as he brought it over to the table. "I thought this might come in handy. I believe we need all the help we can get in heaven, on earth, and whatever there is between."

Mara placed the bowl on the table in front of them. "Let's see what these two are up to."

Declan sat across from her and took her hands in his. He closed his eyes, but not before he saw a shimmering shape appear at his side. He opened one eye to look around, but it seemed no one but Declan and Annalee could see the gently undulating golden orb.

The child was wide-eyed, staring at the shimmering sphere. She smiled widely and did the familiar opening and closing of her little fists when she was making contact with one of her 'ladies.' He focused on a thought and sent it to the figure. "Brighid?"

The orb pulsed brighter. "Yes. I am here to help. Only you and Annalee can see me. Mara will feel me."

As if in response, Mara smiled softly. She closed her eyes and leaned her head forward. Declan inclined as well until their foreheads were almost touching. They wrapped their hands around each other's wrists and began to chant.

The Others quietly took chairs along the table, watching in fascination. Father Benedict held the container above the bowl and slowly began to fill it as the incantation started.

"We wish to see what eyes cannot
We need to know intention, thought
Of that which seeks to do us ill
We seek to bind and keep it still
This is our will, so mote it be
We pass our hands,
Blessed be."

Father Benedict had filled the basin, crossed himself, and whispered, "Amen." He stepped back and took his seat.

Declan and Mara did not move their hands, but he saw the shape stretch itself to accommodate the width and length of the bowl and suspected she did as well. It pulsed and swept over the surface of the basin. Declan saw the dark-haired man kneeling before the man they had seen before: Zlo. Declan gasped as his mind connected with Tomas's. A fear that Declan had never known filled his body, and he felt his own mind twist. His eyes flew open.

"What do you see, Declan?" whispered Father Benedict.

"It's so strange. I see the forest floor. I can't seem to see much above a log. Wait. I see an ocean and sand. I see cliffs. I think I am on a seashore, looking up, but my eyes don't seem very strong. I can smell everything though. I can hear everything around me."

Ho'kee narrowed his eyes and leaned forward. "I don't think Tomas is in human form anymore," he whispered.

Mara nodded slightly and watched the water. She lifted her hands from Declan's wrists and passed them over the bowl. An image rippled up to the surface. A face divided. On one side was the face he now knew as Tomas. The other side of the face was a honey badger.

Declan could see through the animal's mind and eyes, small black paws lifting to claw at a black-and-white head. He felt a pull from the creature's mind to enter the woods and set a course for somewhere else. There was a shriek at the window and a sharp scrape against the glass. Ho'kee leapt from the table and bolted outside.

Declan released the connection with what was left of Tomas; there was nothing there to help them. He opened his eyes and fixated on the picture of the second man in front of him. He closed his eyes again and bent toward the basin. He drew on the lessons learned from Inanna and used the ability honed by Brighid. Joining forces with Mara made them stronger and sent out a wave of energy, seeking Henrik.

In the basin, the image of Henrik appeared, his face sharper than the image created from Shemar's memory, but definitely him. Declan probed gently at first. If the man was working closely with Zlo, Declan did not want to alert anyone to his presence or powers yet. The wraith slid into Henrik's mind. The image in the basin slapped a hand to his ear. Declan could hear his thoughts.

My ear is ringing, Henrick thought. *That's annoying.*

Declan was in. He could feel Brighid with him. She nudged him forward. Declan began to speak the words that Henrick was thinking.

"Mr. Zlo is going to be so glad when he sees the progress made on this building. We will be worthy of the world we are going to live in when he is leader and his army rules with him. He will make me a General, like Gorgo. Weird name. Kind of a weird guy but I like him. I wonder if he notices me in any way except as a fellow Visionary. Why am I thinking about this?

Why is my ear still ringing? Oh man, those idiots are putting in that door for the special guest backward..."

Declan felt a firm pressure against the side of Henrik's face as Henrik cupped his palm, built pressure, and lifted it off his ear in an attempt to stop the ringing. Declan would not be able to stay much longer.

"Henrik!" someone called. "Why are you abusing yourself, friend?" Gorgo's amused voice drifted into Declan's mind. He knew that voice. He knew that name. It was so long ago though.

Henrik smiled sheepishly and looked up at Gorgo. "Ah. Tinnitus. Strange. I haven't been swimming or been around loud noises, other than the regular construction chaos."

Declan felt anxiety within Henrik. He read his thoughts.

Why is Gorgo looking at me that way?

Gorgo didn't say a word. He beckoned Henrik to follow him by crooking his finger. Henrik felt a momentary rush of adrenaline and excitement. He walked with Gorgo, side by side, in silence. His excitement turned to alarm when they walked up to Mr. Zlo, who was watching them with his cold, black eyes. Gorgo turned to Henrik and put his finger to his lips, indicating to keep silent.

"Master...I apologize...I mean, Mr. Zlo...our dedicated chief soldier is reporting a sudden onset of tinnitus."

Zlo's eyebrows lifted, then settled in an angry vee. His facial features became stonelike, and he took Henrik's face in his own huge hands. Henrik would swear Mr. Zlo was working out like a fiend. He seemed to grow stronger, taller, and more dangerous daily. Mr. Zlo bent his forehead to Henrik's own and a clear, blood-curdling *"get out"* was shrieked into Henrik's mind, causing him to wrap his own hands around Zlo's wrists as he crumbled to his knees in agony.

The shriek blew Declan's energy wraith out of Henrik's mind. Temporarily dazed, Declan's eyes became blank. Mara looked worried and pressed his forearms. She saw the golden orb of Brighid flash brightly from within Declan, and his eyes returned to focus.

"That's probably the last time I will be able to go into that mind. There are going to be blocks inserted."

Mara passed her hand over the bowl, and the water remained blank. Zlo was moving fast.

The Others at the table passed worried looks back and forth. They knew who the 'special guest' was intended to be, and they were going to die before they would allow Zlo to get his hands on her.

Chapter Twelve

S hemar sat by the bay window watching the perimeter with a close eye. He looked up at Yenay when she awoke and padded over to him. As he pulled her down into his lap and wrapped his arms around her waist, he smiled.

She placed a kiss on his head. "Your turn, security guard. Get some shut-eye."

Shemar nodded silently and caught the disquieting blue gaze of the large silver wolf outside. The huge, furred head shook, ruff and ears tossing raindrops. The wolf remained seated, its thick chest glistening in the dark. When it moved its tail slightly, the little fox yawned, made a circle, and dropped back into the warmth of the silver fur.

Shemar caught sight of the crow making a quiet, direct line from the top of the trees to the sheltered area above the unlikely pair. It grabbed at the branches, called out, and settled itself in. He glanced over at the bed beside the one he and Yenay shared. Annalee was sleeping peacefully, an aura of silver surrounding her. Whether it was from the moonlight or from the Goddess, he wasn't sure, but she was heartbreakingly beautiful.

Yenay planted her feet on the floor and stretched out her hand to him. "Come. The watch is changing."

Downstairs, Declan put his book down and rubbed his eyes. He looked beside him to see Brighid staring into the fire, her hands resting on her pregnant belly. She looked over at him, her emerald-green eyes warm. "Your relief will be down shortly."

Declan smiled uneasily. "Are you sure about this? Mara is...well...elderly. I can stay up."

Brighid shook her mane of amber hair. The cascade of silver in the front glinted in the firelight. "You have already been awake too long. Mara is ancient and quite used to working her magick in the dead of night. You may have complete faith in her. We do."

Declan looked fondly at the mother figure. "All right then. Will she see you?"

"No. Not yet. There will come a time, but not yet. She speaks to us, she hears us, and she can see us in aura but now is not the time for us to show ourselves to her. Only you and Annalee." Brighid's beautiful face took on a worried countenance. "Chernobog is planning and building. He has appropriated Zlo's body. True to his nature, Chernobog has devoured his young. His demon Gorgo is with him. He is every bit as evil as Chernobog and will also be in human form. Chernobog is aware of you all, knows who you are, and now knows your abilities. He is an impatient creature, given to fits of rage that don't lend themselves to rational thinking, especially when time is running out for him."

Declan stared into the fire before replying. "Time is running out. Meaning, he can't stay in human form for long?"

"No, he can't. He may have taken over the mind and used his magic to keep the body going but his vessel will start to decompose eventually. His magic is not strong enough to stop that process completely. He can't inhabit a human body indefinitely."

"Because he isn't human."

"Yes. That is why he relies on his Descendants and his followers so heavily." Brighid placed her hand on Declan's arm and squeezed gently. Her voice took on a slightly urgent tone. "We can help you, but we can't fight him for you. Do you understand? We will always fight beside you, but we cannot take your place in battle."

Declan's mouth tightened and he crossed his arms over his chest. "When he shows up, we will be ready for him."

Brighid shook her head. "He doesn't work that way. His followers have to willingly go to him. He can't force himself upon them or in them. Once they accept him, love him, worship him, then he has all power. Annalee is protected by this group, and by the magic of the Goddess. He will not hesitate to use deceit to get her to come to him. He can't touch her, but he doesn't need to in order to render her powerless. She is Quan Yin, but she is also just four years old."

They both looked up to see Mara enter the room.

Mara nodded to Declan and noticed that the empty rocking chair beside him moved as if its occupant had just left. She pulled out a cylinder of salt and sprinkled it generously around the room. She glowered at it when she noticed the contents were quite low. She'd used more outside than she'd thought. She put her hands on her hips and tried, unsuccessfully, to look sternly at the beautiful man. "You. Get into bed."

Declan threw his head back and laughed. "Mara! I thought you would never ask—or demand—either way, I am yours to do with as you will."

He bowed gallantly before her. Her eyes crinkled in delight, and she laughed with him, before shooing him out of the room. She took up her post at the bay window and lit three candles—two black and one white. She crossed her arms and watched for the devil.

Abe walked up behind Ethel and put his hand on her shoulder. She was at the kitchen table, a rifle in front of her. She had just completed the perimeter check of the house. The group was leaving the forest guard duty to Ho'kee and his disparate pack.

"Annalee still sleeping? Father Benedict?"

Abe nodded to both. "She is an angel. And I would take bets on our priest being one as well."

Ethel was thoughtful as she looked out the window. She placed her hand over Abe's and her voice was barely above a whisper. "Father Benedict. He seems to be getting physically weaker. Is there anything we need to know about him? Medical condition?"

Abe shrugged and raised his eyebrows. "I haven't been told a thing. And if the good Father knows, I don't think he's told anyone." He dropped a kiss on the top of her head. "Go to bed, my queen. Did you see Wolf outside?"

"Yes. He and his funny little gang have been circling the perimeter all night. They have chased off a few critters but nothing that set alarm bells off."

"That is one ugly frog."

Ethel laughed and clapped a hand over her mouth. "Shh! Stop that! Mara loves that odd-looking little toad."

"Good thing you beautiful women love funny-looking creatures. I would be wifeless without you."

Ethel kissed Abe soundly on the mouth, and walked away from the table, leaving the rifle. Abe settled in her spot with coffee. He watched his son, as a great silver wolf, wrestle gently with a little red fox.

Yenay spooned her child into her own body, curling protectively. She was so very tired. She didn't understand how this group of warriors for Annalee maintained their energy. They seemed unsinkable. They didn't seem to tire, even old Mara who was seventy-some years old if she was a day. The one exception was Father Benedict.

He seemed to tire more easily since she had met him. He was such a wonderful man. She loved Shemar, but even he intimidated her with his raw power. The only one she felt completely comfortable with was the priest. She could be vulnerable with him because he showed vulnerability. The others were... well...they were otherworldly, and she still could not get a handle on the Descendant thing. Even her daughter frightened her a little. Who and what she was going to become was unthinkable.

Tears slipped from Yenay's eyes. She closed them tightly and pulled Annalee closer to her. She wasn't going to sleep. She was just going to rest her eyes for a minute. She would certainly feel Annalee stir in her arms, if she did, and there were guards everywhere. She was just so very, very tired.

Wolf bared his fangs in a black-lipped snarl, his eyes glittering in the dark as he scanned the area. The circle of animals stood still, ears pricked, noses in the air. An unfamiliar scent had entered their perimeter. It was foul and heavy with danger. The crow was silent, tilting his head from his advantageous lookout point in the tree. The fox pushed his snout into the air, detecting which way the owner of the stench was going or coming. The bullfrog emitted a loud, silence-shattering croak, and Mara appeared at once at the bay window.

Moments later, Mara and Abe, with a rifle in his hands, came outside.

A large, male raccoon stood on its hind legs and took stock of the group of animals. It rubbed its paws together and drew them over its black ears. Its black eyes appeared silver in the darkness, shining brightly from its dark mask. It made little snuffling noises, not loud enough to warrant a full-on attack from the group, but its presence alone made them wary.

Wolf's eyes, glinting silver, locked on the raccoon. His glistening lips were drawn back from long, sharp white teeth. The raccoon did a quick assessment and decided that he had adequately pissed the wolf off. Now it was time to lead him away from the house. The raccoon emitted an ear-piercing scream and scrambled into the forest with the fox hot on his heels. The wolf, more cautionary, sank low to the ground and put his ears back, moving silently and quickly in the raccoon's trail.

Mara straightened in shock at the sound. Abe lowered his rifle and looked back at her.

"Raccoon," he said. "They scream when under stress. Could be an indicator that something is out there that shouldn't be. Wolf has gone after the raccoon, so has the fox. That tells me there was something about the midnight visitor that is not sitting right with our security detail. I'll follow behind a bit, but I won't go too far from the house."

Mara nodded. She looked over at the bullfrog on the moss-covered log beside her. He was moving agitatedly, and his guttural communication was constant; both very unlike her familiar. She glanced up to see if his new companion, Crow, was still there, but he was gone. Mara's eyes narrowed. Something about this whole scenario was off. Her witch's intuition was never wrong. She had learned to trust it over her 'logic' time and time again. She shook her head and decided to do a cursory check of the surroundings but no more, she had to get back into the house. Yenay would be wondering what all the noise was about.

Annalee's dark eyes flew open at the sound of the raccoon screaming. She was aware of her mother holding her closely and the quiet in the room. She turned onto her back, trying not to wake up Yenay. Poor Mommy, she was so tired, and she hardly ever slept now. Annalee was glad that Shemar was Yenay's boyfriend. She liked him. She could tell Mommy felt safer with him around.

Annalee's long dark lashes fanned her cheeks as she blinked, her eyes becoming accustomed to the darkness. Then she heard it; that familiar cute snuffling noise she'd heard before.

Very carefully, she moved out of Yenay's arms and slid her feet to the floor. She padded over to the window, iguana in hand, and looked down below. There, in a pool of light, the stinky weasel was up on its hind legs, its little paws stretching up toward her. Annalee, delighted, softly clapped her hands together and giggled. Yenay stirred, and Annalee held her breath. Yenay didn't move again. Annalee turned back to the window and opened and closed her fist to the badger. In turn, he rubbed his ears and nose, and stretched his paws up toward her again, his black eyes shining in the darkness.

"Are you hungry, Mr. Weasel? Why are you back here?" Annalee's smile fell when she saw the badger drop back to the ground, and move in a semi-circle, but on only three legs. He held one paw curled closely to his chest and had trouble balancing. He was hurt.

Annalee looked back at her mother and opened the door of their bedroom quietly and carefully. She paused at the staircase and looked around. She should get Shemar or Declan. She really should get the pretty man. She toddled toward his room but heard the little creature outside give a plaintive, small cry. She would go out and see Mr. Weasel first and tell him to stay where he was so she could get a grown-up to help them. Mind made up, she carefully slid down the staircase on her bottom so she wouldn't slip. Once there, she opened the kitchen door.

Mr. Weasel cocked his head at her, and it looked like he was smiling at her! He took a few tentative steps forward and stopped, reconsidering getting so close.

Annalee crouched down. "Come here, Mr. Weasel. I won't hurt you. I promise. If you come here, we can go wake up the pretty man and he will help you, I know he will."

The badger halted abruptly and rose again on his haunches. He stuck his pointed black nose in the air and sniffed. He tilted his head to the other side to focus on the child. His movements seemed uncertain before he turned away from her, limping toward the forest.

"No! Mr. Weasel, don't go! Please don't go! Don't be scared. I will take care of you."

The badger stopped, looked back, and continued to limp to the end of the clearing. Annalee looked quickly around her. Her outside shoes were on the deck by the door. She sat down and struggled to put them on. The badger watched her attentively. She stood up and her sweet smile brought dimples to her cheeks when she located the creature.

"I am coming to help you, Mr. Weasel."

She took off, following the waddling bundle of black and white.

Declan was awakened by a deafening yell in his ear.

"She's gone! She is going after that badger!"

Declan sat upright and tried to make sense of that half-baked message in his head. What kind of dream was he having that involved a woman and a badger? What had he eaten before going to bed?

"Annalee! The child has been lured by the badger!" Brighid was standing before him, surrounded by an iron-colored glow. Her voice was commanding. "Wake the others! Chernobog has put blocks around the child, we three can't reach her. She is completely focused on the badger."

Declan was already on his feet and flinging open the bedroom door. "Yenay! Yenay!"

Yenay's eyes flew open at the sound of her name. She reached over to gather Annalee to her and grasped nothing. A cold fear gripped her stomach and closed her throat. The bathroom. Annalee was so determined to go to the bathroom herself now she rarely woke Yenay to help. That's it, she was in the bathroom. Yenay lurched over to the bathroom and wrenched the closed door open. Nothing. She put her hand to her mouth. "No!"

She dropped to her knees and looked under the bed and then flung open the closet door, tossing clothes aside. She stared at Declan, standing in her doorway. Her voice, shaking, started small, but built quickly in a panicked crescendo. "Where is she? *Where is she?*"

Shemar thudded into Declan, knocking him painfully against the door frame. "What's going on? You are all yelling loud enough to wake the house. Wait, where is Annalee?"

Yenay's head began to shake, followed by the rest of her body.

Shemar went to her and grasped her hands. "We will find her. She is probably playing hide and seek." Even as he said the desperate words, he didn't believe them. He could feel the danger everywhere. She was gone. He glared at Declan, his eyes burning with fury. "Where are the Others?"

Abe and Mara came into the foyer together, looking up at the gathering on the landing of the winding staircase. Mara closed her eyes, and her face sagged into her decades of wrinkles.

Abe gripped the barrel of his rifle hard and shouted. "What's going on?"

Ethel and Father Benedict joined Mara and Abe on the first floor, shrugging into their robes. Father Benedict's eyeglasses sat askew. He fiddled with them while looking up at the landing. "Where is Annalee?"

Shemar looked below him. "She's gone."

Ethel tightened her robe, her mouth making a straight line above her chin. She shook her head. "No. No, she is somewhere in the house. We would have seen someone come in. There is no way anyone could have gotten past Abe and Mara."

Declan sighed heavily and pulled his hand over his face. "It wasn't a someone. It was a something. Chernobog can't take people. They have to go willingly. He found a way to make that happen."

Abe was out the door before the Others made the connection. "That fucking badger. She is following that fucking badger while we went looking for a raccoon! *Goddamn it!*" Abe stood on the porch, locking his dark eyes on the silver ones of the huge wolf in front of him.

The wolf's teeth, matted fur, and lethal claws bore bloody evidence that the raccoon had joined the spirit world.

"She's gone, Wolf. She went after the badger."

The wolf's huge back hunched forward and his eyes closed. He leapt with astounding grace for such a massive beast and heaved himself back into the forest. A blood-curdling howl reverberated through the woods. The crow, who had been cleaning its beak on the branch, stretched out his wings and answered the call with his own caw. It plummeted from the tree to soar above the wolf. The little red fox, panting and laying under the tree after the raccoon experience, gazed after the two and tried to get onto its feet again. The bullfrog behind him let out a loud reprimand, and the little fox sank back to the ground.

In the house, Declan took a shotgun that Ethel handed to him. It was locked and loaded.

Shemar, vibrating with anger beside him, had not spoken since Abe's declaration. His fury was barely contained in his tense body and seemed to be seeping out of his pores. Declan had a strong feeling that if Shango was unleashed at this moment, it may prove next to impossible to bring Shemar back.

His stomach clenched, knowing that this suggestion, or command, was even in his realm of thought. Anything for the child.

Declan knew Ho'kee was already on the scent, but it was hard to anticipate how much farther the child and the badger could be from here, and how far they had to go before Chernobog's forces would meet the two.

Abe threw ammunition at Declan, and gave him a long, hard look. Declan matched his dark gaze, his own eyes reflecting no emotion at all.

Yenay frantically pulled on clothes, her heart ramming hard against her chest, sputtering orders that no one could understand in her panicked voice. She tried to stop the rampant and graphic images running through her head, unable to get a full breath as each image inhibited her breathing further, but the spinning thoughts in her head refused to dissipate. Mara tried to put a hand on her shoulder, but Yenay wrenched her body away and pointed a finger at the group.

"I don't trust any one of you! Not one! You pledged to protect my baby girl, and she is gone. She is four years old! A child who was supposedly protected by the Descendants of gods has walked out of a guarded house, and for all I know, right into the hands of the one entity in heaven and earth that wants her dead! Get away from me, all of you! Get out of my way and let me find my baby."

She spun on her heel and slammed hard into Shemar's brick wall of a chest. He reached out to take her hand and she leapt back from him as if he were on fire.

"*No*! Don't touch me! You've done enough! Especially you!" She glared at Declan, her eyes shimmering with tears. "You convinced me she was safer with you, that this *thing* couldn't get to her if you were guarding her, and yet here we are—my daughter is missing." She clutched at her stomach as grief and fear gripped her. She caught her breath, steadying herself. Her words were low and precise. "This is my fault. This is all my fault. How did I not feel her slip out of my arms? She is my heart! Annalee is my life; she is my sole reason for being! I gave birth to that angel! I had one job—to protect her— and she's gone."

She sank to her knees, sobs tearing her from the inside out. Father Benedict moved in front of her and dropped to his own knees. He reached out and pulled her into his embrace, his hands stroking her hair. Her heart-wrenching sobs tore at his soul, and he clasped her tightly.

"We will find her, my child. We will find her, and we will stop him. This is not your fault, none of it. My child, you gave birth to a savior of humanity, and her village will help you protect her and raise her. Sometimes, that village will have to raise an army and do battle for her, like right now. But we will save her, Yenay, we will."

Chapter Thirteen

"Mr. Weasel, it's very dark and I am going to get in trouble if we don't go back soon. My friend Mara will take care of you. She has lots of animals around her all the time. Please, Mr. Weasel, let's go back," Annalee called to the waddling little creature. It stopped and looked back at her. It looked down at its lame front paw and back at Annalee. The little girl sighed. "Okay. I will carry you back. But you have to stay put! You stay right there, now!"

The badger turned in a semi-circle, sniffed the air, and plopped his bottom on the ground. Annalee clapped her hands and squealed in delight. She clambered up the hill and reached out to the badger. The badger took a faltering step toward her and then pulled back. It looked around itself cautiously, and crawling forward, reached its black snout to the child.

Annalee gingerly stretched her tiny hand out and touched the badger on his wet nose.

A large pale man with white hair and almost white eyes stood in front of her and smiled down. "Are you lost, little one?"

Annalee felt very cold despite the man's nice words and handsome face.

The badger shook himself violently and pawed at his nose and eyes. He turned pleading eyes back to the child and dove forward, sinking its teeth into the white man.

The white man didn't seem shocked at all but looked at the badger with disdain. "You fool. You touched her."

Gorgo kicked the badger away, but the badger charged toward him again, claws extended and razor fangs sinking deeply into his calf. Gorgo pulled out a pistol and took aim. Annalee shrieked and threw herself on the badger. Gorgo yanked back his pistol and it fired into the air. Around him, men in green army clothing came out of the bushes, talking into radios on their shoulders and holding what looked like huge butterfly nets.

Annalee became still and quiet. She looked up at Gorgo. "You are taking me away."

Gorgo smiled that bone-chilling smile again and nodded to Henrik, who advanced with one of the nets. Gorgo's words were kind, but there was no warmth in his voice. "We aren't going to hurt you, Annalee, I promise. We aren't allowed to, and we don't want to. You are a very special little girl. You are a butterfly, and we are going to scoop you up like a butterfly. We aren't allowed to touch you either, that's how special you are."

Annalee's eyes widened, and she seemed to be studying something around Gorgo. He looked around himself, disturbed at the child's composure and wondering what she was seeing. He watched her with interest as she gave a slight nod.

"You aren't allowed to hurt me."

Gorgo shook his head. "Absolutely not. You have to come with us to see a very special man who has been waiting a long time to meet you. We are going to take you to him very carefully, little butterfly."

Annalee watched him from inscrutable dark eyes. They were not the eyes of a child. "You should let me go."

"Dear one, the woods are filled with dangerous animals."

"They are not dangerous to me. You are."

Gorgo's jaw tightened, and a flash of anger marred his usually animated face. "Do not resist, young Goddess. It is futile, and the Others could be hurt in the process."

Annalee's stoic expression did not alter. She looked intently at the men beginning to surround her.

Henrik was beginning to feel very uneasy. The child wasn't screaming or crying, all which he expected. At that moment, she looked directly at him, into his eyes. He swore she gazed into his soul and found him wanting. All he saw in her was compassion for the badger and a tenacious resolve. She was four years old. How was this happening?

He felt a tug at his pant leg and looked down. That badger had its teeth in his pant leg and was tugging at him. He was about to kick at it, but there was something different about the creature, something familiar. He stretched his hand out to the creature, but a pistol shot tore up the ground between them, causing both to jump back. The badger bolted into the forest and Henrik looked up at Gorgo in alarm.

Gorgo walked over to him, and gave him his cold, thin-lipped smile. "The secret weapon has completed its mission but has been compromised. I do not miss when I shoot. Don't do that again." Gorgo reached over and traced a finger along Henrik's strong jawline.

Henrik felt a warm flush, followed by an unpleasant jolt in his stomach and an invasive, clear thought in his mind.

He's toying with you. It's what demons do.

He almost slapped his hand against his ear again, but remembering what happened last time, he held himself rigid and nodded brusquely to Gorgo. "I understand, sir."

Gorgo watched him suspiciously but said nothing. He turned back to Annalee, who was watching the exchange carefully, almost as if she was recording every word, every nuance. Almost as if she were no longer a child in that little body. She remained still as netting was cast over her, and she was raised off the ground. The collective stared forward, waiting for Gorgo's command. Gorgo scanned the area, his eyes lingering on the area the badger had darted through.

"Fool," he muttered. He put his hand on Henrik's shoulder. "You, our devoted general, may pick three others and stand guard here. Mr. Zlo has informed me that the child's self-appointed guardians are on their way to 'rescue' her. What a complete waste of time and lives. Mr. Zlo has directed that none are to be taken captive. Kill them. For this one time only, you have the authorization to kill an animal. If you see an extremely large silver wolf, destroy it on sight. If you notice it has blue eyes...you are already a dead man."

Henrik inclined his head abruptly and stood at full attention. Almost full attention. He could not get those words out of his head. *A demon was toying with him.* Why did he feel he knew exactly what they meant, but had blocked any part of his mind that would give them credence?

Ho'kee's nostrils flared as his massive paws barely touched the ground beneath him. He had caught Annalee's scent. For a brief time, it was only the child and the badger. Now there was an underlying scent, getting stronger with each lunge forward. Men, and many of them. He flattened his ears against his head in his run, but then he stopped. His ears pricked up, twisting, and his nose drew in the scents around him and in front of him.

There were too many of them for Ho'kee to take on alone, but he couldn't wait for the Others to catch up. Nor could he risk losing Annalee's scent. He caught an accustomed smell and turned his head to see the little fox gingerly stepping into the wolf's tracks. He heard a familiar call and looked up to see the crow gliding over the tree line. The crow landed and called back to Ho'kee.

The abduction army was not too far ahead, but they were heavily armed and there were at least two dozen of them. They were flanking the center soldiers who were carrying a child in an intricate butterfly net. She was alive and physically unhurt. Ho'kee crouched low and followed the scents.

Mara filled the basin with water and carried it into the kitchen, setting it on the long, low table. Yenay and Father Benedict sat beside her. Mara passed her hand over the bowl, recited an incantation, and peered into the water. An image floated to the surface.

Ethel was leading, her tracking skills second to none. Behind her, Declan and Abe looked somber, holding their rifles. Bringing up the rear, his face a stone mask, was Shemar. Yenay could tell he was fighting the rage building within him, aware that if he lost control of it, he would not be able to reign it in.

He needed to think clearly and be able to follow directions. He knew that Shango would not submit to anyone's direction. It wasn't time yet. Declan touched the vial of bioluminescent water Brighid had given him before they left. She only said he would know what to do with it when the time came. Mara sensed that Declan hoped Brighid's faith in him would be rewarded, as he wasn't so sure himself.

Abe and Ethel exchanged looks several times. Mara sensed their minds were on their son, far ahead of them, who, in typical Ho'kee fashion, would be ready to take on an army with his motley crew of creatures.

Mara passed her hand again. "Show me the child."

Yenay's eyes hungrily stared at the bowl, clearly desperate for an answer. An image floated up, an image only Mara could read. Her eyes filled with tears, seeing little Annalee wrapped in a net cocoon, carried by expressionless soldiers, all very careful not to touch her.

Yenay slowly shook her head. "No...no...please God, no..."

Mara looked up and placed her hand over Yenay's trembling fingers. "She is all right. She is unharmed."

"She is in the woods? We can find her in the woods! You can do that mind thing with Declan and tell him where she is!" Her voice took on a frenetic tone.

"I am sorry, Yenay. She has been abducted, but she is unharmed. They seem to have wrapped her in some kind of net. She is being carried. She is awake, alert, and watching."

Father Benedict whispered a grateful amen and crossed himself.

Yenay glared at him at looked back at Mara. "Tell Declan where they are! Tell him!"

"Yenay, they are tracking them. I cannot tell where they are. I cannot see where the abductors are going. The man who is directing this is being very careful. He has put blocks in several places. Declan is trying constantly to find a way into the abductor's minds. He has had some success, but it doesn't last long. He will not stop, I promise. We will get her back, Yenay. The Goddess will not allow them to hurt her."

"She is already hurt! How can you say that? She has been abducted! My little baby...the panic she must be feeling. She is wondering why I am not there, why I let her get so far without me." Yenay's face crumpled and she struck at her tear-streaked cheeks with the back of her hand. "This is bullshit. I am going to find her. I am leaving right now, and I am going to..."

Father Benedict reached over and took her chin in his hand. "Yenay. They are an army. A well-trained, well-armed one. They can't hurt her, but they won't hesitate to hurt you. Annalee needs you to stay safe. She needs you to be here when the Others come back with her."

Yenay slapped his hand and pressed her palms on the tabletop. She squeezed her eyes shut. "Fine. Fine, yes, I understand. I hate it, but I understand." She reached out and took Mara's hands. "Tell me. What else do you see? Tell me everything."

A quarter mile from the compound, Gorgo lifted his hand as an order to stop. His army stood still. He looked down at the body of a large raccoon. Whatever had killed it, had not intended to eat it. He scanned the area warily. He spoke into his shoulder, his words clipped and controlled. "My Liege. One scout was found dead. The perpetrator is not in the area. Initial scan appears that scout was attacked far from the compound but attempted to return to the site although gravely wounded."

There was silence. Then a dark, smooth voice filled his ear. "Leave the body of the scout. Continue to bring the child. Have soldiers fall back to the location of abduction and repeat orders to kill any human on sight. Whether they are part of the Others or not."

Gorgo dropped his hand and stood aside, the army passing him by. He stopped the rear guards. "You are to return to the location. You are under the command of esteemed general Henrik. You are to obey any order he gives."

The men saluted and turned back. Gorgo gave a final look to the scout and gently pushed it with his toe. He sighed and continued on.

Henrik listlessly prodded a patch of blackberries. Around him, Zlo's men stood with rifles in hand, watchful and alert. They didn't think for themselves or take action without direction. This made a perfect soldier in the Visionary army but a lousy conversationalist. He missed Tomas. He even missed Lorraine. He missed the hospital. He missed Mr. Zlo, the one he knew before he became whoever he was now.

Henrik had held the recruitment drive and was unpleasantly surprised when Mr. Zlo told him he was to be in joint command with Gorgo. He was prepared to put this guy in his place when they met again, but when that happened, Henrik was once again slightly flustered by this disarmingly handsome general. With all the other soldiers, Gorgo was rigid, direct, and merciless. With Henrik, he was attentive, respectful, and discreetly flirtatious—a heady combination. Henrik found himself lusting for this tall drink of white-capped water.

Henrik still believed in the Vision and was willing to kill and die for it. He was prepared to end the life of that addict at the rectory who wouldn't cooperate, just to rid the already overwhelmed earth of one more pointless drifter who demanded handouts and gave nothing in return. But Tomas wouldn't let him deliver the killing blow. Tomas had a moment of weakness, of compassion, that he tried to cover up as ruthlessness by telling Henrik to 'let the junkie suffer before dying.' That was how Mr. Zlo saw it, so in Henrik's mind, that is exactly what happened. That's probably why Henrik didn't see him around anymore. Tomas obviously couldn't handle the direction the Vision was taking. Tomas didn't understand how absolutely necessary it was that they ramp up plans to have Visionaries take over the leadership of the world before there was no world to lead.

Henrik continued to stab at the brush in his reflective state, and his hearing picked up a sound in distant woods. He tilted his head. A few of the other soldiers glanced his way, but he held up his hand for them to stay put. It was probably that pesky badger, always hanging around. Annoying creature, but for some reason he really liked it. He reached into his pockets for some jerky and decided to take a quick look for the little guy.

Ho'kee's snout was raised slightly from the ground, and his lips drew back in a black-gummed, sharp-fanged grimace. He locked eyes on the badger, who was peering out from under a canopy plant. The badger's scent was different, not as foul as it had been before, but Ho'kee's focus was on torturing the creature until it showed him where they had taken Annalee. Ho'kee knew the badger had seen him, and was watching him, but wasn't making a move to run away. Ho'kee didn't trust anything that went against nature, and this refusal to take flight or engage in fight troubled him. The badger was on his haunches, and it ran its front paws over its head, over its eyes, and down its snout. It was deliberately breaking eye contact and showing Ho'kee that although it feared him, it wasn't challenging him or running from him. It was almost as if the badger wanted to be with him. Ho'kee decided it wasn't the right time to kill the creature. At this moment, it was worth more alive than dead. Ho'kee didn't need help to track the soldiers, he didn't need its help there, but he knew in his heart that Annalee would not want him to kill it. She was compassion. She was mercy. He watched the red fox gingerly step toward the badger, and the badger slowly emerged from the canopy.

At that moment, Ho'kee heard a rustling ahead of them. His senses picked up one lone man, the scent of danger thick around him. He crouched low, his muscles coiled, ready to spring. His long tail fanned out behind him, still on the ground. His ears pricked to full alert and his eyes unblinkingly stared at the area the man would emerge from. He uttered a low growl.

Henrik heard the low growl and moved his rifle to a ready position. He looked up at the sudden shriek of a crow and lost his focus momentarily. He heard the spine-chilling howl of the great wolf before he saw a wide mouth and enormous paws reaching out with lethal claws in ready hooks. It was the largest wolf he had ever seen. No one would believe the size of this thing. Henrik's finger pulled at the trigger just as the wolf sank its teeth into Henrik's jugular. Henrik's last thought was the unbelievable blue color of the wolf's eyes.

A rifle shot rang out and the search party stood still, horror and disbelief crossing all faces at the same time. Ethel screamed, her mother's instinct rolling in her stomach. "Ho'kee! *Ho'kee, no!*"

She charged into the brush in a panic. Abe was close behind her, his face grim. Shemar's dark eyes were rimmed with red, indicating a simmering anger. Declan saw the fox and the badger come out from the brush together, agitated. The fox was whimpering, anxiously hopping and pawing at the ground.

Declan looked at the badger; paws reaching forward, no hostility or subterfuge in its scent. Declan closed his eyes and forced his way into Henrik's mind.

Nothing. There was no life there. Breaking his promise to Ho'kee, he forced his way into the young man's mind. A collage of memories greeted him. Childhood visions, an image of an old Navajo chief at a campfire. Memories of a life seeping out from a dying mind. He then forced his way into Mara's mind.

"Ho'kee has been hurt. Send Father Benedict. Have him follow the red fox."

The little fox darted out between Declan's legs, back toward the retreat. The badger turned around to look at Declan. Declan hesitated for only a second and felt a strong hand on his shoulder. He looked over to see Brighid, glowing beside him.

Her face was expressionless. "Follow the badger, he touched Annalee. He will take you to Ho'kee. I will clear the path for Father Benedict. We don't have much time. Declan O'Neill, it is time to anoint one of your soldiers. We will need the God of Fury."

Declan met Brighid's brilliant eyes, his own clouded with concern. "I am concerned we won't get Shemar back. I don't know that Shemar is strong enough at this time to overpower Shango when he is unleashed."

Brighid inclined her head slightly and did not break eye contact. "We are aware of that chance. Shemar is the only one who can make that sacrifice."

Declan's peripheral vision caught sight of a veiled, older lady drifting through the trees, her feet not touching the forest floor. He watched her glide, ethereal. "Is that Crone? Please, tell me she isn't here for Ho'kee."

Brighid shook her head gently. "She is not here for Ho'kee."

Declan turned toward the others who were breaking through the brush. Ethel's eyes were wild, Abe's were haunted, and Shemar's burned with a dangerous fury. Declan caught sight of the badger. "This way."

They broke into a collective sprint and followed the badger.

Father Benedict stopped, put his hands on his knees, and bent forward to catch his failing breath. His heart pounded so hard and fast he thought it might burst from his chest. He gulped air and gasped at the little fox, pacing worriedly in a circle in front of the priest. "I am coming, little one. I will give my last breath to our friend, but I have to have at least one to give him." He straightened and followed the fox further into the brush.

Ho'kee's breath was coming more slowly. His mind had slipped to a collection of life memories. He could feel his grip on life loosening, and he was so tired. He couldn't open his eyes, but in his mind's eye, he saw Old Dan, in ceremonial robes, smiling at him.

Old Dan squatted beside him and spoke, his voice low and reassuring. "Ho'kee. Son of Shapeshifter and Skinwalker. There will come a time very soon now that you will feel you must choose between the two lineages. Choose both. Embrace the dark and the light. Each has its power, each has its weakness, but together they create an unbreakable entity. You are moving toward it, Ho'kee. Do not resist the darkness. Welcome it."

Ho'kee saw the terrifying figure of the Keelut lurching its way toward him. It stopped short, unsure of Ho'kee. It dropped to its haunches and stretched out a long-fingered hand to touch him.

At that moment, Declan broke through the brush and kneeled in front of Ho'kee, reaching for his hand to find a pulse. Shemar dropped to the ground, tearing off his own shirt and shredding it into ribbons. He gently disengaged Ho'kee's hands, which were clasped tightly over the belly wound. He deftly tied the strips around the bleeding gunshot wound. Words drifted in and out, but Ho'kee couldn't focus on stringing them together. He was watching the Keelut behind them, and invisible to them. The Keelut's focus never strayed from Ho'kee.

"Gunshot. He's bleeding out. There's internal damage." Shemar's words were clipped, his expression grim.

Ethel fell to her knees beside Ho'kee and gathered her son into her chest, her sobs breaking unevenly. Abe wiped his forearm across his eyes and sat cross-legged at her side, his arms encircling them both. Shemar rose slowly to his full height, his huge chest expanding. Declan watched as a red aura began to seep from Shemar's body. It spiked away from him, creating sparks. Shemar's eyes had clouded over. The red that had rimmed them earlier was becoming a haze over his dark orbs.

Declan caught sight of Brighid in a copse in the woods, a small fire burning in her bare hands. He looked back at Ho'kee, who drew a last, catching breath, and sank into his mother's arms. Ethel closed her arms tightly around her son. A keening wail filled the air, sending all creatures except the badger scurrying further into the forest. Abe gathered them both, his cheeks streaming with tears.

Brighid's message entered Declan's mind. "It is time. Bring Shemar."

Declan stood beside Shemar and forced his way into the big man's mind. "Come with me. There is someone you need to meet, something we need to do. You will have vengeance, Shango."

Shemar turned his massive head slightly and regarded Declan from a place Declan could not reach. He knew his words had reached the right entity when Shemar turned his head again and stared directly at Brighid standing in the copse. He strode toward her, Declan close behind him.

Shemar stood in front of the Goddess, and dropped to one knee, bending his head in respect. Declan handed Brighid the vial of bioluminescent water. She opened it and touched droplets into her hands. She pressed a drop to Shemar's third eye, his temples, and his heart. He pulled out the curious little figurine he had in his pocket and gripped it tightly between his palms.

Brighid's voice thundered through the forest. "Ascend, Shango. Ascend!"

Declan stood back and watched as his friend's body and face twisted before him. Shemar slowly rose from his knee as his muscles expanded, heaved, and split the clothes he was wearing. Shemar roared as the red aura became a flame around him, erupting from within him, and his eyes became orbs of fire. Declan stood further back as the God of Fury roared again, his head and body towering over the majestic trees. He spread out his arms toward the mountains, seeming to tower over those as well. Brighid did not break eye contact with Shango.

She raised her hands toward him, and his great head inclined slightly. "God of Fury, Shango, you who are dedicated to the saving of the innocent and the destruction of those who threaten it, I come in solidarity to ask you to join us in the rescue of Quan Yin, and for the punishment of those who seek to harm Her. Does the Goddess have your pledge of allegiance to this cause? We will not seek to interfere in your justice. We ask only for the rescue of our child."

Shango's mask of fury did not alter, but he dropped the artifact at Brighid's boot-clad feet. It made a delicate clinking sound. Brighid did not move, but the artifact drifted up to her outstretched hands. The pledge had been made.

Shango, flames surrounding his body, walked in fire to a destination no one else could see. He did not wait to see if anyone was following him. For all his enormity, he seemed to pass through the trees and rivers rather than over them. He left no footsteps; he left no destruction of forest or wildlife. Declan looked over at Brighid. She held both the vial and the artifact. She nodded at Declan to follow Shango.

Her words were cautionary in his mind. *"Shemar will need you to be able to come back. No matter how much Shango fights you, do not give up on Shemar."*

Declan nodded, lifted his rifle, and followed the God of Fury.

Brighid looked down with affection at the honey badger, sitting quietly at her feet. She sank down and lifted the animal to eye level. "You did the right thing, Tomas. I cannot undo what Chernobog did to you, but I will show you mercy for your bravery. I will grant you a painless death, or you may continue to live in this form for as long as your life may be, amongst my forest creatures."

The badger wiped at his eyes and nose with his paws, snuffled, and wriggled. Brighid put him down. The badger looked behind himself apprehensively, and saw the crow and bullfrog behind him, also sitting quietly. The crow strutted forward and touched its beak to the badger's nose. The badger looked up at Brighid, tilted his head to the side, and waddled off to join the little group.

Father Benedict and the little fox broke through the brush, both following the unearthly keening of Ethel's grief. They stopped short. The little fox yelped, crying and pushing his snout into the lifeless body of Ho'kee. The boy's color had already begun to drain to gray.

Father Benedict clutched at the cross around his neck. "We are too late."

He felt his eyes fill with tears and he removed his glasses and knelt beside Ethel and Abe. The little fox cried and curled itself into a ball on Ho'kee's hip.

Father Benedict looked heavenward and clasped his hands together. "My Lord, I have received too many blessings from you in this life already. My life of service and gratitude has been a full and joyous one. Your servant St. Raphael bestowed on me a gift in this last year that I have been eternally grateful for. I ask you, Lord. I ask you, St. Raphael, to bestow on me that gift in all its abundance and all its risk, that I might, through You, give life back to this young man who has dedicated his life to the Goddess of Mercy and Compassion. He has given his life for the salvation of humanity. I beg you both, this world needs him.

"I am not a possessive or jealous priest. If there are entities surrounding this boy that would seek to intervene on the part of our united, collective, other-worldly intent to bring him back, so be it. We will need all of you. St. Raphael, let me once again be your healing hands."

The Keelut crawled forward and put its long-fingered hands over the boy's eyes, unseen by anyone except the white-clad Crone. It awakened the gift Ho'kee had been reluctant to accept—his heritage of both skinwalker and shapeshifter.

As the priest spoke, he felt the familiar icy twinges in his hands, but it was different this time. He looked down and gasped as his hands were engulfed in a green aura that throbbed. The aura spread from his hands, up to his arms, his shoulders, his chest. Father Benedict felt the aura overtake his entire body; the icy stabs were replaced by white-hot shards.

Abe and Ethel had stopped weeping. They were watching the priest in dreadful anticipation. The little fox unwound itself, looked at the priest, and grabbed at the hem of Ethel's sweater, pulling her away from Ho'kee. Abe put his arm around his wife's waist and pulled her backward as the priest leaned forward and pressed his hands against Ho'kee's blood-soaked stomach.

Abe held Ethel back from grabbing at her son.

In the copse, unseen by the group, Brighid drifted to the veiled old woman, whose snow-white hair flew around her in a wind-whipped torrent. Brighid lay her hand on the old woman's translucent shoulder and drifted away. The old woman reached up to pat Brighid's disappearing hand, a sad smile on her face, and she watched the priest in silence.

Father Benedict moved behind the boy and lifted his limp body against his own chest. He wrapped his arms around Ho'kee and pressed his glowing hands against the boy's bare chest. The green aura pulsed around him, and Abe swore he could hear a heartbeat in that glow. The aura rolled from the priest to Ho'kee, enveloping them both in its undulating coils. Father Benedict continued to pray, even though he was feeling weaker by the second. He rested his chin on Ho'kee's dark head, squeezed his eyes shut, and used every breath he had left to gather the boy closer to his heart.

The Veiled One cast her eyes skyward and inclined her head to an entity unseen. She folded her hands in front of her.

A thin, sharp blade of dark green shot from the sky to the priest. The aura swelled and buckled, obscuring the two from view. Abe and Ethel heard a cry and saw the fox dart into the green circle.

Slowly, the aura dissipated, leaving Ho'kee still leaning against the priest, but raising his fist to cough into his hand. He placed both palms on the earth and looked around him, confused. He tilted his head back and felt himself connect with something soft but unyielding. He saw Ethel and Abe run toward him, crying and reaching out before they got there, and the fox dancing in happy circles. He looked behind him curiously, and saw Father Benedict, clutching his chest, gazing at Ho'kee fondly.

Ho'kee snapped to attention, on his knees, and held the priest's face in his hands. "Father, no! Father, you can't do this. I can't let you do this!"

The priest patted Ho'kee's hand and smiled gently at him. There was a warmth suffusing him. For the first time in many years, he felt completely pain-free. He felt so free, he could fly. "My son, it was never in your hands to make that decision, but I sincerely appreciate the love behind the statement. My work here is done, and I am very, very tired."

Abe and Ethel sat on either side of the priest. Ethel started to sing a beautiful song, dedicated to the souls of the dying.

Father Benedict closed his eyes in peace. He felt very aware of an older woman drifting close to him. In his mind's eye, he lay his gaze on the Crone from his dreams, the elderly lady he had grown so fond of. "You are here! You are real!"

Crone smiled gently and reached out to cup the priest's face in her strong, withered hand. She was achingly beautiful in an ethereal way. "Yes, old friend,

I am here, and quite real. I am going to help you leave this realm and enter another."

Father Benedict smiled sadly. "I am glad for your company, old friend. But I must confess, I had hoped to see another dear friend that I have kept company with for longer than yourself."

Crone's smile widened and she stood up, offering her hand. Father Benedict reached up and took it. He felt himself drift forward effortlessly. Standing in front of her, she clasped both of his hands in her own and nodded behind him. "Benedict, there is someone here who has been waiting a very long time to greet you. You have much to discuss."

Father Benedict turned, and his eyes shone with glory, love, and peace. He dropped to his knees and was raised up by two firm hands placed on his shoulders. He looked into the face of unconditional love. "My Lord!"

Ethel continued to sing, and Abe drew Father Benedict's eyelids over clouding blue eyes.

Chapter Fourteen

R everend Mother Beatrice watched Annalee from the command center window, and she was irritated. Annalee sat cross-legged in the middle of the quiet, white room.

Why this child? She is barely old enough to walk or speak in full sentences. Why not that strange mind-reading young man? Or that feral Navajo boy? This is ridiculous.

She was very careful to keep her internal dialogue to herself. To speak these words was akin to high treason.

The Mr. Zlo she used to know would reprimand her for such thoughts. She was afraid the new and improved Mr. Zlo wouldn't bother to reprimand. It was more likely she would never be heard from or seen again. She liked the old Mr. Zlo better.

Sighing, she folded her arms over her chest and stared at the child who had refused all food and drink in the last twenty-four hours. She had also refused to speak. She didn't sleep either. She sat there in the middle of the room in that folded-up position, her eyes closed, and said nothing. It was eerie. This was not a normal child.

The Reverend Mother just wanted to go in there and shake the girl, but Mr. Zlo's strange-looking new 'right-hand man' had glared daggers at her, then leaned into her face and snarled, "You *do not touch* the child. She is the special guest of Mr. Zlo, and you do not speak to her or touch her. You do not want to know the penalty of disregarding this order."

Beatrice shuddered and poised her finger above the intercom to admonish the child. She did not mind being told what to do by Mr. Zlo, but she really disliked being told what to do by that peculiar man of his.

Honestly. This should be easy! People should be more than willing to conform to the Vision ideal. They should be lining up! A world of one race, pure and white. A world of one religion, devoted to a terrifying, possessive, and punishing God who would stand for nothing but absolute conformity. A world of uniform wealth and abundance worked for and owned only by those who deserved it. No charity for those with their hands out, expecting a free ride on the coats of those who worked hard.

Mother Beatrice was not a hard woman, she understood there were children, of course. However, under the Vision, children would be a luxury, not a right, and only those designated as worthy and deserving would

be granted that gift. The children would be cultivated, like precious flowers, in accordance to keeping
the world appropriately populated. There would be
no errors in these children. They would be perfect
in physical, mental, and spiritual health. This would
be possible because they will have been carefully
cultivated and then placed in a deserving woman's
womb. One father, one mother, maximum two children apiece.

Mother Beatrice curled her finger back into her
palm, watching the child in front of her. This little
one would not understand the Vision. She would certainly never have a place in it, with her odd little demeanor and her apparent 'gifts' which seemed more
of a hindrance to the Vision than help. Seriously. Mercy and compassion had given this world an overflow
of homeless, addicted, self-centered, whiny, spoiled
'what about *me*?'s that the Reverend Mother simply
could not stomach.

She shook her head. The Vision was on its way to
fruition, she could feel it. It was disconcerting that
Mr. Zlo did not seem as interested in the Vision as he
used to be. He seemed much more intent on 'eradication' than on reeducation. There was a coldness in
him these days that concerned the Reverend Mother
but not enough to warrant abandoning what she had
worked so hard for these years. He was probably just
getting tired. All he wanted was a sustainable world
of good people, and, for his work, he was adored by

many and hated by just as many. She really should be better about supporting his every decision and not questioning his actions. He certainly did not question her loyalty. These days, he barely acknowledged her existence. He was intent on the child. He had spent hours doing nothing but watching her, trying to communicate with her. He would sometimes smile strangely and whisper, "Remarkable. Absolutely remarkable."

Other times a mask of fury would take over his handsome face for a few seconds and he would stare at the child as if his look could kill her.

He and that Gorgo fellow had gone off to investigate when some distant warning signal had been triggered, telling her to watch the child. Mother Beatrice was not to let the child be taken by anyone and, above all, she was not to touch her. She swelled with pride, being entrusted with such a responsibility. She wondered briefly why Henrik had not been given the duty but just as quickly decided she didn't particularly care. She always thought there was something off about that man anyway. He and Gorgo were closer than two men should be, really. It wasn't right.

The enormous dark eyes of the child flew open, and that disarming gaze settled on Beatrice's own. She remembered the first day she met the child, how the little one had walked toward her in an unguarded, open moment before her mother had closed her grip and stopped her. Mother Beatrice leaned forward, the ghost of a smile tugging at her lips. The child's bow mouth smiled sweetly, and dimples appeared in her soft, chubby cheeks. She was so tiny. Ordinarily, Mother Beatrice didn't like children. They were noisy, smelly, dirty, and undisciplined; but this was not an ordinary child. An unbidden thought was thrust clearly into her mind.

She is very special. To all of us, as the human race, not just to your employer. You will be tasked with a life-altering decision, Reverend Mother Beatrice. It will be a choice your own conscience will have to make. Be ready.

That beautiful young man! He was in her mind again! She whipped her head around but saw absolutely no one. There weren't even any guards.

In the distance, she could hear a loud air siren and men yelling. She looked back at the child. She was still watching her from those mesmerizing, calm eyes. The initial warning siren was quickly followed by an ear-splitting alarm ricocheting through the building.

Mother Beatrice punched out the numbered sequence of the control room code to get out. She had been ordered to get out if the siren went through the compound, but to leave the child. Mr. Zlo had assured her that there was no doubt the child would survive. At this moment, Mother Beatrice had a gut feeling that was not true. She scanned the control panel and located the button that would open the door to release the child. The little girl rose up from her sitting position and stretched her open hands out toward Mother

Beatrice. The Reverend Mother Beatrice pressed the button and flung open the door, bending to scoop the girl into her arms.

Mara smiled as she read the bowl.

Yenay scrutinized her. "She is all right?"

Mara nodded. Declan had been able to get through to that old cow. Now, wrapped in Annalee's embrace, she would be the fiercest protector in that compound of the child.

Yenay slumped back in her chair and whispered, "Just bring her back, Declan. I don't care what happens to anyone else. Just bring my baby back."

Mara's eyes clouded as she passed her hand over the basin again, and an image of Ethel, singing a haunting requiem, drifted up. Ho'kee was behind her, his arms wrapped around her shoulders, and he was crying. She looked closer, and her own tears slid down her cheek and into the bowl as she saw her friend, lifeless, gathered against Ethel's chest. Abe stood over them, wiping at his own eyes, rifle at the ready.

Yenay reached out and touched her hand. "Mara?"

Mara patted her hand and spoke quietly. "Father Benedict has joined His Lord."

Yenay lowered her head and started to sob.

Gorgo was having difficulty maintaining his human appearance. His Liege was not attentive. They were both shimmering between their true form and the human bodies they had taken to occupy.

Chernobog had been weakened by trying to maintain the both of them for as long as he had. He watched his demon companion's fingernails lengthen, his back hunch forward and his face elongate. They had been so very close this time. He had seen his followers all over the world get stronger in the face of apathy and fear. So many countries' leaders falling in love with absolute power and falling in hate with signs of compassion. They had been so very close to eradicating hope, compassion, and mercy. So very close to eradicating the human race from the Earth. He knew when he saw the God of Fury advancing toward the compound that he would have to abandon his mission. For now.

It wasn't that he wouldn't love to do battle with Shango, it was that he was positive the Others would follow. The Mother Goddess had that vial of damned bioluminescent water which could ascend them all, and they were all willing to die for Quan Yin. While one God could kill another God, he wasn't about to start that war in this realm. He did not have enough power here. This was not his place, or territory. Not yet, anyway.

He watched apathetically as Gorgo continued to shift in front of him. That tall man with the icy good looks was no more. The body vessel crumbled to the ground, and the demon kicked it away with talon-tipped, webbed feet.

The demon watched Chernobog's human face melt off his chiseled features. The body of Mr. Zlo joined that of Gorgo. Chernobog nodded in approval of the complete sacrifice his Descendant had been willing to make for him. Well, not exactly willing, but he had been so easily overtaken, it was like taking candy from a baby.

Baby.

Chernobog's silver eyes glowed, and he focused his thoughts. He searched his mind's eye and saw that weak-willed, traitorous woman scooping Quan Yin into her arms. He watched coldly as the woman's body, mind, and aura changed. She was holding the child tightly to her, emerging from the room, eyes darting about, looking for any sentry that would block her. He saw her put the girl down and put her fingers to her lips as she negotiated corners, then tugged the child behind her. The woman was prepared to be directly in the line of fire to protect Quan Yin.

Chernobog's mouth was a grim line. Quan Yin was alive and well and protected. If he could have kept her just long enough, she would have continued to refuse food and water, and would have succumbed to death. He could have kept her chained forever. He may have been able to turn her to his cause, and she would have been magnificent.

The power of that child, once it had been polished and reached full potential, would be staggering. Oh, the things that could have been. He debated sending army personnel in there, but he was running out of time. He had to get himself and his demon back to his realm, and he was already weak. If he didn't go soon, he would get caught in some space, in some time, and he would not be able to continue his work.

He snapped his fingers, and the demon crouched at Chernobog's feet. He placed his skeletal hand on the demon's misshapen head and raised his hand from the ground up, wrapping them both in a tight black cloak. The two figures dissolved to particles—black, red, and glowing like coal. They disappeared, leaving the bodies of their human hosts lying on top of each other. The decomposition of the bodies, temporarily halted by magic, was now accelerating.

The sentry that had triggered the air siren lay dead on the perimeter of the compound, crushed under the foot of a Giant. He'd only had time to raise his head to see a burning God in warrior dress advancing toward the compound, and to say to himself in terrified wonder, "What the actual fuck?"

The colossus could not be called a man. His height and breadth were reminiscent of the Trojan horse.

He had slowly shed some of his size as he got closer to the compound, now within his vision. His eyes glowed red. He stopped in front of the compound and gripped his *oshe* in both hands.

His skin was obsidian, slick with a golden sheen. He wore nothing but a red warrior kilt, a beaded necklace, and red sandals. His chest was decorated with a white symbol, and the same symbol was painted on his upper arms.

The second sentry had seen a lot, and done a lot, in his soldier of fortune service. The sight of this God, and being so close to this unleashed fury, caused him to rethink his career choice. He really should have become a plumber, like his mother wanted. He raised his rifle and called out to the inner perimeter guard to sound the invasion alarm.

Shango strode over to him as the sentry dropped to one knee and emptied his barrel into the God. Shango swung his *oshe*, cleanly slicing the soldier in two pieces. Another alarm sounded frantically and a wave of soldiers emerged from the compound perimeter. Their noise was deafening; orders were being barked and followed blindly. He stood above him and opened his mouth.

Fire bolts shot from Shango's mouth, lighting on soldiers and consuming them while they screamed.

Shango reached the compound and raised his arms to the sky. His size reduced again to allow him to enter the compound. He would have to wait to demolish the building. He had to ensure the safety of Quan Yin first.

He swung his weapon, connecting with the 'indestructible' doors. The walls crumbled into piles of concrete and mangled rebar. He strode through the ruined frames of the compound, swinging his weapon, striking at the human and inanimate with equal fury. The sword was covered in blood, hair, and body matter. Bits of concrete and dust clung to the wet remains.

The second-in-command watched from a far tower as the outer compound fell in front of him. There was clearly no mercy in this rampage. This God was uninterested in taking prisoners or hostages. The soldiers had thrown everything they had at Shango, and still, he came forward.

There was only one thing left to do. He would follow the orders of Mr. Zlo to his own death. He reached over to press the black button which would implode the entire compound, beginning with the control room. Neither the special guest nor the Reverend Mother was to be spared. He hesitated for only a second, then pushed it to activate the sequence.

His mouth set in a grim line as he pulled his pistol from his belt and pressed it against his temple.

Declan and Wolf stopped short in their race to follow Shango's footsteps. Declan covered his ears as the compression waves from the implosion thundered through the ground, shaking the trees. Chunks of debris flew over them as they both crouched low to the ground but continued to move forward. Declan heard Brighid in his mind.

"Hurry, Declan. The Goddess could protect Annalee from physical harm by Chernobog, but She can't protect her from humanity and the choices mankind makes."

Declan swore and fought repeatedly to reestablish a connection with Shemar, without success. He attempted to contact Shango but was blocked. He then grappled to establish a connection with Mother Beatrice and Annalee. He knew Shango would not hurt Annalee; she was his reason for ascending, for this rampage. He also knew Mother Beatrice would not be spared.

"Where are you?" He forced himself into the frantic mind of Reverend Mother Beatrice. He saw, through her mind's eye, a labyrinth of concrete and steel, all imploding, all crumbling. He could see a faint trail of blood running from her forehead into her eye. He saw her hands come up to wrap protectively around Annalee's head, her arms tightly binding the child to her body.

Beatrice did not stop to question what she was hearing in her head, she completely accepted what was happening. She knew when she touched Annalee that the Vision was wrong. It was morally, ethically, and spiritually wrong and she had been blindly following it for years. She felt that young man enter her mind and, rather than fear the sensation, she accepted his presence there gratefully.

She had wrapped that child in her arms and, as she rose with her, she felt a strength, power, and unconditional love that she had never known in her lifetime. Warmth started in her chest and belly and radiated to every fiber of her being. She gathered the child tighter and felt scales fall away from her eyes and her heart. She felt hope. She was going to willingly give up her own life to save this child from anything or anyone who would hurt her. She whispered out loud, knowing the young man would hear her thoughts if not her spoken words.

"I don't know. I am just trying to keep us ahead of the falling debris. What is going on out there?" She reared back when an image was projected into her mind. The compound was being destroyed, outside and within. Bodies of Visionary soldiers were scattered everywhere; bloody, burned, and, in some cases, severed in two.

She saw an enormous man in ancient Orisha warrior dress. Wait...this wasn't a man, that was wrong. This was a Thunder God, a God of War and Fury. She held Annalee even tighter. "He can't have her."

Declan's words were soothing in her mind. *"He is here to rescue and protect her, he is one of her guardians. Like the Others, like myself. And now, Reverend Mother, like you. This is Shango. You knew him as Shemar."*

Mother Beatrice closed her eyes. Shemar. Shango. The episode at the ER. It was beginning to fall into place. She pressed her lips against Annalee's forehead, and the child tightened her clutch around Mother Beatrice's neck. "I've got to get her out of here before the building collapses on us."

Declan tried again to reach Shemar, but was thrown back by a light so searing, so bright, that he thought it would scald his mind. Shango was methodically working his way through the compound leaving destruction in his wake. Shango's only mission was to rescue the child, but the self-destruction explosion was bringing the building down on them all.

Declan's eyes searched the area for help and landed on the huge gray wolf bounding in beside him, growling and baring its teeth. It paused beside Declan long enough to push its snout into his shirt. Declan smiled broadly. "I can't tell you how good it is to see you, my friend."

Ho'kee began to weave his way through the crumbling corridors, snout in the air, guiding them toward Annalee. Ho'kee leapt over a heap of rubbish. Declan scrambled over, his purchase on the hill of debris precarious. Ho'kee guided him down the heap, side-stepping. They both landed on firm footing, both listening carefully.

Declan cast another message into Mother Beatrice's mind. *"Don't say a word! There are still guards around."*

Ho'kee was sniffing around a scorched area of concrete flooring, covered with ashes. In the middle lay two bodies. Declan recognized the face of the man from the image in the basin. Zlo, but in rapid decomposition. He sent a message to Mother Beatrice's mind. *"Zlo is dead. There is a second body with him, I believe it to be his henchman, Gorgo."*

Declan sensed the peace wash over her before she said, "But his orders live on. We have to find you two before the remaining guards do. Or Shango."

Declan knew he didn't have to worry too much about the guards. They were completely occupied with saving their own lives, for the most part. But there were a few willing to die for the Vision, and those were the ones to fear. He heard the screams of those men as Shango took hold of the fortress and cut them down mercilessly.

In his mind's eye, Declan watched the sun glint off the blade of Shango's weapon and come back into the sunlight dripping with blood. He sent another message to the prioress. *"What does it look like around you,*

Mother Beatrice? What do you see? Open your eyes but say nothing."

Declan watched through her eyes as she slowly raked her eyes over their surrounding area and then he dropped down to look Ho'kee directly in those startling blue eyes. "I need to put images in your mind. Will you let me in?"

The wolf blinked once, slowly, and its ears folded back in acquiescence. Declan started to move the images from Mother Beatrice's mind to Ho'kee's. They both knew what they were looking for now. Wolf charged forward, muscles rippling beneath coarse gray fur. Declan ran fast behind him.

Mara stood in the foyer, stoic. Yenay stood beside her, wiping away the tears streaking her cheeks. Ethel and Abe carried in the body of Father Benedict and laid him on the bed in his room by the kitchen. They all stood, lost in thought.

Ethel broke the silence. "Who do we call?"

Mara shook her head. "No one yet. We need to get Annalee back and make sure Chernobog is disabled long enough for us to ensure her safety. That is what the Father would want. Then, we call Cardinal Josef."

"Declan and Shemar went ahead. We haven't seen them since." Ethel paused, the next sentence a strangled sob. "Father Benedict died giving life back to our son."

Mara lifted her heavy skirts and hurried back to the water bowl. She passed her hand over it and saw the frightened face of Mother Beatrice, her lips pressed against Annalee's cheek. She watched with open horror as Shango decimated what was left of the buildings and the people within. The God of Fury's rage had been unleashed. She closed her eyes and pressed a droplet of water to her third eye. "Goddess. What do I do?"

The answer came to her immediately. She opened her eyes wide and nodded. She took Yenay's hand, leading her outside.

Surprised, Yenay went willingly. "We are going to get my daughter!"

Mara nodded and raised a finger. "Something is going to happen, and you can tell no one. There can be no fear about what you are going to see and be part of. Do I have your trust?"

Yenay locked eyes with the old babushka. "Absolutely."

Mara led her into the copse and faced her. She closed her eyes and raised her hands. She began to chant an incantation. Yenay watched, fascinated, as wind spun around them, slowly at first but picking up speed.

The wreath was dotted with thousands of fireflies, but three stronger lights within it were growing in size and they seemed to be breathing. The wreath was binding together with thick strands of gray, silver, and platinum. One orb in particular pulsed stronger than the other two and hovered in between Mara and Yenay briefly before drifting to the ground. It expanded upward and outward in a blinding flash. Mara opened her eyes, continuing to chant.

Yenay shielded herself from the intensity of the light.

When she pulled her hand away, the most beautiful woman she had ever seen stood before them; proudly pregnant, a sage-colored silk dress draping her body. Her wild red hair tumbled around her, a shock of platinum running down one side from her crown to the tips of her curly mane. Her emerald eyes glittered, and Yenay knew She was not of this world.

The beautiful woman inclined her head toward Yenay. Yenay did not know why, but she felt compelled to bend her knee and bow deeply to this otherworldly Queen. Mara attempted to do the same, but the firm hand of the Goddess stopped her, taking her elbow and lifting her to stand again.

Yenay was finally able to breathe a few words out. "Brighid. The Goddess, Brighid."

"Mother of Quan Yin. Mara, Descendant of Baba Yaga. Come forward, both."

Both women stepped forward, but Brighid moved to face Mara directly. "You need to go to Quan Yin. You will provide safety. You will take the mother of Quan Yin with you. The child needs her mother."

Mara closed her eyes as Brighid removed the vial of bioluminescent water from her belt. She opened it and pressed a drop against Mara's third eye in the center of her forehead. Yenay stepped back, watching Mara begin to glow from within.

Brighid's voice thundered through the forest, at once both terrifying and comforting. "I anoint you, Baba Yaga. Ascend!"

Brighid reached out sharply to pull Yenay away from the figure of Mara. Yenay watched in frightened fascination as Mara folded into herself, and the structure of a building began to take her place. Boards and floors appeared, a chimney and a window, frames, and a door. In seconds, a small, curious home was in front of Yenay.

Yenay turned to ask Brighid what had just happened, but the Goddess and the wreath had disappeared. The door was flung open and a wizened old witch, looking very much like Mara but hundreds of years older, greeted her with a wide smile.

"Mother of Quan Yin! Enter my home. We are to get your daughter."

Yenay remembered her pledge not to question anything. Refusing the command was not a consideration. Her daughter needed her. She took the Baba

Yaga's hand and entered the gleaming, warm home. The Baba Yaga sat cross-legged on the floor and beckoned Yenay to join her.

"You will need to sit. This will be a bumpy ride."

Yenay joined her, cross-legged, and immediately felt the house rise somewhat unsteadily, gather strength, and lift itself from the ground. Yenay's eyes widened. She whispered, "Are we flying?"

Baba Yaga laughed delightedly. "No, child. We are walking. Look below."

The old witch cast her hand over the floor, making it transparent. Yenay looked below, and immediately regretted doing that. She pressed her hand to her queasy stomach, but she couldn't look away.

Beneath her, the little house was rising on thick, scaly legs that were tipped with savage talons. Yenay couldn't stop herself from watching as the strong legs carried the house surely over the tops of trees. The house knew where it was going. Baba Yaga and Yenay watched out the window, seeing plumes of smoke rising from behind a mountain in the distance.

The witch closed her eyes, whispering again, and the legs of the house moved more quickly.

The sorceress smiled as she welcomed Declan's message. *"Baba Yaga! Brighid told me you were on your way."*

"We are almost there, Declan. I do not sense Chernobog or his demon, but I do sense Shemar is unreachable in Shango."

"Chernobog is gone. He and his demon fled their human hosts. Shango is destroying anything and anyone in his path that is not already being demolished by a detonation device. Ho'kee is with me. We are close to Annalee. We need your Safe House."

The thick, strong legs of Baba Yaga's house carried them closer to the compound. The witch halted their progress and waved her hand toward the door, flinging it open. She grabbed Yenay's blouse as the young woman bolted toward it. "Child. You are several hundred feet in the air. Declan will bring her to us, the door will close, and she will be safe. Be ready."

Yenay's eyes filled with tears, and she folded back to the floor, clasping her hands in prayer.

Shango tore his *oshe* from the ceiling, bringing it down in a wide arc, slicing open the chest of a sentry standing in front of him, as the man tried to pull the trigger on his rifle. Blood spattered Shango's massive chest, creating a disturbing image of the white symbols spanning his body. The ceiling split, dumping layers of debris on the cracking floor. His fiery eyes blazed. His mouth released lightning strikes each time he emitted a war cry. It was good to be back. It was glorious to be back. It was time he was back.

A sentry dropped his gun and raised his hands in supplication to the God of War. Shango did not seem to even see him as he strode forward, his *oshe* swinging, liberating the sentry's head from his body cleanly. Thunder rolled through the ruins of the building, echoing his roar.

In the corridor of the basement area, Annalee pressed her hands over her ears to stop the sound, and Mother Beatrice broke out in a fresh sweat.

They heard Shango's footsteps above them, and Mother Beatrice looked worriedly at the fractured walls. The floor beneath her developed fine, spider-web cracks, which began to expand. She held Annalee even tighter. She looked up to see a sentry bearing down on her, gun poised and at close range.

His words were clipped and emotionless. "Reverend Mother Beatrice. You touched the child. I have orders to destroy anyone who has touched her. Put her down so I only have to kill one of you."

Annalee buried her face into Mother Beatrice's neck and whimpered. The prioress would not risk it. She disengaged the child firmly and put her on the ground, away from the pointed gun.

She closed her eyes and cast off a thought to Declan. *"What do I do?"*

At that moment, a huge silver-gray wolf leapt over a six-foot pile of debris, clearing it easily. It had mesmerizing blue eyes that sparked with intelligence and focus. Its long ears were pinned back against its head, and it landed with grace at the Reverend Mother's feet. It pivoted sharply to face the surprised sentry and that second's hesitation of the soldier was all Wolf needed.

Wolf lunged, a muscled mass of teeth and claws, and snapped the guard's head back. The guard slumped to the ground, his rifle at his side.

The prioress looked around for a rock to hit the beast with when Annalee reached her arms out pleadingly to the wolf.

"Woof!" The child buried her face in the wolf's thick ruff. In turn, the beast licked her face and pushed its snout so forcefully against her stomach that she fell onto her bottom, giggling and holding on to the animal's fur.

Behind him, a filthy Declan pulled himself up and over the pile. Annalee put her arms out to Declan and started to cry. "Dagda! I miss Mommy. This is a nice lady. She came and got me from the room when it got all dusty and smoky and I saw the bad man fly away with a doggie. I think it was a doggie. It wasn't a cute one though."

Declan swept her up hard and fast, drinking in her sweet scent. Wolf stood at the ready, his eyes locked on the Reverend Mother, his tail stiff behind his back, black lips in a snarl. He gave a low growl.

Declan reached out and placed his hand on Mother Beatrice's shoulder. "Thank you."

Mother Beatrice's own eyes filled with tears. "I am so, so sorry. I was so very wrong."

Declan inclined his head briefly. "Yes, but you admitted your mistake and sought to rectify it and did just that. You have the human race's gratitude. Well, most of the race, anyway."

Declan put Annalee down and raised his finger to his lips for silence. He heard thunder in the corridor. Shango was coming. He caught Annalee up by her armpits and settled her on the wolf. She gripped the animal's ruff fiercely. "Ho'kee, get her out of here. Don't wait for us. Baba Yaga and Yenay are outside. You will know what to do when you see them. We will follow as closely as we can, but Annalee is our priority."

Mother Beatrice nodded in assent and placed her hand over Declan's. She spoke in a resigned tone. "You go, it is me he wants."

Declan shook his head firmly. "Shango doesn't know who we are and in his battle rage, he won't care. He has one goal and that is to find Annalee. Everything and everyone else will be collateral damage. I have to try to connect with Shemar. He is in there somewhere; I can feel it. Hanging on by a thread, but he is there."

The wolf cleared the debris pile again, uninhibited by the weight of the child. His paws skidded slightly as he sought purchase on the ground on the other side. His ears pricked with danger. The God of War was close; the wolf could smell the smoke and feel the thunder. His sharp eyes picked up a small crevice at the end of another corridor with light shining through it. It was just big enough to accommodate a child and her wolf. He crouched low and moved with stealth toward the light.

Declan took Mother Beatrice's hand and pulled her with him away from the debris, opposite from the advance of Shango. He heard the *oshe* swinging, cleaving both people and structure.

Declan stood under a dome in the basement corridor and listened. He closed his eyes and pushed his thought into Shemar. *"Shemar. I know you are in there. Annalee is safe, but Shango is unleashed. I am afraid he has no concept of who we are or which side we are on. He has declared war on everyone in this compound. Shemar, we need you to make peace with this ancestor."*

Down the corridor, Shango stopped suddenly. His mouth closed and the fire in his eyes abruptly flashed out. He looked startled and gazed down uncomprehendingly at his *oshe*. His voice was deeply shaken as he croaked out, "Declan?"

As suddenly as the fire was extinguished, it flamed up again. Shango gripped his *oshe*, fire shot from his eyes, and he opened his mouth to roar. The thunderous war cry shook the unstable walls, and a window somewhere shattered. Shango turned and strode toward the source of the sound.

Ho'kee ran as fast as he could, turning nimbly around corners and staying in the middle of the corridor. He kept the sunlight in his focus and picked up speed. He put his ears back, and Annalee gripped his ruff tighter. It was going to be close. He had to clear a hurdle of twisted steel, deadly sharp edges jutting into the air. Annalee crouched so low she was almost flattened against his broad back, and he leapt.

He sailed through the crevice and his paws touched on firm ground. Annalee straightened and looked around. Her eyes widened, and he would have echoed her gasp if he could have. A tiny, centuries-old house sat serenely balanced on what appeared to be giant chicken feet.

Annalee clapped her hands. "Baba Yaga!"

The door was flung open, and Yenay stood in the frame. "Baby! Annalee, my baby!"

"Mama! Look! I am riding Ho'kee!"

Yenay laughed and clapped her hands together. "I see that, honey!"

An ancient and wizened old crone peered out from behind Yenay. She looked like Mara, but not. She waved her withered old hand and shouted down. "Make haste, young ones! Shango has not released his hold on Shemar!"

Ho'kee backed up, measured the distance, and in his mind said a prayer to the Creator. Annalee crouched low again as Ho'kee's trot became a gallop, and he sprang. His back legs hunched forward to meet his front paws, and he slid on the polished wood flooring. Yenay caught her daughter and wrapped her tightly against herself.

Annalee squealed and squirmed. "Mama! You are crushing me!"

"Tough. Let me know when you can't breathe. In the meantime, just let me hold you."

Annalee sighed and gave in, and soon her long dark eyelashes were fanned against her cheek in sleep. Ho'kee had padded off to another room. Baba Yaga was lighting candles and cooing at the bullfrog that sat on a kitchen chair, its heavy-lidded eyes blinking slowly.

In the bedroom, Ho'kee leapt up onto the bed and stretched out. He closed his eyes, and the transition back to human form began. He formed an image and sent it to Declan.

Declan smiled as the thought entered his mind and whispered it to the prioress. "They are safe."

Beatrice whispered back, "We are not."

He stopped smiling as prickles went up his back. Declan turned around. Shango filled the room. He lifted his *oshe* above his head, but paused. He lowered the weapon to chest level and stared at Declan's open hand. In his palm was the ancient artifact the God had tossed to Brighid. "Shemar. Ho'kee is alive. Annalee is safe. We are all alive and safe because of Shango. His work here is done. Shemar, come back."

Shango stood silent, and the fire in his eyes died. His monstrous size began to decrease to Shemar's smaller, but still formidable, height and girth. Shemar looked down at the cracking foundation. He stared at the blood on his body and dropped his hands to his sides—the *oshe* had vanished. He quickly assessed his surroundings and the two people in front of him.

He met Declan's gaze and spoke quietly, "We have to get out of here."

The three were jolted by an avalanche of debris. Declan curled his body protectively around the Reverend Mother and pushed them both toward the opposite wall. Shemar covered his eyes with his forearm against the rising clouds of thick dust. They watched in desperation as the entrance to the corridor was blocked off. That was the way in, and that had been the way out for Wolf and Annalee.

Declan whispered, "Reverend Mother, do you know this fortress well? Do you know the layout?"

The prioress shook her head. "I only came here yesterday at Mr. Zlo's command."

The three crouched again as another wave shook the crumbling building. Declan and Shemar exchanged a resigned look, then they heard a familiar caw.

They looked around to see the crow perched precariously on top of a heap of debris that used to be a wall. It leaned forward and squawked at Declan. Declan smiled, relief in his face. If the crow got in here, it could get out as well, and they could follow it. "I never thought I would be glad to see you, corvid, but you are my favorite sight on this earth right now."

The crow bobbed and squawked, then opened its wings and flew to the opposite end of the corridor where the most recent cave-in had occurred. The three dodged tumbling grit to get to the end and watched as the crow pushed his beak, and then his body, through a dark opening near the bottom.

Declan dropped down and looked through the small hole. "The corridor continues, but there is a door at the side! Quick, you two, help me get rid of this debris."

The three began to tear at the cement rubble until their hands were scraped raw. An opening large enough for Mother Beatrice to squeeze through formed. Declan put his hand on her back and gave a firm push.

She stood just as firmly. "No way. I am partially responsible for this, and I am not going through that hole before both of you. So you can either tempt a few more avalanches by pushing and pulling me, or you can go first and, if this opening lasts, I will follow."

The crow shrieked as the corridor behind them began to shake again, heaving stones onto the floor.

Shemar put his hand on Declan's shoulder. "Go, Declan."

Declan shimmied his body through the crevice and emerged out the other side. He saw the bolted door at the side, and it was slightly askew. The crow strutted over to the opening, poked his beak in, then moved the rest of his body through the door.

Declan reached his arms back through the crevice and called out. "Come! It's not falling as rapidly here, but it won't hold long. There is a door to somewhere. Crow says we take it."

Mother Beatrice put her hands on her hips and inclined her head toward the crevice. "Go, Shemar. I am not going until you get through."

Shemar's mouth tightened, but he didn't fight her. He knew by her stance it would be useless and time-consuming. They had no time that could be wasted. The three rapidly tossed rocks aside until the opening could accommodate Shemar's girth, albeit tightly. Shemar wriggled through and felt Declan's hands on his shoulders, guiding him. He slid one leg out, then the precarious opening shuddered and groaned. Declan and Shemar watched in horror as the temporary entryway seemed to convulse, and another avalanche poured stones over the small opening. They heard the sound of the corridor collapsing on the other side of the obscured opening.

Declan yelled, "Mother Beatrice! Can you hear me?"

There was complete silence in response. Declan sprang forward.

Shemar grabbed him around his chest and pulled him backward. "No, Declan. No. Remember, this is about Annalee. Mother Beatrice made a sacrifice—for Annalee."

The crow shrieked again, and they swung their gazes to the door. Above the doorway, cracks were beginning to noisily form, and dust was sliding down the frame. Shemar forcefully grabbed Declan's hand and pulled him in front of the door. He grabbed the side of the door and, using everything he had left in himself, scraped it open just enough to accommodate the two of them. He pushed through, Declan right behind him, and they stood in a quiet, reinforced corridor.

The crow was standing a few feet in front of them, its black eyes glittering. It beat its wings and took flight down the passage, dimly lit by chaotically bouncing flashlights. Declan and Shemar realized there were others in the passage making their way to the outside.

Shemar paused briefly and reached for a knife in the hilt of his garment.

Declan put his hand on Shemar's and shook his head. "They are fleeing. They are not interested in us, just in survival."

They followed the dazed, broken soldiers through the darkness to an iron ladder leading up to a hole surrounded by glorious, beautiful outside light. They climbed the ladder and heaved themselves onto the earth. Around them, distressed and beaten men stared uncomprehendingly at the pile of detritus that used to be The Facility. Not one of them spoke.

Declan looked up and saw the crow perched on an Arbutus tree. The crow dipped his beak and yelled at Declan before taking off. As tired as they were, Declan and Shemar walked forward to follow the crow.

A few minutes into their journey, Shemar spoke. "How are the Others?"

"All safe. All together. Except for one of our fallen members. Father Benedict didn't make it. He died giving Ho'kee life again."

A muscle worked in Shemar's face as a myriad of emotions fought within him. "Zlo?"

"He is dead. Chernobog had taken him over."

"And The Dark God?"

"Crossed back to his own realm."

"Then it's really over?"

They both fell silent as three shimmering lights appeared in front of them.

They both heard Brighid speak. "No. He can never come back. We need the Others to gather and fight again in Chernobog's realm. This is not over yet."

Declan put his hand on Shemar's shoulder. "We go into battle one more time: as Descendants."

Shemar's face broke into an unexpected, but bitter, smile. "Good! This will be for Father Benedict."

Chapter Fifteen

B aba Yaga's house trod through the seawater easily, the light from its windows illuminated the
rough cliffs and wind-bent Arbutus trees.

Annalee peered over the windowsill. "Where *are*
we?"

Declan stood behind her and a smile spread over
his face. "This is Dodd's Narrows. My mother used to
take my brother and me here often for picnics. Well,
I think she brought us here to beat on each other
outside the confines of her nice clean house, but it was
still good to be outside."

"The tides look like they are at war with each other,"
Ho'kee remarked.

"It can be a challenge getting through here. Good
sailors in a good boat can do it. Orcas, sea lions, and
seals have no problem. But a man swimming wouldn't
survive."

Baba Yaga laughed. "Good thing we have a strong houseboat."

"On weird chicken feet," Ho'kee blurted.

Shemar turned and looked down at Declan. "Why are we here?"

Declan looked out over the channel, to three shimmering lights hovering above a violent sea. The waves were standing on end, clasping each other in frenzied embraces and crashing back to the sea. No boat, or man, would survive that. "The Goddess told us to meet Her here."

Shemar looked back at the wild current. "All of us?"

"All of us."

Yenay shook her head. "Absolutely not. We have had enough. This stops now. We almost lost her once. I am not going to risk it again."

Declan put a hand on Yenay's shoulder and pressed his forehead against hers. She wanted to fight him off, but she couldn't. She reached up and wrapped her hand around his strong wrist.

"Annalee's work is done for now," he said. "She has brought us together. She has made us the Others. She has one job left here, but she will not be coming with us. She will stay here with you, in that lighthouse. You see where that ugly, old, fat man is waving at us?"

Yenay gazed over at a sturdy lighthouse and stifled a laugh.

A man barely older than Declan, and almost as handsome, waved heartily at them. "That is my much older brother, Niall. He will be with you for support. You don't need taking care of. You are a warrior and so is your daughter. However, she is four years old, and she is going to expend a lot of energy with the one more thing she needs to do. The Goddess will be with her, and you will be with her. When she is done, all three of you will wait in the lighthouse until we return."

"Tell me we are going after him." Ho'kee growled out the words.

"We are going after him. We are going to finish this."

Baba Yaga watched the three lights lengthen and widen, moving into a triangle formation. "It is time."

The house strode across the narrows, the silver-capped ebony waves flinging themselves furiously at the scaled legs. The current swelled, and the house rocked slightly. A collective breath of air was taken, and the house settled outside the lighthouse.

It lowered itself to its knees, and the waves thrust themselves against the windows and doors. Annalee watched, wide-eyed with wonder. The Baba Yaga opened the door, and the three lights in front of her house formed a silver triangle. Within the center, a portal seemed to open and the water beneath the lights went still.

Niall flung open the lighthouse door.

"Now," ordered the Baba Yaga, "jump into the portal. You will not fall."

Ho'kee took a few steps back and made a running leap. He flew with ease and grace onto the concrete porch of the lighthouse. Niall embraced him and they moved aside, putting their hands out for the next. Yenay collected Annalee and put her on her back for a horsey ride. The triangle pulsed, and Yenay leapt forward. She drifted, suspended, to the lighthouse. Yenay felt her child getting heavier and heavier until, at the end of the portal, she could no longer carry her. As soon as she set her feet on the ground, Annalee jumped from her back.

Yenay straightened, wincing, and spoke as she turned around. "My girl, what has your Babushka been feeding you? You are getting...." Her words died on her lips.

In front of her, dressed in shimmering robes of green silk and red satin, was Quan Yin. Her dark hair was piled high and adorned with jewels. Her hands were pressed together in prayer. She smiled in perfect beauty and peace. Yenay fell to her knees. Shemar and Declan looked at each other and then at the Baba Yaga.

She inclined her head toward Shemar. "You next, Descendant of Shango."

Shemar stepped into the shimmering triangle.

They all looked back at the portal, which had moved away from the lighthouse and the Baba Yaga. The Others looked at each other in confusion and alarm. It was settling in an area far off the point of the lighthouse and hovering there.

Niall started yelling. "Hey! Hey, you forgot my brother! Get back here! You can't leave him there. Get back here!"

Declan watched the triangle shift and elongate. A fourth shimmering light appeared and drifted in front of and above the three. It pulsed with a gentle light, not as intense as the other three. It drifted closer, and the four created a rectangle over the most violent part of the channel and widened. The fourth light was softer, not as powerful, but joined with the three, creating a space Declan knew was for him alone. He knew who the light was.

"Mom," he whispered.

Ho'kee kneeled before Quan Yin. She stood in front of him and, from a vial she held in her hands, she pressed water to his forehead. She then raised graceful arms into the air.

"Ho'kee, son of land, sea, air, and fire. You are anointed with the water blessed by the Goddess. You have embraced the dark and the light. You are not one nor the other. You are all and everything. You are what you call upon. Descendant of Shapeshifter and Skinwalker, *ascend*!"

Ho'kee stood, and swan-dived into the churning waters. Yenay screamed. Shemar gathered her into his arms and Niall stood rigid. Quan Yin remained standing, arms lifted, eyes closed. The white water erupted. An orca sailed into the air, cutting a smooth arc and splitting the waters on its return into the waves. It pointed its snout into the air and an ebony eye watched Quan Yin.

"I bid you seek the Goddess and the Others, child of the Creator, my warrior."

It smacked the water hard with its tail and moved in a determined line to the house of Baba Yaga. Declan watched carefully as the orca positioned himself below the door. His dorsal fin was slick and strong on his back. The orca drifted beneath him. Declan looked back at Baba Yaga and over at the lights.

He called out, "Coming, Mom!"

And he leapt into the thrashing waves below.

Shemar kneeled in front of the Goddess of Mercy and closed his eyes. He felt her press something hard and warm into his hands. He looked down to see the artifact that had made transitioning back to Shemar possible. His eyes felt perilously close to tears, and he squeezed them shut again.

Quan Yin dipped her finger into the vial and pressed a drop of bioluminescent water against his forehead. "Shemar, son of God of Fury, you are anointed with the water blessed by the Goddess. We call on you now to join the Others in battle. Soldier, warrior, Descendant of Shango, God of War, *ascend!*"

Shemar's mouth opened wide to scream as fire ripped through his body, but no sound came out. He folded in on himself and a lightning bolt shot from the sky into his body. Rolling flames climbed to form the figure of a man, and an ebony silhouette appeared. Fire blazed from his eyes, and his mouth was an orb of fire, lightning striking out from its sides. The artifact Quan Yin had given back to him was around his neck on a leather thong, and the white symbols on his arms and chest glowed.

Yenay put her hand to her mouth. Quan Yin shifted her gaze slightly to Yenay. Shango stared forward, but his focus was entirely on the Goddess before him.

"I bid you seek the Goddess and the Others, Shango, my warrior."

The burning God clutched his *oshe* and stepped into the water, walking toward the triangles.

Baba Yaga looked hopefully over the edge of the porch of her house. She watched the orca rise again with Declan on his back, and she sighed with relief. The Descendant of Dagda would be fully ascended in the other realm. The Dagda was going to need all the power The Goddess could share with him, and for that to happen all at once, he had to be in the other realm.

She looked over at the glowing figure on the shore and marveled again. She was gazing upon Quan Yin. "Blessed be," she whispered.

Declan held fast to the orca's dorsal fin as it plowed through the frantic ocean toward the portal. The orca picked up speed. Declan looked back, and saw Shango in the distance, walking on the water toward the portal. Baba Yaga's house strode purposefully through the channel in tandem with Shango. The maelstrom began to glow more brightly, pulsing. Declan instinctively took a gulp of air as he felt the orca descend sharply. His chest felt like it might burst, but he hung on.

The sea was not as dark in the depths. He watched jellyfish pulse by and crabs scrabble across the sea floor. There was green light down here. Then he remembered; it was bioluminescence. The orca shot up and forward in a graceful arc, breaking the surface, and Declan expelled his breath. They were flying. He gripped the fin with both hands as the orca turned in midair gracefully and dived through the portal directly into the most violent part of the channel. Declan closed his eyes and held on for dear life.

Immediately, he was transported to calm waters. He looked around and above him. He knew this place, but he hadn't been here before...had he? He gazed around him in wonder as the orca moved into shallow waters.

When the orca could go no farther, Declan slid off and wrapped his arms around as much of the great whale as he could. "See you soon, my brother."

The orca emitted a high-pitched squeal and shifted itself back into deeper waters, its fins slapping the surface. Declan stood at the shoreline and looked up at high cliffs dotted with weather-beaten trees, but not a species he recognized from the island. He looked under the cliffs and saw three women, each raising a torch toward the sky. The youngest one lowered her torch and turned toward him, platinum hair flying from an ethereal, ageless, and impossibly beautiful face.

"Inanna! I have missed you, my beauty."

She inclined her head slightly, her smile radiant. He could swear love shone from those incredible eyes.

The next woman turned toward him, lowering her torch slightly. A mass of red hair swept around her shoulders, and her emerald eyes shone in the firelight.

"Brighid!"

She inclined her head, and the final woman turned toward him, lowering her torch. She had an ancient, timeless elegance.

"Crone!"

Overcome, he fell to his knees.

The three women drifted over to him in unison, their bare feet leaving no marks on the soft sand. They gathered around him.

The Crone cupped his face in her hands and lifted his chin. "See me, my child. You are here in mortal form because your full ascension is too great to take place in the earthly realm. Look behind you, Descendant of Dagda."

Declan turned to see a flaming Shango stride ahead of a quaint old house on dripping, scaled legs. A huge silver-gray wolf advanced from the sea, stopping to shake the water from its fur. They stood at the edge of the beach.

Shango dropped to one knee and bent his head to the Goddess. The house's front door flung open, and Baba Yaga stepped onto the porch. She sank to her knees and bowed her head. The great wolf stretched his body out beside Shango and put his head on his paws. Declan turned back to The Goddess.

The Crone addressed them all. "There is a final battle to take place in this realm. Chernobog is here, as is his demon. Declan, we are asking you to help us ensure he will never travel between realms again."

Declan, non-plussed, looked up at the Crone. "My Goddess, I have no idea how."

Crone smiled gently and stroked his cheek fondly. "No, of course not. However, Dagda does."

She backed away and motioned for him to rise. He stood in the middle of the circle, and the women began to walk around him, chanting, their torches raised together. He felt lightheaded and a bit sick. He wondered if he should sit down a moment. That orca ride must have made him seasick. He tried to bend his knees, but he couldn't move. He looked down to see a silver-gray wreath beginning to bind his ankles. It slid effortlessly through his feet, through his pants, around his hips and torso. His arms spread of their own accord, and the wreath began to expand as The Goddess' speed increased, the chant grew stronger, and the single flame of the three torches shot up into the sky. The wraith surrounded him and threatened to choke him. Panicked, he sought the eyes of Crone.

She gazed at him from warm brown eyes. She stepped forward, and Inanna presented a chalice. "Declan, son of our sister. You are father, brother, and King. You are anointed with water blessed by The Goddess. We call on you to join the Others in battle against that which would see the death of humanity. We call on you as our King to lead us into battle against Chernobog. Dagda of the Tuatha De Danann, ancient God of Druidry, Magic and Wisdom, *Ascend*!"

The Others watched silently as the wraith that had slid inside Declan's body imploded. In a blinding, brilliant flash, Declan had disappeared. In his place, on one knee, was a majestic, enormous man whose stature surpassed Shango's.

The Dagda's head was bowed toward the Goddess. His thick, shimmering white hair cascaded in careless waves down his broad back. His cobalt-blue eyes, filled with mirth and mischief, settled on the beautiful redheaded Goddess. An enchanting smile spread over his handsome face, and his great, strong white teeth shone brightly.

Crone stepped forward and tapped his shoulders lightly with her wand. "Rise, Dagda. Rise in all your glory."

The God stood slowly, and the Others watched, spellbound. The Dagda spread his massive arms wide, and his voice rolled over the beach, up the cliffs, and through the trees, startling birds into flight. "Brighid! My beautiful daughter! My favorite daughter! But don't tell any of my other favorite daughters that!"

Brighid passed her torch to Inanna and sprinted as fast as her legs and pregnant belly could carry her. She flung herself into the massive man's arms. He held her tightly but gently, and she buried her face in his hair. "Father! I have missed you."

"Aye? And what of your mother, The Morrigan? Has she missed me as well? You let her know I have been completely faithful to the old witch."

Crone snorted and the Dagda stood, pressing his hands to his solid belly as he let out a laugh that barreled through the area and infected the Others.

Shango, not used to laughter, stifled a snort. Baba Yaga's house shook with laughter, and the silver-gray wolf opened his wide mouth in a gleeful smile.

Brighid slapped her father playfully. "Mother says you are as trustworthy as a hyena, but she loves you and misses you as well."

The Dagda looked Inanna up and down and lifted an eyebrow flirtatiously. He gallantly bowed and drew her alabaster hand to his mouth to press a kiss against it. Inanna flushed and looked downward, a pleased smile dimpling her soft, young cheeks.

"Most fetching. I have missed you most of all, you enchantress."

Crone rolled her eyes and pointed behind the Dagda. "Your army, my King."

The Dagda placed his hands on his hips which were covered in a thick green tunic. His leather boots were tied securely around his calves, and he wore a glinting silver Brighid's cross around his neck. He put his hand out to the great gray wolf.

"Mai-Coh! Descendant of Shapeshifter and Skin-walker. A blessing to see you again. Best stay in animal form for now. Only a God can destroy another God and take his power; however, we will be in need of your unique abilities."

The wolf lowered his head, his eyebrows twitching in disappointment. The Dagda went down on one knee and put his hand on the gray wolf's head. "A demon can slay another demon. And I do believe that like it or not, you have that in you, Mai-Coh."

The Dagda winked at Wolf and stood up. He stood in front of the Baba Yaga and grinned brightly. "Baba Yaga! It has been eons! You don't look a day over thirteen thousand years old. I look forward to our magic together again."

The Baba Yaga grinned and waved at him.

He moved to stand in front of Shango, God of War. The Dagda folded his hands respectfully in front of his stomach and lowered his eyes. "Great Oshiri warrior, Shango. I am indebted to your service here. You do me an honor I cannot hope to repay. I know you join this mission as a service to our Goddess Quan Yin. I am honored to fight alongside you."

Shango's eyes blazed, and the god inclined his head slightly in acceptance. The Dagda stepped back and called over his shoulder. "Daughter! My *lorg mór*."

The three Goddesses once again formed a circle and touched their torches together. A flame shot up skyward, spitting sparks and roaring with power.

The Dagda put his hands on his hips and laughed again. "I love it when they do that."

The flame died down. Suspended in the air, twisting in a spherical arc, a deadly club mace gleamed. One end would slay nine men in one well-swung arc;

the other end could restore men to life. The Dagda reached into the subdued flames and took hold of the weapon. The weapon was heavy and solid in his grasp.

He sank to one knee before the Goddess, one hand wrapped firmly around the *lorg mór*, the other touching the earth. "Goddess, we have lost one of our soldiers in battle before ascending to this realm. I ask that you bless us with another warrior, at this time only, in this realm only, to complete the mission the Descendants have pledged to."

Crone studied the God before her. She smiled sadly and answered him. "So you have. Your realm has lost a good man, and his Heaven has gained a great soul. Very well. We will ask another warrior to join this battle."

She turned back to the two at the cauldron. She inclined her head, and their torches were thrust into the cauldron. The three began to chant, and a thick plume of nightshade smoke began to twist into the sky. It expanded and darkened until the sky was a rich amethyst. A clap of thunder shook the ground. A tear in the blanket of purple appeared over the ocean that the Others had come from, and an outline began to form.

The Dagda's eyes narrowed to focus on the figures moving toward them. He tilted his head, recognizing the animal carrying a woman. He counted the arms of the Goddess riding the beast. He smiled broadly and said quietly, "I'll be damned."

The Others pivoted slightly to allow a walkway for the incoming warrior Queen. Sitting astride a flame and coal-colored Sumatran tiger, Durga stared forward, approaching the Goddess. The tiger moved with the controlled poise of lethal power; bunched muscles rippled under thick fur. Durga's thick swath of black hair fell in a heavy curtain past her hips. Her arms were outstretched to the side, each holding a sacred symbol.

A discus spun on the index finger of one hand. Her other hands held a trident, a conch, a lotus, a *kharga* sword, a bow and arrow, a mace, a thunderbolt, a snake, and an ax. Her wrists and upper arms were wrapped in gold, and she wore a headdress of gold and rubies. Luxurious silk robes in crimson draped over her breasts and hips and her bronzed midriff displayed a multifaceted dark ruby in her navel.

She smiled slightly. Her large, almond-shaped black eyes met the direct gaze of each of the Descendants. She inclined her head to each as she passed. They inclined their own heads in deep respect.

The tiger constantly rumbled deep in its chest as it prowled closer to the Goddess. Its sage green eyes lighted upon Wolf and it raised its lips slightly to show cutting canines. Wolf returned the greeting, drawing back black lips to display his own predatory teeth. Their eyes met, and each blinked slowly. The tiger circled in front of the Others so he and his Goddess could direct their gazes to everyone.

Durga's voice was low, her words clipped and direct. "Who has summoned a Goddess of war, strength, and protection?"

Crone stepped forward, her staff beside her. Her voice matched Durga's in authority. "We three."

Durga inclined her head slightly and regarded Dagda.

"And The Soldiers of Gaia," he answered.

Durga pressed a finger to her third eye and spoke again. "And why do you seek the assistance of Durgatinashini?"

Brighid stepped forward, her hand on her belly. "Chernobog has crossed realms once again, seeking to provoke the destruction of the human race. This time he set his sights on the elimination of a treasured Descendant."

Durga inhaled sharply, her hands tightening on her weapons as she scrutinized the Others. Her gaze slowly returned to Crone. "The Descendant of which Deity, Crone?"

"He seeks to destroy the Descendant of Quan Yin."

Durga's fist closed over the discus, the weapon she used to destroy evil, one that could be used to build an environment that would bring Quan Yin's promises of hope, compassion, and peace to fruition. Her beautiful, full mouth curled upward, an intrigued smile playing at her lips. "He has his demons with him, I would assume?"

The Dagda nodded his confirmation. "You are correct, my lady."

"Splendid. I especially enjoy battles with demons. I accept your request. Lead us, Dagda."

Dagda turned to face his army. Durga and her tiger took their place beside Wolf. Wolf looked up at Durga and sniffed her hand. She smiled down at him and scratched his ears. The Dagda inhaled deeply. "It is with great pride that I announce I have never led a more powerful army. Now. Let's go deal with the Dark God."

Chernobog made a fist with his hand after passing it over the basin and slammed the wood table. The basin tilted, spilling water on all sides. Chernobog paced his outer courtyard and pushed his hand through his long, dark hair. An unfamiliar anxiousness surged through his being.

He could still win this, but he had to be careful. The Dagda leading the charge was a Druid with a mastery of magic and deep wisdom. He honored fairness. Chernobog had an advantage in this area; he was not interested in fighting fairly. The Dagda sometimes showed great mercy, and Chernobog may be able to use that against him.

However, the Dagda also had Shango in his army, to whom mercy had no meaning and who thrived on chaos and war. The Fire God was committed to justice, and his extraction of that justice as payment for Chernobog's acts in the earthly realm would not bode well for the dark god.

The Dagda had the allegiance of Wolf, and no one, not even Chernobog, knew the extent of that boy's abilities now that he had embraced both darkness and light; both shapeshifter and skinwalker.

The Dagda had the Russian High Priestess of magic, Baba Yaga. Chernobog pinched the bridge of his nose in a gesture that once belonged to Zlo. That old bat had lived more years in each realm than Chernobog himself. She was exhausting and beyond tenacious.

And now the Dagda had Durga, the fiercely protective Goddess whose sole ambition was to eradicate evil and establish peace and harmony. Her viciousness toward demons was almost akin to his own hatred of humanity. Chernobog rubbed his forehead. He was going to lose many of his followers in this battle. He wasn't pleased. While he loathed humanity and encouraged them to kill each other off, he did have affection for his demons.

He had known this day would come when he would meet each one of these Gods again, but he had never anticipated that they would gather themselves into an army against him. He pounded his fist down again. This was ridiculous! He had followers in both realms, they worshipped him!

Why couldn't his own kind understand? The earth could be restored to its beautiful glory—its rich landscape, its unique animal kingdom—if they simply destroyed humanity. Granted, it was doing a fine job on its own: turning against each other in escalating violence born of hatred, ignorance, intolerance, and greed. But it wasn't fast enough for Chernobog. Someone, or something, always stepped in to save that ridiculous species.

As long as he was able to travel between realms, he could wreak havoc on the earthly plane, but each time he went, it took him longer to regain his strength and full power. He sensed he was getting closer, but this time was different. Something was shifting in the world now, and he was concerned that with the involvement of Quan Yin, he was going to be defeated.

This time, this battle, Chernobog was on his own with his demons. His black eyes roved the area. Maybe, just maybe, he could convert one of the Others. Shango! Oh, he would be a most excellent soldier in Chernobog's army. But upon reflection; no. Shango literally lived to serve Quan Yin.

He did not trust the Navajo shapeshifter. The boy was too volatile. There was a demon in him, and that intrigued Chernobog, as did the shifting. However, the human in him was dedicated to Quan Yin.

He stood and strode around his courtyard again. His demon, Gorgo, was high in a tree, watching. Chernobog thought quickly. A demon could destroy another demon. If his own demon took out the Wolf, that would leave Chernobog with one less member of the Dagda's strange crew to deal with. His demon had little to do these days and had done such a fine job as a human. He smiled cruelly and snapped his fingers. The demon looked over and scrabbled down the tree on his lethal talons, serpent tail winding behind him. It crouched in front of Chernobog and lifted its pupil-less eyes, wide in their sockets.

"I have a special job for you, Gorgo."

The Dagda strode behind the Others, spinning his club mace. The wolf led them, moving with stealth and silence. His paws made no indentation on the forest floor. Close behind him, Durga, her tiger, and Shango kept their eyes focused ahead. The Baba Yaga's house brought up the rear, easily stepping over trees and boulders.

The Dagda gave a low whistle. "Aye. I'd forgotten how beautiful this realm is. Without the creepy crawlies like Chernobog."

The Baba Yaga hissed at him from her house behind him. "Brother! We are trying to be silent."

The Dagda looked confused. "Why? It isn't as though Chernobog doesn't know we are coming, the old snake carcass. Probably has his nose shoved into his water basin as we speak, snooping for clues."

Baba Yaga thought about this for a minute and acknowledged his explanation with a wide smile.

An unexpected sound behind stopped him. Wolf, seeming to feel a shift in the Dagda's focus, stopped and looked back as Dagda raised his hand in a gesture to halt. Wolf spun around and crouched, stopping Shango, Durga, and the tiger, in their steps. The tiger's growl rumbled low and dangerous in its chest. Wolf left the lead and seemed to glide in silence back to the Dagda.

Baba Yaga hissed from inside the house. "He is close. He has henchmen."

The Dagda swung his club mace up and caught it in both hands. He caught Shango's glowing red eyes as he swung up his *oshe* and held it tightly. The Dagda nodded to Durga, and she swung a *kharga* in front of herself.

He called back to Baba Yaga. "My sister, protect yourself now. Weave your spell of protection, and I will bind it!"

As soon as those words were spoken, an incantation was started by Baba Yaga and the Dagda. A thick, impenetrable fog rose from the ground and began an elaborate entwinement around and through the legs and structure of the house. The Dagda lifted his hand and uttered a sealing incantation, and the fog became invisible but no less impenetrable.

He addressed his army. "My brothers and my sisters. I believe we have all had occasion to come up against

Chernobog in the past, but you may not remember. At times the good has beaten back the evil, and other times, the outcome was not as hoped. He battles using demons and sorcery. Demons are cunning, malevolent, and merciless. We can show no mercy to these creatures. Do not underestimate Chernobog. He is one, and we are few, but he has legions of demons, and he will not hesitate to kill you. A God can kill a God, and I cannot resurrect a fallen deity."

The Dagda thrust his club mace into the air and roared with a voice that shook the boulders of the cliffs. "*A-steach don bhlar*! Goddess, *dion sinn!*"

His battle cry of 'Into battle! Goddess, protect us!' was repeated in the ancient languages of the Others, carried over and through the trees.

Chernobog heard the battle cry and picked up his *bardiche* in one hand and his morgenstern in the other. Nothing would give him greater pleasure than finally giving the death blow to that monstrosity of a Celtic God. Well, that and eradicating humanity. One could certainly lead to the other. This might turn out to be a good day after all. He stood at his castle walls and called his demons forth.

Wolf halted abruptly and gave a low growl, hearing Chernobog's voice and recognizing the war cry. The tiger bunched his muscles, his massive head low to the ground, and snarled in tandem with Wolf.

The brush in front of them began to rustle. Wolf's eyes caught sight of multiple movements, and his keen ears heard a cacophony of muted whispers and hisses. Suddenly, a red-skinned, hunching demon dropped in front of him and bared its razor-sharp teeth.

The Dagda grimaced and made a noise of disgust. "Looks like a Venus flytrap with legs. Smells worse than that badger."

Wolf shifted his weight onto his back legs, his haunches tense. The demon mimed slitting his throat and pointed to Wolf. It then took a step forward and Wolf lunged, sinking its teeth into the screaming demon and forcing it to the ground under his massive weight. The demon reached up with claw-tipped arms and tried to force its fingers into Wolf's eyes. It tried to scream again, but Wolf tore out most of its throat. Wolf forced the demon's face to the ground and shifted position. He lunged again, and the snap of the demon's spine ricocheted through the area. Wolf raised his head to see another demon drop to the ground behind the first slaughtered one. Another demon dropped, and still another.

The Others backed up into a circle, so no one's back was exposed, and began to sidestep, all eyes scanning for numbers and weapons. The demons were crawling, dropping, and scuttering from all areas.

One demon in particular, larger than the others, sat hunched on the castle wall, overseeing and shrieking. Wolf recognized the scent. It was Gorgo. His black lips drew back in a vicious snarl, and he stepped forward, but the Dagda's hand on his ruff stopped him. "Not yet, Mai-Coh. That's what the demon wants you to do. He wants you to leave the pack. Not yet, soldier."

Wolf backed up as well and joined the circle. The demons began to advance slowly, unsure of this group. They were exposed but protected each other. The demons stopped their advance and crouched.

Gorgo shrieked an eardrum-piercing command. The tiger shook his immense head and roared back, his declaration of attack echoing through the area. Shango bent forward, opened his mouth, and expelled a war cry. Lightning bolts flamed out from his mouth and shot into demons on the front line. Their screams equaled those of their leader as their scaled bodies became engulfed by fire.

Durga lifted her sword, and the tiger rose on its back legs. Her *kharga* swung down in a graceful arc and beheaded the demons closest to the tiger. Demons crawled to the tiger's feet and stood to attack, she swung again, dividing them cleanly in half.

The Dagda rose his weapon above his head, swinging in a lethal circle. Gorgo screamed from his post, and a large band of demons attempted to leap onto the Dagda from trees, logs, and nearby boulders. The club mace stroked down in a deadly arch, tearing heads and limbs from red-skinned bodies.

"Now, Ho'kee! Get me into that castle!"

Wolf sprang forward, savagely tearing into anything in his path. The Dagda left Durga and Shango and followed Wolf, the club mace circling with deadly accuracy. He shouted up to Baba Yaga, "My sister! I am moving forward!"

Baba Yaga nodded from the window, watching with sardonic amusement as the scaled creatures tried to climb, leap, drop, and dig their way into her home. The protective shield held. Baba Yaga stoked the fire in her chimney, scattering thorns over the spitting sap. She chanted, and the wreath that surrounded the house broke out in thorns of double-sided blades, impaling demons that had leapt from the trees and cliffs to get to the house. She chanted again and flung an evil-smelling liquid over the logs, which caused the flame to expand in a contained explosion. She heard the screams of demons who were burning to death, having come too close to the house. The odd-looking house stood safe.

She looked over at the bullfrog on her kitchen table and smiled. "Are you hungry, my sweet one?"

Seconds later the bullfrog was tossed out the window and landed on the forest floor beside Durga.

She recognized the ugly toad and looked back at the house. Understanding suddenly, she reached over and pulled Shango by the arm out of harm's way. The bullfrog let out an ominous croak and began to expand itself. Within seconds, it was half as tall and again as wide as the house, and its sticky long tongue unfurled to collect demons, rolling the shrieking bodies into his ravenous mouth.

Durga dismounted the tiger and stood back-to-back with Shango again and felt his fiery body. The tiger snarled at a pod of advancing demons. They looked at each other and stepped backward.

"How many more do you think, Warrior King?"

Shango's eyes burned and his mouth opened. Lightning shot out between his words. "There are hundreds. Chernobog must send all he has, and he will, Warrior Queen."

Durga's hands expertly loaded a bow and arrow at the same time as she poised her trident. Her dark eyes glittered dangerously, and her full lips smiled. The discus spun frenetically on an index finger. "There will be no mercy shown by me to those who serve the Dark God, Chernobog!" An ax flew from another of her hands and cleaved the forehead of a demon.

"Nor by me, warrior Queen." Shango stepped forward, lightning surrounding him. He pushed his arms forward and opened his mouth. Fire engulfed, burned, and melted a swarm of howling malignancy.

Chernobog paced between his castle windows and the scrying bowl. The Druid was on his way. Chernobog closed his eyes and sent a telepathic command to Gorgo at the castle wall.

"Send in the rest of the demons. And be prepared, Gorgo. Your time to take on the earth realm demon is at hand. You will have a wonderful time dismantling him."

The large demon turned its blank, unblinking eyes toward the castle and back to the road leading between the building and the forest. It screamed out a command. There was no reply.

It left its sentry post and slithered down to the grounds, tail flexing. Chernobog stood within his walls. He knew what was at hand before Gorgo had left his position to gather what was left of the decimated demon army. He was going to have to go face-to-face with the Dagda...again.

Outside the castle gate, the Dagda stood motionless. Wolf sat, curling his tail around his haunches and tilting his head to his side, focusing on the castle. He looked up at the Dagda, who was staring unblinkingly at a dark figure in a window.

Chernobog sent a telepathic message to the Dagda. *"Come in, Druid. Kindly leave your dog outside. As you no doubt noticed, my demon is not at my side."*

The Dagda frowned and placed his hand on the wolf's head. "Chernobog is calling me in. I will go in alone, Mai-Coh."

The wolf's eyes glittered, and he growled deeply.

"I realize the danger, Mai-Coh. This is not my first encounter with this creature. I will need you out here. The demons can slow us down and they can bind us. They can greatly wound us to the point that all that is required is a final blow from Chernobog, but they can't kill us. Only he can do that. I need you to prevent any of his demons from getting back into the castle. This is between him and me now."

Wolf stood aside in a ready position and watched as the Dagda dropped his club mace to thigh level and strode to the castle, long white hair flowing over his broad back.

Wolf lifted his snout and stretched his neck out to give a wild call, and felt a heavy weight collapse on his back, wrapping tight legs around his chest and pressing taloned fingers into his eyes. He snarled and snapped, rearing up and against the castle walls to dislodge the creature, but it held fast and steady. It gripped harder, squeezing the breath out of Wolf, and driving its fingers into his eyes, looking for the sockets to wrench the eyeballs from. Wolf saw nothing but darkness, and he could no longer breathe. An image floated in front of him.

Old Dan looked at him with kind but stern dark eyes. He heard his firm voice, *"Descendant of Skinwalker and Shapeshifter, embrace the dark."*

Ho'kee brought a clear vision into his mind's eye and, with his last gasp, breathed life into it.

The creature was flung from his back, and it stood absolutely still, facing Ho'kee. Its wide eyes were unable to process what it was looking at.

Gorgo's own demonic eyes stared back at him, mirroring his image. Gorgo hissed at the twin demon, and reared back when the demon hissed back, with twice as much venom. He extended his taloned hands toward the twin, raising his arms and springing forward. The twin demon slashed at Gorgo as he fell upon the twin, and Gorgo felt his chest wall open and the warm surge of black blood spill over his belly. Gorgo rolled over and leapt up, facing his twin again. The twin was anticipating every move Gorgo was making. Each step he took forward or to the side, the twin blocked him. With a screech of frustration, Gorgo leapt again, and spread the talons of his hands and feet wide to shred the twin demon. The twin moved slightly to the side and vaulted into the sky, higher than Gorgo. It twisted midair and wrapped its legs around Gorgo's throat, pulling him to the ground. From behind, the twin demon's thighs crushed Gorgo's windpipe. It placed its hands over Gorgo's eyes and pressed down.

The Dagda pushed the heavy wooden door open, and his massive frame blocked the light. Chernobog stood in front of the fire grate, arms at his sides. He stared at the Dagda with cold eyes. "Why do you persist in enabling this useless species, Dagda? You have seen what they do to themselves. What they do to Gaia. You have seen what they do to each other, and yet you and your kind never stop rushing to their rescue."

The Dagda's dark blue eyes gazed at Chernobog steadily. "If you would leave them alone, there would be no need for rescue, Dark One."

"Before I kill you, help me to understand, Dagda. What is it in humanity that cleaves you to it? Is it the worship? Is it pride and ego? Is it the sacrifices they make to you?"

"They are my children. You should understand, Chernobog. You have Descendants of your own. Maybe, if you stopped devouring them and started raising them, you might have a different take on humanity."

Chernobog shook his head slowly in complete disbelief. He didn't hate the Dagda. Hate was a completely useless and altogether too human emotion. But he could not, in the eons they had spent in these realms together, understand this love for human beings.

Chernobog caught a glimpse of white over the Dagda's shoulder, outside in the courtyard. He peered closely, and his lips drew together in a thin, tight line. An old lady was hanging laundry in the courtyard. Many dying people have reported seeing such a scene, surely a symbol that death was near.

She turned to look directly at him. It was the Crone.

Chernobog grabbed his weapon and sank into his battle pose. Dagda lifted his *lorg mór* and mirrored the stance.

Chernobog nodded toward Dagda's ax. "You think you will need both weapons? I will kill you, and I will only need this one." Chernobog threw his weapon on a table behind him.

Dagda looked down at him from his towering height and flung the ax into the wood table. "So be it."

Chernobog yelled out a battle cry and swung his morning star at the Dagda's head. Dagda's *lorg mór* intercepted and forced it down. Recovering quickly,

Chernobog heaved the morning star back up, spun, and used the motion to deliver a propelling force behind the weapon, directing it perfectly to its target of the Dagda's chest. Dagda, larger and heavier than Chernobog, stepped quickly to the side and swung the *lorg mór* to counteract, but the morning star managed a glancing hit.

The Dagda did not look down at the open gash below his rib. He could not trust the viper to fight fairly. Indeed, he put his faith in knowing that this viper would cheat, lie, and drag honor through mud pits to win. If he looked down at the wound, Chernobog would use that second's hesitation and, for all his wickedness, he was a skilled and savage fighter.

The Dagda gripped the *lorg mór* and swung it in a sharp incline, ripping the spiked mallet from Chernobog's hands and then driving the weapon into the wooden floor. Chernobog looked up, and the Dagda stepped backward, motioning Chernobog to retrieve his weapon.

Chernobog smiled a tight, mirthless smile and shook his head. His pupils narrowed to slits as he looked at the Dagda and he growled, "You will never change, most *honorable* foe."

"Nor will you, most contemptible serpent."

Chernobog lifted the weapon and wheeled, aiming for the Dagda's open wound. The Dagda's *lorg mór* protected that side, and he plowed a heavy fist into the side of Chernobog's head. The Dark God stumbled, anger suffusing his features. He reached for his ax on the table, but his hand was stopped by a sharp rap on the wrist by the *lorg mór*. Chernobog turned hate-filled eyes to the Dagda, who winked at him.

"Your rules, Dark One."

Chernobog began to speak, a rhythmic chant in an ancient language.

The Dagda's silver eyebrows raised when he recognized the incantation. "You would use magic against me, Chernobog? I, the God of Magic and Druidry? You are desperate."

"I use magic to show you what is happening beyond these walls. I scry so you can see that my demon is seconds away from killing your pet. I have the power to stop that, Druid."

The Dagda watched a watery orb evolve between himself and Chernobog. He stayed motionless, but wary, as he kept one eye on the Dark God and another on the orb. He saw a vision of a demon standing over the lifeless body of a gray wolf. He inhaled sharply. "Mai-Coh."

"The shapeshifter is not dead yet but will be. I can stop this, Dagda. Lay down your arms and surrender yourself and your army to me. Not all of you will be executed. You most definitely will be, but two of the Others have great potential."

The Dagda lifted his hand and the watery orb crystallized, hovering in a precarious glass formation. The Dark God stepped backward, feeling the fury building in the Celtic God before him. The Dagda's thunderous voice shook the castle walls. "You would *dare*? How low you have slithered, Chernobog. How pitiful you have become. Your power is almost at an end here, and you *dare* to use sorcery and my love for my soldiers to bring me down?"

The Dagda swept his hand downwards forcefully, and the orb shattered on the floor into thousands of pieces. "Ho'kee would not forgive me for giving you control over his life and death. He would die a warrior first, in service to Quan Yin. He would never, ever serve you."

"He has a demon in him, you know that, Dagda. How long do you think you can keep it harnessed?"

"Ho'kee has guidance from others older than I, Chernobog. I do not concern myself with keeping any of my soldiers 'harnessed.' Again, something you would never understand."

Glass shattered above the Gods. They both looked up to see a large, bloody demon squatting on the inside of the window frame, pulling out shards of glass from its talons with its payara fish-like teeth. It looked down on them and shrieked. Chernobog's countenance was confident and gloating as he spoke.

"Ah, Gorgo. Hand me the ax. I have decided I don't have as much time as I thought I did to waste on this battle, entertaining as it is. I have decided to change the rules in my favor."

The Dagda looked at Chernobog with contempt. He then glanced over at the demon, who in turn, stared back at him. The eyes glittered, and the sockets that should have been inky black blazed blue.

Chernobog, unaware of what was going on behind him, took a sterner tone. "Gorgo. If you are wounded, I will end your life painlessly and quickly, but serve me one last time and give me the ax."

The demon leapt from the windowsill onto the table, wrenched the ax out of the table, and held it in his hands.

Chernobog scowled. "Gorgo, give me the ax. As much as I appreciate you wanting to make the kill, a demon cannot kill a God."

The demon began to twirl the ax like a baton. It then gleefully tossed it up and out the window it had come through. A laugh erupted from the Dagda.

Chernobog dared a look behind him, and his fury flashed to horror when his eyes met the unblinking stare. The demon had blue eyes. "Skinwalker!" he yelled.

The demon laced its talons together and bent its head toward its clasped hands in acknowledgment. It then leapt to the window and took its place as a sentry for the side of the Others.

Enraged, Chernobog swung up the morning star, taking aim at the Dagda's head. The *lorg mór* blocked the spikes from piercing, but they lay deep, bloody scratches across his skin, spattering his long, white beard. The Dagda's weapon came up from the ground and struck Chernobog in the chest, driving him backward into the long wood table, blood spattering the chairs and floor. Chernobog reached over and retrieved the Dagda's own ax from the table. The demon leapt from its post in the window to the table and grabbed at the ax in Chernobog's hands.

The Dagda called it off. "I need you more now as lookout, soldier. The remaining few demons will be crawling back to lick their wounds, or to be killed, any second now."

The demon reluctantly removed its talons from the ax, moved its face into Chernobog's, and spit. It then leapt back to its post.

Chernobog wiped at his cheek with disgust and picked up the ax.

The Dagda's voice was laced with scorn. "You get worse every eon, Chernobog."

Chernobog emerged from behind the table, brandishing both weapons, swinging them expertly. He let go, and the weapons made a direct line for the

Dagda's chest. The Dagda watched for a split second, then squatted. As both weapons made a direct line for his chest, the Dagda jumped sideways, his *lorg mór* spinning in a savage circle. It bit off the head of the ax and broke the neck of the spiked weapon. The Dagda stopped the *lorg mór* from spinning and thrust the weapon with full force against Chernobog. The Dark God was sent flying against the concrete wall behind him. Chernobog sank to the floor. Dagda strode over to Chernobog, who put up his palms up toward the God in a gesture of surrender.

The Dagda leaned down into Chernobog's face, his *lorg mór* pointing into Chernobog's neck. "I have had it with you. You are more trouble than you are worth, but I won't make you a martyr to your loathsome cause. I will make sure you stay in this realm, though."

Chernobog looked up at the Dagda in horror as the Dagda leaned in, wrapped his hands around the labradorite amulet, and wrenched it from Chernobog's throat. Chernobog whispered, "No! Kill me instead! Don't take the realm-crossing stone!"

"You are unworthy of its power. Stay here and wreak all the havoc that The Goddess can stomach from you, but you are not coming into the Descendant's realm again anytime soon."

The Dagda backed up, taking two weapons in each hand. He looked over at the demon. "I need to see my friend Mai-Coh."

The demon dropped to all fours. Its scaly red skin began to darken, and a soft undercoat of silver fur covered its body. It began to pant heavily, and beads of sweat began to form on its forehead. Its talons receded and darkened, becoming thick and heavy wolf claws. Its thin, grotesquely long teeth shortened to white canines. Its sunken ear canals stretched and elongated, thick fur covering the tender skin. The transforming demon heaved, and the remnants of its being were shaken off by a magnificent silver-gray wolf. The wolf turned brilliant blue eyes to the Dagda, then dropped into a predatory position and drew back its black lips, directing a savage snarl toward Chernobog.

Chernobog sat mesmerized. His voice was barely a whisper, "You would have made a magnificent re-placement for Gorgo."

Chernobog's eyes dilated slightly, almost slitting.

The Dagda stared at him as the Dark God began to mumble an incantation. "Save your dwindling energy, Chernobog. Did you not think that I would anticipate your attempts to play with sorcery? We are protected by a power far greater than yours. Even now, Crone has wrapped a binding on you, now that the amulet no longer protects you."

Chernobog closed his eyes and sighed heavily. "Get out."

The Dagda smiled and bowed gallantly. "We will see ourselves to the door."

Wolf backed away from Chernobog, snarling until he was out the door. The Dagda gathered his two weapons and walked out behind Wolf.

In the clearing, Shango stood at attention, the forest floor slick with demon bodies and blood. Durga sat atop the tiger, two hands cleaning off each one of her weapons. As the Dagda and Wolf approached, the three Others wordlessly fell in behind.

The Dagda stopped at the witch's house and called up. "Sister! We are moving on!"

A loud croak from the vicinity of the Dagda's feet caused him to look down. The bullfrog blinked slowly. The Dagda put his hand down, and the bullfrog pulled itself into his palm. The Dagda tossed the frog through the open front door of the house.

Baba Yaga leaned out and waved. The house lifted its feet and followed the Others.

At the beach, The Three built a fire, and each lit a torch. As the Others approached, the Goddesses raised their torches to produce one flame. They put the torches in the sand and stepped onto the water in front of the Others. Inanna looked back at the Dagda, a tear on her cheek. He swallowed the thickness in his throat as she began to sparkle.

Their bodies shimmered, atoms scattering, and became three lights. The lights moved out over the water and hovered. The Others walked into the water, but Ho'kee paddled as far as he could, and despite his effort not to, a whimper came out.

The Dagda moved ahead him, bent forward, and looked back. "On board, my friend."

Wolf gratefully climbed on the back of the Dagda, his paws on the God's shoulders.

One by one, the Others stepped through the portal, except Durga and the tiger. Durga looked up at the lights and spoke. "My Descendant is not yet ready for me. I would like to spend time in this realm. Is there a position open for a Warrior Goddess in your circle?"

The three lights pulsed softly, and she watched as the young Goddess Inanna formed. She, herself, looked nonplussed as her ethereal body took an earthly form again. She stood beside a gently smiling Durga and reached out to stroke the soft ear of the tiger.

They heard Crone's voice. "Brigid is about to give birth to another Maid. Inanna has served long and well. It is time for her to transition. If Goddess Durga is willing to complete our circle, until such time as your Descendant requires you in the earthly realm, we would be most honored."

Durga laughed as Inanna's mouth fell open. She gave the young Goddess a slight push toward the path that the Others had already crossed. "Go, child. It is time to embrace an earthly life."

On the other side, Annalee opened the lighthouse door. The Baba Yaga's house stood several feet away, firm in the rolling tide. The sun shone warmly, and a faint prism of multicolored light bound the two structures together over the water. Niall and Yenay stood up. Yenay started to cry as Mara stepped over the sill, the bullfrog in her arms, and took Niall's offered hand. Shemar stepped through, and Yenay flung herself into his tight embrace as he moved inside. They all smiled as they heard banter being carried on from one house to the next.

Declan stepped over the sill, piggybacking a gleefully grinning Ho'kee. "Dude, what the hell does your mother feed you? You weigh a fricking ton!"

Annalee jumped up and down and climbed up Ho'kee.

Declan's face had a tight smile. He hugged his brother and then Yenay. They all watched as the Baba Yaga's house began to disappear into the prism. Declan looked down, closing his eyes tightly.

Then he heard awe and wonder in Niall's voice. "Who on this magnificent God's green earth is that beauty?"

Declan whirled around, just in time to catch Inanna as she wrapped her bare legs around his waist, clinging to his shoulders, her cutoff denim shorts and white T-shirt clinging to tanned, young skin.

He wrapped his hands in her thick hair and pulled her face slightly away from his. "Truly?"

She cried as she held his face in her hands and pressed her forehead to his. "Truly."

Annalee clapped her hands loudly and Mara joined her. Yenay and Shemar joined in as well. Ho'kee leaned against the counter and gave two thumbs up.

Niall pushed Ho'kee and said in a stage whisper, "How long has he been hiding this secret?"

Ho'kee laughed. "It was never much of a secret, Niall."

Declan let Inanna's feet drop to the ground but held her waist tightly.

Annalee pulled at his pant leg and pointed to Declan's closed fist. "What is in your hand, Dagda?"

"This is a promise that it will be a very long time before our world sees that particular entity again."

He opened his palm. A striated labradorite amulet was tightly wrapped around a strip of leather.

Epilogue

Joe closed the door after Cardinal Josef left. Kibbles leapt onto the couch beside him as he opened the package the Cardinal had given him. Father Benedict had few material things, but he had wanted Joe to have these items. Joe's eyes filled as he gently fingered the papery thin pages of the priest's well-loved Bible. He clasped the crooked glasses to his heart and allowed the sobs to flow freely. He then reached in and pulled out Father Benedict's rosary. He gazed at it in wonder. A little note dropped out.

"If these beads ignite something in you, Joe, the gift has found the right person."

Joe looked at the note quizzically. Then he noticed that his hands were becoming very cold...and then very hot. He watched his own hands in wonder as they took on an aura of soft green.

Lorraine sat on the toilet seat and stared at the stick in her hands. Two colored lines appeared in the window. She expelled a heavy breath and placed a protective hand over her belly. Bittersweet memories washed over her, and she closed her eyes. She leaned back, a sense of peace settling over her, knowing Zlo's legacy would live on with their child.

Acknowledgments

I want to acknowledge my best friend and sister of the heart, Debbie Frost Peterson, for being my rock, my armor, my shield, and my soft place to land for so many years; my patient, creative, wickedly funny editor Marci without whom this story would never have left my head; my friend Alita, who waited for each chapter with anticipation and read each chapter eagerly; and my husband Doug who encouraged me, provided feedback only when asked, and asked all the right questions about the character's characters.

About Author

Born, raised, and happily retired on Vancouver Island, Lacey finds inspiration and peace in the rugged coast, dense forests, and lush valleys of her home. She is guided by her belief in the powers of the elements around us (as above, so below). When she isn't pushing her cat Benny in a stroller along the waterfront, she is getting happily lost while wandering hiking trails with her dog Morgan.

Lacey is married to a wonderful man who tolerates (and often indulges) her bit of an obsession with the wives of Henry VIII. An English literature major, she is most content driving a forklift and slinging soil in the garden center. She is a poet, a bohemian, and a Crone whose desire to preserve Nature's surroundings inspires her writing.

CPSIA information can be obtained
at www.ICGtesting.com
Printed in the USA
LVHW041726210423
744922LV00001B/49

9 781738 854103